THE NIHILIST PRINCESS

Louise M. Gagneur

III Publishing
P.O. Box 1581
Gualala, CA 95445

1ˢᵗ printing May 1, 1999

ISBN 1-886625-05-0

An earlier version was published in the United States by Jansen, McClurg & Company in Chicago in 1881.

In memory of Sophi B. Fleming, who was given a copy of this book by Will on March 9, 1882.

Edited by William Meyers, who takes responsibility for any errors in this edition.

Introduction

She was young. She was pretty. She stayed out late at night without her father's permission. She was also the daughter of one of the most powerful men in Russia and a relation of the Czar himself.

Though Wanda Kryloff, the nihilist princess, was a fictional character created by Louise Gagneur, she was not without precedent in reality. Russia in the 1800's was so corrupt, so backward, that even some members of the nobility, usually young people, joined the revolutionary movement.

The nihilists do not fit easily into the modern categories into which reformist and revolutionary movements have organized themselves. By 1920 clear lines had been drawn: one was expected to be an anarchist (libertarian socialist or anarcho-syndicalist), a Marxist-Leninist (authoritarian socialist), a democratic-socialist, or a progressive (non-socialist).

Today those who care about such things want to go back and pin modern categories on the Russian nihilist movement. But the nihilists, who began their work around 1870, defy such easy labeling. As a group they were diverse. Many were influenced by Marx's writings, but others tended more towards anarchism, since their rebellion was against unjust authority. Russia's two best-known revolutionary figures of that era, Peter Kropotkin and Mikhail Bakunin, were anarchists, and both inspired the nihilists. The French social-anarchist Proudhon was another important influence.

The nihilists wanted nothing to do with religion, for they saw how the Orthodox church worked with the aristocracy to keep the lower classes in ignorant slavery. But they did not wish for society to sink into chaos once they destroyed the church, state, and capitalists. They proposed legislative bodies, democratically elected by the people, as a first step towards reforming Russia. That is, they asked only for what already existed in the United States (except they would have given women the vote). But they did not wish to trade rule by the Czar for rule by money. At the same time that the American corporations were learning to systematically bribe Congress, the nihilists fought to end the power of the Russian aristocracy and begin the process of creating a primarily farm-based egalitarian and libertarian socialist society.

What happened to the nihilists? Many were executed, imprisoned, and exiled. They successfully assassinated Czar Alexander II in 1881, but his successor was even more reactionary. Many later joined the various political factions that struggled for power after the Czar finally allowed a legislature, the Duma, to be formed in 1905. Those who survived long enough were doubtless happiest during the brief 1917 Soviet period before the Leninist counter-revolution. Most nihilists were too independent in their thinking to support the charade of socialism conducted by Lenin, Trotsky and Stalin, but some probably sided with the Bolsheviks even as others joined the anarchist rebellions against Lenin's dictatorship, most notably at Kronstadt.

And what of Louise Gagneur, the creator of much marvelous fiction? Besides *The Nihilist Princess* she wrote *An Expiration* (1859), *The Black Crusade* (1865), *The Story of a Priest* (1882), *The Crime of the Abbe Maufrac* (1882), *An End of the Century Devotee* (1891), *The Reprobates* (1887), *Crimes of the Heart* (1874) and *The Women's Calvary* (1867), that I know of. She was born in France in 1832. Her works were best-sellers in France and were translated into a variety of languages. Yet today, as I write, not one of her books is in print in the United States or France. Information on her is difficult to find. Was she some 19th century version of a hack writer, someone who's writing simply was not worth preserving?

I very much doubt that. Ms. Gagneur was a feminist and a radical at a time when both were anathema to the established authorities of law, society and literature. Her popularity was systematically strangled after her death in 1902 by a conservative male academic establishment and an equally conservative publishing industry.

I hope that this new edition of *The Nihilist Princess* will begin to establish Louise's place in literature. Her works, when republished, will give great insight into life in the second half of the 19th century. Her novels will prove to be powerful even today, for the issues she raised are still with us.

– J.G. Eccarius

CHAPTER I

A BALL AT THE WINTER PALACE

The fall of Plevna had put an end to the Turkish campaign. The Czar, as conqueror, had returned to Petersburg.

Towards the end of December, 1877, there was an official reception and full dress ball at the Winter Palace. The fete was given in honor of the victor.

The interior of the palace looked like fairy land. Western luxury, with its quiet elegance, can give no idea of the oriental magnificence of the Czar.

The superb suite of apartments, beautifully lighted, and the splendid St. George's Hall, of gigantic proportions, presented a scene of enchantment. Hundreds of enormous chandeliers, suspended from the lofty ceilings, glittered through a misty vapor.

Through the vast halls a living, dazzling flood of people moved. It was like a river of gold, of jewels, of radiant faces, of sparkling smiles, of fair hair and snowy shoulders.

The superb uniforms of the Emperor's bodyguard, the golden breastplates, the epaulets starred with diamonds, crosses, the jeweled pins and stars, all reflected the brilliance in which they moved. Nowhere in the world were the decorations so numerous and so rich as they were in Russia; nowhere were the dresses so splendid, so diversified, so loaded with gold and embroidery.

The Asiatic costumes worn at this fete gave it a very original appearance. A Circassian prince, a Mongolian officer, a Mohammedan prince, and an Arabian chief, each displayed his oriental vestments, strange in their form and warm in their coloring.

The costumes of the women were equally rich, but more modern in their elegance. The airy grace of their Parisian fashions could well compete with the enormous wealth of the military and national costumes. These pretty dresses of gauze and lace were fastened, here and there, by clasps of pearls and knots of diamonds, by sapphire or ruby tags worthy to figure in a royal diadem. And then, the beauty of the Russian women—their superb figures, and thin, bare shoulders, were worth all the jewels of the world.

And what a variety of types! A Circassian, with aquiline nose, dark skin and purple lips, stood side by side with a captivating little Finn, all white and pink, with turquoise blue eyes and pale golden hair. A Greek maiden from Odessa, with great black eyes and straight profile, danced opposite a Calmuck princess, whose oriental eyes recalled to mind the Chinese beauties.

Everyone important in society was at the Winter Palace that night. This society presented the most discordant elements. In the same room with the old boyard noblemen stood the representatives of all the conquered countries. Germans, Poles, Tartars, Circassians, Finns. And now that the boyards were nearly ruined and the construction of railroads had opened up a vast field for enterprise, a sort of financial aristocracy was growing up in Russia, to which high society had slowly opened its doors.

A few wealthy bankers were to be seen in this official crowd. In the ballroom some young people were trying to dance, but they were only trampling on one another's feet.

A young French diplomat, decorated with medals of the Legion of Honor and the order of Saint Wladimir, was leaning against a pillar in the long gallery, idly watching the crowd, when, suddenly darting from his place, he pushed his way through the stream of people. He laid his hand on the shoulder of a young man, simply dressed in evening costume.

"Why, Chabert! Is this you!"

"At last I have found you, my dear Count de Prieu! I hoped to meet you here. I went to the French Embassy this afternoon to see you, but you had just gone out."

"How long have you been at Petersburg?"

"I have been here two days."

"Are you traveling for pleasure?"

"No, I am on business. As far as I can see, I should never come to Russia for pleasure; stupid place, wretched climate, a country only fit for thieves and wolves."

"Oh well, you have to take a little time to get accustomed to it. What business have you to bring you out of France?"

"Since I last saw you, my dear Horace, much has happened to me."

"You look so sad, Raymond! Have you had any ill-luck?"

"It is a mistake that I am still alive, for truly I have been very near the other world."

"Ah! Nonsense!"

"Yes, while your life has been running on here, quiet and cool as the waters of the Neva, mine has been drawn into a whirlpool of stormy passion, and nearly dashed to pieces."

"You talk about passion. You! The coolest man I ever met! You astonish me more and more."

"My dear fellow, never count upon anyone. But let me tell you my very strange story."

At this moment there was a murmur in the crowd.

"Look," said Count Horace de Prieu. "Here comes Emperor."

It was indeed Alexander, followed by the Imperial family and great dignitaries of the court.

The Czar wore a uniform which set off to great advantage his fine figure. His effect was superb. His features, as regular as an antique cameo, had a noble but sweet expression. He returned the enthusiastic greetings of his court and of his nobles with a sadness that was habitual to him, as though the recollection of his greatness and of his despotism were oppressive to him.

"He seems thoroughly good," said Raymond Chabert.

"He is, too; his goodness borders on weakness."

"But he looks very much depressed."

"He ought to be."

"Why, he is worshiped by his nobility and adored by his people."

"His people are very wretched, and misery is a bad friend. As for his nobility, I doubt very much whether they have ever forgiven him for freeing the serfs, and for his liberal views."

"Why, I thought that the Russian nobles were very liberal."

"Yes, apparently, particularly when they live in France. The Russians love admiration, and they will sacrifice the truth any day to gain applause. I think they hate these reforms, which threaten to diminish their privileges."

"Yes," answered Chabert, "their privileges are as exorbitant as they were in France before 1789."

"The Czar," said Horace, "although he is an Emperor, thoroughly understands his century; he is trying to escape from the revolution which is constantly threatening him."

"Is there really any danger?"

"The revolutionary spirit has made great progress in Russia. I cannot tell whether it is as dangerous as some people think. But their placards show a wonderful audacity, a wonderful amount of courage."

"What placards?"

"Why, constantly large red placards are put up, purporting to emanate from a Republican committee, summoning the Emperor, in most disrespectful terms, to give a constitution to Russia, and to abolish the secret police. These placards have cut the Czar to the heart, and, at the same time, have very much cooled the loyalty of the people."

"Most probably that is what the revolutionists wish to do; arouse the public feeling, and the Czar's likewise."

"Perhaps, since I saw you last," said Horace, "you, too, have become a democrat, a revolutionist, a socialist? Come on, tell me the rest of your story. I am really interested."

"Well, in fact, it is stupid enough. I only fell desperately in love with a woman. I am well cured of it now, so that I do not even care to talk against her. The vices of the poor creatures are more the result of our conduct than of their own will. They are what they are obliged to be in the filth that they call society."

"Oh! How philosophical!"

"My dear fellow, there is nothing like death," continued Chabert, laughing. "When we come back to earth we look upon things from a higher standpoint. I loved that woman, I wanted to lift her out of the mire ; I would even have married her, when I found that she was deceiving me. I was a fool, for I tried to save her. That was the cause of all my wretchedness. I ruined myself for her sake, because of the inheritance, which fell upon me like an avalanche.

"You are strange to complain of an inheritance ."

"Yes! But that blasted legacy cost me the two best years of my life, kept me from doing my work, and ruined my career. If I had not had money she would never have looked at me. But I managed to get rid of it soon enough. When I saw that I was nearly bankrupt, I went to Monte Carlo to spend my last thousand francs; and there I swallowed a bottle of laudanum."

"You tried to kill yourself?"

"I was in despair, for I really loved that woman, or rather I thought I loved her, when it was only my vanity which suffered. There was a Russian doctor living at the same hotel with me at Nice, who restored me to life, while the other medical men contented themselves with formally diagnosing my decease. I tell you I have been really and truly dead—you see before you one raised from the dead."

"Who is this Russian doctor?"

Horace interrupted himself again, and touched his friend.

"Look," said he, in a, low voice, "here is the real Emperor."

He pointed to an old man with a fine, expressive face and dignified bearing, a person of the most distinguished appearance: the Chancellor of the Empire.

"Is that Gortschakoff?"

"Yes, a statesman who is always on stilts. His haughtiness would not go over well in France, but here he is looked upon as an oracle. He speaks very slowly, giving the most profound reasons for everything that he does. He allows no discussion whatever; what he says is the law—hence his power. The Emperor desires reform; Gortschakoff will not suffer it. The power of that man consists in his imposing manner and his long sentences. His patience is wonderful. He has a perfect talent for seizing his opportunity. He is conservative, but he is neither ignorant nor blind. He understands the current of popular feeling and is always trying to direct its aim. There have been few men who have taken so much trouble to fetter the progress of a nation. He passes for a liberal, however, and he is old."

"But the progress that you speak of is making rapid strides."

"Yes. In spite of the secret police, there is a nihilist Revolutionary Committee here in Petersburg, that holds its sessions, issues proclamations, pronounces sentence on offenders, and, worst of all, inflicts punishment. The most mysterious assassinations take place constantly. I heard this morning that a large red envelope was thrown into the Emperor's carriage, without any one seeing where it came from."

"Are there many of these nihilists?"

"Some people think there are, others do not. I was speaking to one of the officers of the Third Section about it the other day, and he told me that he thought they would be very dangerous if they were better organized. The head of the organization is not in Russia. By the way, that Russian physician who saved your life is very probably some nihilist who is obliged to live outside of this country. The society here receives all its orders from foreign parts, so many Russians have left their country for political reasons. What is your friend's name?"

"I know nothing of his political status," said Chabert, with an air of reserve. "His name is Michael Federoff. He has been of great service to me, and has put me in a fair way to better my fortune."

"Indeed! Your friend must have a great deal of influence. You say you have only been here two days, and have already been invited to the Winter Palace?"

"I had a letter of recommendation from Federoff to a prince, or rather a princess."

"Is she young?"

"Yes, young and very pretty."

"Ah! Perhaps your heart is already touched."

Horace did not listen to his friend's reply, but hurriedly whispered to him: "Here comes General Mezentzoff. He is the head of the Third Section of the Imperial government. Look at him: he is talking to Trepoff, the chief of police."

The young diplomat pointed out a gentleman in a light blue uniform covered with crosses and decorations.

"Do you see him? All the light blue uniforms belong to the same amiable administration. On account of the color of the uniform they call it the blue police—a terrible institution."

"Why! Does the secret police walk about publicly, dressed up in uniform?" said Chabert.

"Yes, and it is the elite of the police. The chief of the Third Section is one of the most important officers of the government; Prince Orloff and Count Shouvaloff both held that position; they were both, you know, intimate friends of the Emperor."

"Then a man can be a spy in Russia and still be respected! It is so in Germany. However, I can well understand that without their police the tyrants would not have one moment of peace."

"Don't talk so loud," said Horace. "There are always spies hanging around. In Russia, you can truly say,'Walls have ears.' And ever since these incendiary placards have made their appearance, the number of the secret police has been increased... Who is this, right near us, this cheaply dressed individual, with a German looking face? I would not trust that fellow. We must be cautious here; for a mere nothing you can be arrested, slapped into prison, and hurried off to Tobolsk or to Irkutsk, without even a trial."

"Delightful country!" said Raymond Chabert. "Happily I have only come here to make some money, and not to dabble in politics."

"What are you going to do?"

"I am an engineer, and I am trying to get a permit to build a railroad through Southern Russia. I am in the employ of a company of French capitalists."

Just then a hush stole over the vast crowd, followed by a murmur of admiration, as the Princess Wanda Kryloff, the famous beauty, entered the hall. She came forward, leaning upon her father's arm, a woman of exquisite beauty, tall, slender, statuesque, her shoulders and arms like marble.

Wanda was the highest type of the Slav: original yet imitative, full of imagination and of power; her mind was quick and witty, her movements slow and languid; her charm was irresistible, at one moment unreserved as a child, at the next full of dissimulation, with a vast, reserved force. Balzac says of these women: "They have the brain of a man, the heart of a woman; at the same time they are angels and demons."

Wanda had a noble, though rather haughty, presence. Her straight, pure Greek profile brought to mind the statue of Diana. But when she began to waltz, her motions recalled the graces of a houri. Her features expressed every feeling, every passion.

Her nostrils were rose-pink, transparent, and trembled with each emotion, but the line of her black eyebrows, although narrow, was bold. Her pearl-white skin enhanced the deep red of her lips; her dark brown hair, turned slightly back from her temples and waved loosely, was held in place by bands of dull gold. Her eyes were grey, with a lurking golden fire that now and then shot from under the long, fringed black lashes. This glance was wonderful, darting, electrical.

As she passed in front of Chabert she smiled upon him.

"Was that smile intended for you?" asked Horace.

"Yes, that is my friend I was speaking to you about."

"Is that your Princess? She is like a Princess in the fairy tales!"

"She is Princess Wanda Kryloff," answered Chabert.

"Oh, yes, I know her. It would not be easy to forget her. And, of course, you are in love with her already. Did your doctor give you a letter of introduction to her?"

"Yes."

"You are lucky. You'll get along. How did the old Prince, her father, receive you?"

"Very well."

"The Russians are very nice to strangers. Prince Kryloff is an accomplished gentleman; he has traveled a great deal; he has the English elegance and the French charm of manner; but they say that on his own lands he is a fearful tyrant. He used to have one hundred thousand serfs—in those days the wealth of the nobility consisted of the number of men they owned. He was, and he still is, a perfect autocrat. They tell dreadful stories about him; some people believe that he walled up his wife alive with her lover—however, that is only whispered about. According to another version of the story, he had her transported to Siberia, for complicity with the Polish insurrection in 1863, and they say she died there. The Princess was a Pole, and a very beautiful woman; that accounts for the beauty of Princess Wanda. The Prince is devoted to his daughter who, I believe, cares very little for him. Some people say that this fair girl, who is clever and generous, is tainted with these socialist, Nihilist ideas. Of course she is merely an amateur nihilist. Z would not, for a moment, confound her with the mob of starved, drunken brawlers who call themselves revolutionists, nihilists and the like."

"Indeed," said Chabert, with some heat, "I have found her very clever and big-hearted; she is as good as she is fair."

"If you are so touched, at first sight . . ."

"I have known her for six months."

"What ! You told me just now that you had only been in Petersburg for two days."

"Yes, but I have been in Russia for six months. I have been engineering the railroad in the south of Russia, and I am here trying to get the permit from the government to build it."

"For six months! And you have let me chatter away about a lot of things that you know better than I do."

"No, I wanted to hear your views about this country that I shall probably have to live in for several years, particularly as you are in the government employ."

"Has your fair Princess undertaken to get you a grant from the Emperor?"

"I depend a great deal upon the Prince, because this railroad will increase the value of his property. After the emancipation of the serfs, the Prince turned manufacturer. He has large factories on his property, but he has difficulty selling his goods because of the lack of transportation. If he had any means of communication with a suitable market, he could make up for the great losses that his fortune has suffered. I have been of some service to him, for these lords, when they want to turn manufacturers, are apt to ruin themselves without some practical guide. They are like children."

"Has he ruined himself?"

"Oh no! He is still very rich."

"Do you know him well?"

"He received me in the most democratic manner. His daughter, too, has been very polite to me."

"Well, then, you ought to know if she is really interested in this revolutionary movement."

Chabert said only: "Look at her! Could a Nihilist, a revolutionist, waltz like that?"

Wanda was whirling along, thoroughly given up, it seemed, to the pleasure of the dance.

"Whom is she dancing with?" said Raymond.

"Are you jealous?" answered Horace, laughing. "That is young Count Alexis Verenine, aide-de-camp to the Emperor. He seems much taken with his beautiful cousin."

The two friends, engrossed in their talk, had not noticed that the mysterious person with the German face had gradually drawn near them, and while watching the Princess, was eagerly listening to their conversation.

The young man Wanda danced with was tall, slender and fair, covered with decorations, and very distinguished in his appearance.

Wanda was speaking in a low tone to her partner, who seemed completely fascinated by her.

"Has the Emperor read the address of the Committee?" asked Wanda.

"Over and over again."

"What impression do you think it has made upon him?"

"He seems preoccupied and very much disturbed."

"Much so?"

"Yes. He walked up and down the room with feverish haste, then sat down and seemed lost in thought; then he sighed and murmured something that I did not catch."

"How could you see him?"

"I drew aside the doorway curtain, and watched him from behind it. I thought for one moment that he heard me."

"What?" cried Wanda. "Tell me! speak, Alexis."

Alexis blushed painfully.

He hesitated, but Wanda's eyes forced him to speak.

"Are you sure," he said, "that what I say to you will have no evil consequences for the Emperor?"

"What a lukewarm disciple you are, dear Alexis! If our great cause had no better champion than you! What is any man in the presence of a great idea, of a great people?"

"The Czar," answered Alexis, "is more than a man. Upon his life hangs the whole order of society."

"The disorder of society, you mean. It is this very disorder that we wish to destroy. We are not conspiring against the life of the Emperor," she added, in a lower voice, "but against the secret police. Your conscience may rest in peace. Tell me, what did you hear?"

"These words: 'I have had the will but not the power.' Then rising to his feet, with great dignity, he continued: 'I am the Czar, and I will show it!' He called me, and ordered me to summon Trepoff and Gortschakoff; but, suddenly recalling me, he told me to wait. I saw him fall into his chair in an attitude of exhaustion."

The waltz was over; Count Verenine led his fair cousin to her father.

"Papa," said Wanda, "I have waltzed until my head is quite dizzy; I do not feel well, I want to go home."

"Why! We have just come," exclaimed the Prince. "I have not even paid my respects to the Emperor. Do you know that I have made quite a conquest?"

"Yes," said Wanda, in a most indifferent manner.

"That young man there."

"That Nuremberg toy, covered with ruffles? He is a German."

"Yes."

"I hate Germans."

"That is Prince von Stackelberg. His wealth is enormous. His father has a great deal of influence with Mezentzoff, and he has obtained for this young man a high official position in the government of the Ukraine."

"An official position?"

"Yes, Southern Russia and the Ukraine, particularly, are infested with nihilists. I have urged the government to make a rigid search in that quarter. Mezentzoff has just presented to me this young man, who has authority to make the search, and is, besides, furnished with discretionary powers."

"Ah! That is different," said Wanda, with a strange light in her eye. "Present him to me; I shall be delighted to know him."

"I have promised to help him in every way in my power. These vermin who threaten the safety of the Empire must be crushed."

"And which threatens our safety, too."

"I beg you, my child, receive him politely."

"Certainly, certainly," answered Wanda, who could not suppress a smile. "It is only necessary for you to wish, and I will be as agreeable to him as I can."

"Try and moderate your democratic views a little! Sometimes you put forth such theories . . ."

"Oh! Everybody knows what the liberal views of the Russian nobility mean. I shall not be astonished to hear Stackelberg call himself a liberal too. And still, you will see that in his official capacity he will do his work conscientiously."

This admirer of Wanda, this young German Prince, was the same person who had made such a disagreeable impression upon the two Frenchmen.

Prince Kryloff beckoned to the young man, who came rapidly forward.

"My dear Wanda, allow me to present Prince Vassili von Stackelberg."

Wanda bowed haughtily, and as her eyes rested upon his face the German seemed completely captivated.

"My father tells me that you are going to travel in the Ukraine. We shall be there in the spring; I hope you will come and pay us a visit."

Stackelberg bowed very low, and made his thanks in a confused manner, for the words, the voice, the glance of the Princess embarrassed him excessively.

"Princess," he said, "will you condescend to dance the next waltz with me? I have been watching you dance for some time, and my highest desire is that you will grant me this favor."

This forced compliment betrayed the embarrassment of Vassili.

"With pleasure! I'm mad about the waltz!" answered Wanda, speaking gaily, so as to conceal the feelings which strove within her breast: the hatred with which this German inspired her and her joy at having captured a high officer of the secret police.

They were soon talking freely together.

"Then," asked Wanda, "are you really attached to the Third Section of the Imperial government?"

"Understand me: I am simply a deputy reporter. I like this duty very much; it gives me considerable authority, and, I hope, will be a step to a more important post. I am of German extraction, but I am a Russian at heart. My family has been in Russia for two generations, and we have always been attached to the court."

"How long have you been in the employ of the Imperial government?"

"For three years."

"Then you know your way around a little," said Wanda. "What do you think, at the Third Section, of these placards that the Revolutionary Committee are putting up everywhere?"

"We laugh at them. There is no Revolutionary Committee in Petersburg; the police would surely know about it; they have their agents everywhere."

"But," said Wanda, with wonderful dissimulation, "such insolence should be put down, and I suppose that the Chief of Police will take measures for the prevention of such things."

"They are going to make a number of arrests tomorrow, which will strike terror to the hearts of these nihilists."

"Unfortunately," answered Wanda, "nothing terrifies them. Their courage would be called heroism, if it were but enlisted in a better cause."

"To my thinking, all of these people are lunatics, who should be condemned to hard labor in Siberia, to cool their burning zeal."

"Bravo!" cried Wanda, ironically. "Ah! what a noble mission the government has confided to you, and how proud you ought to be of such an honor!"

"I am, and I hope to prove myself worthy of it."

"And . . . when are you going south?"

"In a few days."

The waltz, which Wanda had interrupted several times, so as to converse more at her ease, was over.

The Prince led her to her seat, when suddenly she shuddered. Her eyes met a burning glance fixed upon her.

Leaving Vassili and going straight up to the man who was looking at her, she asked:

"Where is Nadege?"

"She did not come, she is not well," answered the fresh arrival, in an agitated voice.

"Please tell her that although I have not been to see her, my thoughts and my heart are with her."

"When are you coming to see her?"

"Perhaps I shall be there tomorrow."

She passed on.

"Do you know that crazy Stepane Litzanoff?" asked Vassili Stackelberg.

"His wife is my most intimate friend."

"Is he married?"

"Yes. Why does that surprise you ?"

"He is very much talked about just now on account of his affair with a horrid woman."

"Ah!" said Wanda, shivering all over, but instantly recovering her self-possession.

"Let us go home, let us go home at once," she exclaimed to her father.

"But you look so well tonight," said Prince Kryloff. "Your face is brilliant."

"Yes, but I have a headache."

"You are the queen of the ballroom; let me enjoy your success a little longer."

"Oh no! Let's go," she insisted.

As they were leaving the room, Raymond Chabert stood in their way. Prince Kryloff very politely held out his hand to him. "Come see me tomorrow at noon," he said. "We will go together to see the minister; I have spoken to him about you. He has promised me to do everything that he can."

Chabert bowed and glanced at the Princess.

Wanda struck her fan twice against the palm of her hand. And as her father drew her away, Chabert managed to whisper these words in her ear:

"At two o'clock, at the club?"

She made an almost imperceptible sign with her head.

CHAPTER II

A TWO-FOLD LIE

Prince Kryloff loved his daughter as parents do who have ceased to live and love save in their children. She gratified his vanity as well as his affection by her beauty, her perfect grace, and her cleverness, and by the admiration which she excited wherever she went. He was therefore much troubled at Wanda's sudden headache and dizziness.

"It is not anything serious," she said. "A few hours of sound sleep will put an end to it."

As soon as she got home, she ran up into her own room. "Quick, quick, Katia," she said to her maid. "Let us make haste! They must be waiting so impatiently for us."

She tore off her bracelets, the gold band in her hair, and the clasps that fastened her dress and threw them all with the greatest haste upon a little round table.

"You look beautiful this evening, dear Princess!" exclaimed Katia.

"What do you mean, Katia? I have told you expressly that I desire you to call me Wanda, not Princess."

"Some one might overhear us," objected Katia. "A servant calling her mistress by her first name!"

"But who is there to overhear us? Sometimes I am tempted to doubt the sincerity of your convictions."

"It is true, that the scholar has gone far ahead of the teacher."

"Ah, no! I can't acknowledge that. Sometimes the Princess within me revolts at the role that I am playing. I am not yet as 'simplified' as you think I am, but I shall be after a while, I am determined."

She gave great stress to this last word.

"Dear Wanda, your logic astounds me."

"Now, then, do we or do we not desire equality, the abolition of rank and of every privilege that comes from birth and wealth?"

"Certainly we do."

"Well, I do not only not consider myself better than you, but I consider myself your inferior in point of devotion. Did you not give up your independence to come here and teach me the New Faith?"

Katia was brushing the Princess's superb hair. She took her lovely head with both hands, and stooping over, kissed Wanda on the forehead.

"We have heard compliments enough," she said. "Now that there is so much to do for the cause, we must not waste our time in words."

"You are right. Make haste. Is my dress ready?"

"Yes."

"You must hide my hair completely, so that they will not think that I am a woman."

Katia Lawinska was the daughter of a Pole who served the Russian government. Her father had obtained an important post in Poland and harried his countrymen in the most oppressive way.

Katia, disgusted with the conduct of her father, left his house and went to Zurich as a student. Then she came to Petersburg to study medicine, so as to be able to support herself. At Zurich, as well as at Petersburg, she found herself thrown in with a set of socialist students. Their doctrines inflamed her youthful imagination. She had met at Zurich a celebrated Russian physician, named Michael Federoff, who had confided to her a secret mission in Petersburg.

There she had been presented to Wanda Kryloff by a Pole named Padlewski. Finding that she had not money enough to continue her studies, she applied for help to the Princess, who was known to be very generous towards her mother's fellow countrymen.

Wanda became deeply interested in Katia Lawinska, and the young woman, very probably following out her secret instructions, asked to be allowed to enter the service of the Princess. In this humble capacity she had undertaken to convert her mistress to her own doctrines.

She had succeeded beyond her fondest hope.

Brought up among the wild steppes of the Ukraine, Wanda's nature was deep and dreamy. A spoilt child, whom her father adored, she had known no obstacle to her will. Her independent nature brooked no control, and yet her keen sense of justice revolted at the tyranny of the strong over the weak. How often she had implored her implacable father to lighten the unjust punishment of some unfortunate serf!

Among the souvenirs of her childhood there lingered dismal recollections: men beaten like dogs for a mere nothing, women scourged without mercy, whole villages razed to the ground for insurrections against their lord. Often, in her dreams, she saw again these scenes of desolation— groups of old men, women, and children bathed in tears or flying from the vengeance of their persecutor.

Then would rise before her the sad, fair face of her mother, whom she remembered but indistinctly. Wanda was herself a Pole at heart, and she loathed the Russian despotism. In her mind, the cause of Poland was the cause of humanity.

Left entirely to herself, she had read a great deal, particularly French literature. In it she had discovered the breath of modern life, the mighty seed which impregnates Art, Science and Liberty. Her ardent imagination was captivated by these noble ideas. The great characters of the French Revolution aroused her enthusiasm. She idolized those heroes; she would willingly have died, a martyr, for their cause.

At her father's estates she looked upon the peasants, bending under their burdens, ignorant, passive, and brutalized, and she thought how great a work it would be to lift their drooping heads, to cast a ray of light upon their dull minds, to make men of these slaves. Though officially liberated in 1861, little had really changed for them.

In spite of her father's opposition, she founded several schools and presided herself over the examinations. So, when she met Katia Lawinska, her mind was already prepared to receive the New Faith; Wanda was a born revolutionist, and her soul, fired with the love of justice and the longing for high deeds, found in its creed a noble and all sustaining food. She was romantic as a Pole and violent as a Cossack; she delighted in conspiracies, in secret correspondence, in running out at night, in every extreme measure.

Intrepid and enthusiastic, as most of the Slav women are, she loved danger, adored acts of heroism, and thrilled with delight at every heroic deed.

She was a very valuable recruit for the revolutionary party, on account of her position, her influence, her beauty, and her wealth, which she offered most liberally to carry out her views.

From the moment that she joined the party, a complete change passed over her. She had been in the habit of openly expressing her liberal views; and every one had been surprised to hear her talk as she did, in Prince Kryloff's drawing-room. They laughed at it, as they laugh at everything that falls from the lips of a pretty woman. The Prince attached no importance to it whatever, and was amused at what he considered a piece of juvenile exaggeration.

But, once initiated into the society, Wanda became prudent, and even artful. She was learning to look into the hearts of others without revealing her own.

When Wanda had put on her disguise, Katia exclaimed: "I think you are more beautiful dressed up as a man than you are in an evening gown. Just look at yourself!"

"Indeed, I have no time," answered Wanda.

She wore a fur cap, which entirely concealed her superb hair, and a full-length coat lined with sheepskin. A Circassian belt, worked in gold, confined it at the waist. By her side hung a small dagger. Her feet were thrust into high felt boots. Her slender figure set off this national costume to great advantage.

Katia wrapped herself in a long cloak and placed upon her head a hat lined with fur.

"I am ready," said Wanda. "Are you sure that Fedor is at the corner?"

"Yes. He has been waiting there for more than an hour."

"Very well, I will leave you off at the club and then I will go on to the place where they expect me."

Katia did not even know who expected Wanda.

"You know that you cannot come with me," said the Princess. "Believe me, it gives me the greatest pain not to be allowed to tell you everything."

"I do not expect it of you," answered Katia. "Absolute secrecy is necessary for the success of our great undertaking."

They left the house by a back staircase, which led to the offices, and passing through a little door found themselves in a narrow, dark street.

At the corner of the Palace Bridge, they found Fedor waiting for them in a sleigh. Wanda jumped into the light, graceful vehicle and took the reins; Katia seated herself by her side; Fedor climbed up behind. The spirited little horse dashed away, striking fire from the stones of the street in its rapid pace.

It was a lovely winter's night, one of those polar nights in which the moon shines with a clear, icy light, in which the starlight is intense, and the crystallized snow glistens like powdered marble. The cold was sharp and cut like a knife, but the ardor which burned in Wanda's heart rendered her quite insensible to the weather.

She did not even glance around her to gaze upon the spectacle that Petersburg presented as it lay clothed in the blue rays of the winter moon. Before her the Merchant's Exchange, the Custom House, and the University Buildings stood out, clearly defined in the cold light. Behind them, upon the island of Petersburg, could be seen the black outlines of the port, while above them all towered the bold spire of the church of Saints Peter and Paul.

Across the river could be seen a corner of the Winter Palace, Alexander's monument with its angel, the immense palace of the admiralty, and the gigantic silhouette of St. Isaac's Cathedral, with its four bell towers, its tiara of columns, and its golden cupola. Over all, flakes of snow, like touches of light, brought out the effect of the architecture. The great river looked like a white valley. Here and there lay a few boats frozen stiff in the ice.

Wanda, instead of turning up towards the Nicholas bridge, drove towards the Neva, which is frozen so hard in winter that it can be driven over without danger. The sleigh creaked on the bald snow, as a diamond sounds when it cuts a pane of glass.

Leaning back, Wanda held the reins in her small nervous hands, for her animal needed to be held in. He trotted across the river as securely as though he were on the high road. The steam flew from his nostrils. His whole body was steaming, and his tail was covered with little icicles, shining like diamonds.

She turned her horse's head into Vassili Oatrow, and drove quickly through a perfect labyrinth of streets.

She stopped before a tall, large house, such as the speculators were then building in Petersburg. Katia jumped down. "I shall be here again at two o'clock, or at half past two at the latest," she said.

"On! On!" cried the Princess.

The horse started off like the wind.

At the end of five minutes Wanda stopped her sleigh again and, throwing the reins to Fedor, got out.

"Wait for me," she said to the servant.

She went up a little alley. About midway she perceived, standing in a doorway, a human form muffled up to its eyes in a fur cloak. She involuntarily gave a start, and instantly entered a house that she had evidently been looking for.

A porter came towards her.

He said: "Russian."

She answered: "Liberty."

Then he opened a door. He led her into a room on the ground floor where, by the dim light of a lantern, she could distinguish his features.

"Ah! Is it you, Korolef?" she said to the pretended porter. "Just now, as I came in, I saw a man, who seemed to be watching me."

"I suppose the house has been denounced," answered Korolef, very quietly. "It doesn't matter if they do surround it; they won't find anything."

"I trust to your prudence," said Wanda. "Go on. I will follow you."

They crossed several large rooms, poorly furnished. They heard nothing but the sound of their own footsteps, and yet the house seemed to he inhabited.

"Have you heard from the police?" asked Wanda.

"No."

"They are going to make some arrests. Take care."

Then they entered a long passageway.

"Where are you taking me?" questioned Wanda.

"I am going to take you before the Revolutionary Committee."

They stepped before a door opening into a sort of cellar in which were some panels and a chest. Korolef pushed aside the chest and touched a spring. A small, skillfully concealed opening in the wall was disclosed, revealing a narrow stairway.

Korolef began to descend the steps, Wanda following him. When they reached the bottom, they found themselves in a low, damp cellar, and Wanda heard steady thuds, like the throbbing of an engine.

"What is that noise?" said she.

"You will soon see," answered Korolef.

CHAPTER III

THE SECRET COUNCIL

In an underground room, adorned with neither paintings nor hangings of any kind, five persons sat around a table littered over with pamphlets and papers of every description. They were discussing in the simplest manner matters of the greatest import.

These five men were the leaders of the Nihilist party, the recognized chiefs of a propaganda group which, properly speaking, is not a secret society; in Russia every one knows the danger of secret societies. The members of this confraternity were bound by no oath, but they understood that traitors must suffer death. A small number were wealthy, and belonged to the nobility.

At the time there were about five hundred in all, men and women. The Russian women played a very important role in this movement. They proved themselves to be even more ardent and enthusiastic than the men.

The world was astonished at the female element which was mixed up in this social struggle. The deep sense of justice and sisterhood, that, despite of the atheistic radicalism of the Nihilists, permeated their doctrine, touched all young and tender hearts with indignation at the misery, the corruption, the iniquity of their country. The Petersburg women mingled very little in public life. They had escaped the degrading servility which was found everywhere in Russia, which early in life blunted all sense of independence and dignity. These apostles offered up their bodies, their affections, their fortunes, their very lives, even, to the cause. They did not promise unreasoning obedience to any one; for the Russian socialist acknowledged no fetter to his individual will. The greater part were anarchists and resisted every kind of authority. But, with one accord, they give their adherence to the printed directions of the Committee. Their every act, their every thought, had but one aim: the freedom of Russia, and the total transformation of society. They devoted themselves to this work, quietly, unostentatiously, unenthusiastically.

But the enthusiasm was within; it fired their breasts, it burned within their hearts, it showed itself by a ceaseless activity, boundless self-sacrifice, heroism such as great periods of revolution can alone produce. Such was the birth of Christianity, of the Reformation, of the French Revolution; great injustice brings forth great lovers of justice; terrible sufferings arouse avengers; the wrath of the people rises in arms against despotism.

Russia, half barbarous, half civilized held within her the vices of these two social conditions.

"The Russian falsehood," wrote Hertzen, "the Russian contagion, commences at the Emperor and goes down: from soldier to soldier, from jailer to jailer, even to the little hanger-on of the Commissary of Police in the most remote district of the Empire. Thus it rolls on, ever gathering, like Dante's Bolgi, a fresh power of evil, a greater intensity of depravity and tyranny, a living pyramid of crime, of abuses, of shocks, of blows, of tyrants, heartless and rapacious, of ignorant, drunken judges, of fawning aristocrats; all bound together as accomplices, as sharers in the booty, and, last of all, supported by one hundred thousand bayonets."

The camp opposed to this official Russia had consisted but yesterday of a handful of individuals, threatening, striving to unveil the truth. Now the camp held a legion of men and women.

Noble army! They saw one another tortured, dragged to prison, exiled to Siberia, condemned to work in the mines, that is, to a slow death. They accepted the martyrdom, they continued their gloomy and unequal struggle, without knowing how it would end, so that they might, even at a far off day, make sure the freedom of the Russian people, the triumph of their democratic and egalitarian views.

Five men composed the famous Revolutionary Committee which already had, more than once, by its swift punishments, thrown terror into the official camp. What was their appearance? One could read in their faces firmness and calm courage. Besides, they were men of mark, representing the university, the clergy, the army, and journalism.

Andrew Padlewsky was descended from a noble Polish family. In the insurrection of '62 he had seen his father and his brother killed by his side. At heart, he hated his country's assassins. He held, nevertheless, a very important position in the Russian government, but he had only taken the job so as better to understand its machinery in order to serve his vengeance. He had all the ardor, the mettle, the romantic fearlessness, which characterize the children of Poland. He first conceived the idea of the revolutionary society and gathered together its earliest members. At court his influence was so great that it placed him quite above all suspicion.

Doctor Arcadius Poloutkin was a learned professor in the University. His mind leaned, in more ways than one, towards the modern school of philosophy. The study of men's physical and moral nature had led him to this conclusion: the social system, based as it was upon violence, was false, fatally engendering every corruption, every deflection, every misery; the true system of social order would be in harmony with human nature and would assure to every individual the full development of his powers and of his faculties.

This formed the subject of an important work, lately published, called

The New Law. Another book, which bore as its title *Discarded Opinions*, cut down, as with an axe, by its inflexible logic, the numerous philosophical errors of our pretended enlightened century.

Sophronius Komoff was a journalist with a biting but vigorous pen. It was he who edited the *Secret Gazette*.

Kostia Narkileff held a high position in the Russian Orthodox Church. Consequently he thoroughly understood the vices of both the white (married) and the black (unmarried) clergy, both of whom were equally hated for their greed and for the odious manner in which they work upon the superstition and ignorance of the people. Kostia Narkileff possessed much personal influence and a large fortune, both of which he offered unreservedly to the work of regeneration.

The fifth person, a very dignified man, seemed to be the president of the meeting, as much by reason of his age as by the weight of his opinion. He was Woldemar Siline. He was seventy-five years old; an old soldier. At twenty-two years of age he had taken part in the insurrection of 1825; he had passed thirty years of his life in Siberia. At Alexander's succession, thanks to the amnesty, he had been allowed to return to Petersburg, but in all these twenty years he had never ceased plotting. A Prince in his own right, nearly allied to the Romanoffs, he had entered into the revolutionary movement, he said, to wash out the stain in his blood.

There were two vacant places at the table; one was the chair of Michael Federoff, who was engaged in publishing a revolutionary paper at Geneva; the other was that of an officer of the army, high in rank, who at that moment was serving in Turkey.

Sophronius Komoff had just finished reading an article which was to appear the next day in the revolutionary *Gazette*:

"The war is over. What has it cost? Naive question. What cares our Little Father the Czar how many millions have been spent, or how many men killed? Has it not all been for his glory? From cabin to cabin, as far as the frontiers of China, his officers will go, gathering afresh the wherewithal to fill his imperial treasury. Among the three million souls who yearly see the light in his domains, he can always provide enough handsome men to keep guard at his palace-door, or to furnish food for his cannon to mow down with grape-shot.

"And yet, the Czar dare not lay his hand upon his booty. There are other wolves standing around, and watching it with jealous eye, and the Chancellor of Germany, just now the most powerful man in the world, has not uttered his deep voice.

"As soon as he shall speak, fifty-one million men who adore success, will take their cue from him to form public opinion, to which Bismarck can easily add five hundred thousand guns and ten thousand cannons. These persuasive reasons the government of Petersburg will understand at a glance.

"To be sure, we cannot see into the minds of those who arrogate to themselves the right to dispose of the fate of the people. Yet the cause of contemporary history leads us to foresee that the smaller states will be drawn into the orbit of the great powers. Might is stronger than right.

"And, as for us, nihilist warriors, what are we in the presence of these great states, of the enormous machines of war and destruction?

"We are Free Thought, we are Conscience, we are Science and Justice, we are the Modern Idea, we are Progress which nothing can shackle, which moves, which advances ceaselessly; we are the stream which soon will break through every embankment.

"Tremble, despots! Tremble, slayers of mankind! You may triumph today; but ye are destined soon to be overcome."

The article having been warmly received, the journalist disappeared behind a curtained doorway that concealed the opening to a dark passageway.

At the end of this passage could be heard the steady sound of a printing press in operation. This was the noise that had astonished Wanda.

CHAPTER IV

THE SECRET CORRESPONDENCE

Narkileff, who was in charge of the correspondence, was reading aloud the letters. Most of these were numbered; they were forwarded either by special couriers or in other indirect ways, for they could not trust the government post office.

They were made up in two packages: the foreign correspondence and the Russian correspondence.

"I have read them all through," he said. "I will sum up the most important matters for your consideration."

Vienna.

"Arrest of a number of Polish and Russian socialists for having disseminated throughout Hungary certain prohibited books and pamphlets."

Athens.

"Organization of an anarchist newspaper, *The Democrat*; the editors have been sent to prison."

Berlin.

"The socialist party in Germany is making such daily progress that even Bismarck's nerves are so excited that he cannot sleep. As he is unable to control the movement, or to bribe the leaders, he has found a man of straw, who has organized a government-backed Working-Man's Guild. The working men join it, but laugh at it."

England.

"The situation grows more intense, more gloomy."

"The price of all produce and manufactures has been reduced. From this has resulted horrible misery and a series of strikes in the agricultural as well as in the mining districts.

"Throughout the country ill feeling, agitation, and protests from the workmen in London; strike of the stone-masons."

Belgium.

"The struggle between the masters and the workmen is on the increase. Serious insurrection at Seraing. Several killed and wounded."

Italy.

"Troubles at Ferrara and Vallarnbrosa. Frightful poverty, which helps on the socialist cause. They stretch out their hands to us across the distance, and cry out be strong."

"We will be," said Prince Siline. "This important foreign correspondence must figure in our next issue."

"All the nations," added Narkileff, "are, as it were, in the throes of child-birth, and they will soon bring forth Freedom. Now let us read our Russian correspondence."

Samara.

"Mascha Soubotine, condemned as a Nihilist, has just expired, at the age of twenty-two, in a little village where she was confined, far from her friends, with neither money nor supplies. Others are dying."

"We must immediately send them assistance," said Doctor Ploutkin.

"The difficulty is," objected Padlewsky, "how to get it to them without our being discovered."

"We must send someone expressly for the purpose," said the Prince.

"The martyrdom of Mascha, far from alarming or discouraging her two sisters, has, on the contrary, increased their zeal for the cause. Beautiful, rich, cultivated, they have given up the world, their wealth, the joys of married life, to devote themselves entirely to this apostleship."

"We must," said Sophronius, "publish a biography of these three heroines, and also one of Sophia Bardine, of Olga, and Vera Lioubatowitch, and of Alexandra Kahrjewskaia."

"Here," continued Narkileff, "is something important."

Rostoff on the Don.

"The traitor Akim Niconoff has been put to death by our men. They shot him nine times, and placed upon his breast this inscription: 'Killed for denunciation of the Russian Nihilists.' The letter goes on to say: 'We are tracked like wild beasts; we are arrested, stifled in prison. In order to drag the names of our accomplices from us, they subject us to horrible torture;

and, while we incur the most odious punishments for the cause of the people, there are yet found men void of honor and of conscience, who, either from terror of the government or greed of money, betray us and deliver us into the hands of our implacable enemies. We have the consciousness that we have done a deed of noble justice in striking down the traitor. We shall, in future, take care to protect ourselves against these Judases!'"

Wolhinia.

"Princess Tizianoff writes us that she has decided to conclude a fictitious marriage which will put her in possession of her mother's fortune, as Katarina Kambrecdelidze has lately done."

"We can but approve of such a determination," answered Narkileff.

Province of Kherson.

"Here is a letter from Odessa," continued Narkileff.

"The government, in order to gain the confidence of the peasants and the working classes, has sent among them agents in disguise, to watch our movements. But they were unmasked in a wire gauze factory. When they were threatened with violence they absconded. They were recognized by their conversation, and by the clumsy manner in which they went to work."

"In fact," said Siline, "they are not upheld as we are by a great heart and a burning faith! How many lowborn soldiers can they constrain, even by the promise of high wages, to learn a trade, to work fourteen hours a day, to lead the miserable life of the working-man? We need stand in no fear of such spies; they will soon grow tired of it."

Narkileff continued:

Kiev.

"Our friends in Kiev have succeeded in getting up an enthusiastic little community, but they are so followed by the police that quite a number have passed over into Wolhinia."

Moscow.

"News excellent. Everything goes on as we could desire. The new Nihilist paper has struck off twenty thousand proofs. There are now two bands of indefatigable workers who have begun to branch out into the province of Vladimir, even as far as Perm."

Ekaterinoslav.

"Three young ladies of good birth have left their families, and have become 'simplified.' They have arrived at Ekaterinoslav dressed as workmen. As they have never learnt a trade, they have nobly undertaken the commonest kind of work. They have only been here a few months, but already in the factory in which they are employed there is it marked change in favor of our views. Every evening they go about among the hovels of the poor and preach the new gospel. At first they were shunned, but the peasants are beginning to be less distrustful than they were."

Nidit Novgorod.

"Ida Petiveff wishes to join our society. She is a girl of abandoned life, who has inspired a passion in the heart of a rich old man named Isaacs. If we will admit her she offers to get the old man to make a will in our favor leaving us one hundred thousand roubles."

"Write instantly that we refuse," interrupted Siline. "The cause is too pure, too fair, to accept of such aid."

"We are asked for fifty thousand copies of the pamphlet 'The Four Brothers,' one thousand of 'Why Is The Land Not Ours?' five thousand of 'A Clean Sweep,' and, finally, a thousand copies of our paper *Land and Liberty*. Korolef will forward them tomorrow."

Grodno.

"Ah! Bad news," continued Narkileff. "The pamphlets that Michael Federoff forwarded us from Geneva have been seized on the frontier. Soubarief has been arrested."

"My dear Komoff," said Siline, "write at once to Federoff; tell him to send us more pamphlets, but to be more careful. Instead of sending them by way of Prussia, let him forward them to Gontonewski, Ostrow, where one of our devoted friends in the customhouse will see that they reach us."

Tver.

"Here is a letter from Sartoff. He will set out for Siberia in two days disguised as a Jewish peddler. He has sent for our dispatches. Are they ready?"

"Yes," answered Sophronius.

"Tomorrow let Korolef take them to him, as well as sixty thousand roubles, a list of the several amounts to be divided amongst our friends according to their position, their age and their health."

"Indeed," added Narkileff, "our last despatches from Siberia are very good. Our best allies are there. The Poles and all the other exiles make a formidable party. The native Siberians themselves hate the Russian rule, and, at a given signal, they and the exiles together will rise en masse."

Geneva.

"Federoff writes to us that his printing press cannot turn out the pamphlets fast enough; they are written for from Moscow, Kiev and Odessa. He advises us to multiply the secret presses in Russia."

"He is right," said Siline.

"We hear from Kharkoff," said Komoff, "that they have succeeded in establishing one at the house of a very distinguished man."

"Federoff goes on to say:

"Above all, be prudent; do not compromise yourselves by too much haste and impatience; follow the advice of Bakunin. It is by conviction, slowly penetrating into the masses, that revolution can alone bring forth lasting fruit. I am working up a clearly defined program and a plan of organization, without which we shall obtain no results. Although some of our friends are opposed to it, we can never train the masses without a fixed plan of action, without concentration of authority, although we may be free to break through this authority after we have succeeded."

Komoff went on reading.

"Again, we must desire that which is possible; we must content ourselves with a certain amount of liberty and thanks to that liberty, we shall attain our final aim."

"That is quite reasonable," added Siline. "We can only free the people entirely by instructing them. I remember that in 1825 the soldiers were so ignorant that in order to get them to cry 'Long live the Constitution!' we had to make them believe that the word meant the wife of Constantine. What can one expect from a race so sunk in ignorance?"

CHAPTER V

THE REVOLUTIONARY MAIDEN

Prince Siline looked at his watch.

"One o'clock! Wanda Kryloff should be here in a minute. She has the highest revolutionary character. According to my advice, and Padlewsky agrees with me, she should be admitted as one of the Committee, on account of the service that she can render to the cause!"

"A young girl twenty years of age," objected Narkileff, "a beauty besides, can at any moment fall in love. Who will answer to us for the revelations that she may make to the man she loves? Is it not rather thoughtless to lay bare the business of the Committee?"

"It is evident," cried Padlewsky, "that you do not know Wanda Kryloff. Not only is she beautiful, but she is also dedicated. There is no loftier mind, no more compassionate soul than hers. Besides, she will be bound to us by a family secret."

"Ah," answered Poloutkin, "as usual, dear Padlewsky, you reason in a very exaggerated manner. Women are very weak and fickle, and when once their affections are engaged. . ."

"How, Doctor?" cried Palewsky, excitedly, "is that your opinion of women? You think, perhaps, that because their flesh is softer than ours, their moral nature is also! If they have less muscle, they have more nerve. Yes, I maintain that a woman, once possessed by an idea, is stronger for her cause than the strongest man. She will perform acts of heroism before which we shrink."

"Is it for us," continued Siline, "who see them at work day by day, to doubt their perseverance and their energy? In devotion, in fearlessness, they prove themselves our equals, and we should treat them as such."

"I have presented Wanda Kryloff. I will answer for her with my head," said Padlewsky.

At this moment Sophronius returned, bringing with him Wanda.

She held out her hand to the Prince and to Padlewsky.

"Ah!" she exclaimed, "I know these other gentlemen; I remember seeing them at the club. These are our friends Narkileff, Komoff and Poloutkin."

Then she cast her eyes around the room that she had just entered.

"You see," said Padlewsky, laughing, "you are now in the Devil's Cave. Here is the place where the darkest plots are hatched, where the most incendiary articles of the underground press are concocted. Did you not expect to sees frightful scenes, black and red hangings, trap-doors, opening occasionally to admit glimpses of hell beneath? Well, here is the hall of the Revolutionary Committee, and allow me to present the five head conspirators, who have undertaken to overturn an empire of one hundred million men."

"Indeed," said Wanda, recovering from her surprise, "this is not at all the idea that I had formed in my mind of this formidable Committee."

"Perhaps," said Siline, "you may have heard of the rather theatrical initiation of the Free Masons. We thought that our situation was too serious for any such child's play. What is the good of test oaths? We only admit into our society persons whom we know to be incorruptible. We kill the traitors. Niconoff has just been killed. This vengeance seems terrible, but it is necessary, in order to prevent informers, to secure our individual safety, and to assure the safety of our undertaking. Do you feel yourself strong enough, Wanda Kryloff, to keep our secrets?"

As he uttered these words the Prince fixed his eyes upon the young girl's face. He could detect there neither agitation nor fear; he discovered there, on the contrary, an inflexible will.

She answered with perfect simplicity:

"I have the strength, the will, and the faith; the strength to keep a secret, the will to act, the faith to succeed. For this righteous cause I am ready to sacrifice my position, my fortune, and my life."

"It is necessary for us to know," continued the Prince, "what motives have drawn you into the nihilist movement."

"The sentiment of justice," answered Wanda; "pity for the oppressed, the hatred of oppressors and executioners. The personal motives which actuate me are the dismal recollections that darkened all my childhood."

"One more question I must ask you," continued Siline. "You will see at once that it is necessary for me to do so. Are you in love with any one, or are you engaged to be married?"

"I do not think of marriage," she said, "and whatever attraction I may have for any one, I have perfect control of my will. I understand that an apostle must devote herself unreservedly to her work. I would never consent to marry any man who did not hold the same views with me and who would not be willing to devote himself unreservedly to the sacrifice."

"Still more is necessary. You must renounce marriage, which is incompatible with the great and lofty mission we wish to accomplish. Will you promise to lead a celibate life until the triumph of the Revolution?"

"Yes, until the freedom of the Russian people."

"Are you ready to swear it?" said Siline, who, as an old conspirator, had a prejudice in favor of oaths, although the present nihilists disowned them as being opposed to individual self respect.

"I swear it," answered the young girl, who offered up her heart as she had offered up her life, with the same calm resolution, with the same sublime self-sacrifice.

"Then, Wanda Kryloff, as we have entire confidence in you, I propose to you, in the name of the five members of the Committee here present, and of the two absent ones, who will ratify what we have done, to admit you into our Committee, in which the female element up to this time has never been represented, and to take part in our private deliberations."

"But allow me to ask one question," said Wanda. "Are you sure that in admitting me to your deliberations you have not been too much influenced by my rank and fortune? Katia Lawinska is a woman far above the average, who has given repeated proofs of her devotion. She is clever, intelligent, a heroic character, and yet you never thought of her."

"These remarks do you honor," answered Woldemar Siline, "and show the nobility of your heart. But in the struggle in which me are engaged we must consider the importance that individual adherents bring to our cause. If we admit Katia Lawinska into our Committee, we should have to admit a great many more equally heroic. But in order to keep our secret, we must limit the number. Every member of the society is devoted to the work; some are wealthy, and occupy very high positions, but we only admit into the Committee those who can render us exceptional service."

"In the presence of all of you, I feel so little and so weak."

"You have the irresistible power of beauty. You can win over to our side men who are absolutely necessary for the success of the cause."

"I do not know," said Wanda, "if my character will lend itself to the role that you wish me to take. However, I made one effort this evening."

And she repeated to them her conversation with Alexis Verenine, and her introduction to Prince Stackelberg.

"But," cried out the conspirators, "this is very important. If you can bring over this young prince attached to the Third Section . . ."

"Turn this systematic German into a revolutionist? "exclaimed Wanda, "that would be difficult indeed, but I wish to lay a little plan before you, that Katia and I have cherished for some months. Padlewsky, you sent Katia to me. She left her father's house, rather than see that father become the oppressor of his brethren. But I, in my father's house, look upon just such a sight. Formerly he used to whip his serfs, now he exhausts his workmen and makes capital of their labor and their misery. In spite of the love that he bears me, I have no influence over him. He thinks himself superior to these men, whom he treats as beasts of burden. I have not the courage to condemn him, because he is my father, but his character is revolting to me. To continue to be a witness to such sights is beyond my strength. I have determined to become 'simplified' like Katia, and to embrace the apostolate. She and I wish to learn a trade, so that we can penetrate into the farms and factories of Russia, and we are impatient to commence our work. In Southern Russia there are a great many agricultural and industrial associations. We want to go there as simple working women, so as to be able to preach our New Gospel to them."

As she spoke thus, filled with the enthusiasm of strong conviction, her inspired glance, her thrilling sympathetic voice, fascinated her five hearers. "You will be the liberator of Russia!" cried out Sophronius Komoff.

"Doubtless," said Siline, "your ambition is noble, but I think you can do something more profitable for the Cause. Among the working classes we have already propagandists enough. Just now we need to attract members of the best society of Petersburg. We desire to abolish the privileges of the nobility, yet it is from their ranks that we wish to make recruits; we wish some one who can touch the heart of society; you exactly fit this role."

"I will take it," said Wanda, "although I dislike to play the part of a coquette, which necessitates a certain amount of duplicity."

"The oppressed are driven to stratagem. Stratagem is allowable in war, and we have declared war."

Wanda assented.

"So," said Narkileff, "according to what Count Verenine told you, the Emperor paid no attention to our declaration of war."

"So he thinks."

"We looked for that," said Sophronius Komoff.

"Well, then," added Poloutkin, "in our next number we must reprint our address to the Czar and comment in strong terms upon his weakness. For twenty years he has promised reforms without ever granting them."

At this moment, Korolef entered bringing the proofs.

"Will you take the Princess out? said Siline.

"I am sure," said Korolef, "that the house is watched on the side of the quay. We will go out the other way." It was two o'clock in the morning.

CHAPTER VI

THE CLUB

Wanda left the underground chamber by a quite different way from the one which she had followed in entering it. Korolef walked with her to her sleigh.

Fedor, still motionless in spite of the intense cold, was waiting for her, soothing his horse to keep it quiet. In less than five minutes they had reached the tall house which Katia had gone into an hour before.

"Wait for me at the quay!" said the Princess to Fedor.

Fedor drove off instantly.

She went towards the doorman, who, as is the custom in Russia, was stationed outside of the house.

"Will you let me in?"

"Whom do you want to see?"

"Alexander Lazareff, the engraver."

The doorman, stupefied by cold and vodka, gave himself a shake and admitted her.

Wanda passed through the entrance, climbed three flights of steps, and knocked at a door.

A small opening, concealed in the woodwork, revealed itself, and an eye, cautiously applied, scanned the landing and the staircase.

Wanda gave her name.

Instantly the door, grating on its hinges, flew open.

The Princess entered a little ante-chamber, furnished as an office; out of this, another door, provided with the same little wicket, led into an inner apartment.

"It is Wanda Kryloff," said a voice from within; instantly she was introduced into the Hall of Assembly.

This was quite a spacious apartment, lighted by lamps hanging from the ceiling. The work tables had been turned into tea tables, upon which stood samovars and glasses, for in Russia they generally drink their tea out of glasses. On these tables were also thrown books, papers, and pamphlets.

About fifty persons were assembled in this hall, taking tea, reading, writing or talking.

Most of them were engaged in conversation, for on this particular evening there was no especial business to be transacted.

It was one of those friendly daily meetings which were held, sometimes here, sometimes there, to put the police off the track, and where the members could read the letters of their friends and prohibited printed matter and discuss the action of the government. Whenever a member of the club had something important to say, the member asked for a moment's silence and instantly every one listened to him or her with attention.

This was one of those clubs which swarmed then in Petersburg and in every city of the Empire; for in the past years the nihilist movement had taken a most accentuated form.

It had been fifty years ago when this movement commenced; for fifty years the intelligent and educated class of men has struggled against Czarism.

After the death of Czar Nicholas the fight had become fiercer. The act of emancipation was more the result of public opinion than of any spontaneous manifestation of the imperial will. At that time the Russian people, which is a young people, made a prodigious stride. Their aim was not to obtain the insignificant, restricted reforms that good-natured Alexander proposed; they desired a true and thorough social regeneration. To make of this slavish Russia, bending under her religious and imperial yoke, a free nation, showed a wonderful daring in the Russian revolutionists, a mighty power which resembled in no way the expediency of the Western nations. In order to accomplish great deeds, we must long for greater. The Russian movement presented to our gaze a colossal sight, not only by the number of its partisans and the monstrous abuses that it had undertaken to reform, but also by its deep radicalism and by the heroism of its apostles.

Russia had suddenly freed herself, had thrown off the religion and the prejudices of her forefathers. Hence this name of Nihilist, by which title the ruling class designated these independent minds, but in reality there were no Nihilists in Russia. There were political philosophers, free thinkers, humanitarians, who pursued a generous idea: the Freedom and Happiness of Russia. They had been so oppressed for so long a time that now they could not content themselves with a half liberty.

The Russians can do nothing halfway; there is a savage streak in their blood that leads them to extremes. The fire within them cannot be quenched, either by blood or by the snows of Siberia.

Agitation increased daily. The nihilist clubs, numerous enough within the past years, had increased wonderfully. At present they embraced almost every intelligent class among the citizens.

And yet the Third Section of the Emperor's government existed as a representative of the Imperial all-seeing eye, of the Imperial all-hearing ear. Why, with the means at its command, could it not close the clubs, unveil these propagandists, imprison these conspirators? It was because they would need agents in every house, in every family, since there was not a house, not a family which did not contain revolutionists among its members.

As Wanda entered she saw, sitting near the door, Raymond Chabert and

Katia, who were waiting for her.

Raymond was very pale, but as soon as he saw her he colored painfully.

"Ah! At last," he said as he bowed to her.

"What is the matter?" she asked, very much astonished.

"We have been very uneasy about you for the last half hour."

"Why?"

"This going out in the middle of the night!"

"Well!"

"Suppose you were to be assaulted?"

"Cowardly, faithless creature!" answered Wanda, laughing. "When we brave the Russian police, we surely run more danger than in wandering about at night."

"Your fearlessness astonishes me."

"You forget, Mr. Frenchman, that we Russian Revolutionists have nothing in common with your Parisian coquettes."

"We alone can save Russia," added Katia, "and we must be equal to our mission."

"You are right," said Raymond. "But on that very account your life should be all the more precious, and I beg you to allow me to protect it."

"You are too French, too gallant," said Wanda, smiling. "We must change all that." But as she spoke thus, she bent her eyes full of a tender gratitude upon Raymond.

Under that glance Raymond seemed to lose countenance. Happily the company had become aware of the presence of the Princess and advanced to greet her.

They seemed to belong to every class of society. Most of them were young people. Some were dressed as citizens, a large number wore the shabby, rumpled clothes of the student, others the garb of the working man. The women were numerous. Rich or poor, noble or low-born, they were all dressed with extreme simplicity. Their faces showed intellect and resolve.

The perfect freedom which existed between the members of this club would have astonished a stranger. A workman talked with a prince in terms of equality, for in this assembly were two princes, several persons of rank, and three members of the clergy.

On this particular evening they were holding an animated discussion about the event of the day. General Trepoff, Chief of Police, in going through the prison inspection, had noticed one man who stood before him without uncovering his head. Upon being ordered to take off his hat, the prisoner had refused.

Trepoff, in a rage, ordered that the offender should receive one hundred lashes.

One hundred lashes for a piece of impoliteness!

The prisoner's name was Bogoluboff. He had written several articles which attacked the baseness of those high in authority and the cruelness of the secret police. But this was not the crime which had brought upon him their infamous, atrocious punishment. The thing which had exasperated Trepoff was the fact that Bogoluboff had refused to bow down before the Chief of Police.

What chastisement was worthy to be inflicted upon the functionary who had dared to humiliate an author of such high intellectual and moral distinction?

The indignation surpassed itself. Everybody spoke at once; there was one universal cry: "Vengeance!"

One woman alone did not open her lips. With her arm resting upon a table, she sat listening and smiling with a bitter, sad smile.

Her eyes were lusterless. In her somewhat insignificant face, a close observer could detect a singular expression of force, of resolution, perhaps of obstinacy. Her hands were broad, short and strong.

She was dressed with a total disregard for appearance.

Katia Lawinska sat down beside her.

"Is this you, Vera Zassoulitch? I have not seen you for a long time."

"I have been hard at work. I have just passed my examination in medicine."

"What are you doing now?"

"I am hard at work for the cause."

"What do you think should be done to Trepoff."

"He should be put to death."

"But the difficulty is to find a man who will carry out the sentence."

"If a man cannot he found, perhaps a woman will do."

"Would you do it?"

"If no one else can be found."

She spoke with a firm, sharp enunciation.

At that moment silence was requested in order to read aloud the extracts from the *Secret Gazette* that Korolef had given Wanda to show to the club. The correspondence excited the greatest interest, especially the execution of the traitor, Niconoff.

"It is time for us," said Lazareff, the president of the club, "to act. We have been in hiding long enough. We are tired of this slavery, of this infernal rule, which for so many years has prostrated our moral powers. The moment has come for us to openly declare ourselves, to let ourselves be known — ourselves and the cause that we uphold. Trepoff has outraged us with every lash that has fallen upon Bogoluboff. Blood alone can wash out such an insult."

Vera Zassoulitch rose to her feet, overcame her natural timidity, and spoke:

"This is not Trepoff's only crime," she said. "Is it not by his orders that we all are hunted down like dogs, and cast into prison?"

"I saw him at Warsaw," added Katia, "when he was Chief of Police there; he used to persecute and track the Polish patriots just as he does the nihilists now."

"Shall we permit such conduct to go unpunished?" continued Vera.

"No, no!" they all cried out.

"Well, I propose," said Lazareff, "that the men present cast lots, and that he upon whom the lot falls shall revenge us upon this criminal."

"I wish to be included among the men," said Vera Zassoulitch.

But upon reflection they determined to wait, and to take the advice of the other clubs before resolving upon any action. So the meeting broke up without having come to any conclusion.

CHAPTER VII

PRINCE KRYLOFF

When Wanda and Katia reached their home it was four o'clock in the morning. To their great surprise, instead of finding everything dark and silent, they saw lights flitting from window to window, and perceived that there was a general commotion. "Ah, your Excellency, may the saints protect us!" cried out the doorman. "The Prince is like a madman. He has found out that your Excellency is not in the house. He has been beating us all; he wants to turn us all out for having allowed you to go out without telling him."

The young girls looked at one another.

"What shall we do? How can we appear before him?"

"Is the Prince up?" asked Wanda.

"Oh yes! He asks every minute if your Excellency has come home."

"Where is he?"

"In the Princess's sitting room."

"Wait here, dear Katia. I prefer to brave his anger alone."

She boldly mounted the marble staircase which led to her apartments.

Upon hearing the noise the Prince had opened the door.

He was very pale; his features contracted with rage.

"Where have you been?" he said, in a choking voice.

"If you will allow me, father, I will not tell you now; you are not in a condition to listen to me."

"Tell me at once; I will know."

"I cannot tell you before I obtain permission to do so. It is a secret which does not concern me alone."

"Permission to answer me? A secret from your father!"

He panted for breath.

Wanda knew these terrible rages, but she never trembled.

"Will you speak? You shall! You know well that no one can resist me."

Wanda did not say a word.

The Prince came towards her in a threatening attitude , then suddenly checking his fury, he lowered his voice.

"You know, my daughter, that I love you more than anything in the world. I implore you, do not irritate me, I am afraid that in a fit of fury I might forget myself. Tell me, my child, where have you been?"

"I cannot lie to my father," answered Wanda, "and I cannot tell a secret that I have promised to keep. I implore you, do not question me."

"You have a lover, wretched girl!" said the Prince.

He struck a little table with his fist and shattered it to atoms.

"If you do not answer me instantly, I will break you to pieces, as I do this table."

"Wait till tomorrow, I beg of you . I am tired. Permit me to go to bed."

"That is it! You want time so as to invent a lie to deceive me! I wish to know, and I will know, if I have to lock you up until you will speak."

At this threat, Wanda's pride revolted.

"Do what you choose. I will not speak."

Motionless, she leaned against a wall and crossed her arms.

Then the Prince, intoxicated with rage, rushed upon her and struck her in the face.

"Your mother's own child! If you leave this house again at night, I will put you under lock and key."

"As you did my mother," said Wanda, fixing her eyes, full of indignation and revolt, upon her father's face.

When he heard these words, shuddering at this look, as if some terrible recollection had overcome him, he said in a low, hollow voice:

"As I did your mother!"

Before the haughty, contemptuous attitude of his daughter, his head drooped and he withdrew.

Wanda stood for an instant as though nailed to the wall by the insult she had received.

She dared not look into her own heart; for at this moment the man whom she was obliged to call father inspired her with naught but aversion. He was to her the very personification of the odious rule that weighed down her country. Doubtless he was the result of the society in which he had been born, in which he had lived, but he was none the less detestable.

As soon as she had come to herself she called Katia and threw herself into her arms.

"I have no one but you, dear Katia! My father has broken the last tie that bound me to him. This man who tortured my mother, who has committed every crime and every exaction, who has oppressed the poor and the weak, has just struck me in the face, as if I were the lowest of creation. Ah! If I could but go away, run away with you."

"Very well! Let us go," said Katia.

"I cannot. I have promised to stay here. Go to bed; as for me, I am so miserable that I cannot sleep."

"Why are you so unhappy?"

"I blame my father, and I think hardly of him, but he was my father; he loved me. It was a tie which bound me to him, kept me by his side, even made me feel tenderly towards him . This tie has been violently broken; it has been torn asunder; that is why I am unhappy. But tomorrow I shall be strong."

Katia, seeing that her friend strove to keep back her tears, retired.

CHAPTER VIII

THE RED LETTER

Towards one o'clock, on the night of the ball at the Winter Palace, just as Wanda was leaving the ballroom, the Emperor reentered his own private apartments. Alexis Verenine, in his capacity as aide-de-camp, was on duty in the antechamber.

The Emperor dismissed every one, and desired to be left alone.

A large red envelope was lying on his table.

He sat down and, laying his hand upon this letter, seemed lost in thought. Bitter thoughts and utter weariness held possession of that fine, intelligent brain, where so much real goodness dwelt. His eyes were sad, his whole body bent as though drooping under some weight. Suddenly he straightened himself up, took up the red envelope, and extracting from it a letter, read, or rather reread, the following singular and threatening words:

To the Czar:

You have confidence in your glory, in the slavish adoration of your subjects, in the continuance of your power, in the future existence of your race. The truth is this:

Your glory is built up by the blood of your people; your magnificence, by their wretchedness and the sweat of their brow; your power, by their ignorance. But your power draws near its end; your dynasty shall not reign forever.

You think you have done a noble deed in granting your peasants liberty, but have you given them bread?

Your people are weary of suffering, weary of working for the tax gatherer, weary of the impudence and corruption of your nobility, weary of your venal magistrates and of your rapacious officials, weary of your clergy who mulct them in every way, weary of your pretended victories in war, which are but useless massacres, costing them the life blood of their youngest and noblest sons.

Yes, your people are weary of your weakness towards your courtiers, weary, above all, of your infamous secret police, which arrests, judges and condemns behind closed doors the most enlightened, the most large-hearted men in your empire.

From the windows of your palace you can hear the cries of these heroes, whose chains are riveted to those walls washed by the icy flood of the Neva. Today the avengers are awake, the conspiracy is everywhere, among your nobility, as well as among your people, who at last understand that they, too, have rights. It is among the army, among the clergy, even within your palace, among your most trusted servants.

The storm is gathering, the thunder rambles beneath you; soon a fearful whirlwind will sweep you from your throne, dynasty, government and nobles.

But there is yet a way to escape this frightful catastrophe. Make the revolution yourself. Give land to the peasants, give a constitution to your people and suppress the secret police; ask the nation if she will acknowledge you for her father. And thus you will save your country from the horrors of a civil war.

Shake off your torpor, put aside your stupid courtiers, act according to the impulses of your heart and of justice.

If you will do this thing you will have a right to the gratitude of the Russian people, and posterity will rank you among the benefactors of mankind.

– The Revolutionary Committee of Petersburg

Alexander fell back in a profound reverie. Far away could be heard the music of the ball and the rolling of the carriages as they bore home the courtiers. The Emperor having gone, they no longer felt any interest in remaining.

He arose, went to the window, and looked out upon the Neva; across the river he saw, indistinctly in the pale light, the black outline of the massive fortress.

And in thought, he saw those heroes, chains upon their feet, hollow-eyed, shivering with cold, crouching in their damp cells, and cursing him. He turned away, and sat down again by the table, upon which lay the red letter.

It was the feeling of his impotence which so weighed upon him. And yet this monarch reigned over the greatest empire in the world. One hundred million people bowed beneath his yoke.

The Swod, or Russian code of law, thus defined the Czar: "An autocrat whose power is unlimited."

He could draw as much money as he wished, and without rendering any account, from the Exchequer of the State. All Russia belonged to him; he could give the land to whom he pleased. He could pardon, or degrade, or exact; he could make a man rich or poor by one word. What would he have that he could not have, this man who was the most complete personification of autocratic power?

He desired to restrict his power, to give a constitution to his people, to break the administrative net that entangled his country and paralyzed it — and he could not. His nobles were banded against him to preserve their privileges.

He had struggled, but he was discouraged. His whole energy seemed to have been exhausted by the one act of the emancipation of the serfs, which had nearly cost him his crown.

This despot, in whose hands the accident of birth had placed unlimited authority, was a liberal man, certainly, but a weak man.

It was not he who governed — it was his ministers and his courtiers.

Now and then, when the rumor of some injustice reached his ears, he wished to make amends for it. He gave the necessary orders; but he was not always obeyed.

"Does this Revolutionary Committee really exist?" said the Czar to himself. "Perhaps they are madmen, maniacs. However, they speak the truth; I am threatened with a revolution! And I would be as Louis XVI. Louis loved his people sincerely, just as I do, and, like me, he was powerless to bend the will of those around him, of a blind and obstinate court.

"And still, I could prevent the catastrophe. Some will resist, but others will hear me. If I would . . ."

Then, lifting his head he said, in a loud voice:

"I will, and thus I shall insure the safety of my dynasty far better than by my conquests. Yes, I will make this revolution in spite of Gortschakoff, Shouvaloff and Adlerberg. And yet, must I break the hearts of the faithful men who love me, and who have devoted their whole lives to my service, to my glory? But, after all, what are these men before the happiness, the prosperity, the resurrection of a nation? I emancipated the serfs because I did not wish to rule over slaves; I will make this revolution because I do not wish to reign over ignorant starvelings. I will do it, even if it costs me my throne! My throne!"

He made a movement of disgust and weariness.

"They say there are conspirators here, in my very palace!"

He rang the bell. Verenine entered.

"Suppose I question this young man, who has always been devoted to me?" thought the Emperor.

"My dear Alexis, this letter states that there are here, among the court officials, certain men who desire the destruction of my authority, and perhaps of my life." The young aide-de-camp became livid.

Alexander was so far from suspecting him that he did not notice his sudden change of color.

"Have you observed any signs of the kind?" continued Alexander. "Has any one made any propositions to you?"

"No, Sire," answered Verenine, but in such a broken, husky voice, that the Emperor fixed his eyes upon him.

"You look very pale! Does anything ail you, my child?"

"No, your Majesty, but what you have just said to me . . ."

"I know your devotion, your attachment to me. Do you suspect any one? Think a moment."

"No one; there is not a person in the palace that you have not loaded with benefits."

"That is true," said the Emperor, with a sad smile. "But ingratitude, dear Alexis, is the independence of the heart; and nowadays, as independence is the fashion . . ."

"Do you suspect . . ."

"Ah! I, unhappily, only believe in a devotion founded upon fear, or upon the hope of future benefits. You will learn, by experience, as I have, that the human heart is not altogether beautiful."

"The human heart is not frightful; but society is."

"You talk like a Nihilist. Society, socialists, I hear these words on every side."

Verenine was very uneasy.

"Does your Majesty suspect me?" he stammered.

The Emperor sighed.

"No, Verenine I do not suspect you. Your father was entirely devoted to me. I made his fortune. You are my son's friend, and it is in your interest to remain faithful."

Alexander did not speak for several minutes; then he said, "I saw you dancing a little while ago with a very beautiful woman. It was Princess Kryloff, I believe."

"Yes, Sire."

"She has fine eyes. It seems to me that I have heard that she, too, is somewhat addicted to the madness of the day."

Alexis felt himself grow pale and tremble. He understood well that his uneasiness might not only ruin him, but Wanda likewise. In the presence of this imminent danger he managed to control his emotion.

"She a Nihilist! Her soul is too lofty, her heart too loving, to allow her to adopt such a doctrine of extermination."

"How enthusiastic!" said the Emperor, smiling.

"She is my cousin, Sire, and besides, we have been friends since we were children."

"And you are in love with her? That is quite natural. Why should you not marry her? Your family is as good as hers; your fortune . . ."

"Prince Kryloff is very rich, and she is an only daughter."

"Is that all? You know that I never forsake my friends when they are in trouble. I have always for your father's sake felt very kindly towards you. Do not forget it, my child."

"Ah, Sire, you overwhelm me with your goodness, but in the first place, I should like her to love me."

"And why shouldn't she love you ?"

"She is such an enigma; she has such an impenetrable character."

"Does she love anyone else ?"

"I do not think so."

"Well, then, will you allow me to arrange the matter for you?"

"Ah, Sire, would you condescend to . . . But, indeed, I would rather first know what Wanda's feelings are towards me."

"Nonsense! You are a handsome fellow, and if you have no rival, she will love you, I am sure. As you have chosen me for your confidante, I give you my word of honor that you shall marry Wanda Kryloff."

"Believe me, Sire, my gratitude is profound. Only if I dared, I should beg your Majesty not to take any steps in the matter until I speak to Wanda myself, for she will never allow a husband to be forced upon her by any one. She would resist her father's will; she would resist the whole world."

"Do you think she would resist the Czar?"

"I fear she would."

"Was her mother a Pole?"

"Yes, Sire."

"Then I understand it. Well, you can tell me what I can do for you, and I will do it. Go back into the ballroom, and if Trepoff and Mezentzoff are still there bring them to me."

He made a sign with his hand for Verenine to leave him. Alexis went out violently agitated. Why had the Emperor sent for the Chief of Police and the General of the Guards? Did he suspect anything? Had he guessed his secret and Wanda's? Alexis's knees gave way under him. He reeled like a drunken man.

"They speak the truth," thought the Emperor. "In my palace, about my person, these men whom I have loaded with benefits are conspiring against me. Even this child that I have loved as my own betrays me. Shall I give him up to the police, and send him off to Siberia? It is no use; Princess Kryloff has turned his head with her beautiful eyes. But she cannot be very dangerous. She is romantic and unreal, like all young girls ; I cannot arrest everybody, and without proof, too. This movement is fatal! It has such an effect upon the young people. It is so dull in this country of clouds and snow, and life in Russia is very monotonous. I suppose they are conspirators from conviction. Perhaps, if I were in their place, I would be a conspirator, too, from ennui and disgust of life. Yes, I will enter into a conspiracy with my people against this government which oppresses me."

At this moment, Trepoff entered, conducted by Verenine.

"Did your Majesty send for me?" said Trepoff.

"Yes, General," answered the Czar, in a severe tone. "It appears there is a conspiracy in Petersburg, a so-called Revolutionary Committee, and that a missive like this can be thrown into my carriage in broad daylight, without anyone knowing who has thrown it."

The Emperor held out the red letter to the Chief of Police.

Trepoff took it with a trembling hand. As he read, he could not suppress his expressions of contempt and scorn.

"Well," asked the Emperor, "what do you think of that?"

"They are maniacs," said Trepoff, "or perhaps some men who have laid a wager to terrify your Majesty. We have discovered that a hundred and ninety-three maniacs are running about Russia, disseminating revolutionary pamphlets. Out of these hundred and ninety-three, but twenty have been found guilty. For four years we have searched in vain for the authors of the plot; there is no plot. With the exception of a few dangerous men, who are under lock and key, these pretended Nihilists, about whom there is so much talk, are really not to be feared. They are narrow-minded, fanatical, idle men, without position, without influence, and with very little intellectual weight."

Far from being convinced, the Emperor struck the table with his fist.

"General," he cried, "your agents are unskillful. You, yourself, seem to me to be blind. I myself do not believe that there is a plot ready to spring at once into action, but I believe there is a conspiracy against my government. These anarchists that you despise are among my nobles, at court, in this very palace itself. I am sure of it."

"In your palace?" cried Trepoff, utterly astounded.

"And you know nothing of it," continued Alexander, "and yet you and Mezentzoff are only here to watch over my person."

"I will discover them. I will punish the guilty."

"No; that is not my intention. Look, if there is a conspiracy bring me the proofs; bring me the list of the guilty, to me alone. I am sure the last trial has had the most deplorable effect, and your agents make so many mistakes! They might deal rigorously with the innocent. I will not have it! No one, particularly those about my person, shall be arrested without my express permission. Do you understand?"

"I will obey, Sire," said Trepoff, bowing low.

Alas! The Emperor had forgotten once more that be was not the master.

CHAPTER IX

REBELLION

Prince Kryloff's palace stood upon the banks of the Neva, not far from the Admiralty Gardens, in the most charming part of Petersburg. This palace, which was one of the oldest and finest in the city, was built, as were most of the Russian palaces, in the old French style, slightly Italianized. The woodwork of the lower story, the Corinthian columns, the pediments of the windows, the ornamentation in carved stone, all were brought out in bold relief by the rose color stucco of the building, which formed a lovely background and produced a superb effect.

One of the wings of the palace was entirely taken up as a Winter Garden. Through the panes of glass, under a roof covered with snow, could be seen palm trees, magnolias and bananas, which reared their tall heads on high.

Within, everything was magnificent. There could be found, as in all the noblemen's houses, every luxury, every article of taste, gathered from all parts of Europe. However, the national character revealed itself in a Byzantine Madonna and a statuette of St. Peter, the patron saint of Prince Kryloff. These two icons, decorated with gold, and each surrounded with a large golden nimbus, recalled to mind that the palace was in Holy Russia.

Wanda's boudoir was furnished in a very original taste. It looked more like a study than a young woman's lounging place. On the Smyrna carpet lay a large white bear's skin. Upon the sofa, a pretty piece of furniture tufted in blue and gold brocade, was thrown a superb robe of blue fox, fringed with crimson tassels. Here and there, scattered among satin poufs and luxurious arm-chairs, stuffed bear cubs, used as footstools, gave a decided polar appearance to the room. The hangings of the doors came from Asia; the tapestries, bought at the fair of Nijni Novgorod, were Chinese, splendid in their rich coloring and marvelous designs. Trophies made of singular and beautiful armor, interspersed with Italian pictures, adorned the walls.

The greatest luxury in Russia consists in furs and flowers, especially flowers. Russians seem to console themselves for the implacable cold of their winters by a profusion of verdure. And so Wanda's room was like a hothouse. In the tall windows banana trees spread their great leaves; English ivy climbed around the gilded pillars; a superb orchid fell gracefully from a lamp of Japanese porcelain. In every corner magnolias and camellias bloomed; jars of Bohemian glass held exotic flowers, and amongst them fine bronzes and cloisonne enamels were arranged with taste.

In the midst of all this, stretched upon a sofa, lay Wanda, idly dreaming. She wore a dress of white cloth, trimmed with ruby velvet. Her slender waist was imprisoned in a gold band set with turquoise.

"Katia, do you know whom I expect to see today"

"No, dearest."

"My three lovers."

"I hope you are not in love with any of them?"

"No," she answered, hesitatingly.

"You seem doubtful."

"No, I am not, but . . ." she sighed.

"I am uneasy," said Katia. "Love is a fatal, absorbing passion. Sometimes it does give a noble impulse to the heart, but more frequently it deadens our generosity."

"Someone said long ago," answered Wanda, "Love is but a two-fold egotism."

"Yes, and when the greater number suffer, have we the right to be happy?"

"It is true it is a crime to think of happiness when our brothers are suffering in prisons and in the mines because of their devotion to their fellow men."

"And yet, you could have such a brilliant life, such a happy, beautiful life!"

"Ah! The world is not as charming as you think it. Now, yesterday, the ball at the Winter Palace was superb, dazzling. I had every success that a woman can desire. Katia, I found it empty, unsatisfying and frightfully tiresome. And these crowds, where I can neither talk nor walk nor dance, are to me the dullest things that I can imagine."

"Oh, I can understand that!"

"I only begin to live when I come home and can take you in my arms; when I meet our friends, to whom I am bound by one great, noble idea. They look upon us as maniacs. On the contrary, we are the only sensible people in Russia; all the other inhabitants of the Holy Empire are mummies."

"That is very true. If every one could but know what a mighty interest we have in our lives, how exciting, how emotional it is, every one would join us."

Just then a footman entered, sent by the Prince to ask Wanda if she would come to breakfast.

"Tell the Prince," she said, "that I'm not well, and that I will not take any breakfast this morning."

"Not well?" cried Katia.

"It is not anything, but I do not want to see my father today. I feel that I would forgive him, I am so weak towards those I love. He will come up here presently; he can't bear to have me cross to him."

"You are very wrong, dear Wanda, to allow any weakness in yourself, even towards your father. A father has no right to our love or to our respect unless he behaves himself properly. Even if my father had loved me, I could never have forgiven the exactions that he practiced upon my unfortunate fellow countrymen."

"You have a firmer and stronger character than I have. I will try to follow your advice."

Just then the Prince burst into the room like a whirlwind.

Katia withdrew.

"Are you ill, Wanda?" he exclaimed. "You look very pale."

Wanda did not say a word.

"Wanda?"

"Father."

"I am the cause of this. When I see you ill my pride disappears, and I only know that I love you. Tell me, have you a fever?"

"I do not know."

"Don't look at me with such eyes."

Wanda cast down her lids; her face was proud and cold.

"I was in a rage last night. You know that at such times I lose all control of myself. I am on fire. Anger controls my very limbs, my whole being. I am not responsible for what I do."

"There are some words that can never be forgotten."

"I take back everything that I said. Well! Are you satisfied? Have I humiliated myself enough before you? Let us forget it all! I forgive you, forgive me. Kiss me, and let this coolness pass away. But you are cold, unfeeling! Kiss me, I tell you."

"I cannot."

"Why?"

"Because you know me well enough to know that I am incapable of a low, mean action. Your suspicion of me was worse than your blow."

"Wanda, look here; put yourself in my place. Didn't you tell me that you felt badly, and that you wanted to go to bed? I was worried about you, and I went to your room. Nobody was there. I called Katia — no answer. And you came home, dressed up like a man, at four o'clock in the morning, and you refused to tell me where you had been."

"Why did you ask me? If I was obliged to use a subterfuge so as to be free, naturally I could not be at liberty to tell you where I was going."

"But, it seems to me, a father has some authority over his child. Your reputation, our honor, was at stake."

"I was in disguise, and you know I am not a woman to compromise our honor, since you desire to confound your honor with mine, although, according to my views, one is responsible for one's own acts alone."

"Hah! What sort of talk is this? Stupid notions."

"If you hope to win back my affection in this manner . . ."

"Come, spoilt child, little rebel, let us put an end to this wretched quarrel."

"No," answered Wanda, firmly.

"What! are you going to be hard against me?"

"Yes."

The Prince was seized with a fit of laughter, which sounded more like anger than mirth.

"Are we to remain at loggerheads?"

"Certainly."

"Perhaps you wish your old father to go down on his knees before you, like a lover?"

"Not at all."

"But what do you wish, then? Tell me. At least I should like to know what conditions are necessary to sign the peace."

"I am no longer a child, as you seem to think I am. In eight days I shall be twenty-one years old."

"That is true."

"Then I shall be of age."

"Well?"

"I wish to be free."

"How free?"

"Free to do what I think fit. Otherwise I shall be obliged to quit your house."

The Prince gazed at his daughter with haggard eyes. He could not speak, so utterly overcome was he by the expression of her intention, uttered, as it was, with an evident and fixed determination. But recovering himself, and forcing himself to speak pleasantly, he said:

"Quit this house! Why, where would you go to?"

"You need not trouble yourself; I have already found a place."

"Found a place! Do you then think seriously of leaving me?"

"I have been thinking of nothing else, all night long."

The Prince walked rapidly up and down the room to overcome the agitation that these words caused him. His brain was in a whirl; anger, paternal love, indignation, the fear that his daughter would carry out her threat, all these emotions filled his mind. He knew Wanda's determined character, and he dreaded an outbreak.

He drew a chair up to the sofa upon which Wanda was lying and sat down.

"Let us see, my darling."

He took her hand. It lay between his hands like a lump of ice.

"I could not sleep, either," he continued. "All night long I was feverish and wretched. Kiss me, to quiet me, to soothe me, and then, afterwards, we can talk about this matter."

"You would not care for a kiss, father, that is given unwillingly, would you?"

"I want you to kiss me lovingly. Must I fall at your feet?"

"It is useless for you to lower yourself to me. Simply consent to give me what I have asked of you."

"Your liberty?"

"Yes."

"Absolute liberty?"

"Yes."

"What do you mean by that?"

"I wish to go out when I want to, and where I want to; I wish to be allowed to receive any person whom I fancy here, without having to ask your permission."

The Prince hesitated.

"Ah!" he said, "this is a declaration of war."

"No, only of principles. My dignity refuses to accept any control whatever over my actions."

"But will you promise me to be prudent, and not to compromise yourself?"

"If I were to promise that, I should at once acknowledge myself capable of abusing my liberty."

"Well, I grant your request. Only I wish your old governess always to accompany you."

"No, I want Katia."

"And why Katia?"

"Because my old governess bores me."

"But Katia is only a waiting maid."

"She is very well educated, as I have told you, and I wish to make her my secretary."

"Your secretary! Do you intend to enter the ministry?"

"Almost. I wish to undertake some serious work. I want to organize a House of Refuge for poor children."

"Bah!"

"I find life so petty, so monotonous."

"Why do you not think of marriage?"

"If I am to marry, I must find a man to suit me, such a one as I have never met."

"But if I were to find a good match for you, a man of old birth, distinguished title, princely fortune, fine appearance?"

"All that would be nothing to me if did not like him; above all, if he did not possess certain moral qualities that I must find in my husband."

"What qualities are those?"

"Why should I tell you? You would not understand."

"I will try."

"Are you then in a great hurry to get rid of me?"

"No, but you are old enough to be married, and I long to have grandchildren."

"To inherit your large fortune?"

"Certainly."

Wanda smiled.

"What is the meaning of that ironical smile?"

"Because I think that you are wrong to trouble yourself about your fortune. Before you have any heirs, very probably your lands will no longer belong to you."

"How can that be?" said the Prince, starting from his seat.

"Perhaps the revolution will have swept them away."

"The Nihilist revolution? Do you believe in it?"

"I believe in it as firmly as I believe that the sun shines."

"Are you still taken up with these criminals?"

"I only observe, and see what is going on; that is all. Revolution is in the air, the atmosphere is charged with electricity, and at any moment the storm may burst."

"You see all that through the medium of your romantic imagination. I spoke to Trepoff about it yesterday. He thinks the nihilists are but few in number, and very weak."

"If you think them inoffensive, why do you pursue them with such rigor?"

"Because they are criminals: men capable of everything, fearing neither God nor man. They would undermine the very foundations of authority, without which no society is possible; their doctrines endanger the government, the established order of things, the safety of the family and of property."

"You have left out religion," said Wanda, laughing. "Be all this as it may, I think we may, in a few years, be reduced to working for our living; and for my part, I intend to learn a trade, so that I can support you and myself, if it be necessary."

"If your prediction should be realized, dear Wanda, you need not trouble yourself about my fate. Rather than look on such a spectacle I should prefer to blow out my brains. But let us put aside these gloomy forebodings, and say, as did the King of France, '*Apres nous, le deluge.*' I want to speak to you today about something of much greater importance."

"What is that?" said Wanda, with indifference.

"I wish to consult you about the fete that I intend to give on your twenty-first birthday. I wish it to be regal in its magnificence. I wish every one in Petersburg to be talking about it. I wish my beautiful Wanda to have a perfect triumph."

"You are very good, father, but you know I hate ostentation. If you really desire a reconciliation with me, give up this fete, and let me have the money that it would cost for my poor."

"How much do you want for your poor?"

"Whatever the fete would cost."

"Well! I will give the fete, and besides you shall have as much money as it will cost. Will that satisfy you?"

"No, I want all."

"How?"

"Twice the money that the fete would cost."

"Very well! I will double the sum, but I must have the fete. I have an idea in my mind."

"An introduction to some one, perhaps? So often you have introduced me to men whom I cannot fancy."

"But this one is really promising."

"I will lay a wager that it is Prince Stackelberg. Possibly he might do; but in the first place I must know him."

"You shall know him. He is truly a distinguished man, with a more than ordinary mind, together with energy and savoir-faire. He will get on in the world."

Just then a footman entered and handed a card to the Prince.

"Chabert!" he exclaimed. "To be sure, it is twelve o'clock. Will you receive him here?"

"Certainly," said Wanda, rising and going towards the door.

"In order to satisfy you completely, I promise you to do everything in my power for this protege of yours."

Chabert entered.

CHAPTER X

THE FAIR PROPAGANDIST

The Prince, whose manners were perfect, received the French engineer in the most charming and cordial way.

Wanda extended him her little white hand, which peeped out from a wide sleeve of ruby velvet.

"Allow me," said the Prince, "to swallow a mouthful of breakfast and put on my coat; I shall be with you in twenty minutes. The minister knows that you are coming. It is rather difficult matter to push through, but I think we shall succeed."

He left the room.

Raymond found himself alone with Wanda for the first time since his arrival at Petersburg. His face glowed with delight.

Without being strictly handsome, Raymond Chabert had a fine, intelligent head. His deep set, dark blue eyes betrayed an intense nature. His high forehead, his delicate mouth and slightly pointed chin, gave evidence, according to the theory of Lavater, of great powers of devotion.

He had none of the frivolity which is attributed to the French, but he had all their noble impulses: courage, honor, chivalry, and above all a wild thirst for liberty and justice.

There was more than one point of resemblance between himself and Wanda; the young nihilist had given him all her confidence and a friendship which amounted almost to tenderness.

"We have not seen one another for two months," said the Princess. "How much we have to talk about and to tell one another, haven't we?"

"Let me come to myself. The happiness of seeing you alone is so great I am dazzled."

Wanda looked at him with a tender smile.

"Yesterday, at the ball, you were so surrounded, so beautiful, that I did not dare approach or speak to you; and last night, at the club, the few words that I uttered were received with so much irony . . ."

"Oh, well! Never mind. Tell me the news from Ukraine. What are they doing? Are they enthusiastic? Did you pass through Kiev?"

"Yes."

"Whom did you see there?"

"Some of the students."

"Are the young people in the schools as discontented as they were?"

"More and more so. Their meetings have been prohibited, and that has exasperated them. The workmen are very ardent."

"And the peasants ?"

"Always indolent and careless. They stupefy themselves with liquor and forget their misery."

"Poor peasants!" said Wanda. "So intelligent, so simple, so resigned!"

"They keep to themselves their opinions; they sometimes listen to our missionaries, however, and the seed is being sowed."

"And, doubtless, it will bear fruit."

"And now tell me about yourself," said Raymond. "You look very pale. Is anything the matter with you?"

"I am tired, and I have been opposed, that is all."

"How long these two months have been!" said Chabert. "If you could but know how my heart and my soul have thirsted to hear your voice! If you could but know how I have missed our walks and talks by the banks of the Dnieper!"

"My dear Raymond," said Wanda, laughing, "you are decidedly too gallant for a conspirator."

"Do you call me gallant because I tell you how lonely and wretched I was after you left me, and what a void your absence made in my life?"

"Forgive me, my dearest friend; I cannot let you go on, for you certainly will propose, and that, you know, according to our agreement, cannot be allowed."

"I propose to you? The worm to the star? It is not love that I feel for you. It is worship, respectful worship. Can the sun prevent us from warming ourselves in its rays?"

"Very Oriental! Bravo! Go on! But you know that we reformers discountenance all gallantry and fine speeches."

"I know it, but my heart is overflowing, and I can find no words to tell you the impression that you have made upon me. Not only your beauty, not the charm of your sympathetic voice, but your great heart, your goodness, your generosity, have overwhelmed me with respect and admiration."

"That is enough, isn't it? Do let us talk sensibly!"

"I haven't any sense left. When I think that you have deigned to interest yourself in me; when I think how kindly you have listened to the tale of my folly, and how, by your eyes, by your words, you have poured hope into my blighted life, I cannot restrain my gratitude. And I would like to prove it to you, not by words merely, but by deeds, if my life can ever be of use to you."

"Take care, I might possibly accept that offer."

"Will you truly?"

"I can't say just now, but there may come a time when I shall ask you for it, although if I remember aright, you offered it once to somebody else."

"How?"

"Do you forget your promise? Suppose Michael Federoff should claim it!"

"He asked me to devote my life to the service of a great cause, but I did not give him a promise."

"That is a delicate distinction. However, as Doctor Federoff's views and mine are identical, we shall probably understand one another."

"Then will you accept the offer of my life? Wanda, my sister, my friend, I am intoxicated with delight! Thanks! Oh, thanks!"

"Speaking of the Doctor," continued Wanda, "have you received anything from Geneva?"

"Yes, a large package."

"What is in it?"

"I do not know."

"Is that all the interest you take in the cause?"

"It was not intended for me."

"For whom, then?"

"For you."

"Why did you not tell me about it?"

"I was ordered not to give it to you until you attained year majority, that is, in eight days."

"Did Michael Federoff write you that?"

"Yes."

"Did he tell you why?"

"No."

"Oh, I am so curious! Give it to me now."

"I am your slave, Wanda. I will obey you. However, let me make you understand that Doctor Federoff insists upon my not giving you the package until the 13th of January."

"Do you think they are political pamphlets?" enquired the Princess, very much excited.

"I think not. It looks like a manuscript."

"A manuscript? Done up in a package?"

"It may be a very long letter."

"Did he tell you why he did not send it to me at once?"

"He was afraid that it would fall into the hands of the Prince."

"Very probably! Well, to show how strong I am, although I am dying with curiosity, I will wait until the 13th."

The Prince entered. "I am ready," he said, "and the sleigh is waiting. Let's go."

Raymond bowed to Wanda, laying his hand upon his heart, in Oriental fashion, and left the room with the Prince.

"What a loyal nature, what a generous heart!" thought Wanda. "If I were allowed to love — perhaps."

She sat down, lost in thought.

But suddenly rising to her feet, she passed her hands across her brow, as though to banish thought.

"No, no," she said aloud. "I will not. Apostles dare not love. I have taken the oath, and this man might possibly cause me to forget the other."

A footman entered bringing a card.

"Ask the gentleman to come up," she said.

It was Count Verenine.

"What is the matter? This troubled face — what has happened?"

"Ah! Wanda! What a night I have passed! How must I love you to play this part! A spy upon the Emperor, upon the man who has loaded my family with gifts, who has treated me like his own child! And I am a very bad conspirator; I almost betrayed myself and you too! I cannot lie, above all to the Emperor, who can look right into my heart."

Wanda made no answer. Her eyes expressed uneasiness and severity, compassion and contempt for her cousin's weakness.

"Do not look at me that way, Wanda, I beg you."

"You are a child, Alexis," said the Princess in a firm voice. "You are grateful to the Emperor for your father's wealth, but every imperial favor is an iniquity. The fortunes that he gives away belong to the people, and every personal sentiment should be blotted out in the presence of the great cause of humanity. Have not I taught you this? Have you not accepted this doctrine and sworn to devote yourself to it?"

"That is true."

"Well . . ."

"My reason goes with you, but my heart revolts against my ingratitude."

"Instead of looking upon the benefits that the Emperor grants to his favorites, look at his government, loading the people with taxes, hunting the nihilists like wild beasts, scourging men with rods . . ."

"He knows nothing of it," interrupted Verenine.

"That may be, but he is responsible for it, because he has absolute power."

"I assure you, he is very liberal."

"Well, then, why does he not act according to his convictions?"

"His kind heart makes him meek."

"When one is all powerful, one has no right to be weak. When the hand is too weak to hold the scepter, it should be laid aside."

"I think he is going to make some great resolve."

"They have been about that so long! If he had been firmer he could have transformed Russia. In circumstances like the present, weakness entails terrible consequences. Take care, Alexis! Do not allow yourself to be guilty of weakness."

"Speak, Wanda! I will do whatever you order me to do."

"Well! Tell me what happened last night. Hide nothing from me."

The young aide-de-camp repeated, word for word, his interview with the Czar.

"And is this the cause of all this emotion?" asked Wanda.

"But suppose the Emperor speaks to me again about this marriage, and his kindly intentions towards us?" asked Verenine, with beseeching look and lips trembling with emotion.

"Well him that the love of Wanda Kryloff is not to be bought; and that she will marry the man she loves, if he is not worth a kopeck, in preference to all the nobles of the world."

"And so I suppose I am not worthy of you. You are perfectly indifferent to me."

"No, good, brave Alexis, I have a genuine, sincere affection for you. If I scold you, it is that I want to make a hero of you."

"You can make what you will of me, Wanda; if not a hero, at least a slave."

"Oh no; not a slave, but an independent man, and so my sisterly love for you will increase."

"Sisterly!" repeated the young man, sighing.

"Yes, that pure love fortifies the soul, while passion weakens it. And you know to what work I have devoted my life."

"But that work may last for a long time."

"That may be, especially if the workers are as lukewarm as you are."

"Well, will you promise me that later . . ."

"I will promise nothing."

But she bent upon him such a loving look and smile, that it completed the overthrow of the tender Alexis.

"What is that noise?" she suddenly said. "Is that my father?"

Verenine went towards the window.

"No, it is not the Prince; it is — I saw him at the ball last night; you were talking to him. It is Prince Stackelberg."

"Are you sure?" said Wanda, rising and looking out of the window. "Yes, it is."

"Will you see him?" asked Verenine.

"Yes. I expected him this morning."

Verenine sighed, took his fair cousin's hand and kissed it. As he went out, he met the young German on the stairway.

Prince Vassili Antonovitch von Stackelberg was descended from one of those German families that Peter the Great transplanted into every administration of the Empire. Thanks to their tenacious rapacity, and their patient faculty for slow infiltration, they had ended up worming themselves into every office of the government.

They were hard workers, careful in detail, punctual in attendance, thorough business men, and good accountants. The Slavs, on the contrary, were careless; their ungoverned, intangible, unstable characters rendered them unfit for steady work which requires application and uprightness. This want in the character of the Slavs had made the fortune of the Germans in Russia.

The family of Vassili von Stackelberg claimed to be of princely origin, and although these German Russians had never had a higher rank than Count or Baron, the Stackelberg family had obtained permission to take the title of Prince.

This young man, about thirty years of age, was a type of his race. A square head, set upon angular shoulders, long, unwieldy legs, which gave him a heavy and plebeian walk, an unhealthy looking complexion, yellow hair; hard piercing eyes made his face look like a mask, and its expression was as impenetrable as one. His lips were like a woman's. His long hands with their flabby fingers indicated a nature which will stop at nothing to attain its aim.

And yet, thanks to his height, his fame and his fortune, he passed for a handsome man; thanks to his haughty, affected air, his reserved and correct manners, for a future statesman.

As he entered Wanda's boudoir he bowed with studied elegance.

"Forgive me, Princess," said Stackelberg, "if I have been indiscreet enough to send up my card in the absence of the Prince, but I wish to ask for some important information from you before I accept the mission with which the Emperor has deigned to honor me."

"Ah, yes, this inquiry into the nihilist movement in Southern Russia."

"Principally in the Provinces of Kiev and Odessa, Ekaterinoslav, Kherson and Kharkoff. It is a great proof of confidence, of which I am justly proud, and I wish to prove myself worthy of it. Therefore I do not desire to accept without knowing something of the moral condition of the country that I shall have to report upon.

"If I understand you," answered Wanda, "you wish to be certain beforehand that you will meet with work worthy of your powers!"

He bowed, with an affectedly modest smile.

"I mean to say that I do not care to go on a fruitless errand. As they have intrusted this to me . . ."

"You must, at least," interrupted Wanda, laughing, "find subject matter for a report which will do you credit."

"It seems to me you are laughing at me."

"I am only trying to understand you, that is all," replied Wanda, with assumed candor.

Vassili continued: "I have heard a great deal of you, Princess, as a woman far above the average. Not only is your mind beautifully cultured, but they tell me you have a rare intellect, and a high toned, energetic character."

"I have some friends who exaggerate my good points, and then my father's fortune and my rank help on the reputation that they are kind enough to give me."

"The proof that you have a real value is, that you have also enemies."

"That is more interesting."

"Should I have a better chance of pleasing you were I to criticize you? I should like to, but I do not know where to commence. You seem to me rather proud."

"I am."

"But in my eyes pride is rather a quality than a fault. Pride gives dignity. I like proud women; I like them not to yield too easily to love."

"It seems to me," interrupted Wanda, smiling, "that we are wandering from our subject."

"How can I always hold the thread of my discourse, when talking to a woman as beautiful as you are?"

"As you have mentioned your preferences, allow me to speak of mine. I do not like the habit that we Russians have borrowed from the French, of only speaking to women in words of gallantry and flattery, as if they were incapable of understanding anything else."

"Very well, then, let us go back to socialism, and you will see that, far from looking upon you as a frivolous doll, I expect from you serious information about the important question which brings me here. They say that you are a nihilist. Of course I do not believe it."

"In fact, as I am a Princess, and enjoy every social prerogative, it is quite natural that I should find everything perfect in this most perfect of worlds."

"But I am told this society contains a great many young persons, men and women, who belong to the nobility."

"I have heard that, too, but I think they can only be nobles that are more or less ruined, or not well received at court."

"There are others, besides. The Slavs are very enthusiastic."

"Are you not enthusiastic, Prince?"

"Enthusiasm is a madness, and God be praised, I am quite sane."

"And still, there is good in enthusiasm. Nothing great and noble is accomplished without it."

"I assure you, I am essentially a positive, practical man. And still at this moment you make me understand that enthusiasm may be a powerful motive power, inherent in some natures."

"I am still waiting to hear your question about Southern Russia," interrupted Wanda, drumming with her rosy fingers upon the table.

"I obey! The opinions about this nihilist question are very diverse; some say that it is making frightful progress; others deny it, and think that the nihilists are very few in number, and make all this fuss to conceal their weakness. Now, tell me, is this party dangerous or not? You will do me a great service in giving me your opinion about the condition of affairs in your domains. I would like also to have the opinion of the Prince, your father."

"Oh! My father!" said Wanda, laughing, "He sees nihilists everywhere. I should not be astonished if he looks under his bed every night for fear of finding one of them there. It is a mania with him. You can't utter their name in his presence without putting him in a fury. I think the minister has set this inquiry on foot at his instigation."

"And you? I want your opinion."

"Well! It is this: there are nihilists. They do exist, but if you find twenty in, Odessa, thirty in Kiev, and one hundred in the whole of Southern Russia, I think you will be doing well."

"A hundred active propagandists — that is possible. But how many converts, how many neophytes do you think there are?"

"If there are any, what means will you take to discover them? The Russian peasant, although apparently so brutalized, is suspicious, crafty, very cunning. It is difficult to make him out."

"Then, would you advise me to refuse this mission?"

"No. On the contrary, it may give you a great deal of reputation. All these investigations and official reports do not seem to be of any use, but they bring those that make them into notice. The nihilists may be much more numerous than I suppose, and your inquiry may be very useful."

Stackelberg watched Wanda closely while she was speaking.

"Would you be willing to help me in my researches?" he continued.

"Certainly, if I can be of any use, or any service to my country. It is true that I pity these wretched maniacs, or, if they are not maniacs, these criminals, who preach rebellion and anarchy. But I know the respect due to the laws of my country, and I will be your co-worker in the noble mission that you are about to accept. You will accept that, will you not ? If there are no nihilists, and if needs must, we can invent a few. I have heard that a great many inquiries have been made after that manner."

Now, Vassili was watching and listening to Wanda uneasily. Was she joking, or was she in earnest? Was she playing a part? Did she suspect the object of his visit?

If she were a nihilist, as they charged her with being, she would be on her guard. But then, her conversation was so easy, her tone so light, that it made him hesitate.

No, a regular socialist could never have kept up this conversation with an agent of the Third Section.

He changed his tactics.

"I am not as unfriendly as you think to the nihilist views. I am liberal, very liberal, perhaps more so than you yourself."

"Who told you that I am a liberal?" said Wanda, feigning astonishment.

"Public rumor."

"The public seems to trouble itself a great deal about me."

"How can it fail to trouble itself about you, if it has once seen you?"

"Another naughty speech, Mr. Inquisitor. If you go on flattering me this way I will not be your co-worker."

"Yes, I am truly liberal," continued Vassili, "and you inspire me with such confidence that I will tell you the whole truth. I shall only accept this mission in the hope that I shall be able, by exaggerating the importance of the revolutionary movement, to help on the truly liberal party."

"Ah, that falls in with my opinion of the manner in which these inquiries are conducted."

"Have you heard anything of this red letter that was thrown into the Emperor's carriage, yesterday?" asked Stackelberg.

"A red letter?"

"Every one is talking about it today."

"No," answered Wanda, "what was in it?"

"I do not exactly know, but it appears to have made a deep impression upon the Emperor. He had a stormy interview with Gortschakoff this morning, who threatened to give in his resignation; perhaps by this time it has been accepted."

As he spoke, Stackelberg watched the Princess attentively, but Wanda saw through his game, and was on her guard.

"This is very important news," she said in an indifferent tone.

"Now, this rupture with the most powerful man in the empire arises from the fact that the Emperor wishes to give a constitution to Russia, and to proceed slowly in the way of reform. Now follow me: if we frighten the Emperor, we can get more out of him than by reassuring words."

"Are you in favor of a constitution, Vassili Antonovitch?"

"Certainly! And you, what do you desire?"

"You insist upon my being a liberal."

"I suppose so; it is impossible to be intelligent, to reflect, to think, without being a liberal."

"Gortschakoff's opinion has something in it."

"What is his opinion?"

"He thinks that a wind of democracy is blowing against Europe, and that, sooner or later, it will carry away our court and all our privileges, but that we, boyards, whose fate is very much to be envied, should not assist the bad wind to blow on us. On the contrary, we should keep it back as long as we can; and when at last it shall reach us, we must endeavor that it may make us as little harm as possible."

"Ah, I do not recognize you in that speech, Princess! Can you reason with such egotism, you, who have so noble a character?"

"That is not egotism, it is common sense."

"I think there is but one way to preserve us from the storm, and that is to turn aside the thunderbolts. The constitution, which I ardently desire, would have the effect of a lightning rod."

"Perhaps you are right. It might retard the revolution for a few years."

"Do you believe in the revolution?"

"It is very much the fashion, and I use the word without attaching much importance to it."

"She will not let herself be caught," thought Vassili. "And still, I am sure that she is a socialist and that she is making fun of me."

He resolved to strike one more blow, in order to surprise her.

He spoke abruptly:

"I am intimately acquainted with a member of the Society of Deliverance."

At these words, Wanda could not help trembling slightly. She winked her eyes quickly, as if she had received a blow.

"I have her," thought Vassili.

"I have heard of that society," said Wanda, in a perfectly natural tone of voice. "Well, what is it, and what is its aim?"

"A large number of its members belong to the nobility. Its aim is to overthrow the government and to uproot society."

"Secret societies always interest me," said Wanda, leaning eagerly forward, as though to show the lively interest that she took in the young German's revelations. "I am very curious, and everything secret attracts me."

"It is not properly speaking a secret society, it is rather a kind of propaganda."

"Are women admitted into it?"

"Among the nihilists women are recognized as the equals of men."

"Are you a member?"

"I? What are you thinking of? Their program is not at all mine. I am not as radical as that, but, in following out the plan that I propose in my inquiry, I shall be of as much use to the nihilists as to the Emperor."

"That is carrying water on both shoulders," said Wanda, laughing.

"You think that I am ambitious."

"Perhaps."

"You are mistaken, my ruling passion is . . ."

"Perhaps it is assurance?"

"You look into my very heart; send me away, I beg you; for, if I stay here another quarter of an hour, I shall completely lose my senses. For my peace of mind, it would have been much better if I were to deprive myself of the assistance of such a dangerous co-worker."

"Particularly," said Wanda, smiling, "as you had made up your mind beforehand about the way in which you intend to carry on your work."

Vassili bit his lips.

"I think," she said, "I have guessed the true purpose of your visit."

"Could you have guessed that, fascinated by your appearance last night, I hastened this morning to express my admiration?"

"That is not it. You came direct from the office of the Third Section, did you not? They told you there that I was a nihilist, and you are curious to know the truth."

Stackelberg blushed up to his ears. "Ah, Princess, do you suspect me of playing the part of your judge in your presence?" He rose and with an offended air stalked towards the door.

"As I have wounded you by my suspicions," continued Wanda, "pray forgive me, and let us part good friends." She held out her hand, but Vassili hesitated to take it. Wanda feared that she had been guilty of imprudence. She needed to redeem her fault and regain the good graces of this crooked individual.

"I was only joking," she said with a fascinating smile. "You are not angry with me, are you?"

"How can any one be angry with you?" answered the Prince, rather embarrassed by this smile.

"When are you going south?"

"When are you going?"

"Not before April."

"I expect to go next month," said Vassili, "but in all probability, the inquiry will take me a long time, for it not only embraces Southern Russia but Western Russia likewise. I shall begin in Podolia, Volkynia, Grodno, Minsk, and Mohilew; then I shall go through Bessarabia, the provinces of Kherson and of Ekaterinoslav and the Crimea, and I shall wind up with Little Russia and Kiev. Then I shall hope to have the pleasure of meeting you."

"We expect that you will make your headquarters in our house."

Vassili bowed. "How can I resist such an invitation?" he said. "I would go to the end of the world only to look once more at your beautiful eyes!"

Wanda placed her finger upon her lips.

"Hush! Or we shall quarrel again."

The Prince kissed the hand she held out to him and withdrew.

He had hardly lowered the portiere behind him when Wanda spoke, making a movement of profound disgust. "What a fair spoken, slimy creature. That kiss was like a vampire's bite."

She rubbed it off with her other hand.

Opening the door, she called: "Katia! Katia!"

Katia came immediately.

"Ah! the sight of you does me good, after what I have just gone through."

She repeated in detail her interview with Stackelberg.

"I should never have had the courage to give him my hand, if I had not thought that the safety of our friends in the Ukraine, and our schools too, were at stake."

Then she told Katia all about her conversation with Verenine.

"Decidedly," she added, "the address of the Revolutionary Committee has produced an effect upon the Emperor, and seems to have aroused him."

"The people," said Katia, "are aroused, too."

CHAPTER XI

PASSION

At this moment the footman entered and handed Wanda a letter sealed with a coat of arms.

Recognizing the crest and the handwriting, Wanda tore it hastily open, and read the following:

Dearest Wanda of My Heart,

You have forgotten me, you have forsaken me, and yet your poor Nadege is the most unhappy of women. If you do not come to me soon I feel that I must die. My husband is false to me. I have suspected it for some time, but today I know it. It is horrible! I am in bed with a burning fever. There is no remedy for my grief, no end but death.

I am such a coward that I am ashamed of myself. I love this man who is so false to me. How can I tell you? I never loved him so dearly as I do now. Jealousy devours me. When I think that another woman has his love, his thoughts, his caresses, I am nearly mad.

I adore him! I adore him! And he loves me no longer. He does not hate me yet, but I annoy him because I cannot conceal my jealousy. It breaks out in spite of me, in reproaches, entreaties and sobs. And he shrugs his shoulders or else yawns.

If you do not come to me I do not know what will become of me. Sometimes fits of madness seize me, I want to kill someone, to kill my rival, to kill myself, and so put an end to an existence too heavy for me to bear. I depend only upon you, upon your brave heart, that can inspire me with the courage to live.

Your wretched friend.

Nadege Litzanoff

Upon reading these heart-breaking lines Wanda grew pale, and seemed very uneasy.

"Nadege. My poor Nadege," she murmured. "If she knew! Wretched Stepane! Only yesterday what a look he gave me, what a gloomy fire, what sadness in those eyes!"

At that recollection Wanda trembled; she placed one hand upon her heart, while the other clutched the hack of an armchair.

"What is the matter with you?" asked Katia.

"Nothing," she said, making an effort to recover herself. "Get yourself ready, and order my carriage; we are going to see Nadege, poor, dear soul!"

CHAPTER XII

THE THIRD SECTION

While Wanda was going to see her friend, Vassili Stackelberg wended his way towards the office of the Third Section

Under this harmless title there existed in Russia a secret police, which had for its aim the surveillance of every suspected person in the Emperor's domains.

The secret police, organized by Ivan the Terrible, had answered in the most wonderful manner for the purpose for which it was intended. Paul the First abolished it, but the Emperor Nicholas reorganized it and gave it the highest official position in the empire. It was under the orders of a secret commission, which acted as an inquisitorial tribunal.

Petersburg was filled with its agents. Hertzen said to his son, about to visit the banks of the Neva, "Trust no one: neither the coachmen who drives you, nor the footman who waits on you, nor even the friend to whom you may send letters. Expect to find a spy everywhere."

This formidable organization extended over the whole of Russia. The secret police arrested and imprisoned at its will. It had at its command impregnable fortresses, the scourge, solitary confinement, starvation, the torture of thirst; black dungeons, into which men were thrust alive; quicksilver mines, in which the strongest man could live but five years; and the snows of Siberia, killing slowly by cold, misery and despair.

No proof was necessary. The denunciation by a blue officer was enough.

In Russia the agents of the secret police, instead of being despised, were held in high esteem. These posts could only be filled by men far above the other officials, for they had to be incorruptible, as they were often called upon to accuse men of the highest rank.

The Chief of the Third Section is, at the same time, aide-de-camp to the Emperor, the first officer in the Empire, and the confidante of the Czar. He sits in the Cabinet, and often decides weighty questions.

But there are, besides, two other police forces: the police of the Minister of the Interior, and the police under the administration, at that time, of Trepoff. These three strived to see which would discover, arrest, and imprison the greatest number of the Czar's subjects.

General Trepoff had gone home in a terrible state of agitation at the severe remarks made to him by the Emperor. He could not close his eyes all night, and the next morning at seven o'clock he went to see Mezentzoff, the General of the Guards, or Third Section, to whom he communicated his conversation with the Czar. At once General Mezentzoff in a rage bore down upon the Third Section and attacked the colonels; the colonels fell upon the captains; and so on, to the little office boys who had no one to scold.

Why had no one discovered where the red letter came from? Why had not the wretch who threw it been arrested?

"You are all," screamed the General, "either in love, or blind, or drunk, or ill! Have not I one single faithful, zealous employee? Must I watch over the safety of the Emperor, and act as policeman? I wish that before this very night, the writer of that insolent letter shall be arrested."

"Perhaps," said one of the colonels, very timidly, "perhaps the letter was written by a crazy man."

"I don't care, find out who the crazy man is. There must be a plot.

Double your police agents. The letter says that the conspiracy is everywhere. Let all persons that are suspected in society be watched, as well as the common people."

Then he ordered the society list to be brought; his finger had just rested upon the name of Princess Wanda Kryloff, as Prince Stackelberg entered.

"You have come in the very nick of time," said Mezentzoff. "Did not I see you last night, dancing with Princess Wanda Kryloff?"

"Yes, you did."

"Well, she is suspected. Her beauty and her rank would make her a very dangerous agent for the revolutionists."

"That charming woman dangerous? To us men, yes, but not to the government."

"My dear Prince, do you know what is actually taking place, now, here in Petersburg?"

And, in a few words, he laid before him the progress of nihilism, not only among the people, but among the nobility, and, above all, among the younger portion of the community.

"As you are about to undertake the inquiry in Southern Russia, you ought to find out about the Princess. Her father, I know, is true, but we can no longer answer for anyone's children. You are acquainted with the Prince, I believe?"

"I was presented to him yesterday, for the first time."

"Very well."

"What am I expected to do?"

"Find out if this young girl is a nihilist, or connected with any secret society. I trust your discretion. I see that you are intended for a diplomat."

Two hours after this conversation Prince Stackelberg returned to the office of the Third Section.

"Well," said the General.

"I have found out nothing. She is clever, proud, witty, coquettish, charming, in fact."

"But what do you think?"

"Watch her," said Stackelberg.

The General wrote down, opposite Wanda's name, these words: "To be watched."

"No, no," exclaimed Stackelberg. "Don't do that! If she really belongs to the nihilist party let me have the glory of finding it out! She has invited me to pay her a visit next spring, in the Ukraine. I shall have time to study her then."

"But suppose you fall in love with her?"

"I fall in love! General, love will never make me forget my duty, nor the Emperor's service."

Notwithstanding, the General did not strike out those words "To be watched," and when the German had left the room he gave orders accordingly.

While Mezentzoff was holding his interview with Stackelberg, Trepoff also had sent out a spy to entrap Wanda.

CHAPTER XIII

A RECRUIT

When Wanda entered her friend's room she found her looking utterly disconsolate, stretched upon a lounge, covered with furs, but shivering all over.

"Dear Nadege! Your letter broke my heart. What is the matter?"

Nadege arose and threw herself into the Princess's arms.

"My life is over," she murmured.

"And you are in this state of mind because a man has been false to you? Why, they are false to every one; don't you know that?"

"But this man is my husband, and he swore to love me. I cannot stand it."

"But, my dear soul, Russian law is elastic enough where marriage is concerned. You can ask for a divorce and get it."

"Do you think that so easy to do?"

"Everything is easy in Russia when you have money."

Nadege gave a great sigh. "Dear Wanda," she said, "there is no cure for me. I love him."

"A man who betrays you, who does not love you any longer?"

"I am weak, I am ignoble, anything you choose, but I love him." And she burst into tears.

Nadege Litzanoff, at the age of twenty, was an exquisite type of Russian beauty. Her light golden hair shaded a brow white as ivory. Her dark blue eyes were almost black. Her cheeks, generally suffused with pink, were today white and spotted with red. Her lovely mouth, usually wreathed with smiles, looked drawn and hard. Her despair was so great that she had even forgotten all the little coquettish elegances of dress. Yet her figure, simply wrapped in a morning gown of blue cashmere, was exquisitely graceful.

"It is so long since I saw you!" she continued. "Your presence does me good, for you are so strong."

"You are just a spoiled child. Your life has always been a bed of roses, and the first thorn that you feel gives you a mortal wound. If you would only look around you, you would see many troubles, many sorrows much harder than yours to be borne."

"Oh, Wanda! There is no trouble like mine. You are thinking of poverty, and the privation that it brings, but if I had his love, I could endure everything without saying a word. Cold, hunger . . ."

"And hard work?"

"Yes; I would go work in the mines if I thought that would win back his love."

"How little you know of the hard life of the common people!"

"How little you know of love, dear Wanda."

"How do you know?"

"You have never been in love, have you?"

"I am twenty-one years old, and women do not generally reach that age without having felt some palpitations of the heart."

"And you have never told me, your best friend"

"I could not tell you. It was a love that is perfectly impossible."

"Impossible?" said Nadege. "Was it one of the Emperor's sons?"

"No, my dear, you will never find out. And I assure you it has cost me a great effort of will to force back this love, which seized me suddenly, powerfully. I do not want to talk about myself."

"Did he not love you?"

"I think he did, but it could not be. Let us talk of something else, I beg of you."

"How did you cure yourself of it?" persisted Nadege.

"I tried to distract my mind."

"Ah! If I could only do that," sighed Nadege, "I feel that I could be saved, but I cannot. I think of him all the time. It is a perfect infatuation. Jealousy gnaws at my heart without stopping. I cannot sleep, and if I do sleep I have the most frightful nightmare. Sometimes I think I shall lose my mind."

"How long have you suffered this way?" asked Wanda.

"For several months."

"Why did you not tell me?"

"I had only suspicions at first, but now I am certain."

"Tell me everything; nothing comforts one like pouring out one's grief into the heart of a true friend."

"Oh!" said Nadege, "My happiness lasted but a little while. I do not think he ever really loved me. I gave my whole soul to him, and yet I always felt that there was something between us. I thought to myself, if it is the recollection of another woman, or even a natural coldness, it must, melt away before my tenderness and glowing love. Sometimes he would seize me in his arms, press me to his heart, with such tender, loving words! And then suddenly he would relapse into a state of perfect indifference; he would stare in front of him without seeming to see anything, and when I would speak to him he would seem not to hear me. I always thought there must be some woman between us, some woman whom he could not forget. After three months, he was away a great deal. He said he went to the club, and as he came home very late, he had a separate room fitted up for himself in the north wing of the house. This broke my heart, and I complained of it."

"You were wrong there," said Wanda. "A woman should never lower herself to complain when she discovers that she is no longer loved."

"You could do it, you are made of stone, but I . . ."

"I think you are made of wax."

"I cannot do as you do," continued Nadege; "I cried, I cried and there was a scene. Gradually the separation was so complete that I did not see him once in three weeks. I went to see you several times, but you were not at home, and I had dignity enough not to confide my troubles to any one else. But I wanted to find out what the meaning of it all was. Three days ago, when Patti and Nicolini were singing at the theater, I went. I was in one of the boxes, and could not easily be seen. Every one in society was there, and I thought that I would possibly see him there, in company with the person who had taken him away from me. Sure enough, at the end of the second act he happened in with quite a pretty woman by the way, she looked like you, but she was not as handsome."

"Ah!" said Wanda, with distended nostrils.

"Yes, she had your eyes, but they were not as beautiful as yours."

"Have you been able to find out who she was?"

"Yes, I told my father, and he went to the police. I found out that she was a Pole, very handsome, but as yet little known in society. Stepane met her accidentally and fell in love with her. He has given her an elegant house, carriages and horses, and for three weeks he never quit her side, even receiving his friends at this woman's, giving entertainments, and doing heaven knows what. However large his fortune may be, it won't take long to lose it in the way he is going on now."

"Well, what did you do?"

"I wrote him such a touching letter that he came to see me, fell at my feet and wept bitterly. But when I asked him why he did not come back to me, he said: 'If I only could.' 'Do you really love this creature?' I cried. 'No! I hate her!' he answered. 'Then what is the meaning of your conduct?' 'Don't ask me,' he said. 'It is a madness; I'm as unhappy as you are.' 'But,' said I, 'why do you not at least keep up some appearance of decency, and come and live in your own house?' 'You are right,' he said, 'for I do not love her half as much as I do you. Let me alone, and I promise you to live here.' I promised him. This morning he has not left the house. What is he doing? I do not even dare ask; I do not dare cross the threshold of his room. Look at me! Is not my wretchedness complete?"

While Nadege was talking, Wanda had risen and had gone towards the window, where she stood looking out, as if to conquer or conceal her feelings; but at last, hearing Nadege's sobs, she sat down by her and drawing her friend's head towards her, she soothed her as one soothes a child to dispel its sorrows.

"Listen to me, Nadege," said Wanda. "I have loved, I have suffered, and yet I am cured and happy. Do you really wish to get over this frantic love for a man who does not care for you?"

"I do not know. I do not see how I can live without my love; it is part of myself."

"Then you like to suffer?"

"Oh no, no! But there is nothing that can give me happiness except his return to me."

"You are mistaken. Any violent distraction . . ."

"Another love!" cried Nadege, indignantly. "The sight of every other man fills me with disgust."

"Yes, I mean another love, but not love for man. The love that I mean is a higher, nobler love."

"The love of God? I don't believe any longer in anything."

"Formerly," continued Wanda, "heaven and the cloister were the only refuge for unhappy human beings. But in our enlightened century, the love of God as presented to us by our priests, is no longer the highest consolation. The larger, holier love of humanity has replaced in my heart the love of God."

"Yes, you have often spoken to me of this new doctrine. It is well enough for you, with your mind, but I am only a weak, loving-hearted woman."

"The heart can lead one to these doctrines quite as well as the head. It is the heart that revolts against the injustice of the world. Have you never thought of the mothers that have no bread to give their children? Of the fathers, sick or out of work, who cannot support their families? Have you thought of the innocent men who pass their whole lives in gloomy, icy dungeons? Of the brave men who expiate their devotion to humanity by working in the mines or by a long, sad exile? Can any one of us dare to seek our own individual happiness, when so many are wretched? If happiness is so rare, joint responsibility becomes a necessary social law."

"Yes, you are right. What you say is true. If I could bring relief to all those sufferings, I might forget my own."

"In these days," continued Wanda, "we can no longer stop to talk about human misery. We must act."

"Have you joined those horrible nihilists?"

"Those horrible nihilists, as you call them, would abolish every injustice, every social horror."

"Are you really a socialist?"

"Well, you may call me what you please; I wish the downfall of every evil. I wish a society in which liberty and equality shall reign, in which there shall be a more equal division of labor and capital. Now, my darling, your chief trouble is idleness. If your mind were more occupied, your grief would not be so poignant. Once more, tell me, do you really want something to take you out of yourself?"

"Yes, I will give myself up to you. I will try. You can do with me what you choose."

"Can I depend upon you?"

"You can speak to me with as much safety as you could to the dead."

"Very well, dear Nadege; I will tell you that there is a vast conspiracy on foot which will soon embrace the whole of Russia."

"A conspiracy against the Emperor?" cried Nadege, in great alarm.

"It is not so much against the Emperor as against the Government. We wish to abolish every iniquity."

"Then," said Nadege, smiling, "you will have to do a great deal in Holy Russia."

"See, you are smiling already."

"I am trying." But at the same time she wiped away a tear that glistened on her long lashes.

"Shall I come for you this evening and take you to my club?"

"Have you a club?"

"Yes, women and men go there together. In the society that we are trying to organize, men and women have the same rights, the same freedom to develop themselves, and for the same quality of work they will be paid the same salary."

"Do you want to make me work?"

"Don't be worried; the work that we expect from you will not soil your white hands. Well, have you made up your mind? Shall I come for you this evening?"

"Yes."

"Suppose," said Wanda, "I take you with me now, so as not to leave you alone with your sorrow?"

"No! Oh, no!" said Nadege. "He has not left the house; he might come to see me. I would rather wait."

"You are wrong to wait. Come. Believe me."

"I cannot."

"Dear, weak creature," said Wanda, kissing her. "I have an idea: I want to see your husband and speak to him, and make him come to his senses."

"Oh, yes. He admires you, perhaps he will listen to you."

Wanda kissed her friend again, told Katia, who was outside in the antechamber, to go down and wait for her in the carriage, and then bent her steps towards the apartments occupied by Count Litzanoff.

CHAPTER XIV

THE NEW ROAD TO DAMASCUS

Count Stepane Danilovitch Litzanoff was still young, and wonderfully handsome. His father, General Litzanoff, had married a Georgian, and the son of this marriage united in his person the beauties of both races. His complexion was creamy white; his eyes were black, with glints of emerald light; his nose was straight; the nostrils quivered with every emotion; fair hair curled around a brow broad and lofty; his head he haughtily threw back. His graceful but flexible figure told of a rare combination of strength and weakness.

It was not merely his physical beauty which fascinated. He had, besides, a ready wit, brilliant and caustic, without any bitterness. He loved the good and the beautiful. He was tender towards the weak and very generous without any ostentation.

He was a sceptic, as were so many in Russia. He had cast to the winds every prejudice of society. He had satisfied his every caprice, his every passion; his father adored him and ruined him. And when, at twenty-five gears of age, he married Nadege, he was a thoroughly satiated man.

In Paris, where he had lived for over a year, and at Petersburg, he had acquired the reputation of being a great gentleman, both from his extravagance and from his eccentricity.

In spite of all this, he declared that he was never amused. "There is, as it were," he remarked to a friend, "a great gulf within me that nothing can either fill or satisfy."

When Wanda sent up her card he was stretched out upon an immense bear's skin that he had thrown down upon the floor. The beast itself had been killed by the Count in the forests of Finland. It had required courage to kill it. He wore a white jacket embroidered in gold thread. It opened in front over a red silk shirt with a rolling collar which showed off his white throat to advantage. His trousers were confined at the waist by a superb Circassian scarf.

He was reading, and seemed completely absorbed in his book.

When he read Wanda's name on the card he shuddered, first flushing deeply and then growing deadly pale.

Wanda, who was very pale also, stood outside the door, and said in a low voice, "Can I come in?"

For a moment he could not speak, but at last he replied: "Is this you, Wanda Kryloff? Do you honor me with a visit?"

Wanda, entering and perceiving his agitation, stood just within the doorway.

"Do I disturb you ?"

"Oh, no, no!"

They said no more. Their voices failed them. They could hardly see one another.

Wanda was the first to recover her self-possession.

"You were reading?"

"Yes, a book of which I am passionately fond," answered Litzanoff.

"You are always passionately fond of something."

"I am always crazy about something. But excuse me, do sit down."

He pushed a chair towards her, but he himself dared not approach her. Wanda sat down. Stepane took a seat far away from her, upon a Turkish divan.

"Will you allow me to ask you what you are reading with such enthusiasm?"

"Oh, you will think I am insane."

"About that, dear Count," said Wanda laughing, "my opinion will not greatly change."

""Yes, that is true; my reputation is made. Well, it is one of these nihilist books. Some time ago one of my friends, Andrew Padlewsky, brought it to me and recommended me to read it. I never thought about it until this morning, when accidentally I came across it. I have read it, scarcely stopping to take breath. I am already on the second volume, and upon my word I am almost a nihilist; at least that would give me something to do."

"You, a socialist?"

"Yes, one scamp the more in the society."

"How slightingly you speak of those poor fellows!"

"I only speak of them as everybody else does."

"Everybody?"

"I have heard that you take up for them."

"It is true," answered Wanda, "that the nihilists do attract to themselves all the unhappy, disinherited, out of place men in society. But did not Jesus attract the common people to him? I have heard there are also many rich, influential persons who have devoted themselves entirely to the cause."

"What delights me in this book is its analysis of men and of society. It criticizes the civilization of which we are so proud, which in fact is nothing but a filthy sewer."

"Bravo! Is that really your opinion?"

"It is, indeed! Yesterday I was ashamed of myself. Nadege has told you everything, hasn't she?"

"Yes."

"Well, do not judge me too severely, Wanda Petrowna," said Stepane, stifling a sigh.

Wanda was silent.

Litzanoff went on, "I have been terribly misunderstood, but this book shows me that the fact of there being so many misunderstood natures like mine, is due to the utterly disorganized and stupid state of society."

"Very good," said Wanda, approvingly.

"The most attractive chapter to me," continued Litzanoff, "was the one that criticized the Russian social system, containing within itself, as it does, every vice and every crime of both the barbarous and the civilized world."

"In fact, we are a pretty people."

"It makes me blush to be a Russian! Everywhere thieving, injustice, cheating, lying, all consequences forced upon us by the Asiatic despotism under which we live. The whole social system must be rebuilt from its very foundations."

"That is what I think."

"And the people are starving. It is ridiculous to say that they are bad, that their instincts are rebellious, when all they have to do is to rise and conquer us, for they are a hundred million to our one million. The truth is, they are a patient race; they work and they groan all their life. They give the sweat of their brow and their life's blood for us, and what do we give them in return? Gallows. They have put up with it for centuries, and perhaps they will go on putting up with it — this good people, this sheepish people, this stupid people."

Litzanoff was magnificent as he thus spoke. He looked like an untamed horse with dilated nostrils and fiery, fierce eyes.

Wanda gazed at him, rendered speechless by her admiration.

"You are on the point of becoming a nihilist," she said.

"From this moment I am one. We must overturn this worm-eaten house, and build another upon a new, logical, righteous basis."

"Above all," said Wanda, "let us prevent this hideous industrial feudal system, as baleful in its influence as the old feudal system, from getting a foothold in Russia. We must give the means of work to the workman himself."

"Why," said Litzanoff, "are you a nihilist?"

"Yes, yes, dear friend, I am."

"Are you an associate of any secret society?"

"There is none; but I am in the very thick of the conspiracy."

"Is there a conspiracy?" exclaimed Stepane. "And I not in it? Wanda, will you enroll me, and take me as the most ardent of your disciples, the most fearless of your propagandists? Tell me, will you?"

"And, if it is necessary, will you sacrifice your life? Will you run the risk of being exiled?"

"Everything, everything! It seems to me that a new existence opens before me. My empty, weary life will have some aim. Ah! If you did but know what a real service you are doing me."

"And I hope I am doing something for Nadege, too. Promise me, won't you, to love her as she deserves to be loved?"

"Yes, as a tender, charming child."

"She loves you so dearly, and you are not good to her."

"Wanda Petrowna, tell me what the nihilists think about love and marriage."

"Does not your book teach you that?"

"My book says: 'Every true feeling is lawful, but every union not based upon perfect sincerity is degrading.'"

"Well, if you did not love her, why did you marry her?"

Litzanoff looked down, overwhelmed with shame.

"I suppose you have heard," he said, "of my wild youth. The first time that I saw Nadege, her fair face, her childlike grace, her goodness, her sweet, tender eyes, all went to my heart, and I resolved to marry her. I was tired of my existence. I wanted to try and lead a quiet, decent, honest life. I hoped for a sort of regeneration from this new love. I wanted rest, and I thought I would find it with Nadege."

"Then the very day of my marriage I saw a woman for the first time who embodied in herself every perfection. Her beauty was but the reflection of a great mind and a large heart. Her eyes — I can never forget them, never. They follow me, they eat into my soul, they madden me. I wanted to love Nadege, but those eyes are always between me and her. I found a woman who looked like her, but although her eyes were of the same color, the same shape, they had not the same effect upon me. For eight days I tried to delude myself, but after that the vulgar creature disgusted me. Then I took to gambling, to racing, to hunting in the wild woods; this bear's skin nearly cost me my life. Life! You ask me if I would give it for a great work. I would give it for nothing."

He buried his head in his hands.

Wanda said not a word, lest her voice should betray her emotion.

He raised his head, and his gaze met Wanda's. It was like an electric shock. Wanda looked down. The sigh that burst from Stepane was like a hollow groan.

"Wanda!" he cried.

"Stepane Danilovitch!" she said, in a sad, haughty tone.

"Forgive me, forgive me!" He threw himself at her feet. Tears glittered in his eves, and Wanda, overcome by this terrible love, fell back in her armchair.

Stepane stretched out his trembling hands.

Irresistibly drawn towards him, she leaned forward, when suddenly feeling her weakness, she drew herself up with dignity and murmured: "It is impossible."

"Oh, why?"

"Justice and loyalty: they are true morality. Goodbye."

She arose to leave the room when Litzanoff rushed towards the door and stood in her way.

This aroused all Wanda's pride. "What do you mean?" she said.

"Nothing. I only implore you to . . ."

"Let me pass."

"I must speak to you or die."

"Let me pass," repeated Wanda, who felt her feelings getting the mastery over her.

"If you leave this room without listening to me," said Stepane, drawing out a little dagger, "I shall be dead before you reach the bottom of the stairs, and you will be my murderer!"

His accent, his gesture, were so determined that Wanda trembled.

"Well! what have you to say to me? What do you want with me?"

"One word from you, one only. Tell me that, that you love me!"

"No," answered Wanda.

"Is it really no?"

"It is really no."

"And you forbid me to love you?"

"Yes."

"Absolutely?"

"Absolutely."

"That is all that I wanted to know."

He drew aside from the door to allow her to pass.

His face wore such a terrible expression that Wanda stopped.

"What are you going to do?"

"What difference does that make to you?"

"Stepane, my brother . . ."

He said not a word.

"I will not leave you until you tell me all your heart."

"By God, I am going to kill myself! Would you rather have me go mad? I have been struggling for two years. I cannot stand it any longer."

"Your wife, Stepane! Poor Nadege!"

"She will be unhappy, but she is only a child. She will soon get over it, but as for me . . ."

"You have just determined to join the nihilists. Will you give that idea up so soon?"

"Oh, I know that after the first blush of enthusiasm has passed away, I shall soon fall back into my old state of despair. If I were upheld by a great love, perhaps I might do something."

"Well, then, Stepane, for the sake of my love, serve the cause of humanity."

She laid her hand In his. "We can have a noble pure affection for one another; I give you mine, and I desire yours. Promise it to me."

"I do!" cried Stepane, in perfect ecstacy. "Tell me, what shall I do?"

"At present, go see Nadege, who is waiting anxiously for you. I have brought her over to the cause. I will come and dine with you at six o'clock, and after dinner I can drive you to my club."

"Can I go in that way, without any preliminaries?"

"The clubs are not secret societies. It is only necessary to know who you are, and as I answer for you, you will be cordially received."

Stepane conducted the Princess to her carriage.

Nadege was watching them from her window. Wanda nodded to her, and said to the Count, "Nadege is waiting for you. Go, tell her I will be back before long."

"I will obey you blindly," answered Stepane, sighing deeply.

CHAPTER XV

THE PURSUIT OF THE NIHILISTS

"**W**e are watched," said Katia to her friend, as she got into the carriage.

"What do you mean?"

"I have seen the same man pass by the house twice. There he is, in that sleigh, getting ready to follow us."

"Do you really think so?"

"I am sure of it."

Wanda looked around and saw the sleigh following them at a distance.

"He has not horses like mine," she said. Lowering the glass she called out to the coachman, "Make haste, drive fast as you can past Mestchauskaia, Perspective, Newsky, and the quays. We will give this gentleman a little trot."

The horses flew. It was three o'clock, and they were beginning to light the lamps, for at three o'clock in January it is dark at Petersburg.

In less than five minutes they had distanced the hired sleigh. They were astonished when they suddenly perceived it standing at the corner of the English Quay! Evidently this spy knew where Princess Kryloff lived.

Wanda found her father waiting for her in her boudoir.

"Where do you come from?" he inquired.

"From some place where I went to enjoy my liberty," answered Wanda, haughtily.

"Who went with you?"

"Katia."

"What is this girl? A nihilist?"

"This girl, as you call her, is worthy of my confidence. This morning I have told her that she shall be my secretary, or rather my companion. Father, you seem to have forgotten our agreement."

"If this is to be the way of it, it cannot last," broke out the Prince in a rage, which he strove in vain to repress. "It is my duty to watch over you and to know what you are after."

"For this one time I can tell you," answered Wanda. "I have just been to see Nadege Litzanoff. But if at some future time it should suit me not to tell you where I have been, your questions would force me to lie. Would it not be better for your dignity, as well as mine, that you should refrain from questioning me?"

The Prince walked up and down the room with hurried steps. Suddenly, throwing a large roll of bank notes upon the table, he exclaimed: "Here are the twenty-five thousand roubles I promised you. Am I to know, at least, where this money is going to?"

"If I am to keep an expense account, I would rather have you keep the money."

Wanda looked at her father. She saw the veins swelling in his forehead, and she knew what that meant. But she was determined she would give up nothing.

The Prince, recognizing her temper, continued more gently. "Chabert and I had an interview with the minister; everything is going on very well. You are satisfied with me in this matter, are you not? And in return, will you not grant me a little favor?"

"What is it?"

"To spend this evening with me."

"Oh! That is impossible."

"Why?"

"I am not going to dine at home."

"Very well," cried out the Prince, completely losing control of himself. "I cannot accustom myself to allow you to go out alone day and night, whenever you think fit."

Wanda listened to this new outburst with calmness.

"Do you know what is said of you?" continued the Prince. "I have just heard it from a friend of Trepoff. They say you are a socialist, a Nihilist, an anarchist; and all this mystery looks very much like it. If I only knew . . ."

"Well!"

"That in my house, my daughter was plotting against the Emperor; if I thought that you had the least intercourse with these bandits, these thieves, these assassins, I would renounce you forever. I would give you up to the authorities. Yes, yes! Examples must be made, or this pestilence will infect the whole of Russia, and society will be entirely overturned."

Wanda saw her danger. If she were discovered everything would be discovered. She must reassure her father and take away all suspicion from him for the future. She hated a lie, but now it had become a duty. All things are fair in war, and surely war had been declared, as she was openly denounced.

Laughing gaily, she said, "Is this the cause of your anger? Are the police so hard up that they need to attack the young girls of noble birth? But how could I have given them cause to accuse me? Ah! I remember. Last night at the ball I was talking about nihilism with Verenine. We were laughing at something, and I said that if nihilism could deliver us from these official gatherings where we are nearly crushed to death it would render society a great benefit, and he told me about an address that the Emperor had received from a pretended Revolutionary Committee. There was a gentleman watching us. I refused to dance with him. I wager he was a spy. But I assure you, father, I am not a nihilist. What earthly benefit could accrue to me from the overturn of society? I would have to lose my senses before I could become a nihilist; you certainly do not think me insane as yet."

Kryloff knew his daughter, her independence of thought, her perfect horror of a lie. This avowal of hers set his mind at rest.

"That is just what I said myself, but why is there this constant mystery about your actions? Tell me, for instance, where are you going to dine today?"

"I am going to take dinner at the Litzanoff's."

"But you have just come from there."

"Yes, I went to make peace between Nadege and her husband; we dine together, and then we are going to the theater."

"And what are you going to do with this money? If I thought that it was going to pass in to the hands of the conspirators . . ."

"I can only say what I have already said, do not question me any more. I want to found a Home for Orphans. For the very reason that I hate the nihilists, and in order to escape the consequences of a revolution, we who are rich, idle and happy, ought to busy ourselves in taking care of the distressed, and in trying to ameliorate their condition."

"Why did you not tell me this before?"

"Because you opposed me so in my efforts to found those schools in the Ukraine."

"The reason of that was that I do not agree with you. The more you educate the lower classes, the more you better their condition, the more do you develop in them hatred of their superiors. They are a race of slaves, a vile lot, who can only be ruled by the knout. Look at the results of the emancipation : the ruin of the nobility, the ruin of agriculture, and general misery."

"Those are not my views. Please allow me to act according to my convictions."

"I passed over your fancy for the schools. I will do the like with this fancy for a Home. Just now liberalism is the rage; it is the fashion, and women are the slaves of fashion. However, do not ruin me with your follies, for it is money put to very bad account."

"My follies! Let me enjoy them. The illusions of youth last but a little while."

"But still, these very follies give color to the accusations brought against you."

"I can always disprove them easily enough. Naughty father, don't let us have any more of these scenes."

"Spoilt child," sighed the Prince, "you know that I always give in to you. I wanted to look over the list of invitations with you this evening, and add a few names to it, Prince Stackelberg's among others."

"Very well! Tomorrow morning we can do it. I will help you with your ball, if you will help me with my Home."

"I wish the ball to be a success," said the Prince.

"Then invite the officers and the generals. I noticed last night what a brilliant effect the military decorations produced."

Wanda was thinking that it would be a good thing if she could make some recruits in the army.

"What is this sudden fancy that you have taken for the soldiers?" exclaimed the Prince. "You, who have always expressed such hatred for war and everything belonging to it. But you are right, and I will think it over."

"Adieu," said Wanda, "I must dress myself."

She went to her own room. Once there, she fell into a chair, overcome with fatigue. Not only had the struggle with her father exhausted her, but also her interview with Stepane Litzanoff.

"What is there about this man to move me so?" she thought. "I always suspected that he loved me, but what is this feeling that I have for him? I will not allow it to be love. No, I will not."

And leaning her pale face against the back of the chair, she thought of Stepane.

The first time she met Count Litzanoff was on the day of his marriage with Nadege. Wanda had been struck by his singular beauty and by his original and independent mind. She felt herself irresistibly drawn towards this being, so refined and yet so untamed. Every time that she met him the impression deepened. She saw her danger, and gradually she stopped going to visit Nadege. She had thrown herself into the revolutionary movement, chiefly to escape from the effect of the sudden and violent feeling that threatened to take possession of her. In nihilism she had found an all-absorbing interest. Raymond Chabert had also interested her; she even felt a sort of tenderness for him, that she thought at one time might culminate in love. But this feeling was nothing in comparison to the one that a single glance from Litzanoff awakened in her. Still, she felt much more confidence in Raymond than in Stepane.

Now she strove to analyze these two sentiments, although so upset by her interview with Litzanoff that she could not clearly see into her own heart. Litzanoff's love seized her as with magnetic power, but it also caused her a sort of uneasy, frightened remorse. Raymond's love, on the contrary, did not take her by storm, but it inspired her with boundless confidence. His tender but timid admiration, his entire devotion, melted her heart.

"After all," she said, rising to her feet, "what does it matter? I owe myself entirely to the cause I have embraced."

She called Katia and asked for a light.

"Make haste, Katia, and dress yourself in one of my dresses. In the future you are to be my lady's companion."

But Katia answered, hardly noticing her sudden rise in rank, "We certainly are watched; I just saw that sleigh again. I sent Fedor to look, and he recognized Popoff, whom the Prince discharged last month."

"Is he sure of that?"

"Yes, and it frightens me, for that Popoff is a thorough scoundrel, capable of anything. He has probably told the police about the trips we have been taking at night."

"Indeed," said Wanda, "then war is really declared."

She then told Katia of her conversation with her father, and of the accusation that was hanging over her.

"The police have their eye on us," she added, "but we shall find means to throw them off the track. As we are going to the Litzanoffs' house, who are certainly not suspected, we may allow ourselves to be followed. Then about nine o'clock, we can dress up two of the maids in our hats and cloaks and send them back in the coupe. Then after they are gone, we and the Litzanoffs can pay our intended visit to Padlewsky."

"Very well," said Katia. "We may escape this time, but after this how shall we be able to hold intercourse with our friends? This is a permanent danger, not only for us, but for them."

Wanda seemed lost in thought; suddenly she cried out: "Eureka! I will seize the bull by the horns. I will get my father to take me to see General Trepoff."

"Well, what will you say to him?"

"I will complain of being suspected by the Government that my father has always loyally served. I will complain of being watched. I will invite him to our ball," and she burst out laughing.

"Go on."

"I will fascinate him. Isn't that an original idea?"

"Charming! But take care, it is dangerous to play with fire."

Katia Lawinska had an energetic countenance; her large head, high cheek bones, deep color, dark brown hair, small, bluish-gray eyes, deep-set and far-seeing, her unbending figure, her careless dress — all these told of a strong, unyielding character. And yet, if she had been more becomingly attired, she might have passed for a pretty woman.

When she had put on the costume that belonged to Wanda, it worked a complete transformation in her.

"You see you are not ugly," said Wanda to her. "It is only your frightful nihilist clothes that make you look so."

"I dress myself this way as a protest against female vanity. Immoderate love of dress ruins women. So that their bodies are adorned, they are utterly indifferent to the embellishment of their minds and of their souls."

"And still," answered Wanda, "I think Padlewsky is right. The love of luxury is innate in human nature, above all in women's nature. We can never get rid of it, and it is, after all, a sociable trait."

"But at this time," answered Katia, "when the common people are clothed in rags, our luxury seems to me an outrage on their misery."

They went out.

Popoff was still in the sleigh, watching the house. He followed the carriage along as he had done at the Litzanoffs'.

Wanda found Nadege happy, radiant with delight.

"There is no one but you that can perform such miracles," said the young wife, throwing her arms around her friend's neck.

Wanda held out her hand to Stepane, and she felt how his trembled.

"Stepane and I," said Nadege, "have become out-and-out nihilists. We will follow you anywhere, even to Siberia. Will we not, Stepane?"

"To the end of the world," he answered.

"Very well, dear friends, I shall at once put your sincerity to the proof. I have brought my maid with me, whom I look upon as a friend, for we democrats know no rank, no state of servitude, no caste. She is as devoted as I am to the cause, and I want you to invite her to dine with us at your table."

"Indeed," said Nadege, laughing, "this is an unexpected proof. To admit a servant girl to my table, however devoted she may be to socialism, is a height of democracy to which I have not altogether attained. If you wish it, she shall not eat with the other servants; I will have her served by herself."

"But if you were to go to Siberia, could you pick your society?"

"But we haven't gone there yet. What do you think about it, Stepane?"

"Well, if Wanda, who is of higher rank than we are, does not think it beneath her to dine with this person, we should be very wrong to show ourselves more hard to please than she is."

Wanda rewarded the Count for this condescension with a loving glance. He was one of the most aristocratic men in Russia. She knew what those words must cost him.

"It was only a proof of your earnestness, dear friends. But your repugnance will soon disappear."

And, telling them Katia's story in a few words, she opened the door and called her. "Come here, dear. Here are two new nihilists who want to know you."

At the sight of this distinguished young girl, who entered with perfect ease of manner, Nadege held out her hand, and Stepane bowed.

The dinner was very gay.

At eight o'clock they sent Nadege's two maids back in the carriage, and the four friends went together in an ordinary hack to Padlewsky's.

"Plotting is very amusing, is it not?" said Wanda.

"With you, above all, dear Princess," answered Stepane.

"The words prince and princess, and count and countess," cried out Katia, "are absolutely prohibited in our vocabulary."

They got out of the hack at the New Perspective. But what was their dismay in seeing behind them the sleigh that they thought had followed the two maids in the coupe! How had the scoundrel found out their trick?

"The girls must have spoken to one another as they got into the carriage, and Popoff knows Wanda"s voice and mine perfectly well," explained Katia.

"We must rid ourselves of him, anyhow," said Litzanoff. "In time of war spies are killed." And he drew out a little dagger.

"Oh! not here, in the open street, at nine o'clock in the evening," exclaimed Wanda. "All the police watching us, and everybody passing up and down the street."

"I can strike him before he has time to move."

"It would be too dangerous," said Wanda.

"Less dangerous than to allow him to follow us," observed Katia. "He is, besides, a scoundrel capable of any crime."

"Kill a man, shed his blood!" exclaimed Nadege in terror.

"We must buy him off," said Wanda. "Have you enough money about you?"

"I have a few bank notes."

He went up to the cab.

"Popoff!" he called.

The fellow, who had no notion he was discovered, bounded to his feet.

"Come down, I want to speak to you."

He came down.

"How much do they pay you for following us?"

"But I . . ."

"No buts, answer me!"

"I assure you, your Excellency . . ."

"I know you; if you do not answer me at once I will have you arrested by the police, for the money you stole from Prince Kryloff. How much will you take for lying to the men that employ you?"

"Fifty roubles."

"Well, here are a hundred, and see to it that you do not get in my way again, for if you do, it will not be roubles that you get, you scapegrace."

Popoff leaped to his seat, whipped up his horse, and drove off quickly towards the Neva.

Then the four friends disappeared down a narrow lane which led into a larger street, built up, as are all the streets in Petersburg, with handsome houses and miserable shanties standing side by side.

They rang a bell at No. 11, mounted two flights of stairs, and knocked at a door, which opened instantly.

CHAPTER XVI

DESCENT OF THE POLICE

They entered quite a large hall and asked for Padlewsky. They were instantly introduced into a room in which a dozen persons were playing cards.

Andrew Padlewsky came forward to meet them. He pressed Wanda's hand.

"I bring you two fervent neophytes," she said.

Padlewsky started when he recognized Litzanoff and Nadege.

"What!" cried he, "this naughty boy, this terrible sceptic, has he found out the truth at last?"

"Here is our truth, our beacon-light!" answered Litzanoff, pointing to Wanda.

"There are about fifty of us here, already," continued Padlewsky, "but I think we shall have a hundred tonight, for there is to he a very important discussion."

"Where are your friends," asked Litzanoff. "This room fitted up with card tables, and wax candles, and shades for protecting the eyes, does not look much like a place for a political meeting."

"This respectable drawing-room is only intended to foil the police. The meeting is not held in this house, it is next door. You came in at No. 11, which has two entrances; you could also have entered at No. 15, which has two entrances; but the meeting is at No. 18. All three houses belong to us. We make the doormen drunk whenever we have a meeting; they do not suspect anything. Besides, we have friends who watch for us, stationed at all the doors. You see these four bells; they answer to the four principal doors. At the least alarm a bell warns us of our danger, and we instantly go out by the other entrances. These four bells are under the care of men whom I can trust as myself. Every time we meet, they change their costume. Tonight they are disguised as superintendents, sometimes they appear as cab drivers, and then they wait outside in a droschka or a sleigh."

"It is all very well arranged," said Litzanoff, "but among a hundred people, how can you be sure that one will not betray you?"

"We very seldom meet together here. The persons that are allowed to enter are perfectly safe. Their position, or their fortune, or their antecedents place them above all suspicion, or above any corruption by the police. We know them, and we answer for them, as Wanda Kryloff does for you. You may be perfectly easy, as far as that goes."

Just then several persons entered.

Padlewsky touched a spring in the wall. A secret door opened, leaving a space large enough for one person to pass at a time.

Through it they entered the Hall of Assembly.

This hall was spacious enough to accommodate two hundred people. It had no windows but was hung with cloth, wadded, to deaden the sound of voices. The floor was covered with a thick carpet. Everything else was very plain: simple wooden benches and a stand, slightly raised, for the speaker.

Litzanoff's and Nadege's were astonished to recognize among those present many members of the best society, and even of the families known for their devotion to the Emperor! There were also Poles, Finns, a prince from Daghestan, Jewish bankers, several Kaskolinks, and political prisoners who had been liberated or who had escaped from prison.

Woldemar Siline was the first to mount the stand. He described the actual situation of Russia, read the most important documents aloud, and showed how an iniquitous war, undertaken for the purpose of uprooting the revolutionary movement, had on the contrary increased the number of nihilists.

Doctor Poloutkin succeeded Siline and eloquently but vigorously exposed the disastrous consequences of the Turkish war. In conclusion, he said, "We are the most wretched nation in the world. In our rebellion against the actual condition of things, we are sure that we express the feeling of the people. Nobles and citizens, workmen and peasants, we are all weary of this odious tyranny. The Czar has sacrificed three hundred thousand souls to suppress in Bulgaria a rule which is much more humane, much less despotic than our own. We have shed our blood and spent millions to free the Bulgarians from the oppression of the pacha, but are we not ourselves under pacha and rajahs? We have sent our soldiers into Turkey to bring them happiness and liberty! What is Lithuanian happiness? What is Muscovite liberty? Before we deliver others, let us try to deliver ourselves. Has a Russian peasant ever owned house and lands like the Bulgarians? Has one of our mujiks ever gathered in crops of grain equal to those owned by the dwellers in the fertile valleys of Sophia and Adrianople?

Has Turkey her Mouravieffs, her Trepoffs?

"Our scourge is Caesarism! It has weakened our bone, it has sucked dry the marrow, it has made of us a degenerate race. In order to take our place among civilized nations we must destroy utterly this structure of our government, our shame and disgrace.

"They say the Czar's intentions are good, but the road to hell is paved with good intentions. In our last appeal to him we strove to awaken his imperial conscience, if an Emperor can have a conscience. What liberties has he granted to us, this magnanimous Emperor? He has patched a few pieces to an old garment, that is all.

"They tell us that today there are laws in Russia, but the governors of the provinces modify or transgress those laws exactly as they see fit.

"There are in Russia judges, and even juries, but the police continue to act as they please. Scourging has been prohibited, but it still goes on in this holy, abominable Russia. They told us that the whips had been cast aside, yet they whipped our brother Bogoluboff outrageously. He cried aloud, not at the pain, but at the insult. That insult has aroused us. Each one of us has felt the lash that fell upon Bogoluboff's back."

In France Doctor Poloutkin's discourse would have been applauded; in England it would have been greeted with frantic cheers; but here there were no applause, no noisy demonstration, although every one present approved of the speech. Enthusiasm in Russia is calm; it is a country of abstract passions, of cool rages, of dogged intoxication.

Then Narkileff rose up and asked in a steady, quiet voice: "Yesterday we discussed, when there were but few of us present, what sort of vengeance should be taken upon Trepoff. I wish to appeal to you as to what punishment he deserves."

"Retaliation!" cried several voices.

"No, death!"

"Let those who wish him put to death stand up!" continued Narkileff. About half the number of those present arose.

"It would be almost impossible to have him whipped" observed Komoff.

"With the means at our disposal nothing is impossible," said Padlewsky.

"The scourge is not a sufficient punishment for that man's crimes," observed Woldemar Siline. "There have been four hundred and fifty prisoners arrested without trial, who have been reduced in number to one hundred and ninety-three; that is to say, two hundred and fifty-seven prisoners have died either by hunger or cold, or have been sent away secretly to Siberia. Do you think that one man's life is enough to expiate such cruelty?"

"No! No! Death! Death!"

Such was now the cry.

"What sort of death?"

The opinions were divided.

"The traitor Akim Niconoff perished by the dagger, said Sophronius," and those who have struck him down have never been discovered.

"Listen to me," continued Padlewsky. "I do not wish to kill Trepoff."

Loud objections drowned his voice.

"Justice must be done."

"Wait," he continued, "for the great day of judgment, the day of the wrath of the people."

"We should have to wait too long," cried out some one in the crowd.

"Reflect one moment, my friends; this would he an assassination."

"Say rather a righteous execution."

"But what good will it do? If you begin you cannot stop with Trepoff. You must go on to the magistrates, the blue officers, all the representatives of tyranny, of arbitrary rule, all those who openly and with impunity practice injustice in the Holy Empire of the Czar. And do not let us pay them back crime for crime. Let us show them that our morality and our justice are far above theirs."

He was violently interrupted.

"No such namby-pamby generosity! They have made martyrs enough; we will avenge them and defend ourselves."

Padlewsky allowed the tumult to subside.

"You forget," he resumed, "that the punishment which you intend might bring very dangerous consequences, terrible reprisals upon us; it might shackle our movements, bring forth a fresh set of repressive measures, and increased rigor against the prisoners and the exiles."

"So much the better," cried out Poloutkin. "That will but fill up the measure. The more they imprison, the more they scourge, the more will public indignation swell and rise. The Russian people is a man asleep with his hands hanging by his sides. We must shake him from his torpor, draw him out of his deadly lethargy, put arms into those hands paralyzed by slavery and by imbecilic submission to his tyrants. One lightning stroke will, I hope, be the signal vainly expected for twenty years by every man who believes in the revolution and desires it." These words raised a storm in the hall.

"Yes!"

"No!"

"Death!"

"By the dagger."

"By the revolver."

"Secretly."

"Publicly."

"Boldly."

"In open day."

"As publicly as possible."

"Who will do it?"

"Do you wish me to do it?" whispered Litzanoff in Wanda"s ear.

"Oh! No, no!" cried Nadege, overhearing him, and pressing close to her husband's side.

"How brave you are," said Litzanoff, laughing.

The meeting moved to adjourn; every one arose and talked together in groups.

Katia crossed the room to speak to Vera Zassoulitch. She was sitting by herself on a bench, listening to the uproar, with her sad smile and inward-looking eyes.

"If they do not resolve upon something definite tonight," she said with much simplicity, "I shall take the matter into my own hands."

She left her seat and drew near to a group engaged in angry discussion, but she did not join in their talk.

"Who is that young girl?" asked Litzanoff of Katia.

"She is a heroine, a martyr. I will tell you her story, it is frightful. She had hardly left school in Moscow when she met Netchaieff, who initiated her into our doctrines. For the crime of having listened to him, she was condemned to be sent to the casemates of the fort. She asked in vain what were the charges against her; her jailors were deaf and dumb, to her entreaties. She had a mother whom she worshiped; she was allowed neither to see her, write to her, nor to receive any message from her. Afterwards she discovered that her mother had been imprisoned likewise; that her sister, with a baby at the breast, had been thrown into prison. The baby died, and its wretched father was condemned to twenty years in the mines. Vera's heart bled more for the sufferings of those she loved than for her own.

"And yet, what a dreadful life she had! She was allowed no occupation; she was tortured by silence, weariness, longing. During those two years, she told me, her eyes rested upon no one save her jailers and the agents of the police. Her ears heard no sound save the noise of the bolts, the click of the guns, the step of the sentinel, the monotonous tick of the clock, telling of wasted hours, long and weary as centuries. At last, when this poor girl came out of her dungeon, and thought herself once more free, the police seized her and sent her into a distant province where she was confined, placed under strict surveillance, hurried from town to town, from village to village, persecuted by sidelong glances, by outrageous suspicions, for a crime that she had never committed. Do you see all the indignation, all the pent-up revolt in that creature twenty years old? Do you understand her hatred for the police and all their men!"

They were still discussing Trepoff's punishment but had arrived at no conclusion, when the same man who had opened the door for Wanda and her friends came suddenly into the room and whispered something to Padlewsky.

"My friends," exclaimed the Pole, "the police are at the door of No. 11."

There was dead silence. Every face grew pale; they all saw themselves on the road to Siberia.

Siline mounted the stand:

"Let there be no stupid panic," he said. "Be cool. There are three other entrances. Let us divide ourselves into three parties so we can effect our escape. I have been engaged in this business for fifty years, and it is at least the twentieth time that the police have broken up our meetings. Let us be calm. Above all, let there be no cowardice! Let us remember that we are ready to sacrifice our lives for the great cause of the people." Nadege was trembling, almost ready to faint. But on Wanda's, Litzanoff's and Katia's face could be seen neither hesitation nor fear.

"You are as brave as an old conspirator," said Wanda to Stepane.

"I assure you, I have never been so much amused in my life. These are genuine emotions." He whispered in Wanda's ear: "This morning, I wanted to kill myself; I am glad that I waited."

She fixed her beautiful eyes upon him.

"It would have been a suicide with no result. You see now that you will have plenty of opportunity to sacrifice your life."

Padlewsky had gone into the drawing-room of No. 11 to shut and bolt the doors, so as to gain time, while the police were forcing them, to cover the retreat of his friends. But he returned in a few moments, and said quietly:

"The situation is serious, more serious than I thought; the four entrances are guarded by the police."

No word was said, no cry was uttered, but each one seemed to hear the beating of his own heart.

Padlewsky went on, still perfectly unmoved:

"It is evident that we have been betrayed. There is an informer among us."

Each gazed upon the other.

"Who is he? It matters but little! The coward shall be punished by the futility of his information. If I seemed uneasy for a moment it was but to try you. Forgive me; you are each one of you a hero. I foresaw all this, and there is a fifth entrance known to me alone. The four doors are strongly barricaded; it will take the police half an hour to break them down. So we can take our escape without any hurry. Only be perfectly silent."

Then Andrew Padlewsky drew aside one of the curtains; behind it was a door, which he threw open; one by one the persons present, passing through it, stepped upon a very narrow winding staircase. Like the captain of a shipwrecked vessel, Padlewsky would not descend until he had seen the last one of his friends safe. Then he pulled back the curtain into position and locked the secret door behind him. At the same moment the blows of the axes as they fell upon the outside doors shook the house to its foundations.

CHAPTER XVII

THE CHIEF OF POLICE

The next morning Wanda woke up fresh and blooming. She looked as if no care had ever troubled her. Her white brow was unruffled by a cloud. As soon as she was dressed, she went to her father's room.

"Father," she said, "I have been thinking all night long about the accusations that have been brought against me. Although they are perfectly false, they might have very disastrous consequences for you as well as for me. I should like very much to prove my innocence to the police. It seems to me the more necessary because yesterday, when I went to see the Litzanoffs, I was followed by that fellow Popoff, that you had sent to jail. How did he get out? And why do you think he was following me? Evidently he has been bribed by somebody. Don't you think he is in the pay of the police?"

"That scoundrel Popoff at liberty?" cried the Prince. "I will see about this. What proofs can you give of your innocence?"

"I want you to take me to see General Trepoff, and I shall ask for an explanation. Do you think he can doubt me when he sees me? Have I anything in common with these young Nihilists who go about dressed up in brown frocks with their hair cut short and blue spectacles on their nose? Am I not a woman of society, a fashionable woman?"

"It is a good idea," said the Prince. "I will think it over while we are at breakfast. And besides, Trepoff is a charming fellow, rather gallant perhaps, but very distinguished in his manners and quite liberal in his views."

"He flogs the political prisoners," interrupted Wanda, in rather an ironical tone.

"He is right. Those nihilists are insolent, audacious beyond expression. Imagine the Chief of Police insulted by such a low-bred fool as that Bogoluboff!"

"He is a man, father, at any rate! "exclaimed Wanda; "I think the General ought to have some respect for the dignity of man."

"Do you call such a wretch as that worthy of dignity? He is a thousand times more culpable than a thief or even than a murderer. A murderer merely endangers the lives of one or two persons, but a nihilist endangers the life of our whole society."

"I think, father, that you exaggerate the importance of the nihilist party."

"Perhaps you are right, but at any rate the Chief of Police ought to uphold the law, for without it social order cannot exist and we should fall into a chaotic state of misrule. Would it not frighten you to pay a visit to General Trepoff?"

"Not in the least; I am strong in the consciousness of my own innocence."

"But suppose there really does exist some accusation against you? Even just now you were upholding Bogoluboff. You could not speak in that way before people without exciting suspicion."

"Well, I want to explain to the General that I have an independent way of thinking, and that it has given rise to the idea that I do not love this Government of satraps."

"There you are again. Indeed, you frighten me! You know well that in Russia you cannot joke about such things."

"I will utter those very words to him in such a pleasant way that he will not mind it."

"Child, you do not understand the police.

"My friend told me — and he knew what he was talking about — that in a hidden place they have a piece of mechanism reserved for special occasions, consisting of rods worked by machinery. Any one who is suspected can be brought before the head of the Third Section and after a few moments of interrogation he suddenly feels a trapdoor opened and finds himself suspended in a dark chamber. Then unseen hands rapidly undress him, and the invisible rods do their duty. Then he is placed upon the trapdoor, it moves back into position, and he is conducted to his carriage with the greatest courtesy. He goes home bearing with him an indelible impression of his visit to the General, and at the same time the consolation that his executioners have never seen his face, and so cannot recognize him again. I am told that several ladies in society have been thus treated."

"Don't you think it is horrible that such acts can be committed with impunity? One does not need to be a nihilist to revolt at such proceedings."

"And you are perfectly capable of saying that to the Chief of Police?"

"I promise you that I will watch over my words."

"But suppose he questions you to find out your opinions?"

"Then I will answer him in a light, trifling way."

"Well, let us go, but take care."

Two hours after this conversation Prince Kryloff's coupe stopped before General Trepoff's office.

Trepoff, who at that time was chief of the Petersburg police, was not a monster. He was looked upon as an amiable man, with fine manners, agreeable in conversation, very fond of art, literature and drama. For a long time he had been one of the Czar's favorites.

In passing through Warsaw, of which he was then Chief of Police, Alexander had met him one day in a droshky drawn by two superb black horses. Trepoff was standing up in the carriage, steadying himself by holding on to all iron bar. The Emperor sent for him, and asked him why he drove about in that attitude. "So that I can see everything, Sire," he answered.

From that moment the Emperor gave him his confidence.

Not only the Czar, but the public likewise, had the greatest confidence in Trepoff. He was independent and fair. The big thieves feared him as much as the little ones. He took as good care of the poorer parts of the city as he did of the wealthy ones. The citizens of Petersburg called him "Father Trepoff," which is a great compliment in Russia.

How had he allowed himself to be so carried away by his temper as to give that order which had in one instant lost him his popularity?

As she mounted the stairs that led to the apartments of the Chief of Police, Wanda felt her heart beat. She was afraid that she would lose her presence of mind before this man, who embodied in himself, as it were, all the crimes of the Third Section.

For three days Trepoff's rage, excited by the reproaches of the Emperor, and by no means appeased by Bogoluboff's flogging, had been on the increase. In three days' search he had still found no clue to the conspiracy. The stupid, unsuccessful zeal of his police had exasperated him. He knew that the nihilists longed to avenge the insult offered to Bogoluboff, and all the scourges in the kingdom did not seem to him severe enough for their crimes, and the sleepless nights they caused him.

And so, when Prince and Princess Kryloff were summoned, he fairly bounded from his seat.

"Ah! Now I will find out something. A woman, a young girl; I will manage to make her speak."

Concealing his bad temper, he received his visitors with politeness, and invited them to be seated.

"General," said the Prince, "my daughter has desired me to bring her to see you, in order that she may lay her complaints before you of the rumors that are circulated in regard to her, and of the manner in which she is watched by your agents."

"Yes," said Trepoff, "I have had several reports made to me, in which the Princess's name figures, and . . ."

Up to this time Wanda had sat with her veil down. She removed it.

The General looked at her, struck dumb with admiration.

She wore a little hat of garnet velvet, trimmed with white ostrich feathers and pearl buckles. Her hair fell over her forehead in soft curls, and her excitement caused her eyes to deepen in color and to glow with intensity.

"I have come here to accuse myself," she said, smiling in the most coquettish, bewitching manner. "I am a nihilist."

"What!" cried the Prince, who thought his daughter had gone mad.

The Chief of Police looked on in utter astonishment.

"Yes," she went on, "I am a revolutionist, a rebel. I rebel against the miserable pavement of Petersburg, against the wretched macadamized roads, against our green roofs that drive the French painters to despair. I revolt against everything that is ugly, against everything that offends my eye and hurts my feet, against everything that shocks my taste, my good sense, or the feeling of justice that nature has implanted within me. Up to this time I have not rebelled against society, for I have nothing to complain of."

"Well," said the General, utterly confounded.

"But if you are accusing me," she continued, "spying on me, persecuting me, I don't know what I shall do. Perhaps turn socialist, nihilist, revolutionist, anarchist; anything you choose, just to find out what it is all about, and to keep your policemen at bay."

At these last words Trepoff felt his face grow crimson.

"And yet," he said, "last night at eight o'clock, you, together with Count and Countess Litzanoff . . ."

"And my companion," interrupted Wanda, not in the least disconcerted.

"Were seen in a part of the town not much frequented by the aristocracy, going in the direction of a house which is looked upon as suspected."

"We were all going to a little theater, which is not very refined, that is true, but we only wanted to amuse ourselves. We had no intentions whatever against the Government."

"How could you make up your mind to go to such a place?"

"Count Litzanoff is so blasé that he always wants to try some out-of-the-way place. We had a very pleasant evening. That is the whole truth."

"But why did you give a hundred roubles to Popoff?"

With wonderful presence of mind Wanda, answered: "To understand that, you would have to know Count Litzanoff. The persistency of that fellow in following us set him nearly crazy. He did not want any one to recognize him, and he had no small change with him, so he threw him that hundred rouble note."

Trepoff listened to all this. If it was not true, at least it was probable, and how could he say to this beautiful creature: you lie!

"You are very clever," he said, "but . . ."

Wanda interrupted him:

"General, do you know why the Russians are always plotting? It is because they are so bored. In Russia the sky is sad, life is sad, we are sad from our birth. When we do not intoxicate ourselves with vodka, we long for political intoxication. In place of building prisons why do you not put up theaters? Russians are crazy about theatrical amusements; do something to amuse us. Think of it, and you will see that I am right."

"This is all very entertaining. What makes me doubt your being a socialist is your fine mind and your very charming manners. You seem to me to have too much sense, too much refinement, to allow yourself to be mixed up with these infidel, dirty, empty-headed democrats."

"And how could you suspect that Litzanoff, that epicure, that king of society, that swell, could become a nihilist? And his charming, airy little wife! How could any one associate her with the viragos whose portraits adorn the daily papers? Poor Nadege! She would faint at the mere thought of such an accusation. General, I particularly want to introduce you to these dangerous nihilists. My father is going to give me a ball on my birthday, which is the 13th of January. I hope you will honor us with your presence. There you will meet these black-hearted conspirators face to face."

As she spoke, Wanda managed to throw into her face an expression of exquisite charm and grace. The Chief of Police, completely captivated, accepted the invitation. His anger had passed away. He complimented the Prince upon having such a daughter.

CHAPTER XVIII

SELF-ABNEGATION

When Litzanoff returned from his evening at Padlewsky's, he conducted Nadege to her room, and then withdrew to his own. He wrapped himself in a fur robe and stretched himself out upon his divan.

He tried in vain to sleep. Towards midnight he arose, and taking up one of the books that Padlewsky had lent him, he went on with his reading. Suddenly he stopped, walked up and down the room, then stood still, lost in meditation; his eyes shone, his breast heaved, his face was distorted with passion. In a moment a change swept over his features, his eyes grew tender, he stretched out his arms towards some unseen form, he murmured indistinctly words of love, of grief, of gentle reproach.

Then for several minutes he appeared stupefied, when, seizing a pistol which lay upon the table in his room, he placed it against his heart, and as suddenly let it fall. "She will not let me!" he said.

About daybreak he fell asleep, and did not awaken until noon.

Nadege came to inquire if he felt badly.

"Not at all," he answered, kissing her tenderly. "I have read the whole night through. And you, dear, how do you feel after last evening?"

"I could not sleep either," said Nadege, "but I was not thinking of last evening's performances, I was thinking of you."

"Are you still always thinking of me?"

"Yes, I am," said the young wife, making a charming little face. "But you cannot say the same to me, ungrateful man!"

"Yes, I am ungrateful, and still my love is sincere, I assure you."

"Stepane," said Nadege, with a gravity, a resolution that did not seem to belong to her, "I want to speak to you about something, and I want you to tell me the truth."

"What is it about, dear?" said Litzanoff, stifling a sigh. He thought another scene was impending.

"You are in love with Wanda."

He gave an involuntary start.

"Are you crazy?"

"Then swear that you do not love her."

"You are so childish."

"I am not childish, Stepane; I am only a woman hopelessly, desperately in love with a man who does not care for her. Our reconciliation did not deceive me."

Stepane thought that by lying he could hoodwink his wife, and he also thought that if he once owned up to his love for Wanda he would lose the happiness of seeing her in his own house.

"You are entirely mistaken, Nadege. I admire Wanda as I do a statue. She could never love any man who is not a hero, and I am not a hero. You are all the time thinking that I am still in love with some other woman. The trouble with me is that I have led a dissolute life; my heart is worn out, my senses are deadened; I am the victim of a terrible ennui, which prevents me from feeling the charm of any gentle, quiet love. Dear child, I thoroughly appreciate all your noble, good qualities. I am touched by your affection for me, and I know that I am unworthy of it. I wish I could love you as you deserve; I wish I could worship you, pass my life at your feet."

"Why don't you love me that way?" sobbed Nadege, throwing herself into her husband's arms.

"Poor little heart! I cannot."

Nadege fell almost lifeless upon the divan.

"Nadege, my darling wife, your reproaches will kill me. Spare me them, I implore you."

Suddenly the young wife perceived the pistol that Litzanoff had thrown upon the floor in his frenzy.

"What is this?" she cried, picking it up. "Stepane, my husband, my love, you have been trying to kill yourself!"

And she frantically embraced him.

"You wished to die. Why, why? Because this woman — I do not know who it is — but I know it is a woman."

"No, I swear to you it is not so. I did want to die, but it was only because I cannot love you as you deserve to be loved," answered Stepane, who really began to be moved by the grief which he was causing. And he pressed his wife to his heart.

"Say that again, swear that you do not love any one but me."

"No one, my love," answered Stepane.

"Thanks, thanks! Do you know what I came to propose to you? Do you know what I have determined to do?" she said, smiling.

"No."

"Well, I came to offer you your liberty."

"How?"

"If you wish it, I will apply for a divorce."

Stepane arose, and walked up and down the room in somber silence.

"Forgive me, forgive me," cried Nadege, who thought she had hurt her husband's feelings. "I know it would have killed me. But I only desired your happiness. I love you well enough to die for you."

Now this was what troubled Litzanoff so deeply. He saw, as it were, his liberty within his grasp, the liberty whose loss he had so bitterly regretted for two years. He hesitated between his desire to seize it and his unwillingness to grieve Nadege. It would be cruel to accept it. Nadege's last words softened his heart.

"How kind you are!" he said, with tears in his ryes.

Nadege believed that he loved her; if not passionately, at least tenderly.

"What book is this?" she asked.

"It is the book which has converted me to socialism."

"Are you really converted and convinced?"

"Yes, I really am," answered Litzanoff; "so really convinced, that I am willing to sacrifice my life to the cause."

"Then so am I," said Nadege. "I say as Ruth did to Naomi: 'Your God shall be my God, and whither thou goest I will go.'"

For four days after this, Stepane remained shut up in his own room. He only left it to get new books from Padlewsky; the works of Bakunin, Lassalle, and Marx. After he had finished those he read Auguste Comte, Charles Fourier, and Proudhon.

The idea of Justice in all its glory burst upon his mind. At first it blinded him. Then around him in every direction he saw the Old World crumbling to pieces at his feet. He saw that a new edifice must be built up, resting on no Roman law or legal rights or atheistic philosophy or barren rationalism. He could and would contribute his stone to this colossal structure and in the presence of such lofty thoughts, such noble desires, his own selfish suffering seemed to pale.

After four days spent thus in almost complete solitude, during which time he had been very good to Nadege, he made a grand resolve.

He sent for his steward. This intendant, Dimitri Kischleff, was an old serf, a type yet quite usual in Russia, who looked upon the emancipation as a mistake, and who still remained perfectly devoted to his master. He was well educated, and possessed some little means, but he was a true mujik, kissing the hand that smote him.

The fortune that Stepane squandered with lavish hand, Dimitri took care of as if it were his own. He regarded the palace as his. He rejoiced in the luxury of his masters, as if their magnificence reflected upon himself. He had completely identified himself with them. Beautiful, fascinating Stepane was a demigod. He adored him as if he had been his fetish.

"My dear Dimitri," said Stepane, "I have not looked over my affairs for a long time. You have advised me several times to cut down my expenses. I suppose, then, that my fortune is somewhat impaired. I wish you would draw me up a list of everything that I own, leaving out the marriage-portion of the Countess. I want you to let me have the statement tomorrow, or this evening if possible."

"My accounts are in perfect order, your Excellency," answered Dimitri. "I can bring them to you in a couple of hours."

"I am waiting for them with the greatest impatience. I want one hundred thousand roubles at once."

"One hundred thousand roubles," cried the steward, looking very much frightened.

"Yes, I want it today."

Dimitri shook his head. "That will be hard to do. I have only about twenty thousand in hand. Your Excellency forgets all that I have had to pay out this month: the house you bought, the horses, and the French dresses for Madame."

"That is true, I forgot."

"I got a bill this very morning from the coach maker for five thousand roubles, and yesterday the upholsterer sent in an account of ten thousand."

"Very well, very well, pay those bills, and pay everything I owe up to this date, but after this I will have no more money spent on that woman."

Dimitri looked delighted.

"Yes, good, faithful Dimitri, I have given up that folly, but I have taken up another a thousand times worse than all the rest you have groaned over."

"Are you in earnest?" exclaimed poor Dimitri.

"One thing I promise you, if I do ruin myself completely, I will take good care that you shall be provided for. So rest satisfied, my good fellow."

"Ah, your Excellency, if there is yet time, do reflect upon what you are going to do! Poverty for any one who, like you, has always rolled in wealth, is a frightful thing."

"Is it more frightful for me than for the mujik, who passes his whole life without one moment of happiness or of prosperity?"

"Excellency, are you in earnest?"

"I am indeed. You know me, Dimitri; you know that I will have my own way. The fancy that I have now is at any rate a noble one and will give me real pure enjoyment such as I have never known. Gather together my money and bring me the hundred thousand roubles that I want."

The faithful servant withdrew, overwhelmed by this new madness of his master's. He had the hundred thousand roubles, but he did not want to give them to Stepane immediately, for fear they would be squandered too quickly.

At noon he brought in the list of the Count's property and prepared to read it out. "Now, your Excellency."

"You weary me with 'your Excellencies;' call me simply Stepane Danilovitch."

Dimitri looked at him with open-mouthed amazement. "Never shall I forget," he said, "the respect that I owe to your Excellency."

"Do you not owe me obedience before everything else?" answered Stepane, smiling. "I wish you to call me Stepane, just as I call you Dimitri."

The steward looked very embarrassed. "Perhaps he is going crazy," he thought, glancing at him with frightened eyes.

Stepane could not help laughing. "Yes, dear Dimitri, I am a man, neither better nor worse than you, and if I had the right to command — which right, however, I do not recognize — I would order you to call me Stepane. You may call me what you like, but I warn you that the oftener you drop the 'Excellency' the more you will please me."

"Ah, I thank your Excellency for allowing me to do as I like, for I cannot forget the respect due your Excellency; and when your Excellency comes to your senses, perhaps your Excellency might punish me for want of respect."

"That's it! Now you are satisfied. And when are you going to bring me the hundred thousand roubles."

"If Your Excellency could do with fifty thousand?"

"No."

"Sixty thousand?"

"No."

"Perhaps I could scrape together eighty thousand."

"I believe you are driving a bargain with me."

"Sometimes," insinuated the faithful steward, "what they charge you one hundred thousand roubles for they will let me have for eighty thousand; and if your Excellency will only allow me to manage the transaction...."

"That is impossible. I want to make a present."

"A present!" groaned the steward, "When it is so hard for me now to make two ends meet!"

"You know I don't like meanness."

In about ten minutes Dimitri returned, bringing with him the hundred thousand roubles.

"This is all that I have saved."

"What do you mean?"

"Well, when I see Your Excellency throwing your money out of the windows, I try to catch some of it."

"Good, honest Dimitri! Give me your hand!"

But Dimitri drew back, throwing a look of astonishment at his master. He fell on his knees at Stepane's feet, took the hand that his master had offered him, and pressed it to his lips.

"How difficult it will be," thought the Count, "to save the Russian people from their servile customs, and to inculcate in their breasts sentiments of equality and liberty! Am I myself sure that I have lost all my prejudice of caste?"

His invested property amounted to three million roubles. He had wasted about as much again. He put the list of his property and the hundred thousand roubles in his pocket, ordered his carriage, and went out.

CHAPTER XIX

JEALOUSY

A quarter of an hour later, Stepane was in Wanda's boudoir. He found there Raymond Chabert, who had brought with him the package of letters that he had received at Geneva. It was the eve of the Princess's twenty-first birthday.

When Litzanoff first entered the room, he appeared perfectly self-possessed, but at the sight of Raymond, the fire that had devoured his heart for two years burst forth in flames of jealousy.

He could hardly speak; his nostrils trembled; his upper lip was drawn back from his teeth like a savage beast.

Raymond looked at Litzanoff with wonder and astonishment. "Who can this strange creature be," he thought, "who loves the Princess, and dares show it in this outrageous manner? Can it be possible that she loves him?"

This suspicion sent a pang to his heart. It was not jealousy that he felt, but a deep despair. He felt that he ought to leave the room, and give place to the new comer; and yet he was as if fastened to his seat by some unseen power. He wished to go, and he could not. However, he saw how ridiculous the situation was, and in an agitated voice he asked:

"Have you any commands for me, Wanda Petrowna?"

"No, thanks," she replied, giving him her hand and bending upon him her tender glance. She guessed the thoughts that passed through his mind, and she wished by that sympathetic look to soothe the trouble that he seemed to feel.

But Litzanoff noticed that look. A sigh burst from his lips which sounded like a groan.

Raymond left the room. When Stepane and Wanda found themselves together and alone, they felt overwhelmed by that feeling which paralyzes the brain, contracts the heart, and shatters the nerves.

They dared not look upon one another; they dared not speak. They feared lest the utterance of one word, the interchange of one glance, would drive them irresistibly into each others' arms.

Wanda, that brave woman who never trembled, feared this man who loved her. She forced herself to break this dangerous silence.

"Well?" she said, affecting an indifferent manner, "what have you been doing all this time? I have not seen you for a long while. Padlewsky told me that you were devouring books on socialism."

But Stepane heard not a word.

"Who is this gentleman?" he asked roughly.

"What do you mean?"

"That Frenchman."

"He is an engineer."

"It seems to me I have seen him somewhere."

"I don't see how that is possible; he has only been in Russia for six months, and in Petersburg but within the last day or so."

"Do you know him well?"

"Yes. He has been laying out a railroad in Southern Russia that goes directly through my father's property. So of course we were obliged to make his acquaintance. And besides, he is one of us."

Litzanoff laid his hand upon the little package of papers that Raymond had left. As he did so he watched Wanda attentively.

"Are these socialist pamphlets?" he asked.

"I think not."

"It is probably the plan of the railroad, and as I have a great deal of land in the Ukraine, this railroad may affect my property, too."

"You are taking a great deal of interest in the management of your affairs just now, are you not?"

"Yes, a great deal."

"Have you entirely come over to our way of thinking?"

"I hope so. Will you let me look at the plan of this railroad?"

"That is not a plan; it is a letter."

Stepane grew livid.

"My dear friend, my brother!" cried Wanda, "what is the matter with you."

"Nothing. I know I am ridiculous. Look! Here are a hundred thousand roubles for your work, and I intend to give my whole fortune to the same object. Goodbye!"

"Stepane! Stepane! You shall not leave me."

"Why not?" he asked, looking her full in the face for the first time.

"Because you are mad, and madmen cannot be allowed to go at large."

"On the contrary, I am very calm; don't you see that I am?"

"Stepane, I see your whole heart."

"Well, what do you see there?"

"Why make me tell you, when you dare not tell me!"

"That man loves you!" said Stepane, in a choking voice. "I know it. And he is jealous of me. Have you given him the right to be jealous?"

"No more than I have to you, but you take the right," said Wanda, laughing.

"Don't laugh; it pains me. It is true, I have no right to be jealous. Forgive me, Wanda. I love you passionately. I am ridiculous, unjust, wild, yes, wild. Just now I could scarcely keep myself from flying at that Frenchman, who looked at you with such eager eyes."

"Remember our agreement, Stepane. I offered you a sister's love, and you accepted it. Those are our terms, and we must keep them; otherwise it will be impossible for me to see you."

But these words, instead of soothing Stepane, roused him to greater fury.

"Is this fellow married?"

"No."

"Then you may fall in love with him; perhaps you are already in love with him."

"I have a real friendship for him, as I have for you."

"As you have for me! I do not want an affection exactly like the one you give to another man."

"Why not?"

"You ask me why not? Because a woman can only love one man. And the love that I feel for you is the most absolute, the most violent, the most jealous love I ever felt for any one in my life. Tell me the truth: if this man loves you, and you love him, I will leave you forever."

Wanda said not a word.

"Ah, I understand your silence!" cried Stepane, in despair.

"I do not love him as I do you," murmured Wanda, in a low, trembling tone, which resounded in Litzanoff's heart, and made him tremble in every limb.

He tried to throw his arms around her, but she drew back, and pale, trembling, she said: "Do not touch me, or I will go away, and you shall never see me again. You forget Nadege."

"No; this very morning Nadege came to me and proposed a divorce. She knows that I love you."

Wanda's face showed the deepest anxiety.

"What!" she exclaimed. "Would she consent to a separation and have you allowed her to see this love of yours?"

"Yes."

"If she did propose it, it was only to try you. She wanted to find out the truth. A separation! Poor child. It would kill her. No, no, you shall never sacrifice Nadege; I will not have it. And besides, I cannot marry you. I have taken a solemn oath never to marry."

"You?"

"Yes."

"When? Why did you do it?"

"I cannot tell you."

"It is not so."

"It is."

"You have taken an oath. To whom? To this Frenchman, I suppose."

"No, to the Revolutionary Committee."

"And what is the meaning of this oath?"

"The meaning of it is that the apostles of this great cause must be men and women free from all family ties. With them the passion for humanity must absorb every other passion. If a woman loves, she cannot keep a secret from the man she loves."

Litzanoff, who, despite of his fiery nature, had in some respects a really noble character, felt himself overwhelmed by the simplicity with which Wanda spoke of her great sacrifice. He felt how low, how vile he was to speak to such a woman of his own personal sufferings.

"Forgive me!" he cried. "I understand that you cannot lower yourself to my level, but try to lift me up to you. I thought my heart was inaccessible to any noble thought; my education was terribly perverted."

"That does not matter, dear Stepane. You will have only the less to forget. We nihilists withdraw our young men from the universities because they only learn respect for official authority, for official science, for official history. In one word, they are taught at the public schools everything that we are trying to undermine."

"Well, I may at least be allowed to model my mind after yours, since that is the only thing you will allow me."

"Yes, Stepane; were we free, I would allow no more, for the most violent passions are those which last the least, because your heart, you say yourself, is worn out, and perhaps this love of yours is but the result of the obstacles that separate us.

"Ah, Wanda!" cried Stepane, "give me one kiss, only one, and you can take my life. Or, if you will have it so, I will disappear from the face of the earth forever. Wanda! I am, its it were, bewitched; one kiss will break the charm, and my reason will return to me."

Wanda, exhausted by this long struggle, did not draw hack. Fascinated by his intense desire, she stood still, but she murmured with trembling lips: "I do not want to. I do not want to."

He suddenly seized her in his sinewy arms. At his touch, Wanda shuddered and tried to free herself. "No! no!" she cried.

"I will have one kiss!" said Litzanoff hoarsely; "I will have one, only one!" He lightly touched her lips with his.

Wanda seized a little dagger that she always wore at her waist, and struck Litzanoff with all her strength on the shoulder. He did not even feel the pain. He crushed the young woman's lips against his own in one long passionate kiss.

"I hate you," she cried, indignant, enraged, magnificent in her anger. "You are infamous! Leave me!"

But Litzanoff heard not a word; he had fainted dead away, with the blood streaming from his wound.

Wanda rang the hell. Katia answered it immediately.

"Take care of this man, my dear Katia."

"Is it Count Litzanoff? What has happened?"

"Nothing; he had a rush of blood to the head; I bled him. If he asks for me, tell him I cannot see him."

As she was turning away, she said: "When he comes to himself, give him this roll of bank-notes. He wished to give them to the cause, but I will accept nothing from him."

Stepane was recovering his senses as he heard these last words.

"If you will not accept them I will throw them into the fire!" he cried.

Wanda withdrew without even looking at him. As soon as she was alone, her angry eyes grew wet with tears.

Suddenly, she heard Katia give a cry. She listened; the door of her room flew open, and Katia appeared, white with terror. "Come! Come quickly!" she exclaimed.

"What is the matter?" asked Wanda, rushing into the other room. She saw Litzanoff lying at full on the floor, apparently dead. He had just plunged the dagger that Wanda had thrown on the ground into his breast.

"Stepane!" cried Wanda. He opened his eyes.

"Forgive me, Wanda!" he could barely articulate. "I could not live, with you angry with me." A strange smile passed over his face.

"Call Packline," said Wanda to Katia, who ran out of the room.

Wanda knelt down, drew the dagger out of the wound, and stanched the blood with her handkerchief.

"Stepane! Stepane!" she repeated in despair. "Do not die! I love you. I cannot let you die. I will not let you die!" and she covered his pale face with kisses. He smiled.

At that moment, Packline, the physician attached to Prince Kryloff's establishment, entered. He sounded the wound and announced that there was no immediate danger. The blade had passed along the rib, and had not reached the heart. He stopped the bleeding and dressed the wound.

"You will be able to be about in three days," he said, "if you are not imprudent."

But how to get he wounded man home! In order to hide his discolored clothes, they wrapped him in a fur mantle.

"When shall I see you?" he asked, in a low voice.

"I shall try end get off for a moment tomorrow," answered Wanda. "But if I cannot, then the day after."

Stepane closed his eyes. "Will you forgive me?" he said very low.

"Yes."

She gave him her hand. He pressed it to his lips, respectfully, reverently.

CHAPTER XX

THE LETTER FROM GENEVA

As soon as Stepane had gone, Wanda fell powerless upon the divan. She remained a few moments, with her head thrown back, in an attitude of overwhelming despair. Sob after sob seemed stifled in her throat. Katia was watching her with great uneasiness, but she dared not speak to her. At last she bent over her and took her hand.

"Be brave, sister," she said. "You have forgotten that letter from Geneva; doubtless it comes from our friends, the poor exiles."

At these words Wanda aroused herself and said, "Give me the letter."

She broke the seals of the envelope. As soon as she had read the first words of the enclosure she uttered a piercing cry, clasped the paper to her heart, and fainted dead away.

The bulky envelope contained, as Raymond supposed, a manuscript. It ran as follows:

My Well-beloved Daughter:

It is your mother who writes to you; your mother whom you believed to be dead; your mother who from the day when she was cruelly torn from the child that she adored has never ceased to think of her.

I have suffered horribly in the past seventeen years, but my keenest suffering has been my separation from you, my darling Wanda. Thanks to our friends I have often heard of you. I know how beautiful you are, and I know that the loveliness of your person is but the reflection of the beauty of your soul.

We sent you Catherine Lawinska. She does not know that I am your mother, but she has been in the habit of writing frequently to my friend, Michael Federoff, and every letter was full of you. How I have devoured those letters, which showed me that you gradually became a rebel, an enemy to oppression, a lover of the victims of tyranny!

Now I can tell you my sad story: I know that you will understand me, will pity me, will excuse me. I have not written to you before to tell you that I still lived because I wished first to be perfectly sure of your sentiments. I feared your father, our persecutor; I feared the police of Petersburg.

Ah, my Wanda! If you could but read my heart! It overflows with tenderness and joy. How I long to press you to my bosom, and to cover your beautiful head with a mother's kisses!

Your mother,
Alexandra Kryloff

Wanda read this letter with inexpressible emotion, and then threw herself into Katia's arms, weeping violently.

"That was the lady," exclaimed Katia, "that I used to meet so often at Michael Federoff's. Do you not remember how often I have spoken to you about her and her splendid, large dark eyes?"

"Is she beautiful still?"

"She looks like you, but her face has a sad, almost severe expression."

Wanda took up the manuscript that had been enclosed within the letter, and commenced reading it. This is what she read:

At sixteen years of age I was traveling in Italy, where I met Prince Kryloff. He was a thorough gentleman, a great lord, elegant in his manners and very fascinating. He was passionately in love with me. He was very gentle and very tender. He was heir to an old name and princely fortune; in one word, he possessed every thing that could dazzle and charm a young girl. I thought that I loved him, and it gave me great happiness to promise to be his wife. The first year of our marriage was perfect bliss.

Nicolas Markewitch, the Prince's private physician, was an old man and entirely devoted to him. One day he said to the Prince: "I am growing old and my health is uncertain. Soon you will have to find a successor to me. There is one of your serfs who has a very remarkable mind. I have been attending to his education for some time past; if you will send him to the university for a couple of years, he will make a first-rate doctor.

"What is his name?" asked the Prince.

"Michael Federoff."

The Prince frowned. "Is he the son of that scoundrel Federoff, who helped the Barkeloff peasantry in their insurrection against me?"

"I am sorry to say he is, your Excellency," answered Markewitch. "But he surely is not responsible for his father's actions. He has an excellent heart and a very loyal nature. It seems to me a pity to throw away this young fellow's powers which could be so usefully employed in your service."

"Markewitch is right," I said, happening to be present at the interview. "Let him come here, and then you can see what you think of him."

The Prince granted my request. Michael had a fine, open countenance, lively and yet grave. There was a great deal of power in his face.

The Prince said that no Russian university would admit a serf. I proposed that he be sent out of the country to finish his education, and he was accordingly sent to Prague. He distinguished himself so much there at the school of medicine that his fellow students forwarded an address to the Prince begging him to give Federoff his freedom. Michael also wrote to the Prince, entreating him most humbly for the same favor.

When he received these two letters, Kryloff flew into the most terrible rage, and when I asked what was the matter, he threw the two letters at me. "Look!" He exclaimed, "how far your protege can push his ingratitude. Blood will tell. The son of a rebel! I have spent three thousand roubles on his education, and now he wants me to give him his freedom!"

I tried in vain to soothe the Prince's rage. "I can sell one of my jewels," I said. "The smallest one that I possess will pay for all the expense you have incurred." He would not listen to me, and grew very angry, while he accused me of sympathizing with the liberalism of the day, which would surely in time, he said, bring about a revolution. This was in 1867. Alexander had just come to the throne, and every one was talking of his liberal views, and of his projects of emancipation.

I dared say to the Prince one day that, as he would probably soon lose all control over this young man any how, it might be as well to gain his goodwill by giving him his freedom in a manner which would insure his gratitude. But my persistency seemed to aggravate him beyond control. In the afternoon I went to see the priest, who returned to the charge, and induced the Prince at last to send Federoff to Paris to perfect himself in his profession.

All that year I tried to bend the Prince's will and induce him to liberate Michael.

"Promise me," I said to him one day, "that if I give you a son you will give me in return Michael Federoff's freedom."

"What a singular interest you take in that boy!" he answered, laughingly. "Yes, yes, I will promise you."

I was in such a weak state of health that they were anxious about me, and I suggested to Markewitch that it would be better for him to have a consulting physician, and that as it would soon be Federoff's vacation, he could summon him from Paris. "That would be an excellent thing to do," answered Markewitch, "and besides, his poor mother is in wretched health and is pining to see her son before she dies."

One morning as I was taking my daily walk, I directed my footsteps towards the cottage of the poor woman. It was the first time that I had ever set my foot within a peasant's house. I was shocked at the wretchedness that I saw there. The old Federoff, sullen, downcast, was standing in the doorway. His continued life was due to extraordinary strength of constitution, for he had received one hundred strokes of the knout as punishment for resistance to the orders of his overseer. Few men have been known to survive that.

When I told him the news about his son, he sneered. "How?" said I, "are you not proud of Michael's learning, and of his splendid mind?"

"Ah, Your Excellence," he answered, "what business has a slave with a splendid mind? The more he knows the more does his bondage weigh upon him."

I saw that he was right, and I told him that I hoped his son would soon be free.

When I entered the cabin I found the sick woman lying on a bed above the stove, covered with miserable rags.

"Here is the Princess," said Federoff. If the Virgin Mary had come to see her in person the woman would not have been more astonished, for she had heard of celestial visions, but never that a Princess could lower herself so far as to pay a visit to a serf. When I spoke to her of her son, the tears commenced to flow. "I shall never see him," she sighed.

"Yes, poor creature," said I, "you shall see him. I will send Markewitch to you, and tell him to take care of you and make you well, so that you can be on your feet again when your son comes."

I thought to myself that if the Prince refused to send for her son, I could easily forward him the money necessary for the journey. When I left those poor people their faces wore a brighter and more hopeful look, and I felt an inward satisfaction such as I had never before experienced.

I have related all this to you in detail, dear Wanda, because it is an important date in my life. In my childhood I had often heard my countrymen talk about the exactions of the Russians and their cruelty towards the Poles, but it made no lasting impression upon my mind. Now for the first time I began to think about the social system in Russia. I asked myself, what right have a few men to own the entire land, and enjoy all the advantages that it gives, without doing the least work, while those who do work not only own no land whatever, but have not even bread enough to keep up their strength? I heard several persons speak of the socialist doctrines. I sent to a friend in Kiev to send me every book which was sold secretly there. When the books came I read them, and they revealed to me a whole new world.

I told the Prince that I was very wretched, very depressed, and at last he consented to send for Michael Federoff, so that he could assist Markewitch in caring for me.

I was alone in the drawing-room when Federoff arrived. It had been three years since I had seen him last. His success at the university, his intercourse with men, had entirely done away with all his former servility of manner. He stood before me, a handsome, distinguished gentleman. I received him as my equal, and asked him to be seated. He was perfectly unembarrassed, and we entered into conversation. He opened by thanking me in the warmest terms for my kindness to his mother.

The Prince had been out hunting; he came into the room and looked curiously at Michael, whom he took for some gentleman of the neighborhood.

"Well," said I, laughing, "Don't you recognize the doctor?"

"What doctor?"

"Doctor Michael Federoff."

I shall never forget the look that he cast upon poor Michael, who stood up, evidently awaiting the storm about to break.

"What," cried the Prince, "is this gentleman whom I find sitting in my drawing-room, talking to my wife as if he were one of us, is this gentleman the son of my serf?"

I asked him to sit down. "Dear," I said, "I was asking him about his studies."

"Who gave you permission," yelled the Prince, "to clothe yourself in this manner? Go put on the livery that befits your rank. Then perhaps I may allow you to present yourself before me and the Princess."

"But," I said, "my dear husband, you forget that he has graduated as a physician, and is treated with perfect equality by every one."

"What is that to me? He is my serf, and I intend that he shall behave himself with all the deference that a serf owes to his master."

And as he spoke, he strode up and down the room, overturning the chairs, gesticulating with his hands. Suddenly stopping in front of me, he exclaimed: "What books are those that I found this morning in your room?"

"They are some books that I borrowed," I stammered.

"Who lent them to you? This famous doctor I suppose. I wager he is mixed up in the nihilist movement. He has got all these notions in Paris, and be sent you those books."

"Indeed he did not."

"Who did, then? Tell me."

I was so frightened I could not speak. He went on in this way for a long time, raging, overturning everything in his way declaiming against the insubordination of the serfs, against Michael, against his rebellious father, against the disobedience to himself. He was angry with me for the first time, and I fainted.

I became very ill. Markewitch was sent for, and becoming very uneasy, insisted upon summoning Michael to his aid. It was some time before he could be found. The Prince was in a rage at his delay. At last he came, dressed in the coarse garb of the serf, but this vulgar costume could not conceal the beauty of his features or the intelligence that beamed in his eye.

"Where have you been?" screamed the Prince. "My wife's life is in danger, and you delay to come to her assistance."

"I was looking for some serf's clothes," answered Michael. "I had not any of my own, Your Excellency."

"Very well, doctor," answered the Prince, sarcastically; "you have an opportunity to prove your skill. If anything happens, I hold you responsible for it.'"

I was ill for three days and nights, and at last my child's life was sacrificed to mine. The child was a boy. The Prince laid all the blame upon Michael, who had watched continually by my bedside, and by his skill and unremitting care had saved my life. And do you know how the Prince rewarded him? He loaded him with chains, and had him locked up in a dungeon. I cried, I begged, I fell at his feet in vain. Michael was thrown into prison.

From that moment, I felt nothing but disgust for my husband.

One day I told him that it was he who had killed my child, and not the innocent one he had kept in prison. He was so furious I thought he would murder me. After that my life was a perfect hell. My health became affected.

I induced Markewitch to go and see Federoff in his dungeon. He brought me back word that Michael had been ill, but was now better, and that my interest in his welfare supported him in his sufferings.

As soon as I could, when the Prince was absent, I went to see him in his prison. I could hardly recognize him. He was as thin as a ghost. His suffering, his insulted dignity, had imparted to his bearing an air that was almost sublime. I held out my hand to him; he pressed it between his own and carried it to his lips.

"Oh, Your Excellency, how can I ever repay you for the happiness your presence gives me!"

"Michael, my brother!" I exclaimed, "can you pardon me for being the cause of all your trouble?"

"I pardon you?" he whispered.

"You are a nihilist, Michael, are you not?"

He looked at me.

"Are you afraid of me? I am a nihilist myself."

"You? You? Your Excellency?"

"Yes, I am."

"Then," he cried, "Russia is saved! If minds like yours can see the power of our ideas; if you, one of the privileged class, acknowledge the justice of our cause, then we shall soon see the renovation of our barbarous land."

I had guessed rightly: he belonged to the new school of science and philosophy which was beginning to take root in Russia. He was, in fact, one of its leaders.

From that hour I did all that I could to mitigate Michael's sufferings. I sent him, through Markewitch, linen, food, papers and books; and whenever the Prince was absent from home I went to see him myself. These visits were hours of ineffable happiness. There was no feeling of love between us at that time; his gratitude to me, my compassion for him, drew us together, and we discussed the new ideas of liberty and justice by which we both were inspired.

One day the Prince undertook to visit the prisons in the village. While I was sending comforts and assistance to Michael, I had done a great deal for the other prisoners. The Prince found luxuries in every cell. He asked who had sent them, and he was informed that it was the Princess. Then came a scene, but I merely said to him: "Will you kill your second child?"

The Prince grew quiet. He yielded to my entreaties, and set Michael at liberty.

You, my dear daughter, were born soon after. and although he desired a son, your exquisite beauty made him love you.

After that, I spent a few months of real happiness. The Prince went to Paris for the winter, but I alleged the health of my child as sufficient reason to keep me at home, and he departed by himself. My whole time was taken up with study, and with the care of you, my child, whom I loved.

The Prince returned home in the spring. One day he went to pay a visit to a gentleman in the neighborhood, and returning unexpectedly found me and Michael reading a work of Bakunin in the library. You know that his rage is like an epileptic fit. He seized a cane and beat Michael violently. It was his right, for Michael was his serf.

I cried out with indignation. He rushed towards me to beat me too, but Michael, who had endured his own punishment without a word, threw himself between us, and said: "No, Your Excellency, if it cost me my life you shall not strike the Princess, for in an hour afterwards you will regret it."

The Prince, intoxicated with rage, threw himself upon my defender, but suddenly his face became purple. He tottered and fell heavily to the floor. Michael, still suffering from the effect of his blows, lifted him up and cared for him. For two days and nights he never left his bedside, and he cured him.

This accident had saved Michael's life. But the Prince was not touched by the serf's devotion to him; he was a serf, and devotion was part of a serf's duty. As soon as the Prince's health was completely reestablished, he forgot everything that he owed to Federoff. There was no insult that he was not forced to submit to, and as a serf he had no right to complain. The Prince always tried to humiliate him before me. How often I have seen the blush of shame mantle that noble brow!

One day I said to him, "Michael, I cannot stand this any longer. Here is a considerable sum of money; take it, and leave the country. With your talent you can easily make a way for yourself."

At these words he grew very pale. "But my poor father," he said, "my sick mother, my young sister Akoulina. What would become of them? I am afraid the Prince would visit his anger upon them, and you know my father is not very submissive. What a terrible punishment he has already received! And then," he continued, in a lower tone, "I cannot leave you, who have been so good to me. Besides, the little Princess needs my constant care. I love the child as if she were my own. Forgive me for expressing myself so familiarly; your kindness has emboldened me."

I gave him my hand; he knelt down and pressed it to his lips.

Once when you had been very ill, and Michael's care had saved you, wild with joy, forgetting everything, I threw my arms around his neck and kissed him. At that time the masters and mistresses used to embrace their serfs; no one would have refused to kiss his serf at Easter. But I had treated Michael as my equal, and had never kissed him, lest by so doing I might recall his slavery to his mind. That embrace of mine overwhelmed him. He fell back, as pale as death, in a chair. Your father was there. He looked at both of us; the basest suspicion — ferocious jealousy, vengeance, hate, every evil passion — seemed concentrated in that look.

"Ah," he said, "this, then, is the result of your nihilism. The serf faints when his mistress kisses him! I will put an end to all this, I promise you. I have seen your little game, Madame, for some time. My wife, the Princess Kryloff, in love with a serf! What a noble love. But, my little doves, you have reckoned without your host: I will teach you what it is to betray a Kryloff."

As long as your health needed his care, Michael was allowed to see you, but one morning the Prince came into my room and, with a horrible smile, said to me: "Your lover is arrested."

"Do you mean Michael?" I said, feeling myself grow pale.

"Yes; he has failed in his respect to me; he has dared to love you, and he must be punished."

"Indeed, he does not love me in the way you think he does. I swear to you he does not!" I cried.

"Oh, you love him too! Look at yourself in the glass! Would you turn as pale as that if I told you I was going to give the knout to another man?"

"The knout! You are going to give the knout to Michael?"

"Yes."

"No! No! You shall not do it. This man has saved your life, has saved your child's life. I implore you on my knees, spare him. I assure you that I have no feeling for him but one of gratitude."

"What, gratitude to a serf?"

"If you suspect us," I cried, "send him away. But spare the savior of Wanda's life!"

"It is out of my power to save him; the judges have condemned him to one hundred lashes of the knout."

"Then he is condemned to death! He is innocent, perfectly innocent. He has never said one word to me to lead me to think that he loves me."

"If he does not love you, your manner is sufficient to convince me that you love him, and that is enough."

Then I completely lost control of myself and screamed like a maniac: "Tiger! Barbarian! Savage!"

I do not know now what I said nor what he answered. I can only remember these words: "Yes, you shall look on at his punishment. If you dare to refuse, he shall have two hundred blows instead of one."

That day was one of the darkest of my wretched life. The horrible scaffold was set up in the midst of the market place of Barkileff. It was a kind of board, low to the ground, and inclined at one end, upon which the victim was to be stretched.

When our carriage drove up neither the condemned man nor his executioner had as yet arrived. About a hundred persons had assembled to witness the execution. A dozen or more Cossacks, lance in hand, kept back the people at a respectful distance.

I was so weak, so shattered, that I could with difficulty keep myself from swooning. "None of your ridiculous affectations!" said the Prince, severely. I tried to I keep back my tears as I gazed upon that plank stained with blood upon which Michael was about to suffer. I felt that henceforth I should love him with all my strength, with all my heart, with all my soul.

A few moments after the arrival of our equipage, the crowd opened to give way to a man whose very appearance made me shudder. He was a sort of Mameluke, of herculean proportions, with a low forehead, high cheekbones, red hair, flat nostrils, and the eyes of a beast. His sleeves were rolled up and exposed to view his hairy, muscular arms. He held in his hands a collection of thongs that he seemed carefully to select and sort.

"Who is that man?" I asked.

"He is the executioner," answered the Prince.

The crowd opened a second time to give way to Michael, who appeared between two soldiers, accompanied by an officer of the police. He walked with a bold step, his head up. Never had I seen him look so handsome. Why could I not fly to him, tell him of my love, press him to my heart ? I dared not; the least demonstration on my part would have doubled his chastisement.

He saw me. His pale face colored, and he sent me a glance that thrilled through me like an electric shock. My eyes sought his in return; in that look our hearts became forever one. This union had the scaffold for its altar, the hangman for its priest; it was the union of two rebels who vowed there an implacable hatred of their oppressors.

The Prince detected that glance, and said to me, in French: "Look at him well, Madame, for in all probability you see him for the last time."

The police officer unrolled a paper, and read aloud the sentence which condemned Michael Federoff to receive ninety-nine blows of the knout, as punishment for repeated and grave injuries and misdemeanors against his liege lord and master.

Michael listened to this sentence with a smile of compassion upon his lips. Having read the sentence, the officer withdrew, and the Mameluke came forward, crying out in a hoarse voice: "Now, my fine fellow, it rests between you and me. We will see after awhile whether you will laugh or not."

He went up to him to take off his clothes, but Michael motioned him back, unfastening the sheepskin that covered his shoulders, and let it fall at his feet. He was merely dressed in a linen blouse. I looked upon him with horror.

"Ah, my *galoubtchick!*" said the executioner, "you spare me all trouble, but I assure you I shall not spare you. In the first place, I must tie you."

"Do your cowardly duty," answered Michael. Without another word he stretched himself upon the plank. The hangman fastened Michael's hands beneath the board, then he fastened his feet firmly with ropes and with a knife cut his blouse open behind, so as to leave his back bare.

Then the knout whistled through the air, as, with all his strength, the ruffian brought it down upon Michael's body. I heard a cry, which pierced my heart. I stopped my mouth with my handkerchief.

The police officer, who, unmoved, was watching the execution, said "One." The execution went on. "Two," said the officer.

I heard a second stilled cry. I saw before me the bloody knout waving in the air, the blood flowing from my beloved and then saw no more. I had fainted. My executioner held a bottle of salts to my nose and brought me hack to consciousness. Michael was insensible. They thought he was dead, but they gave him a cordial which restored him to life and went on with the scourging.

"I implore you," I said to the Prince, "spare me this sight. You see that I cannot endure it."

"But if he did not see you here he would die," said the Prince. "That hangman has a fist of iron."

I said no more. At the fiftieth blow I fainted again. The Prince sent me home, but he himself remained until the end.

When it was over Markewitch, who loved him dearly, took

Michael in his arms, weeping bitterly, and restored him to life.

Here Wanda stopped reading; her breast heaved; her eyes kindled with indignation and horror.

"Is this man my father?" she cried. "Mother! Michael! I will avenge you! Someone is coming; I hear footsteps. Katia, quick! Hide this manuscript; he would take it away from me. He would read it. Perhaps his blows might fall upon them again, far off as they are." Katia was hiding the letter as the Prince burst into the room.

"What is the meaning of all this?" he cried. "I hear some man has shot himself in my palace."

Wanda made no answer. She simply gazed at him with horror-stricken eyes.

"What has happened?" he continued. "I will know. I insist upon it."

"I do not know."

"You do not know?"

"I do not know anything," she said wildly, passing her hand across her brow.

The Prince thought she was going mad.

"Here, Katia, can't you answer me? "

Katia made no reply.

The Prince looked first at one and then at the other. He took Katia by the arm and shook her roughly.

"What does all this mystery mean? The day has gone by for suicides, assassinations, and the like; this must be some new fashion introduced by the infernal nihilists."

"Your ferocity has produced the nihilists," answered Wanda. "The bringer-forth of revolution is the blood of the martyrs, of the apostles — of such men as Michael Federoff."

At the sound of that name the Prince started, grew livid, fixed his scared eyes upon his daughter, and stammered:

"That name. Who told you?"

"I know everything."

"These nihilists!" screamed the Prince. "They have crept into my very palace. They have stolen my daughter's heart from me, as they did her mother's. But I will find them out! I will unmask them. I will punish . . ."

"It is unfortunate, is it not, that the knout is abolished," said Wanda.

"You will drive me mad," cried the Prince, seizing his head with his hands.

Wanda looked at him with a severe and crushing glance. It terrified him. He left the room, banging the door behind him. As soon as she was sure that he would not return, Wanda resumed the sad task of reading her mother's letter:

At the end of eight days I wrote to Michael by means of Markewitch, and told him that henceforth my life was bound up with his.

The Prince, perceiving the horror with which he inspired me, determined to send you and me to Perm, at the foot of the Ural mountains, where he had an enormous estate and a handsome castle. Upon the estate were quicksilver mines worked by his serfs. Now-a-days only criminals or assassins or socialists are condemned to work in these mines, but then the good-natured, patient peasants labored for their masters, without any complaint, to bring forth the precious metal, whose value availed not them, from the bowels of the earth. In return they received a scanty ration of food, and if they refused to work they were flogged.

And these poor people never rebelled. One hundred million men patiently accepted this state of slavery imposed upon them by one million of men in no way their superiors. I asked myself if these wretches had within them any sense of justice, and if the progress of civilization could ever reach their reason or their dull intellect.

I considered that we would have to prepare a new generation for the new ideas, and that popular education alone could bring about the regeneration of the Russian people. I founded several schools, but as soon as your father arrived, he objected. "Why instruct the people? Learning would only make them discontented and unhappy with their lot. It would inspire them with disgust for work and insubordination against their master!" He closed my schools. The winter was coming on, and I wished to go to Petersburg. He refused, alleging that at Petersburg I would manage to affiliate myself with the liberals.

Towards the end of October you were taken very ill. Markewitch and the physician at Perm gave up all hopes. I asked for Michael, and the Prince, frantic at the thought of losing you, sent for him to come.

For the second time he saved your life; for the second time your father, suspecting us most unjustly, struck me.

These continual scenes humiliated me to the point that I resolved to run away. I told Michael, who was terrified at my intention, but at last he yielded to my entreaties and consented to take me under his care. Your health was perfectly reestablished, so that I could take you with me. I sold my jewels at Perm and realized a sufficient sum for our journey and for my establishment in a foreign country.

Once out of Russia, I knew that Michael could support us. At any rate, I preferred poverty with him to princely luxury built up by the blood and sweat of the serfs. We obtained false passports and in the Prince's absence we left his house in the middle of the night.

We were told that the navigation upon the Volga was still open. We intended to sail down the Volga to the Caspian Sea, but when we reached Kazan, to our horror we found the river frozen. We were obliged to change our route and make for the frontier of Prussia. The roads were bad, the weather was bad; it was five days before we reached the frontier, and there we were arrested.

"Michael was torn from my side. I was not even allowed to know what fate was in store for him. I was conducted back to Krylow, guarded between soldiers like a prisoner.

I expected violent outbreaks, reproaches, scorn, even blows, but I was astonished and alarmed when I found the Prince perfectly calm. He ordered your old nurse to take you from me. Then, as I was going into my own room, he said, "Not there; follow me." He led me into an uninhabited wing of the castle where I found a room ready to receive me. Nothing was in it except the essentials of life.

"Henceforth this is to be your apartment," said the Prince, "and you cannot leave it without my permission." I did not dare speak; I only said, "Where is my child? Can I not have her with me?"

"She shall be brought to see you daily."

"What!" I cried. "Am I to be a prisoner in my own house?"

"In your house, Madame? Excuse me, in mine."

"I shall write to my family."

"You can write if you choose," he answered, smiling grimly.

Then I understood that I was tied to this man, that I was forever his property, his slave.

I was completely worn out, morally and physically. I could make no resistance. I heard the noise of chains, the grating of the bolts and locks. Overcome by weariness and fatigue, I fell asleep.

The next morning when I awoke I found my breakfast already served upon a table. I jumped out of bed and, running to the door, shook it violently. It was locked. The whole truth burst upon me. I was a prisoner, a prisoner for life. I threw up the sash of the window and looked out. Beneath me was a deep ditch. For a moment I thought I would throw myself out, and so end my wretched life. But the recollection of you and of Michael crossed my mind. I determined first to learn his fate. If he was dead I determined that I would die, too.

Now and then my jailor would pay me a visit. He tried to excuse his conduct. He was punishing me, he said, to bring me back to my duty. He was very jealous of me, he said, and in spite of my misconduct he loved me still.

Six long months I passed in that martyrdom. At last the Prince was obliged to go to Petersburg. As soon as I heard that he had gone, I began to breathe freer. I could think of nothing but how to escape.

It was a beautiful, brilliant April morning. The snow was beginning to melt, and with its rays some sort of hope seemed to creep into my heart. I seated myself by the window and looked idly out upon the green steppe that lay stretched out before me. Suddenly I saw in the distance a human figure. It was a mujik. As he drew near I watched him with beating heart, for I had a presentiment that this man was to be my liberator. At last he came near enough for me to distinguish his features. Carefully looking around and perceiving no one, he held out to me a paper. It was Michael.

My heart stood still. I knew well the danger he ran, but as the Prince was away I was not so terribly alarmed. I answered him by signs, and I tore up some pieces of my clothing into thin strips and knotted them together until I had made a string long enough to reach to the ground. I tied a little toy that you had left behind you to the end of this cord and lowered it from the window. I remember thinking to myself, that if they discovered me I would say that I had been trying to draw your attention up to my window by means of that plaything.

Michael ran quickly forward and fastened a letter around the little toy. I pulled it up hastily. With what joy did I hold that letter in my hands! He had been condemned to work in the mines, but he had managed to make his escape and had come to look for me. He had heard that the Prince had gone away. There was not a moment to lose. They had not as yet had time to find out his absence from the mine, but they would soon. He proposed to climb, at nightfall, the fir tree that grew beneath my window, and from there to throw up to me a coil of rope. I was to fasten the rope firmly to the iron bars outside my room. At midnight he would climb up with the necessary instruments to file away the grating. Then he would help me down on the rope.

We had no money, so we should have to hide in the mountains, and gradually make our way into the country of the Kirghis. It was exactly the plan that I had laid out myself.

At midnight I fastened the cord and let it down. In a few minutes I heard a dull thud, as though something had fallen on the ground. I looked for the cord; it had been badly fastened and had given way. All night long I watched, dreading the morning light. I heard no sound save the sentinel pacing his round, and the beating of my own heart. Perhaps the fall had killed him; perhaps he was lying, wounded, helpless, in the bottom of the ditch. At last day broke, and peering through the fog that obscured the sun's light, I saw Michael seated in the fir tree nearest to my room. He held the rope in his hand, and motioning me away from the window, he threw it dexterously into the room.

Just then I heard the door open. I thrust the coil of rope under my sofa. The Prince's confidential servant entered. He had seen my motion, and glanced towards me suspiciously, but he merely asked me what I would have for my breakfast. I was so troubled that I could hardly speak, and he perceived my agitation. He left the room, and I ran to the window to warn Michael. But Michael was no longer there.

I threw myself upon the sofa, wondering what I should do. At last I determined that I would not open the window, and I would keep my light burning all night. Then he would understand that we had been discovered. He had understood, in fact, and he had hid himself, but towards midnight I heard the report of firearms, and I knew that they were after him. But as the noise gradually died away in the distance, I supposed that he had escaped.

The day after that the Prince returned. He came at once to my room, went up to the sofa and kicked it with his foot; but the coil of ropes was not there.

"Where is the rope?" said he. I knew there was no use for me to deny anything, and I opened a closet where I had hid it.

"Here it is."

"Very well, they told me the truth. But I warn you, you shall not escape me."

He left me, and returned shortly with his confidential servant. He opened the door of a small dressing room attached to my chamber and asked me to walk in. His calmness and politeness froze the very blood in my veins. I entered; they turned the key on me. In a few minutes I heard the noise of axes and hammers, and for many hours I was left in total solitude, wildly conjecturing what new torture was being prepared for me. When at last they unlocked the door, I found that my bright sunny room had been transformed into a gloomy dungeon. The windows were walled up, and high up, just below the ceiling, two little openings had been made about twenty inches square.

"Now, my love," said the Prince, laughing, "you cannot well make signals to your convict-lover. I warned you that I am jealous. I shall have to leave you for two or three months, and I cannot allow you to have any communication with him in my absence. I shall have the door walled up as well as the window."

"And my child!" I cried. "My child! She belongs to me! I would rather die than be separated from her."

"I shall take her with me," he said.

I fainted. When I recovered my consciousness I found myself lying on the sofa, and I heard the noise of the masons walling up my door. They left a little grating through which my food was passed to me.

I had no books to read; I had no light; I could no longer solace myself with the beautiful view from my window; above all, I had lost you, my child. The only reason why I did not kill myself was because I was too weak to make up my mind, too powerless to put my desire into execution.

The three months passed. To me they seemed three years. One night I was awakened by a great noise and tumult in the house. Suddenly I heard the cry, "Fire! Fire!" I sat up in bed and reflected. Fire was deliverance or death, and death was deliverance, but, such a death! I opened the grating and saw a torrent of flames. No one was thinking of me, so I lay down upon my bed and waited for death.

Suddenly I heard a voice. "It is Michael; don't be afraid. Everything is ready for our flight." I heard pickaxes knocking at the wall. In five minutes the opening was large enough for me to pass. He took me in his arms, but the fire was raging in the passage. "Put your arms round my neck," he said, "and be cool."

"I call walk," I answered. "Here is a staircase; let us go this way." He dragged me to a window, fastened a rope ladder to it, and almost threw himself out with me in his arms. At the same moment I heard cries behind us: "Here they are! Here they are!"

Instantly, when we had reached the ground, Michael took out a cape from under a mound of earth, where he had hidden it, and threw it over my shoulders. Taking me by the hand, he said, "We must run; do your best, for your own sake as well as for mine."

We found a horse awaiting us at the park gate. He mounted, swung me up behind him, and we galloped off. When the day dawned we had reached the first ridge of the Urals. Then we allowed our horse to take a little rest. Such was our excitement that we felt neither hunger nor fatigue.

During this halt Michael told me all that had happened since his last effort to deliver me. He had dressed himself as a miner and had worked in the mines; the Prince had never thought of looking for him there. He perceived a great discontent among the workmen and discovered that they all bore a sullen hatred for the overseer, who pushed them unmercifully. As an apostle of socialism, Michael preached to them our doctrines. He so worked upon their imaginations that, upon the infliction of an unjust punishment upon one of the band, he aroused them to proceed in a body to the castle and set it on fire.

When our horse had sufficiently rested, we continued our journey through mountain defiles that Michael had studied for months. In less than two months we were beyond all pursuit. At last we were out of Russia.

As I crossed the frontier, I turned around towards that accursed country and looked back in a sort of intoxication upon that land of misery and anguish, that empire of evil, where the weak are at the mercy of the strong, where injustice rules, where for five years I had suffered every humiliation, every agony of which the human soul is capable.

It is needless to tell you of all our adventures in the country of the Khirgis, where we spent six months.

Michael's skill as a physician supplied us with means. We sailed down the Caspian Sea to the port of Lissa. We crossed Persia and Armenia to Trebizond. Then, by way of the Black Sea, we arrived in a steamer at Marseilles.

I wrote to my father to ask for assistance. He was very poor and could not help me, but an old aunt of mine, dying just at that time, left me quite a little fortune. I thought for a while that we could live in peace. Then I heard that the Prince was searching everywhere for us, having denounced us as criminals and incendiaries to the foreign governments. We were obliged to change our names and again go into hiding. In 1863 the insurrection in Poland broke out. We had one moment of hope, but in a little while my wretched country was more oppressed than ever.

For seventeen years I have been exiled, separated from you. Thanks to Padlewsky and Katia, we have at least the same creed, the same hope.

I have wished to tell you all my life. Now you know the truth. I hope, my beloved child, that your upright mind will absolve your mother.

I waited to make this revelation to you until you were of age, because now you are free to dispose of yourself, and you can claim your inheritance from your father. This fortune will at least make you independent. As for me I do not need anything. Michael's practice is quite sufficient for both of us.

If you do not care for your fortune, I desire that you will give it over into the hands of the Revolutionary Committee. Ah, if Geneva were not so far away, if you were not necessary where you are, I would ask you to come to your mother, who for seventeen years has hungered for the kisses of her child. But the cause before everything. At this time we must concentrate all our efforts, all our means, to one aim: the freedom of the Russian people. Besides, Michael and I have a project, which, if we can push it through, will permit us to see you and to embrace you soon.

Your mother presses you to her heart and covers you with kisses.

Alexandra

"Poor mother!" murmured Wanda, wiping away her tears. "How she has suffered! And I am the daughter of her persecutor!"

She threw herself into Katia's arms.

"Oh, thanks! Thanks!" she cried. "You have opened my eyes and made me worthy to know and love this noble woman."

CHAPTER XXL

THE BALL

Prince Kryloff's ball to celebrate Wanda's coming of age was royal in its magnificence. His palace, one of the finest in Petersburg, was decorated for the occasion by a French artist. Flowers, lights and mirrors, mirrors of lights and flowers, were everywhere.

Wanda wore a dress of satin and Canton crepe trimmed with patterns of water-lilies and seaweeds. Her emerald necklace, with its wavering light, and the dark green leaves of the lilies upon the dead white of her dress heightened the effect of her pale skin and wonderful green-tinted eyes. Every one in society was there. Although the army was still in Turkey, there was no lack of uniforms, for the officers of the Imperial bodyguard and the aides-de-camp of the Emperor added the *éclat* of their scarlet uniforms and numerous decorations to the brilliant scene.

All Wanda's adorers were there. She saluted them each in her usual friendly way, but when she perceived Stepane Litzanoff, hardly able to stand, gazing at her with despairing eyes, she went straight up to him and said: "You here? How imprudent! How is your wound?"

"It is nothing."

"You have a fever now."

"You promised to come to me; you did not come. I would not wait any longer."

"This folly will put back your recovery."

"Well, what if it does?"

Stackelberg was watching them. He read in Litzanoff's eyes his consuming love and, in Wanda's suppressed pity, her suppressed tenderness.

Stackelberg loved Wanda as well as such a nature could love. He had sworn to himself that she should love him, and here was a rival. A bitter jealousy awoke in his heart.

At midnight, when the ball was at its height, General Trepoff was announced. Wanda received him and, taking him by the arm, led him to her father.

"Well, General," she said gaily, "do you see any suspicious persons present? Have you discovered any of these wicked and dangerous nihilists?"

Just then they were passing through a small drawing-room in which several of the guests were engaged in an animated discussion. They were Padlewsky, Raymond Chabert, Alexis Verenine, Horace de Prieu, Stepane Litzanoff, and Vassili Stackelberg.

Litzanoff was speaking.

"Russian society," he said, "is rotten to the core. Beneath its elegant manners and refined tastes lurks a savage selfishness and brutal passions. In this Holy Russia, we are all either oppressor or oppressed, lords or fawning lackeys, peacocks or vipers, treading down or trodden upon. Our lordly vices gloss over our moral decrepitude. But alongside of this society, ready to crumble to pieces, a vigorous, young, lusty tenacious generation is arising. It is the popular element, which will soon absorb the aristocratic element."

Then, perceiving a cold sneering smile upon Stackelberg's face, he went on more excitedly: "Is it among civilized nations that such men as Trepoff are allowed to flog political prisoners?"

At that very moment General Trepoff stood at the entrance of the room.

"It was not Trepoff who flogged Bogoluboff," answered the General. "It was the Chief of Police, who was obliged to force his authority to be respected."

Litzanoff did not know Trepoff. He turned around and saw Wanda leaning upon this gentleman's arm. Seized with jealousy, in the most insulting manner he said:

"That does not alter the fact. I maintain that any nation in which a Mister Trepoff, whatever his rank may be, can with impunity outrage the respect due to humanity, is not entitled to be called a civilized nation."

"Hush, Stepane Danilovitch!" cried out Wanda, but Litzanoff would not hush.

"And why," said he, "should Bogoluboff have saluted this Mister Trepoff? Was it his place to thank Mister Trepoff for keeping him locked up as a prisoner?"

"Stepane, you are speaking to General Trepoff himself," broke in Wanda, who was as white as a sheet.

Litzanoff smiled at Wanda. She, leaning on Trepoff's arm — could it be possible? But carried away by the fever that burned in his veins, by his vanity, by a sort of bravado, he bowed to the General and in the bitterest tone continued:

"I ask General Trepoff himself if there is any law here in Russia which compels a man to take off his hat to any person! I maintain that Bogoluboff was right and that the Chief of the Police was not right. But in Russia justice has two weights and two measures; in Russia justice does not touch the rich and great; it only flogs the weak. And still the Czar calls himself liberal."

Wanda, in despair, drew Trepoff away. "I beg you, General," she said, "do not pay any attention to this crazy young fellow."

The Chief-of Police was trembling with rage, but he controlled his temper, and even smiled as he answered Wanda :

"Here, at least, is one of our nihilists."

"Oh, no! Tomorrow you will be surprised to hear him argue on the other side of the question. He does not know what he is talking about. I assure you he has something the matter with his brain."

"I think that is what ails all the nihilists. But they are dangerous, and that is why we lock them up." Wanda looked at him with her lovely, beseeching eyes.

"Do not arrest Litzanoff, General. His wife is my intimate friend; she adores him, and it would kill her. It would be a dreadful blow to me to have such a thing happen on my birthday. It would ruin the happiness of that little family."

"I could forgive him if he had attacked me alone, but I think I heard him declaiming against the Emperor, criticizing the Government. However, I shall know exactly what he did say."

"General, have you brought your spies here?" exclaimed Wanda, forgetting to dissemble her indignation.

"No, I have not. But you must acknowledge yourself that I have good cause to do so," he answered, with a hard laugh.

"I grant you," she replied, "that he has been impertinent, and audacious, and very ill-bred, but for my sake, forgive him."

"I will forgive him, if I can," said Trepoff, and in a few minutes he withdrew.

Wanda went back into the little drawing-room. No one was there but Verenine.

"What has become of Litzanoff ?" she asked.

"He went out of the room with Prince Stackelberg."

"Stackelberg!" exclaimed Wanda.

"Well, what is there extraordinary about that?"

"Did you hear what they were talking about?"

"No, I did not. I only noticed that they seemed deeply interested in one another's conversation."

"Oh, for pity's sake, Alexis, go and find Stepane! Tell him I want to see him; tell him Nadege wants to go home; tell him anything you choose, but get him away from Stackelberg."

Just then Chabert came up. Wanda's anxiety and uneasiness increased her beauty tenfold, dazzling Raymond with her appearance.

"Can you come to see me tomorrow?" she said to him. "I have something important to ask of you."

"Of me? Whatever you ask is granted beforehand."

"Oh, you are a true Frenchman. Do not be too rash in your promises."

"What promises have I made you?"

"You offered me your life, did you not?"

"Yes."

"I shall not ask you to die for me, but what is more difficult, to live for me, upon my own terms."

"I vow to you that . . ."

"Do not vow before you know what it is."

"You have excited my curiosity. Please give me some idea of what you mean."

"I mean something about marriage."

"Marriage? Whom am I to marry?"

"You shall know tomorrow. Good night."

CHAPTER XXII

PROVOCATION

It was Stackelberg who had incited Litzanoff to that diatribe against the Government and the Chief of Police. As soon as Wanda had got General Trepoff out of the room, he led the Count on to a discussion about political and social questions. He was, in fact, playing the same game with Litzanoff that he had tried with Wanda. Wanda, being a woman, and more quick to discern, had seen through him and foiled him. Not so Count Litzanoff, who, careless at all times of danger, had no conception whatever of the German's motives. The smoking-room was unoccupied as the two young men sauntered in.

"My dear fellow," said Stackelberg, handing the Count a cigar, "although I appeared to contradict you a few moments ago, I am, at bottom, entirely of your way of thinking. Between you and me, I am not far off from becoming a nihilist like yourself."

"Who told you that I am a nihilist?" said Litzanoff, startled.

"Why, you talk like one. You wish to overturn the government, the laws, the religion of the country. I should like to know something of this movement. We Germans — for I am of German descent — are not so quick, not so intuitive, not so clever as you Russians, but when an idea once has penetrated into our thick heads, take my word for it, it is not so easy to get it out. I should like very much to be admitted into your secret society, The revolutionary movement interests me intensely. You said just now that Russia is debased and corrupt, but believe me, a nation which can produce such characters as Myschkine, for instance, cannot be looked upon with contempt. I have heard that there are amongst these Nihilists persons of the highest rank, who have given up everything — family and fortune — for the cause.

"We are not nihilists," answered Litzanoff, completely thrown off his guard. "We are socialists, humanitarians, revolutionists. We only desire to overthrow the existing state of things because it is wholly evil."

"You desire, then, a revolution which shall be both political and social?"

"We do."

"Are there many of you? Is the organization an extensive one?"

"At this question Litzanoff came to his senses. He looked at the face of his interrogator; and that flat, smooth, pale countenance made him tremble. He suddenly perceived that he had betrayed his secret to Stackelberg; not only his own secret, but that of his whole party.

"Truly," he said, "I am a strange sort of fellow. But yesterday I was reading a book which I came across accidentally, a socialist book, very probably left in my room to attract my attention, and here I am talking about it as if I were a prominent agent of the revolution. If an idea appeals to me as just, I accept it; if, on the contrary, it strikes me as false, I criticize it. Clearly, you know nothing of me or of my past life, if you take me for a socialist, unless, indeed, you consider my nihilism as the last of my eccentric extravagances, or extravagant eccentricities. I believe in nothing, that is true, and consequently I respect nothing, but that does not imply that I am mixed up with any party. In the first place, I should have to know where this Party is to be found. Where is it, where does it meet, where does it hold forth? I have heard a great deal of talk about these Nihilists, but I have never seen them. I should be infinitely obliged to you if you will introduce me, to some of them, for like yourself, I am dying to belong to some secret society."

Stackelberg bit his lips. "I have gone too fast," he thought.

"Princess Wanda," said Stackelberg, "is thought to he a nihilist. What a notion! Do you know how I think these Nihilist women look? Cut out of wood, with thin gray hair trimmed short, red noses adorned with spectacles — they are all midwives and drink vodka. Do you think Wanda Kryloff could associate with such creatures? You know her very well, do you not?" asked Stackelberg.

"Yes, she is my wife's most intimate friend."

"Are you marred?"

"Yes, I have been married for two years."

"You married! Why I have seen you everywhere with . . ."

"Well, in fact, my married life has not been altogether irreproachable."

"You Russians are great flirts."

"Although I have a beautiful wife," continued Litzanoff, "I am not so blind but that I can see the beauty of other women. I love everything that is pretty."

"Even Wanda Kryloff?" asked Stackelberg, fixing his eyes upon Stepane.

Litzanoff blushed painfully. "I love Wanda," he said, "as I would a goddess; but she is too perfect for my taste. She wearies me because she makes me feel my inferiority."

"Excuse me, Stepane Danilovitch; you are desperately in love with that beautiful girl."

"I? It is a platonic affection. You do not know me."

Just then Wanda, who had been looking for them everywhere, appeared at the door of the smoking-room.

"At last" she said, "here you are. Nadege is looking for you, Stepane Danilovitch. She told me to tell you."

"Shall I retire?" asked Stackelberg, hurt that Wanda took no notice whatever of him.

"Oh, I only want to give Stepane the message his wife left for him."

Stepane threw down his cigar and followed Wanda into the conservatory adjoining the smoking-room.

"Wretched man," she whispered, "what have you said to him?"

"To whom?"

"To that German."

Stepane felt a cold sweat break out all over him.

"I believe I let out that I am a nihilist. We were speaking of the nihilists, and I said 'we.'"

"As if you were a member of a secret society?"

"Yes."

"Well, Trepoff suspects you, and Stackelberg will convict you. You must leave Petersburg tonight. If not, you will be arrested tomorrow."

"Who is this Stackelberg?"

"An agent of the Third Section."

"Ah! I see now."

"Promise me that you will leave the city!"

"I will hide; but I will not leave Petersburg as long as you are here."

"I must leave you now," said Wanda. "We must not be seen together." Stepane tried to take her hand. "Are you mad!" she said.

"Yes, more so than ever."

"I insist upon your going at once to some friend's, who will conceal you. You are worn out; you look livid; you need rest."

"I will obey you, but pity me. Give me your hand."

He seized it and pressed it to his lips; at the same instant they both heard a slight rustle among the leaves of the shrubbery which hid them from sight.

"He is listening to us," she exclaimed in terror.

Stepane made a sign of farewell, and returned to the smoking-room. Stackelberg was lying on the sofa, carelessly puffing away at his cigar, as though he thought of nothing but the rings of smoke that floated upwards before his eyes.

Litzanoff crossed the room without looking at him. He was just outside the door when Stackelberg called after him: "Stepane Danilovitch!"

Litzanoff did not turn around; the German arose and rushed after him.

"Sir, I spoke to you!" he said.

"I heard you," replied Litzanoff.

"You made me no answer."

"No."

"Will you have the goodness to tell me why you did not?"

"Because I did not choose to answer you."

"Will you please to explain this sudden change in your behavior to me?"

"Simply my fancy."

"In fact, Count, as you said just now, there must be something." And he touched his forehead with the end of his finger.

"I can say that myself, but I allow no one else to say so."

"Who will prevent me from saying so if I choose?"

"I will!" said Litzanoff, in a tone of defiance.

Stackelberg had resumed his cold, phlegmatic manner, and looking at his enraged adversary with a satirical smile, he handed him his card.

"Tomorrow at ten o'clock," he said, "I will send you a friend who will arrange this matter."

"Very well," answered Litzanoff, turning his back.

"Ah, that was a happy thought!" chuckled Stackelberg, who had overheard the conversation between Stepane and Wanda. "This duel will keep him at home. I will see that he is locked up by eight o'clock."

On the other hand, Litzanoff, who could not conceive such baseness, said to himself: "This is first-rate; I have the whole day before me. He will never have me arrested before the fight comes off."

As soon as she had quitted Stepane, Wanda went in search of Nadege.

"Dear friend," she said, "your husband must disappear for a while. I am afraid he has compromised himself, and he might be arrested."

"Arrested!" cried Nadege, in horror.

"It is only a dread that I have. Watch and see if you notice any commissary of police walking frequently by your house; if you do not, after a few days he can come home again."

"Where can he go to hide?"

"Wherever you think is the safest place. I am going now to speak to Padlewsky about it; he knows all sorts of mysterious holes and corners in Petersburg."

She looked for Padlewsky everywhere, but he was not to be found.

CHAPTER XXIII

THE ARREST

As soon as Nadege reached home with her husband, she begged him not to sleep in his own house, but he laughed at her fears. Nadege knew well that arrest often meant disappearance forever, and her love exaggerated the danger. She begged Stepane on her knees to seek some place of concealment, but, raising her from the ground, he said, "I would go away to quiet your fears were it not that I have made a positive engagement to meet some one here, in my own house, at ten o'clock tomorrow morning."

"Why can't you write and put off the engagement?"

"That is impossible."

"If you will only break this engagement and conceal yourself, if you will do just this one thing, I will forgive you all your neglect for these two long years."

But Litzanoff would not consent. So Nadege passed the night in anguish. She could not close her eyes without seeing her husband before her living in a gloomy dungeon, or loaded with chains on the road to Siberia. She awoke very early, covered with a cold sweat.

At seven o'clock she dressed herself and went over to Stepane's apartments, and again renewed her entreaties.

"Why cannot you break this engagement?" she urged. "There must be some woman mixed up with it."

"No, dear child, it is a debt of honor, and I have promised to pay it at ten o'clock punctually."

Nadege withdrew, but she had scarcely reached her own room when she heard a noise in the courtyard. She looked out and saw two soldiers guarding the entrance, while two more, preceded by a commissary of police, were walking in the direction of Stepane's apartments. A hack was standing outside the door.

At that moment her maid entered.

"They have come to arrest the Count!" she said. "The house is surrounded."

Nadege, wild with terror, rushed over to her husband. He was in bed.

"Make haste!" she cried. "Get up! The police . . ." She had no time to say another word before the commissary and his men entered the room.

"Is this Count Stepane Litzanoff?" asked the commissary.

"It is," answered Stepane, rising.

"I have orders to arrest you."

"Of what am I accused?"

"Of conspiracy against the government."

"It is false."

"I know nothing but the orders that I have received. You can explain your conduct to the judges."

"Where am I to be taken?"

"To the fortress of Petropavlosk."

Upon hearing these words Nadege fainted.

This fortress was the Bastille of Russia. The darkest stories were told of the horrible martyrdoms and mysterious crimes of which it has been the silent witness.

"Can you not at least allow me a short time to arrange my affairs? I give you my word of honor that I will make no effort to escape."

"It is impossible. My orders are strict; I must obey."

Litzanoff was not well. In his desire to be at Prince Kryloff's ball the night before, he had gone out too soon. His wound was but partially healed, and the agitation and annoyance of all this produced violent pain and a raging fever. Nevertheless he dressed himself and followed the soldiers.

As he crossed the threshold of his door, he heard one piercing cry. It was poor Nadege.

The fortress of Petropavlosk has its rocky foundations deep under the waters of the Neva. It is situated nearly opposite the Winter Palace, on the other side of the river. Built to protect Russia against the Swedes, it remained to imprison the Russians themselves. It defends Petersburg, but still more does if threaten it.

What dark stories could that fortress tell! How many sobs, how many groans, how many cries of rage has it stifled within its gray walls? The day may come, and that soon, when the people will arise, and with avenging power penetrate into the terrible depths and darkness of its dungeons.

Russia has its laws, its judges, its juries and yet an inquisitorial tribunal can arrest, condemn, and pronounce sentence without trial.

Litzanoff was led away to the Governor of the fortress. He could hardly stand up. To overcome his physical weakness he had exerted himself to the uttermost.

The Governor looked at him attentively. "You are not well?" he inquired.

"I have two slight wounds, which are annoying, and they have caused me a very high fever."

"Unfortunately," said the Governor, "I have nothing at my disposal except Cell 9, which is very cold; in a day or two I can give you a better room."

He gave an order to the turnkey, who, followed by the soldiers, accompanied Litzanoff out of the room. He stopped before a door and threw it open.

"Follow me," he said.

They went down the steps and came to a row of cells, but they did not stop there. They descended ten more steps, and entered into a dark passage-way which runs below the level of the river. Lamps suspended from the ceiling gave a flickering and uncertain light. On either side, heavy doors, bristling with chains and bolts and locks, added to the gloomy look of this labyrinth. At the end of the corridor was an enormous grated door more overloaded than the rest with bars of iron and other defenses. This opened upon the Neva. How many have gone through that gate to their death!

Each one of those cells had its own sad story. It was in No. 12 that the fair Princess Tarakanoff, who was inconvenient to Catherine I, was drowned by the overflow of the Neva. After the waters had fallen, they found her body partially eaten up by rats. In No. 11, Batenka underwent twenty-three years of torture rather than betray his benefactor, Speransky. When he came out, he could no longer speak nor bear the light of the sun. It was in No. 8 that Netchaieff, who was chained to the wall, went mad.

Still more horrible stories than these are told. Some dungeons are built in the shape of an egg, so that the prisoner can neither sit down nor lie down nor stand upright. Gradually the weight of the body, always thrown out of position, dislocates all the joints. They say that there are other cells in which the captive, chained by the middle of his body to a heavy beam, is forced to gaze ceaselessly upon the Neva which flows beneath him. His imprisonment is a continual vertigo.

Alexander had certainly abolished all these tortures. But Litzanoff knew the legends attached to the fortress. He also knew that, once within its walls, a man might remain there forgotten for years, or perhaps forever.

They had come to the cell intended for him. It was eight feet high; the walls were green with damp; the floor was of brick, oozing with a slimy moisture. This gloomy enclosure was lighted by a small grated window, funnel shaped, which admitted a melancholy, doubtful light. And all the time a hoarse murmur could be heard; it was the waters of the Neva, beating against the walls.

There was neither bed nor sofa nor chair. The only piece of furniture was a long wooden bench.

At first Litzanoff saw nothing. Exhausted by his fever, he wrapped himself in his fur cloak, and lay down on the bench. The only thing he asked for was water; for, in spite of the cold, he was consumed with thirst. His mind wandered. Wanda's dazzling form passed before him, and then Nadege's touching face: the two women that he loved.

Gradually the delirium passed away, and the horrible reality forced itself upon him. He looked around him, and he saw the walls of his dungeon.

Then he arose, oppressed by an inexpressible terror. He was stifling. He wanted air and light; he shook the bars of his window, he beat out his strength against the heavy door. He, who had never known a fetter to his will, to his desires, here found invincible, brutal obstacles, walls of granite, and a will put over him which he knew well to be implacable.

Wanda! He could not see her. Perhaps he would never see her again. He wept, he cried aloud, he buried his nails in his flesh; he turned upon himself, as does a lion in its cage; at last, utterly exhausted, he sank powerless upon the bench.

A man brought him some tea and his ration, a piece of black bread and a porringer full of cabbage cooked with hemp-seed oil.

Litzanoff asked for paper, pens and ink. The man paid no attention to him and did not answer him a word. The Count longed to fly at his throat.

Now he understood his situation. He was condemned to silence.

Night came. In Petersburg in winter it is dark at three o'clock, and the day does not break until nine. So the wretched prisoners are left in darkness for eighteen hours.

He was sitting up motionless when something soft ran over his hands.

It had to be a rat. He shuddered with horror, and thought of Princess Tarakanoff.

That first night was frightful. The fever covered his body with an icy sweat and filled his cell with horrible shapes. At times he thought he was going mad. His head was bursting, then sinking fits seized him, and he thought he was dying.

Suddenly, in the very middle of the night, he heard the most awful shrieks in the cell adjoining his own. He listened. Where did the cries come from? There could be no doubt about it: some poor wretch next door to him was in agony. What were they doing to him? Those were not cries of pain. Was he laughing? Was he singing, in a wild, incoherent manner? Certainly the man must have gone mad.

Stepane felt sure that if his confinement lasted any length of time the like fate would overtake him. Lose his reason. How much better would it be to die! But then he had powerful friends with some influence at court. Nadege would go to her own family. But on second thought, he feared they would not do much for him; he had alienated the affection of all his wife's relations. Besides, when a man is in disgrace his friends soon forget him, particularly when they are under a government which for the slightest suspicion may exile or imprison.

When the day began to break Litzanoff grew calmer. He remembered the promise he had given to Wanda two days before, to devote his life to the nihilist cause. The hour had come, and he must not hesitate.

At this thought his courage returned, and he determined to show himself worthy of the love that Wanda had promised him.

When, at ten o'clock, the door of his cell opened, he was perfectly calm, almost resigned.

CHAPTER XXIV

THE EXAMINATION

Two soldiers entered to conduct Count Litzanoff before the judge. In a few moments he found himself in the presence of a tribunal composed of two blue officers, the judge, and his clerk.

Litzanoff understood that the situation was a serious one, that his life was at stake. And still he thought of nothing but Wanda. To be worthy of her, to turn away all suspicion from her, to sacrifice himself if necessary, these were his only thoughts.

"Count Litzanoff," said the judge, "you are accused of having yesterday, in Prince Kryloff's drawing-room, attacked the Czar and his government in the most outrageous terms, calculated to bring contempt upon the Emperor and his Imperial government."

"I did not attack the Emperor. I confined myself to criticizing Official Russia. Every one knows that the privileges of our nobility are exorbitant. I blamed Trepoff, who has flogged a political prisoner. But, gentlemen, do any of you approve of that act?"

"We are not here," said one of the blue officers, "to answer questions, but to ask them."

"You give us to understand," said the judge, "by your mode of conversation, that you are connected with these dangerous nihilists, who desire the destruction of the Government, and the utter upheaval of society."

"I belong to no community," answered Litzanoff. "This is the whole truth: I was reading a book criticizing our social system; it struck me very forcibly, and I allowed myself to be carried away by its arguments so as to quote them in an excited manner, and to lose my temper in the presence of a dozen gentlemen, in a way which I fear will cost me dearly."

"It is not a question of temper," said the magistrate, "but of a violent, bitter diatribe that you permitted yourself to utter, resembling exactly the nihilist modes of speech. At this moment we hold in custody at the Palace of Justice one hundred and ninety-three prisoners, who express themselves in the same manner with yourself."

"I do not understand you, as I am not acquainted with any nihilists."

"How did you obtain your socialist books? They are prohibited," said the judge.

"I did not obtain them."

"Who gave them to you?"

"I do not know."

"What? You do not know?"

"No. I found them laying on the table in my study."

"I adjure you, for your own sake," said the judge, "tell me the truth, and the Emperor, in consideration of your honesty and your youth, may pardon you."

"I have told you the truth. I am entirely innocent of any plot against the Emperor."

"And yet you gave a hundred roubles to an agent of the police to prevent him from following you?" Litzanoff repeated what Wanda had said to Trepoff.

"How long have you known Princess Wanda Kryloff?"

At this question, Litzanoff could not prevent a slight shudder.

"Ever since my marriage," he answered.

"Your friendship with her has been interrupted from time to time?"

"Yes."

"From what cause?"

"That I cannot tell you, for I do not know. Some woman's fancy, I suppose."

"Within the last eight days you have seen her frequently. How often?"

He answered without any hesitation, "Four times."

"Have the goodness to say under what circumstances."

"There are some details of my private life that I am not willing to reveal."

"Take care your silence will only compromise the Princess."

That is true, thought Litzanoff, and at once he related his connections with the Polish adventuress and his reconciliation with his wife through the mediation of Wanda. The judge asked a great many questions about the Polish lady, and then, reverting to the Princess Kryloff, he asked: "What was the meaning of the stabs that you received in the Princess's boudoir."

"I struck myself."

"Why? From what motive?"

At this question, Litzanoff lost his temper.

"Am I not to be allowed to scratch without giving an account of it to the Government?"

"Has Princess Kryloff ever spoken to you on the subject of the nihilists?"

"Never."

"Do you suppose that it was she who had those books placed upon your table?"

"Not at all; on the contrary, I am certain it was not she."

"What do you base your conviction upon?"

"Upon the relations which exist between her and my wife, relations of a purely friendly character."

"Are you acquainted with the other friends of the Princess?"

"The Princess, by her rank, has the highest position in Petersburg society. I do not think you will find many nihilists among them."

"And yet yesterday you used these words: 'We, the nihilists.'"

Litzanoff's pale face colored. The judge noticed it, and fixed his eyes intently upon the Count. This exasperated Litzanoff.

"I don't remember having used any such language," he exclaimed, petulantly.

"You pronounced the words in Prince Kryloff's smoking-room, in the presence of Prince Stackelberg."

"If that gentleman repeated our conversation, you know by this time that he is much more of a socialist than I am. How do you know that I was not trying to find out his real opinions? I thought it was he who wanted to join the revolutionary party."

"The Government knows what to think of the character and opinions of Prince Stackelberg."

"And so do I," answered Litzanoff, with a sneer.

At these words the other member of the court, who up to that time had not spoken, interrupted.

"Take care, Count Litzanoff," he said. "You are aggravating your situation, which is already bad enough. We are upon the track of an extensive conspiracy. You can obtain your freedom by assisting us, for in spite of your denial we are certain that you are in collusion with the enemies of the Government. It is a matter of the highest importance to us to know the name of the person who initiated you into this nihilist society. Give us his name, and you are instantly released."

At this, Litzanoff was seized with a sort of delirium. His fever was raging, his blood was on fire.

"Who initiated me! You want to know who initiated me! You have done it yourselves! From this moment I am a nihilist! You have no right to put an innocent man to such torture, to ask me such questions, to . . ."

"Count Litzanoff," interrupted the grave personage, "remember the respect due to the magistrate."

"You ask me if I am a nihilist. I answer, I am a nihilist, and I protest against your inquisitorial tribunals, your arrests, your arbitrary judgments. I complain, as Bestucheff did, that the Emperor can do everything, and that the people can do nothing. I complain that you can arrest me unjustly, and that I have no redress. And now you can ask me what you choose. I will not answer another question."

But the judge went on with his examination, while all the time Stepane held a sullen silence.

"You are only aggravating your situation," said alternately the judge and the blue officer.

"What does it matter?" at last he cried. "Perhaps tomorrow I shall be dead."

They asked him several questions about Princess Kryloff. They were asked in vain.

Then the clerk handed the examination to the prisoner for him to read and sign. Litzanoff cast his eyes down the page. As he read the veins in his forehead swelled, and he uttered the most indignant exclamations. His answers, as well as his silence, were so interpreted as to bear witness to the existence of a secret society, and to acknowledge that he was connected with it.

"I will not sign that!" he said, throwing the paper down with contempt. "It is an infamous tissue of lies."

"You will not sign it?" said the judge.

"No."

"Is that your determination?"

"It is."

"Then we who have signed it are liars?"

"If you call lying not telling the truth."

"You are indeed a rebel," added the grave personage.

"We want no other proof."

"In truth," cried Litzanoff, beside himself with rage, "I want a revolution to deliver us from Russian justice. I see your aim: you will have a conspiracy and conspirators, cost what it may. You want a victim, and as I have fallen into your hands, I am to be sacrificed. I hope that the nihilists will avenge me."

"Do you still refuse to sign this paper?" asked one of the blue officers.

"I do refuse."

"Then we will wait until solitude and silence bring you to a better state of mind."

"Yes," replied Litzanoff, "you expect darkness and the torture of solitude to produce their usual effect upon me. But my will shall triumph over the weakness of my body."

The blue officer turned to one of the soldiers. "Remove the prisoner," he said.

For more than an hour Litzanoff had been battling with his fever. It was now at its height, and as they advanced to seize him, he fell senseless to the floor. They were obliged to take him up in their arms.

When he came to his senses, he had chains upon his feet.

CHAPTER XXV

SOUND REASONS

The Emperor had said to the Chief of Police, "There is a conspiracy on foot against my government and my person; it extends to my nobility, even to my army. Discover it."

For fifteen days, the Third Section sought and found nothing. Litzanoff had dared address General Trepoff with insolence; naturally he must be a nihilist, attached to some secret society. His antecedents, his eccentricity, his contempt for public opinion, his courage, his youth, all pointed him out as the proper person to suspect.

He must be forced to speak. That would be no difficult task. This volatile young fellow, well known for his indolent and effeminate life, was not made out of the stuff of heroes. So instead of sending him to the Third Section and treating him with the usual forms, they shut him up in one of the gloomiest cells of the fortress and exercised towards him the utmost severity. They thought that a few days of solitary confinement would bring him to his senses and make him communicative.

It is true that Trepoff had promised Wanda that Stepane should not be arrested for his insolence to the General. But Stackelberg's subsequent report had put another face on the matter. He repeated his conversation with the Count, carefully aggravating and falsifying its sense.

"After all," thought Trepoff, "what is a promise made to a pretty woman, when opposed to sound reasons which affect the State?"

As soon as Nadege had sufficiently recovered from the shock caused by her husband's arrest, she realized that there was not a moment to lose and hastened to see Wanda.

Wanda was in bed, fast asleep. Nadege threw herself into her arms, sobbing convulsively. "Save him! Save him!" she cried. "You and Padlewsky have been the ruin of him. This accursed nihilism! Where can I go to find him, to take care of my poor Stepane? He is ill, and they will murder him. Perhaps they will send him to Siberia!"

Wanda did not say one word. She sat up in bed, and looking straight before her, seemed lost in thought.

"Who signed the order for the arrest?" she asked.

"I don't know, but I think they want his life, for as I came out I met two persons on the staircase, who said they came from Prince Stackelberg. I insisted upon knowing the motive of their visit, and they answered that, as the Count was arrested, they could tell me without hesitation. They had come to arrange the preliminaries for an affair of honor, a duel."

"At what time did you meet them?"

"At nine o'clock. It must have been this duel which prevented him from going away last night, as you recommended him to do. He was waiting to see his adversary's seconds."

"I see through it all," said Wanda. "That scoundrel Stackelberg managed the whole affair. The coward! I will avenge your husband, I promise you. But first of all we must get him out of the hands of the police."

"Oh, yes, make haste," said Nadege. "Poor Stepane! He in prison, he who could never bear the least restraint. Tell me, what can we do?"

"You must go to your father; he has some influence with the Emperor. No one but the Czar can open the gates of the fortress. We will not have recourse to violent measures until we have exhausted all others."

"But," answered Nadege, "my father is very timid; he hates the nihilists. And then he has seen my unhappiness for the last two years. He is not likely to trouble himself to set at liberty the man who has caused me so many tears."

"I know all that, but you must go to see him. Perhaps he may do something for us. The main thing is to see the Emperor immediately. I will write to Verenine to come to me at once. He has access to the palace at all hours of the day, and we can send through him a protest against this arbitrary arrest."

She jumped out of bed, wrote a note to Verenine, and then proceeded to dress herself.

Her grief was terrible. She reproached herself with Litzanoff's arrest.

She knew he was ill and wounded, and she feared that the severity of the prison, together with his bad health, would kill him. In her dark eyes could be read an intense anger as well as an intense sorrow. With whom was she angry? With the Chief of Police, who had broken his word to her, and with that flabby German, Stackelberg.

Following Wanda's advice, Nadege went to her father's house. To him the Czar was a idol. When the Czar spoke, it was as though God himself had uttered his voice. If he had been imprisoned, exiled, flogged, by the order of the Emperor, he would have accepted it with resignation, perhaps even with gratitude. It is thus with all the pious inhabitants of Russia; they look upon the Czar as the earthly representative of the Deity.

When Nadege told him of her husband's arrest, he raised his eyes to heaven, and sighed:

"May the will of God and of the Emperor be done in all things, my child."

"But," exclaimed Nadege, "we must save him; we must get him out of prison. He is ill, and perhaps they have locked him up in one of the dampest cells in the fortress."

"No one can get him out except the Emperor."

"That is just it. I want to know if you will not see him for me."

"In the first place, tell me of what do they accuse Litzanoff?"

"Of being a nihilist."

"A nihilist!" exclaimed Nadege's father. "He has he fallen so low as that?"

"Dear father, it is altogether a mistake of the police."

"Ah, well, then they will soon find out their mistake and set him at liberty. If he is guilty, he ought to be punished."

"I assure you he is innocent. If you would go to the Emperor you might lessen the severity of his punishment."

"His punishment," continued the old man. "It is wrong to accuse the police of unnecessary severity towards the prisoners. It is the nihilists who represent the government of the Czar as cruel and unjust. And how could your husband be accused, if he has not given them some reason to suspect him?"

Nadege told him in a few words what had happened the night before at Prince Kryloff's ball. This tale filled the old man with indignation.

"He dared blaspheme in that manner against the Emperor, and you say he is not guilty? If the nobles attack our society in this manner, whom can we expect to defend it? Nihil, Nihil, nothing, nothing — that is their whole system of philosophy. Nihil, that is to say, no God. Nihil, that is to say, no authority. Nihil, that is to say, no Emperor. Nihil, no government. Nihil, no property. Nihil, no family. Nihil, no religion. Down with morals, conscience, human respect. Nothing to guide a man but his brutal instincts. Every principle upon which society rests is a prejudice. Yes, yes; I have no doubt that Stepane is a Nihilist. I have often heard him express opinions which have made me shudder. And his conduct looks like it. He respects no one; he revels in every baseness; and how has he not tortured you, poor child, who adore him? And you can forget all that, and ask me to obtain his pardon? Never, never! If they send him to Siberia, well and good; he will be dead in the eyes of the law, and you will be free to marry another man who may make you happy."

"Father," said Nadege, "I love my husband, and if he goes to Siberia I will follow him."

"You would leave your old father to follow that miserable fellow?"

"It is my duty. I loved him when he was rich and happy, and now that he is unfortunate, I love him still more. I beg you, dear father, intercede with the Emperor for him."

"I will never ask the Czar for a favor to an anarchist. If your husband is arrested, there are sound reasons for his arrest. He will be tried, and then we shall see whether he is innocent or guilty. After all, a few months of confinement will do him a great deal of good."

"But suppose they do not give him a trial? You know that political prisoners are often hurried off to Siberia, or allowed to perish in their cells."

"Those are fables invented by the nihilists."

Nadege mentioned several persons who had disappeared very suddenly from society.

"Without doubt there were sound reasons for condemning them," answered her father. "And take care, my child, not to talk disrespectfully against those put over us in authority."

"Well," exclaimed Nadege, exasperated, "if they will not give me back my husband, I will turn nihilist too! I hate a government that tolerates such iniquity."

The old man rose up and said in a severe tone, "If you do, Nadege, I renounce you as my child forever."

Nadege left her father in a state of violent grief and despair. She returned to her own house. It was being searched. All Stepane's drawers had been broken open; all his papers and books were seized.

"Take everything!" said Nadege. "Search everywhere, and you will find that he is innocent."

She did not know that the very day before Padlewsky had sent a parcel of prohibited books to Stepane.

The commissary of police, who was directing the search, gave a singular smile at her words. That smile alarmed her. She set out again to go to Wanda.

CHAPTER XXVI

THE PETITION

Verenine answered his pretty cousin's letter immediately. He was in a disturbed state of mind himself. He had gone that morning to the palace, where he was on duty, and had been informed that, by the orders of the Emperor, his position was filled.

He was in disgrace.

How long would it last? Doubtless the Czar suspected him of being mixed up with the nihilists. Litzanoff had been arrested; he might expect the same himself.

"Why don't you hide? "said Wanda.

"That would be confessing myself guilty, and how can I run away?" he added, sighing, and casting a look of mingled anguish and love at Wanda.

She understood that look, and it touched her with a species of remorse. But since Verenine was in disgrace he could be of no use whatever to the cause, and his lukewarmness and vacillation might lead him to commit grave mistakes. He was too timid, too susceptible, to keep a secret. Under these circumstances it was quite useless, nay, even cruel, to lead him to believe that she could ever love him.

"Dear Alexis," she said, "I have something to tell you, but I do not know how to begin, for I am afraid it will distress you."

"Are you going to leave Petersburg?" asked Verenine.

"No, not just now."

"Ah, if I should not be able to see you."

"You love me, I am sure, and that is precisely the thing that embarrasses me."

"Wanda, are you going to be married?"

"Yes and no."

"What do you mean?"

Verenine could hardly speak; he was livid. Wanda took pity on him.

"Yes, I am going to be married without being married. The cause demands all my energies; I am not allowed to think of any selfish affection. Always on the point of arrest or of transportation to Siberia, I have no right to dream of love, nor of any great happiness."

"Explain what you mean, Wanda; you are killing me."

"I am going to marry so that I can come into possession of my mother's fortune, which is now held by my father. Do you understand?"

"But why do you not choose me for your husband?"

"Because you are in love with me."

"But I will promise to respect you as if you were my sister."

"No, Alexis, it is impossible. Besides, I have other reasons. You are a nobleman, you are rich, you are a Russian; I wish none of these things."

"Ah, I understand," said Verenine, looking down to prevent her from seeing the tears in his eyes, "you have selected Monsieur Chabert. But he is in love with you, too."

"How do you know that?"

"I saw it plainly enough. Wanda, Wanda! Before you enter into such relations with him, reflect what you are doing. Are you sure of him? Can you trust his honor, his loyalty, his unselfishness, his disinterestedness?"

"His disinterestedness? He knows nothing of my intention."

"Then," said Verenine, "listen to my last entreaty. Remember how long I have loved you; since my childhood I have always been devoted to you; have I not always tried to please you and to keep my love from troubling you?"

"But, dear Alexis, it would be unendurable for me to have a husband who would be always complaining about my cruelty, my coldness, my insensibility."

"But don't you think that other men will be just as importunate as I am? As it is not a question of love with you, why cannot you trust yourself to my honor? Wanda, let me be your husband, at least in name. It would be something to me to see you every day."

"My good Verenine, I have perfect confidence in you, but I cannot do what you ask me. I have confided this secret to you because I do not wish any longer to be an obstacle in your career. I do not think there is in you the stuff for a conspirator. Listen to me, and take my advice: marry some sweet good woman who will love you. You are neither romantic nor adventurous. To speak plainly, your timidity would be embarrassing and even dangerous to me in the career which I have marked out for myself."

"You are punishing me very heavily for my hesitation."

"We have to be what we are, my dear Alexis. There is nothing that I have said which should possibly wound you."

At this moment Nadege came in. She told her friend of her unsuccessful interview with her father. She was in despair.

Wanda looked at the two loving, gentle, weak creatures before her, and said to herself, "How happy these two could have been together!"

She stood lost in thought for some time, then said, "We must address a petition to the Emperor. Will you take it, Alexis?"

"Yes, I will carry it to the Grand Duke. If the Emperor is kind and liberal, the Grand Duke is still more so."

"You adore despotism, Verenine," said Wanda, severely.

"I condemn the system, but I render justice to the men."

Nadege seized a pen and tried to write; her hand trembled so that she could not. Wanda took the pen out of her fingers and in a large, bold, rapid hand, traced the following words:

Sire:

An act of injustice has been committed in your name by the agents of the secret police. Count Stepane Litzanoff, my husband, was arrested this morning, and is now confined in the fortress of Petropavlosk. What was the cause of this arrest? A few words of disapproval elicited by the conduct of General Trepoff in flogging Bogoluboff, a political prisoner. As corporal punishment has been abolished by command of Your Majesty, why is it considered a crime to blame an officer for disobedience to your law?

Count Litzanoff, who is ill of a fever, was dragged from his bed to be immured in a damp, cold dungeon. This arrest may cause his death. I come before Your Majesty to ask if a few imprudent words are to be punished by death? I appeal to your great goodness, to your lofty sense of justice, to obtain his immediate release, or at least his transportation into a hospital, where I can be near him, and take care of him.

I remain Your Majesty's humble subject,
Nadege Litzanoff

Verenine went away at once, taking the letter with him.

"If this does not succeed," said Wanda, "I will try something else."

"What will you try?" asked Nadege.

"I cannot tell you, dear. I do not think you are strong enough to be trusted with our secrets. With your weeping eyes and pale face, you do not seem to me made of the stuff of which heroes and martyrs are formed."

"You do not know me, Wanda; I am a Slav, and although I look so frail, I have within me a mighty power. If they will not give me back Stepane, you will see of what I am capable."

Wanda touched a bell, and Katia appeared.

"Bring me my hat and coat; if Raymond Chabert calls while I am out, tell him to wait for me, or else to come back tomorrow morning.

She drove off with Nadege, whom she left at her own door. Then, asking her to lend her carriage for a while, she drove on to Padlewsky's.

Padlewsky lived on the right bank of the Neva, in a little house full of flowers and birds and animals of all kinds. After passing five hours of each day in the office of the Minister of the Interior he came home to this little place, which he called his hermitage.

In fact, this quiet, respectable hermitage was a rendezvous for the nihilists. All his servants, of whom he had ten, were nihilists in disguise. Although this was his home, he was but seldom to be found in it.

Wanda was unwilling to bring Nadege with her because she knew in all probability she would have to look for him in one of his secret hiding places.

She rang the bell. The faithful Korolef came down to open the door.

"Is Padlewsky in?" she asked.

"Is your business urgent?"

"Yes."

"Come on," he said, curtly.

Wanda got into the carriage again. Korolef seated himself beside the coachman. They drove along the quay as far as Vassili Ostrow. Then Korolef got down and opened the door. "Send your carriage away," he said in French. Wanda ordered Nadege's coachman to drive home.

Vassili Ostrow was the largest and most considerable of the islands in the Neva. It was not only an important commercial center, as it contained the Exchange, but it was also the part of the city in which the University and the Public Schools were situated. Formerly Vassili Ostrow was called the German quarter, for then both science and trade were in the hands of the Germans. And German still was as frequently spoken as Russian in this populous portion of Petersburg.

It presented quite a different aspect from the fashionable part of the town. There were no brilliant uniforms, no elegant dresses, no handsome equipages. Along the quays the boatmen and the sailors were at work. In the large squares and the narrow streets men and women could be seen with books under their arms. The private houses were small; there were no handsome warehouses, such as could be found in the Perspective Newsky, but little modest shops where one could buy the necessaries of life.

Korolef led Wanda into a shop outside of which were hanging old clothes.

"Come in here," he said. "You cannot go with me dressed as you are in that handsome cloak and hat."

"Can you loan me a coat and hat and pair of felt boots for a few hours?" said he to the shop woman, who hastened forward at the sight of Wanda.

"Here is a very good cloak," she said.

"That will do," answered Korolef, taking off Wanda's covering. "We will leave this with you until we return. Now give me that waterproof and that black straw hat."

"They belonged to a nihilist who has just been arrested," said the woman. "His landlord sold them to me to get rid of them; he was afraid they would compromise him."

"Put on this waterproof," said Korolef to Wanda. "Pull the hat down over your eyes; now let us go."

They turned into the street that runs between the Academy of Fine Arts and the School of Cadets. It was the first time that Wanda had ever penetrated into this part of the town, curious both in its aspect and by the strange population that inhabited it.

To what class did these strange beings belong? These young men were invariably dressed in greasy, ragged fur clothes; they had intelligent, expressive faces; but at the same time they were cold and sad. They walked slowly and quietly. There was no laughing nor singing in the streets. These were men who thought, yet dare not express their thoughts. The women make no attempts at elegance or grace. Sometimes under their hideous black straw hats one detected a pretty face, but they seemed to like to wear blue spectacles. And they walked on, sad and silent, like the men. Here, more than anywhere else, one seemed to feel the heavy weight which pressed upon the Russian people.

Wanda watched them with a growing interest.

"They all belong to us, Korolef, do they not?"

"They are students, otherwise nihilists."

"Where are we going?" asked Wanda.

"To the Jew Isaac's tavern."

"Shall we find Padlewsky there?"

"Yes, he has gone there to meet two agents of the Third Section."

"Of the Third Section?" said Wanda, in dismay.

"We have our men in the Third Section," answered Korolef.

"But can you trust them?"

"To be sure we can."

"Do you pay them very high?"

"No, they are nihilists. Through Padlewsky's influence they were taken into the employ of the Third Section, and they keep us apprized of all our enemies movements. We have some of our men among Trepoff's police, likewise."

At the corner of a little street, Korolef stopped. "This is our place," he said.

Taverns are very numerous in Russia, especially in Vassili Ostrow. They are a species of cellars, in which Greeks, Jews, and industrious mujiks have established coffee houses, restaurants and bakeries.

"Be careful," said Korolef to Wanda. "Take hold of the banister."

Wanda went down a staircase of eight steps covered with slippery snow and ice. At the bottom was a grated door. Korolef lifted the latch, and they entered a little room in which a quantity of fur cloaks were hanging. The cloaks were greasy, dirty, torn in places, slimy, and covered with snow.

A young mujik, who seemed half asleep, took Wanda's cloak. They crossed a long dirty hall where red lamps shed their light upon splotchy tablecloths. These tables were served by Tartars dressed in black — princes perhaps, who had been unfortunate.

The room was full, and yet not a word was spoken. All the people present ate and drank slowly, without making the least noise. It was a feast of phantoms. As they passed through this room Wanda shuddered. "What is the matter with all those frozen men and women?" said she in Korolef's ear.

"They are philosophers, scientists, energetic characters, almost all of them nihilists," answered Korolef. "They do not speak because they wish to act. And it is so dangerous to talk."

Korolef opened a second door. He ushered Wanda into a small study. There sat Padlewsky with two strangers, all three disguised in true nihilist fashion.

On a table, lighted by a smoky candle, stood some glasses, the eternal samovars, and a bottle of kvass.

"Have you heard the news?" said Wanda, as soon as she came in. "Count Litzanoff is arrested."

"We were just talking about it," answered Padlewsky.

"His wife is nearly crazy. That is why I have come here to see you, and to tell you what we have done."

"I have news of the prisoner," said Padlewsky, "brought by our friends here. This is the Princess Wanda Kryloff," he said, turning to the two individuals, "you can be perfectly easy."

"Well, what have you found out?" asked Wanda.

"Litzanoff's arrest is a serious affair," answered Padlewsky.

"He is confined in the fortress," said Wanda.

"Yes, he has just undergone an examination. He was superb, magnificent, but his answers have very much aggravated his situation, and he will probably be sent to Siberia."

"But he is ill," interrupted Wanda. "He may die in prison. Upon my advice his wife has written a petition to the Emperor, asking that her husband may be sent to the hospital."

They all approved of this. "If we can obtain that, we can easily liberate him. What do you think, Korolef?"

Korolef simply bowed his head.

"Is there any other important news?" asked Wanda.

"Yes; the Minister of the Interior has been blaming Trepoff for his violence in regard to Bogoluboff. And there is a quarrel between the Third Section and the Minister of the Interior."

"If we have any one in our interests in the fortress," continued Wanda, "why cannot we obtain news about Litzanoff, especially about his health?"

"I shall hear tomorrow. I hope, indeed, to be able to hold communications with him."

Wanda's face shone with delight.

"Oh, try to encourage him! Tell him that we think of him, that we will never forsake him. I am so afraid that in a moment of weakness he may allow something to escape him."

"Oh, no," said Padlewsky, "never! Litzanoff is imprudent, but he is the noblest man I know, certainly the bravest."

"When can you give us some news about him?"

"Tomorrow."

"Where shall I see you?"

"At your own house, if you will allow me."

"No, that is too dangerous. My father suspects me, and watches me closely. But I am going to the factory where Matcha Mikouline is engaged. I can see you there."

"I have a little office near the factory. I shall be there about two o'clock."

"What street is it in? What number?"

"There are no numbers. You will find me in the house back of the church. Ask for Ivan Martyne."

Korolef took Wanda back to the second-hand clothes dealer, where she picked up her cloak and hat. Hailing a cab, he put her in it.

"Drive to the Palace Kryloff," he said to the coachman.

In a short time Wanda drew up at her own door. Her father saw her alight from this miserable little vehicle and could hardly believe his eyes. His daughter in such an equipage? Had she forgotten all dignity, all respect for herself? He feared to give way to his temper, for he saw that by so doing he merely widened the breach between them.

For two days since she had upbraided him with the name of Michael Federoff he had been perfectly wretched. Who had told her? Her mother, perhaps, or Michael himself. Were they in Petersburg? Did she go to see them when she went out in this mysterious manner? This thought nearly drove him frantic. He determined to follow his daughter and demand an explanation.

Wanda heard her Father's footsteps behind her, but she never turned round, nor did she say a word; feeling what he was coming for commenced the blood surging in her veins.

She went into her boudoir. Her knees were trembling, but she drew herself up and in a determined attitude awaited the coming of the Prince.

He came in a few moments and closed the door noisily behind him.

"What do you want with me?" said Wanda.

"The most mysterious things are constantly going on in this house, and I want to know what it all means. Do you understand me? Where have you been."

"I took Nadege home, and as she wished to use her carriage, I came back in a hack."

"You lie."

"Yes. I do."

"Why do you lie?"

"Because you question me. I told you that if you asked me questions I should lie to you. You are asking me questions, and I am lying."

The Prince lifted his hand.

"Take care!" said Wanda. "You did not get the better of my mother; you will not get the better of her daughter. I have Polish blood in my veins. I am more of a Pole than of a Russian. Poles are not cowardly, like the Russians; they will not obey."

"I will lock you up, as I did your mother."

"We shall see about that."

"Would you dare to resist me?"

"Yes, I would."

"Then it is a case of open rebellion?"

"It is."

"I see you are a nihilist."

"I shall become one; you wish me to become one."

"I wish you to be a nihilist? What I wish is that we shall leave Petersburg at once."

"I will not go."

"I will make you."

"I am of age."

"Of age? What is the law to me? Is there any law in Russia for princes of my rank and fortune?"

"It is true, there is no law for you, but there is law for me, and I will not go."

The Prince began to laugh in a terrible way, breaking the furniture around him at the same time. Suddenly drawing out a little dagger, he exclaimed: "Do not exasperate me too far! I might kill you."

Wanda saw that she was in danger. She thought of Litzanoff, dying perhaps in his dark cell, needing her aid; she resolved to soothe her father's anger.

"I was wrong," she said, "to say what if did. But just as you cannot control your temper, I cannot subdue my pride. Try to be less violent towards me, for our quarrels only drive us farther and farther apart."

She uttered these words in a gentle, tender voice. The Prince drew her towards him, and wished to kiss her, but she thought of her mother, and she could not control herself from shrinking away from his embrace.

"You do not love me," he said. "Some one has turned your heart away from me. It must be that woman who has already caused me such bitter pain."

He buried his face in his hands.

"Yes," he continued, "she has stolen your heart from me, and she has made a, socialist of you."

"Be calm, father. I will kiss you; are you satisfied now?" said Wanda.

"No, no, you do not love me; you hate me, just as she hated me. Ah, I am wretched, wretched."

He completely broke down, and sobbed aloud.

"Be kind to me, be just," said Wanda, wishing to take advantage of this momentary weakness. "Give me my liberty, and you will see that I will love you as I used to do."

"I will leave you," said the Prince, rushing out of the room.

When he had gone, Wanda looked at the clock. It was half past four. Chabert must soon come.

She lay down upon a sofa, for she was exhausted. These violent scenes were killing her. Her relations with her father were growing more and more unbearable. She must have a legal protector, a husband who could take her away from her father's house.

She was waiting for Raymond with genuine emotion. On the coming interview depended her entire life.

CHAPTER XXVII

THE SHAM MARRIAGE

When at five o'clock Raymond entered Wanda's drawing-room, he found her lying on a sofa, very pale, and apparently very much agitated. She told him all that had happened that morning.

"I could not sleep last night," said he; "your words excited my curiosity so that my imagination wandered into the wildest realms of fancy."

"Did you not guess what I meant?"

"No."

"It is very hard for me to tell you," she said, sighing heavily.

"Anything that you say to me will be well received; you know that."

"You don't know what I am going to say."

"I say again, anything that you desire of me shall be granted."

"I wish to speak to you on the subject of marriage."

"So you said yesterday, but I cannot understand what I have to do in the matter. Do you desire me to make a proposal to some one?"

"You have not guessed right. A certain gentleman has to be asked if he will accept a young girl's hand."

"Is the young girl a friend of yours?"

"The young girl is myself."

"Do you intend to marry?"

"Yes."

"And you wish me to undertake this negotiation?" asked Raymond, much stupefied.

"Not exactly."

"Please tell me what you do mean."

"In the first place, dear Raymond," said Wanda, "what do you think of marriage, of the position and of the rights of a husband?"

"In my eyes, marriage is a form which enables two beings to live together openly."

"In your eyes, then, it is merely a form."

"A form and a contract."

"And you don't think that the woman owes obedience to her husband?"

"I think, on the contrary, that the man, being the stronger of the two, should submit his own will to the woman. That is the natural consequence of a genuine love."

"All this gallantry fills me with despair," said Wanda, laughing. "The new doctrine does not admit of any inequality between a man and a woman."

"As for me," continued Raymond, "I look upon the man as inferior to the woman, and in marriage his place is to obey."

"Incorrigible flatterer! That is not so. A man should not obey his wife, but he should respect her dignity. I should never allow my husband to tyrannize over me, even in a matter of affection. This tyranny is excusable between two lovers, who are not bound by any legal tie, but as soon as a man claims this tyranny as a right given him by law, he is odious! Perhaps these new ideas may shock you?"

"Nothing that comes from you, Wanda, can shock me."

"You once told me that you were willing to devote your life to me."

"I did."

"I know well the exaggerations of lovers, for already ten men have offered to devote their lives to me."

"I am not astonished at that."

"Yet there is but one man whose offer I trust, and that man is yourself, Raymond."

"Oh, thanks!"

"Still, you are far from imagining what I am going to ask of you."

"I have told you already there is no sacrifice that I would not make for you."

"You know that I have devoted my life to the cause."

"I know it, and I share with you your convictions and your hopes."

"Are your convictions real, or do they spring from a simple desire to please me?"

"Both. To please you I studied, then I reflected, and then I became convinced."

"Perfectly convinced?"

"Perfectly."

"You know that in our society some of us are forbidden to marry. In the position that I hold, I am not allowed to marry. Do you see why?"

"Yes, I understand that marriage does not fit the life of an apostle."

"And besides, love is talkative."

"Truly, love opens the heart. I could never have a secret from . . ."

"Hush!" interrupted Wanda.

"Why?"

"The word love must never be pronounced between you and me. This is the state of the case," she continued. "In my father's house my every action is fettered, and I cannot fulfill the mission that I will fulfill at the risk of my life. My father suspects me, he watches me; he will soon find out something. There is danger not only for me but for my friends; danger to which I will not expose them. Then, you know that my father and mother are separated."

"Your mother? I thought she was dead."

"No, she is still alive. The letter that you brought me the other day was from her. It was the history of her life. You have seen her. She lives with Doctor Federoff, to whom you owe your life."

"That handsome woman your mother? One can see that she has suffered. Does the Prince know that she still lives?"

"He begins to suspect it, and my situation is growing daily more embarrassing. His temper is fearful, terrible; he kept my mother locked up for years, and he has just threatened to do the same to me."

"And you wish to marry so as to escape from under the control of your father?"

"I wish to marry without marrying."

"I think I understand you."

"I wish to contract a sham marriage, as Princess Tizianoff and Katerine Cambredelidze did. By marrying I shall obtain my independence, and likewise my mother's fortune, which at present is in my father's hands."

"And whom have you chosen as your husband?"

"You, Raymond."

"Me! Me!" exclaimed the young Frenchman.

"I must have a great confidence in your devotion to me, must I not? For I know that the feeling you have for me is not entirely fraternal."

"My feeling for you, dear Wanda, shall be whatever you wish it to be."

"Are you sure?"

"I swear to you it is so."

"I must tell you one thing more, which may perhaps arouse your jealousy."

At these words, Raymond grew pale, but in a moment he answered: "Having no pretension to your love, how could I be jealous?"

"Will you never be jealous?"

"Never."

"Even if I love another man, while I bear your name?"

"Do you love another man?" said Raymond, in a choking voice.

"He is not free to marry, and you ought to know me well enough to be certain that I will never do anything to compromise my dignity."

As Wanda spoke she watched Raymond attentively. He hid his face in his hands, and sat for some moments perfectly still.

"It is as I thought," said Wanda. "You have all the French prejudices in regard to the honor of the husband."

Raymond raised his face; it was bathed in tears.

"Oh!" cried Wanda, "what have I done? Raymond, forgive me! I had to tell you the whole truth. If I had supposed your love for me was so strong I never should have thought of proposing this marriage to you."

"The shock has been terrible," said Raymond, "but it is over. Forgive me for my weakness. Hereafter you will find in me a brother, a slave; the most devoted brother, the most humble slave."

"But the marriage."

"It can take place whenever you will. I belong to you; you can use me as you please. It is great happiness for me to live by your side, to know that you have such confidence in me."

"If you become my husband," continued Wanda, "you will be exposed to a great deal of danger. My father will have a paroxysm of rage. He may apply to the police to get rid of you. You see how they have treated Litzanoff. In Russia one is never secure. I give you eight days to think about all this."

"I don't need eight days to think about it. I have made up my mind. If I am in danger, you are in danger too, and naturally I shall be your protector. You have given me a noble part to play."

"Perhaps you think you are going to marry a Princess. Not so; the day that I leave my father's house I shall lay aside my rank and my fortune. The money that will come to me from my mother will be thrown into the fund of the Society of Deliverance. You are not only called upon to accept a life of danger, but a hard life, a life of work."

"I accept it all with gratitude. Only promise me that you will not cut off your hair, and that you will not wear blue spectacles."

"How French you are!" said Wanda, smiling, as she laid her lovely hand in his.

CHAPTER XXVIII

APPRENTICESHIP

In spite of the opinion of the Revolutionary Committee, Wanda had never given up her idea of going among the common people to teach them her doctrines.

Katia knew a young girl named Matcha Mikouline, who had finished her education, and was now engaged in learning a trade in one of the Petersburg factories. Wanda wanted to make her acquaintance.

It was the first time that Wanda had paid a visit to the factory, although Katia had spoken to her about it very frequently. It was situated in a remote part of the city, in a wide, marshy plain without streets, houses, or pavements. Miserable huts, some of them half sunk in the ground, were reflected in the waters of the Neva. These wretched abodes were the homes of the workmen. For a few kopecks a day they could get board and lodging. To be sure, their diet consisted of cucumbers, cabbage and salt fish. Still it was something to eat, and they did not, at any rate, die of hunger. The population consisted entirely of poor people. The speculators had built a large factory in this place. There were so many inhabitants there, and the living was so cheap, that they could hire workmen at very low wages.

Padlewsky had said to Wanda: "At two o'clock, at the house just back of the church, ask for Ivan Martyne."

It was half-past one when they reached the banks of the Neva. They left their sleigh there and proceeded on foot across the path made in the frozen snow by the workmen. They soon reached an open space in front of the church. Just behind it they perceived a miserable little hut, decorated with a sign, on which a painted samovar and a huge bottle surmounted these letters: VODKA. This was a tavern.

Katia pushed open the door. The interior was as wretched as the exterior. A few rickety tables, some wooden benches, an old clock, and a stove furnished the little room, which had only an earthen floor.

An old woman, with her head wrapped up in the remnants of a shawl, sat by the stove mending clothes. Several children, tattered and dirty, were playing on the ground.

"Is Ivan Martyne here?" asked Wanda.

Padlewsky was waiting for them in an adjoining room. He was writing.

"Whose house is this?" asked Wanda.

"It belongs to my clerk. He only gets twelve roubles a month, and that has to support his wife, his mother, and her five children. I have got his wife into the factory, but she does not receive any pay as yet; they say her work is not good enough. The old mother sells tea and vodka. The whole family is with us."

"Tell us about the prisoner," broke in Wanda.

"He has undergone a second examination this morning, and although weak from fever, he acquitted himself admirably. He has avowed himself a nihilist, and refuses to answer any questions."

"How did you hear all this?"

"We have a friend in the fortress, one of the turnkeys. The jailor, like all Russians, drinks. Our friend soaks him well with vodka, then takes the keys and carries the prisoners their food, and so can hold communication with all the nihilists in the fortress."

"Could we get Litzanoff out by means of that man?"

"Oh, no, that would be against our principles! We could not save Litzanoff without endangering the life of Andrew Kowalski; besides, we should lose our means of communication with the other prisoners."

"That is true," said Wanda. "Is Kowalski a Pole?"

"Yes, and a Pole never becomes a Russian at heart. At the first ray of hope, we shall see them every one forsake this accursed government."

"Has he seen Litzanoff?"

"Yes, this very morning."

"Where is he?"

"In cell No. 9."

Wanda grew pale as death.

"And his health, his wounds?"

"Thanks to Kowalski's care, he is better."

"Has he grown more quiet? He is so violent, so excitable! I dread the results of his outbreaks."

"He is much less agitated than he was. Kowalski asked him if he wished to write to any one. At first he appeared delighted at the thought; but perhaps he distrusts Kowalski, for he put off writing until tomorrow."

"Thank you for your good news. We are waiting now for the answer to our petition; meanwhile we are going to the factory."

"What for? I can tell you everything about the workmen. Our last pamphlets have had a wonderful effect. Almost all of them have come over to us."

"It is not only to preach that I want to go. I am going to begin my apprenticeship today."

She threw aside her fur cloak and showed herself dressed in a faded cotton gown, with a woolen kerchief crossed over her breast.

"Are you in earnest?" he said.

"I am indeed; this morning I cut off my long nails. We simplified women do not allow long nails."

Padlewsky looked compassionately upon that little, delicate, white hand, with its rosy, shell-like palm.

"Have pity upon those lovely hands!" he said.

"Wretched aristocrat!" answered Wanda. "If I were not obliged to live in the society which I despise, I would cut off my hair too."

"Oh, that would be a crime!" exclaimed Padlewsky.

"You are romantic, effeminate, aesthetic!" exclaimed Wanda.

"My pretty little sister, I am in no sense a communist. I acknowledge the monarchy of grace, of beauty, of intelligence and of talent, the hierarchy of nature; for, truth to tell, nature is in no wise republican."

"You are a traitor," said Wanda, laughing, "and I think we will denounce you."

"My dear child, do not fancy for a moment that the rich and powerful of this earth are perfectly happy. There are moral tortures, pangs of wounded vanity, frustrated ambitions, troubles of the heart, harder to bear than poverty and hard work."

"Doubtless you are right," said Wanda. "But at present we can only make the revolution by means of the people, and for that purpose we must live among them and know their life."

"Why not go to the linen warehouse that we have started for the common people? You would learn to sew there."

"That is too confining, and there we have so little opportunity to spread our doctrines."

"The longer I look at you, my dear Wanda, the more am I convinced that you will never, with your appearance, be able to pass as a working woman."

"We shall see. At any rate, I must be something for myself, for I cannot live in my father's house much longer.

She then told him her idea about her marriage.

"Do you think a man can live with you like that? How old is he?"

"He is twenty-eight. It is that young Frenchman that I spoke to you about."

"A Frenchman above all others!"

"He is converted. He is one of us."

"Converted?"

"Yes."

"No doubt he is converted to the fact that you have very fine eyes. A Frenchman! Twenty-eight years old!"

"You evidently do not like the French."

"Perhaps I am jealous that you did not think of me."

"I did think of you, Padlewsky, but you are necessary to the party. You hold too high a position; you have too much to do. I want some one who will be perfectly devoted to me, and this Raymond Chabert will be. But I must say goodbye, we must go."

"I must speak to you alone for one minute," said Padlewsky. Katia withdrew into the adjoining room.

"The delegates from Kiev, Odessa, and Moscow will be here tomorrow. We are going to have a meeting in the night to pass sentence upon several offenders, among others, Trepoff. There will be much discussion. I am opposed to violent measures. What do you say?"

"I am also," answered Wanda, "particularly opposed to the death sentence. I do not think any man has the right to take another's life."

"I depend upon you to support me. Violence is in the air. I am afraid they will do something foolish."

"I wish," said Wanda, "you would speak to them about my marriage. Narkileff, I think, will make out the marriage contract for me, and you and Siline can be the witnesses."

"Think it over well," said Padlewsky. "I do not think the Committee will permit it."

"When they hear my motives I think they will, but I must have a perfectly legal marriage, without my father's consent. Narkileff, I suppose, can arrange it for me. Speak to him about it."

"I will do whatever you wish, but take care how you contract this engagement, which may seriously fetter your actions."

"My dear Padlewsky, it is only a marriage in name."

They left the room together. Padlewsky had a sweet, sad smile upon his lips. He admired Wanda enthusiastically. He had none of the rigidity of a nihilist; he was a socialist, but he was a man who watched his opportunity. He loved Poland and hated Russia. In spite of his genial nature, he was a thorough revolutionist, devoted, and if necessary, resolved.

Wanda and Katia, went on to the factory. The foreman had been apprized of their visit and came forward to meet them. He led them into a room where twenty young women were winding off thread into skeins.

"He is one of us," whispered Matcha to Katia. "We have gained over almost all the factories in Petersburg and the suburbs. I hope soon to be able to go to Orenbourg, where there are no apostles. Beyond the immediate neighborhood of Moscow, Kiev, and Odessa, there is still so much to do."

"The Russian Empire is so vast," said Wanda, "that I think it is a waste of time to attempt to convert the rural populations. It would take too long a time. We had better confine ourselves to more central points. The peasantry are very timid, and unwilling to act in any decisive manner. But once the movement begins I think we may count upon them to rise in a body and rid themselves of the oppressors who have trodden upon them for so many years."

"Before we bring about an insurrection I think we had better be sure of success," answered Matcha. "Look at the rising of 1825. What good did it do? It simply ended in the murder or exile of one hundred and twenty of our men. I belong at present," she continued, "to a new society called 'The Initiators.' We do nothing but preach the truth. We believe that the people must be slowly saturated with our doctrines before any general movement can be made."

Just then the overseer came up to them.

"Say nothing before him," whispered Matcha. "He is one of us, but he knows none of our secrets."

Wanda and Katia began their work; it is easy enough to do, but it required skill which practice alone could give. At the end of an hour Wanda was perfectly exhausted. Katia kept bravely on, but the Princess's muscles were not so strong. Tears of mortification stood in her eyes at the discovery of her own physical weakness. She bit her lips and said to herself, "I will learn. I will be a working woman; why does my body rebel against my will in this manner?"

The girls were watching Wanda with curiosity, and smiling at her. They perceived that she was a person of rank, from her appearance and attitude, as well as from her weak, slender, white hands.

The overseer laughingly handed each of them a ten kopeck piece. "Take this," he said. "You have not gained much today, but we give you this to encourage you. Maybe tomorrow you will do better."

Wanda put the bit of money in her pocket. "Do you know, Katia," she said, "I am very proud of my ten kopecks? It is the first time that I ever earned any money. Up to this time I have been nothing but a parasite, deriving my support from others, and giving them nothing in return."

And this Princess, whose father's income was one hundred thousand roubles a year, kept taking the ten-kopeck piece out of her pocket and looking at it with a sort of loving admiration,

"I shall always keep this," she said, "as a souvenir of one of the happiest days of my life."

As she drove away from the factory, a beggar girl, clothed in an old fur coat full of holes, held up her little hand, blue with the cold, for help. The Princess gave her a "blue-note."

"Alms giving is against my principles," she said. "But perhaps that little thing has a mother in the factory, who works all day long, and can barely make enough to buy food for her children."

CHAPTER XXIX

THE DEATH SENTENCE

The next day, at midnight, the Revolutionary Committee met. It consisted of six members of the ordinary committee: Komoff, Narkileff, Siline, Poloutkin, Padlewsky, and Wanda. There were, besides, two delegates from Kiev, two from Odessa, and two from Moscow, twelve persons in all.

Siline first took the stand. He made a short but powerful speech, very violent, and as eloquent as the orations of the French Convention, whose style he carefully copied. The Russian nihilists, on the contrary, affected a great coolness and simplicity of speech.

After him Komoff arose. "The time has come," he said, "for us to pronounce sentence upon our persecutors. We are tracked like wild beasts, arrested, tortured, thrust into prisons, driven into mines, exiled from our native lands. Today, throughout all Russia, we are dying, martyrs to the cause of justice. The forms of trial that they grant us are a farce. We are allowed no defense. The accusations are tissues of lies and slanders. We must protest in some energetic manner against the ceaseless cruelties of our enemies. We must show them that nothing can shake our faith. They must understand that we too have a court and judge and jury. They kill us; let us show them that we can kill them!"

Padlewsky followed with a very able argument, dissenting from the propositions of his brothers. He represented that the executions by the nihilist party had no good effect whatever; that they merely brought about more strenuous measures against themselves, while they in no way intimidated the Government. Trepoff, for instance, was very popular in Petersburg, and his death would do them much more harm than good, and probably alienate many of those who at present wished them well. Finally, he urged them to be patient, lest they should compromise the revolution instead of hastening it.

"My dear Padlewsky," said Narkileff, "the position of the Russian people is this: for years the revolution has been in swaddling clothes; the time has come for her to stretch her limbs, to throw off the robes of her infancy, to breathe, to move, to feed her own strength. Freedom! Liberty! Thus she cries. She has thrown prudence to the winds; her one longing is for action. The time for study and for meditation is past: she would rather risk and lose all than remain inert under a crushing despotism. We can wait no longer. The movement hurries us on, in spite of ourselves, in its irresistible, passionate, fore-doomed course. Around us the old feudal world is crumbling away; the old creeds, the old political systems totter under the weight of their own powerlessness. In the day of their power did they give the people liberty, did they give the people bread? But a new day is dawning; we live but in the hope of that day. It is for us Russians, the most oppressed people in the world, to raise the standard of revolt; we are bitter, we are sceptics, we are rebels; we scorn death as no other nation does. We have a wild, barbarous power known only to ourselves. And we must have this revolution, if costs us our every possession. If it costs us even our life. And shall we hesitate to put a few criminals to death?"

"I hope I am as desirous of the revolution as you are," answered Padlewsky. "But is it practicable just now? I think not. Transition is a law of nature. Perhaps in a century or thereabouts . . .

"A century! Wait a hundred years for the revolution!" screamed Siline. "Our duty is to hurry it on."

"A few isolated executions will not hasten it," continued Padlewsky. "They will retard it. By these means you will arouse the nations of Europe against you, and you will intimidate the Russian people, who are accustomed to despotism, and who fear their rulers."

Then Wanda stood up, and said with much simplicity: "I represent in your committee the female element, an element which the revolutionists of the West have never admitted into their assemblies, although women constitute one-half of the human race. In the name of all women, I implore you to respect human life; I implore you to shed no blood. Do not stain the purity and nobility of our cause by acts of vengeance and barbarity. We wish to found a social order, based upon peace, clemency and happiness. These are, in my opinion, the only means to revolutionize the world."

She said no more, but the total silence that ensued showed her that her views had not been acceptable.

"Now," said Siline, "we will form ourselves into a court, and pass judgment upon the criminals. The facts are already proved. I will recount them to you. First, Trepoff, chief of Police in Petersburg. I need not recall to you his many acts of cruelty. The last and most revolting one is the flogging of our brother, Bogoluboff.

"Second, Mezentzoff, Colonel of the Armed Police. His latest crime is the iniquitous arrest of Stepane Litzanoff, who, dangerously ill of a fever, has been thrown into an icy prison for a few hasty words thoughtlessly expressed.

"Third, Heyking, Captain of Armed Police, Chief of Police at Kiev. He has arrested and imprisoned a number of our brothers and subjected them to hunger, thirst and total solitude. He has sent off two of them without trial, one to Tobolsk, the other to Iskousk. They both died on the road as consequence of ill treatment.

"Fourth, at Odessa, the son of a wealthy merchant, who was one of us, betrayed us to the police, and revealed our place of meeting. Twenty socialists were arrested and thrown into prison."

"Death to the traitor, and at once!" exclaimed Komoff.

"Fifth, at Moscow, a wretched Captain of Infantry struck one of our brothers with his sword, and then kicked him severely, for refusing to denounce the nihilists of Moscow to him.

"Sixth, the son of a noble family betrayed a friend of his who was striving to enter our ranks. He has been shut up in prison, and we have been able to do nothing for him."

"Kill him! Kill him!" exclaimed Komoff, Poloutkin, and the six delegates, all at once.

"I think," said Narkileff, "that we have no right to strike until we have first warned the criminals of their approaching fate; so shall we have the approval of the popular mind."

"Let us now cast our votes," said the President.

The vote was taken in perfect silence.

Trepoff and the two traitors were condemned to death. Two members only had voted against the sentence: Wanda and Padlewsky. Mezentzoff, Heyking, and the Captain were to receive warnings.

"Who shall execute our sentence," asked Siline.

"Several have offered," said Komoff.

"Name them."

Komoff read out the names; one was the name of a woman.

"Who is this woman?" objected one of them.

"I know her," replied Siline. "She is a heroine. She is a friend and disciple of the unfortunate Netchaieff. Although very modest, she is brave. Let us cast lots, and if it falls upon her you can depend upon her."

"Then," said Komoff, "are we to cast lots now in order to choose from these volunteers those who will carry our sentences into execution?"

"Yes."

Each of the names was written upon a piece of paper, which was carefully rolled up and then thrown into an urn.

"First," said the President, "who shall kill Trepoff?"

Wanda was called upon to draw the lots. She put her hand into the urn and took out one of the bits of paper.

Komoff opened it and read, "Vera Zassoulitch,"

They went through the same form in choosing the executioners for the other offenders. Then they separated, deeply impressed by the results of their meeting.

Two days after that, on the 23rd of January, a young girl was walking with a firm step towards the palace in which the Chief of Police daily received his petitioners.

She stood in the ante-chamber waiting for Trepoff. Vera Zassoulitch held a revolver in her hand, concealed by her long fur cloak. As Trepoff passed in front of her she raised her arm and fired, and the General, severely wounded, fell at her feet.

The telegraph carried the news to the four quarters of the globe. Europe, for one instant, forgot Peace, War, everything, to gaze upon this act of courage, upon this unknown heroine. Two days later, at a grand ball given in Biajan by one of the wealthiest families of the city, the dead body of a young nobleman was found stretched out at the foot of the principle staircase. His assassin could not be discovered.

Also, at Odessa, the son of a rich merchant was found stabbed to death in a lonely street. Upon his breast was pinned a paper, with this inscription: "Killed for denunciation of the socialists."

Mezentzoff, Heyking, and the Captain from Moscow, each received the following letter:

"You have been condemned to death by us, the Revolutionary Committee of Petersburg, for crimes committed against our brothers, the nihilists. In consideration of your ignorance, we confine ourselves to warning you that if your conduct towards these sublime men is not materially modified, we shall be forced to allow your sentence to be implacably executed."

The Captain from Moscow, when he received this strange epistle, sent in his resignation to his colonel. Heyking and Mezentzoff tore theirs up with contempt. This letter, with a few necessary alterations, was placed upon the walls of Kiev, Moscow, Petersburg and Odessa.

CHAPTER XXX

TEMPTATION

After the meeting broke up, Wanda asked for a private conference with the five principal members of the Committee and laid before them her views concerning her marriage.

Siline and Komoff were violently opposed to it, but gradually overcome by her own strong will and by their knowledge of her firm and noble character, they gave their consent. Narkileff promised that he would get everything ready for the celebration of the marriage.

The eight days given to Chabert for reflection had passed away. He went at two o'clock in the afternoon to Prince Kryloff's palace, and, very much agitated, was duly ushered into Wanda's sitting-room. He found her lying down on a white-and-gold sofa. She wore a white Watteau wrapper trimmed with ribbons and lace. It was beautiful and enhanced the effect of her dark brown hair, which, unfastened from its many pins, hung in soft curls upon her shoulders. Behind her magnolia trees, gardenias and other flowering shrubs made an exquisite background to her luxuriant beauty, while the air was heavy with their tropical perfume.

Raymond had never seen Wanda in such a dress or in such an attitude. What did it mean? It was a singular way to receive him, of all men.

She held out her hand to him; it was moist and perfumed. Did she wish to drive him mad? She gazed at him with such a look that his blood rushed to his head.

Was she really in love with him? And was this talk about a sham marriage a joke? He dared not stop to think.

"Well, dear friend," she said, in the tenderest voice, and with a melting smile, "have you reflected upon my proposition?"

"It was not necessary for me to reflect on the matter. I told you once, and I tell you again, my life is at your disposal."

"I do believe you, and I asked one of my friends to find a priest who will consent to marry us secretly. I am only waiting now for my mother's consent."

"After our marriage, if you will allow me to ask, what are we to do?"

"Nothing will be changed, for the present, in our mode of life. I shall remain with my father as long as I can. If I find that I cannot stand it, we must run away together."

"Together?" asked Chabert.

"Why not? In the eyes of the world, will you not be my husband?"

"Yes, that is true."

"And we shall live together like brother and sister, or like two friends."

"Yes."

"It is said that a simple friendship is impossible between a man and a woman when they are young, particularly when they are thrown familiarly together, and a magnetic attraction sets up between them. They say that this magnetic power overcomes the strongest will. What do you think?"

She raised herself upon one elbow and, resting her chin in her hand, seemed to look into Raymond's heart.

He did not lower his eyes, but gazing at her in return, he replied, "If you are sure of your will, I am sure of mine. Never, Wanda, never shall you hear even a word from me that could annoy or displease you."

"Do you know, if I were a flirt, I would hate you for your indifference? And, in fact, there are so many nooks and corners in a woman's heart, that I cannot say what your coldness might not pique me to do. Then what would become of your resolution?"

Raymond looked down. He blushed painfully.

"Stop this game, Wanda," he said, in a low agitated voice. "It is unworthy of you, and it is unworthy of me."

She was indeed playing a game to try Raymond before she entered upon her new and singular relationship with him.

"I want to feel certain," she said, "that you are perfectly sure of yourself; for if you are not, I have of another make-believe husband in mind, in fact, I have thought of two."

"Do you not trust me?" he said.

"I trust you. One of the other men is too much in love; besides, he is a nobleman. I wish to marry someone beneath me in rank. The other man believes in free love."

"That is to say," said Raymond, "that he gives full play to his fancies."

"Oh no; it is not so bad as that. But he will be here in a little while."

"Did you get yourself up in this manner to receive him?"

"Why do you ask? Are you jealous?"

"I have no right to be jealous."

"My dear Raymond, I told you that I love someone, and I want to talk to you about him."

"Are you going to introduce me to him?" he asked.

"I should like you to know him. Do you desire it?"

He hesitated. "Yes, I do. I must know him in the course of time. In spite of myself, I have thought a great deal about him in the past week, and have fancied an ideal and perfect creature, more ideal, more perfect, perhaps, than the reality. When I shall have seen him, I shall feel more at ease."

"I hardly know whether to tell you who it is or not," said Wanda. "I think I will, though. And I am going to ask one thing more of you."

"To love him like a brother?" interrupted Chabert.

"No, but to help Count Litzanoff to escape."

"What! Is it Litzanoff!"

"You see now how impossible this love is. He is the husband of my best friend. There is an insurmountable barrier between us."

"Does he love you?"

"Unfortunately he does."

"Perhaps he is not as scrupulous as you?"

"Perhaps not."

"When two creatures, young, beautiful, loving, desire one another, no obstacle, not even Nihilism, can keep them apart, Wanda."

"You do not trust me!" exclaimed the Princess, very much offended.

"I think you are a true heroine, but there is a law of nature, stronger than human will, more imperious than any theory: it is love."

Wanda started to her feet.

"Raymond, do you think I am a liar?"

"I think you are at this moment perfectly sincere, but the day may come when your feelings will change. Will and reason are weak in the presence of that law of nature which blindly seeks its aim."

"You are a horrid materialist!" exclaimed Wanda.

"No, I merely see what passes before my eyes."

"Have you changed your mind about devoting your life to me?"

"No, I have not. If at any time I see that our fictitious marriage is an obstacle to the fulfilment of your desires, I will help you to obtain a divorce, which is not a difficult thing to do."

"That is all that I wished to know, my friend," she said, reaching him her hand. "I dressed myself in this way and surrounded myself with these appliances of luxury simply to try you. I wanted to find out if you could resist me, and I wanted to know if you were really jealous. Now I only fear one thing: I fear that your sacrifice will render you unhappy."

"That I cannot tell. I only know that in sacrifice can be found intense pleasure."

"I believe you, Raymond, I believe you."

"Well, when are we to be married?"

"Day after tomorrow, at night. Padlewsky has arranged it all. I think I hear his voice in the antechamber; he promised to bring me news of Litzanoff this evening."

Padlewsky entered the room.

"Allow me to present to you my betrothed husband, Raymond Chabert," said Wanda, in French.

"Merely an imaginary husband," said Raymond smiling.

"I think I have seen you several times at our club, have I not?" inquired Padlewsky.

"Let us talk about the prisoner now," interrupted Wanda. "What is he doing? How is he?"

"He is much better. Here is a letter that he sent you through Kowalsky. The note that you sent him had the most wonderful effect upon him; after he had read it, it inspired him with new life. His appetite returned, his fever went down, and he ate the prison rations with relish."

"I only sent him these few words: 'Be brave, be patient, be prudent; we think of you.'"

As she spoke, she tore open the envelope and greedily devoured Litzanoff's letter. As soon as she had read it, she handed it to Raymond. The note, written in lead pencil, ran as follows:

"Since I received those lines from your dear hand, my soul is drunk with joy, my dungeon glistens with light. An adored image is ever present with me. I love this solitude, where I can sit and dream of your heavenly face without distraction. You need not fear for me; my faith is firm; I am glad to suffer for the cause. Above all, I am glad if I can, by my sufferings, buy back the admiration of the woman who is my idol."

Raymond read these lines, and with a perfectly unmoved countenance, returned them to Wanda.

"Litzanoff is fascinated like the rest," he said. "I am not jealous."

"Oh," exclaimed Wanda, "if he gets well will they not take him from the hospital? And then, what shall we do?"

"Don't worry yourself," answered Padlewsky. "We shall manage it somehow. Have you anything more to send to Litzanoff?"

"No, I am waiting for Verenine, who promised me to bring the answer to Nadege's petition from the Czar's son, the Czarowitch, today. Please tell me what arrangements you have made for our marriage?"

"You are to come to my house. The marriage contract will be there in readiness for you; you will only have to sign your names."

As they were talking, Nadege rushed into the room and threw her arms around Wanda's neck.

"At last!" she said, "I have heard from him. He is ill, but they have taken him to the hospital, and through the intercession of the Czarowitch I have obtained permission to see him tomorrow."

"Who has done all this for you?"

"Verenine. He got the Czarowitch to take my petition personally to the Emperor. For eight days I have done nothing but cry."

"Does Verenine expect to get Stepane pardoned?" asked Wanda.

"Oh, no!" answered Nadege. "It is because they cannot pardon him that

I am to be allowed to see him."

Wanda got up from her chair. Her eyes were on fire.

"They are going to send him to Siberia," she cried, "without trial. He must be saved! He must be delivered out of the hands of these butchers. Something must be done at once, or . . ."

She had not finished her sentence when Verenine entered the room.

"My dear cousin," he said, "I have done what you asked me to do, but I found it very difficult."

"Thanks, dear Alexis, but half the work is not done yet. He must escape. The secret police must be taught to understand that we rebels are as powerful as we are bold."

"I will do all that I can for you, Princess," said Raymond.

"And I, too," added Verenine.

"Very well; perhaps I shall need you both."

"As for me," said Padlewsky, "I will go look up Komoff and send him to prowl around the hospital. As Countess Litzanoff has permission to visit her husband, she can communicate our plans to him."

Following Padlewsky out into the antechamber, Wanda said: "Do let us act promptly and quickly, and besides, tell me, is everything ready for the marriage?"

"Have you your mother's consent, Wanda?"

"I expect it every day."

"As soon as you get it you can fix your own time."

CHAPTER XXXI

THE CERTIFICATE OF DEATH

It was very early the following morning when Prince Kryloff entered his daughter's room, holding in his hand a large envelope banded and sealed with black.

"I accused you unjustly the other day, my dear child," he said. "I suspected that your mother was in Russia, but this letter informs me . . ."

"My mother! Oh, what is the matter? Let me read it!" She snatched the envelope out of her father's hand.

It contained two enclosures. One was a letter signed Michael Federoff. The other was a certificate of the registry of the death of Alexandra, late Princess Kryloff. Wanda fell, stunned and broken-hearted, upon her divan.

"Dead! dead!" she cried, "and I was not with her! And you, my father, have caused all this wretchedness! You are truly guilty of her death."

The Prince frowned. "In the presence of death," he said, "I forgive you." He left the room.

Wanda sat still, repeating over and over again the one word: "Dead!

Dead!" At last she summoned courage to read Federoff's letter. It contained a full account of her mother's terrible death.

As she sat there, crushed by grief, Katia burst in upon her, and told her that Raymond Chabert was waiting to see her, with an important despatch.

"Yes," she said, "I suppose it is something about my mother."

"Your mother is not dead!" exclaimed Chabert, almost before he had entered the room. "Here is a letter from the doctor, and one from the Princess also."

These words produced such a reaction in Wanda's heart, such a revolution of feeling, that she threw herself, nearly fainting, into Raymond's arms.

The bliss of holding this woman to his heart, of feeling her lovely form in his arms, intoxicated him with rapture; he would willingly have shed his life-blood for that short moment of ecstacy.

However, Wanda recovered her self-possession in a few seconds, and then sat down to read the two letters.

The one from Doctor Federoff was addressed to Raymond Chabert. It informed him of the Princess's consent to her daughter's marriage, and then went on to disclose a plan which she and Federoff had formed to return to Russia and be near her daughter. At the same time it would enable them to help with the revolution by their personal influence and actual presences. As Wanda could not have entire possession of her mother's fortune during her mother's lifetime, they had taken advantage of a little trip in the mountains of the Oberland, and of their guide's avarice, to bribe him to swear before a magistrate that Princess Alexandra Kryloff had come to her death by a fall into a precipice. The Princess meanwhile, under an assumed name, had taken refuge in the house of one of her friends. Later they expected to sail for Odessa from Marseilles.

The second letter ran thus:

My Beloved Daughter,

I give my consent to your marriage with Raymond Chabert. We saw but little of him while he was in Geneva, but that little impressed us very favorably. And as you think him worthy of your confidence, I rejoice in your choice, although perhaps your marriage may eventually be more real than you at present expect it to be.

I hope soon to see you. To see you, to hold you in my arms! Oh, my child! How can I tell you what I feel! I fear that I may die before that blessed hour comes. You, whom I thought lost to me forever, you, my only child; you, the joy, the hope of my life!

We expect to arrive at Odessa about the middle of next month. Try to get your father to go back to the Ukraine as soon as you can.

There we shall be near one another and can see one another.

Your mother, who is happy at last.

Alexandra

Wanda kissed this letter over and over again. "Poor mother," she said, "poor martyr! Yes, we are going into the Ukraine very soon now. By the way, Raymond, my father told me yesterday that your affairs are almost settled, so maybe we can go together, my dear husband."

"Pretended husband!" sighed Raymond, smiling at the same time.

"Is that a complaint?" said Wanda, watching him narrowly.

"I am only laughing at the idea of what they would think in Paris of this marriage of mine."

"You would be ashamed of it, wouldn't you?"

"No indeed, my affection for you is great enough to brave even ridicule."

"Ridicule! Oh, that is a terrible word, and a very French word, too."

As they were laughing and talking, Prince Kryloff opened the door. He had come back to see how Wanda was, and to his astonishment he found her evidently in a high state of enjoyment.

What could be the cause of it? Had Chabert anything to do with it? Did she love him?

He looked first at the one and then at the other. He hesitated for a moment then held out his hand to Raymond.

"I have good news for you," said the Prince. "I am to see the minister at two o'clock, and I hope today to get the permit for you."

Raymond thanked the Prince and after a few minutes conversation with him withdrew. As he left the room Wanda smiled at him, and made a little motion with her hand.

The Prince saw this, and it worried him. He did not say anything at first, but he walked up and down the boudoir, evidently angry about something.

"What is the matter now?" asked Wanda.

The Prince made no answer but looked at her in a perplexed and suspicious manner.

"Have you any more suspicions about me? Have you discovered something else? This life is killing me. Do let us go to the Ukraine! You will be better satisfied, and so shall I."

What was the meaning of her sudden reaction? Chabert was going, so she wanted to go too; of course she was in love with him.

"What is there between you and Chabert?" said the Prince. "I saw you make a sign to him just now. Have you hatched some plot between you to deceive me?"

"Father, that shows how little you know of Raymond. He has the noblest, the most loyal heart I ever knew."

"Are you in love with him?" said the Prince, fixing his dark angry eyes upon his daughter's face.

"Father, look at me! You know I never lie. I am not in love with Raymond, but I have the greatest esteem and friendship for him. That is the truth, and the whole truth."

"I believe you, my child. I have led a wretched life, my daughter, and that may account for my suspicious and hasty temper. Forgive me! I loved your mother to distraction. She preferred a serf to me. I made her suffer because she made me suffer so horribly. In spite of me, your mother's image always comes between us, and I fancy that I constantly see in you her Polish blood and her obstinacy, her self-will, her ungovernable disobedience. Her death has caused me the greatest relief, but I feel that I can love you better. Truly, you are now the only affection of my life. I do not wish to suspect you. I will do everything you want me to do. If you prefer to go to the Ukraine, let us go. There is something that I want to speak to you about, but I will wait till we go away; meanwhile only tell me that you are not angry with me; say that you love me."

"I am not angry with you," said Wanda.

"But you do not love me."

"Are you not my Father?"

"Tell me that you love me," said he.

"No, I do not."

A light shone in the Prince's dark eyes.

"I will go away now. You are so hard. You have never forgiven me because I once struck you."

Wanda made no reply.

"Must I go down on my knees? What can I do to wipe out the memory of that one act."

"Do everything that I ask you to do."

"I will, if you will only love me, Wanda."

Wanda did not wish to break with her father altogether as the Revolutionary Committee had imposed upon her the duty of preventing Prince Stackelberg's inquiry throughout the Ukraine.

CHAPTER XXXII

THE ESCAPE

When Nadege saw her husband again she could hardly recognize him. Six days of seclusion, of solitude, of burning fever, of moral and physical torture, had not been without their results.

This nervous, fantastic, external, emotional being, if left longer in prison would soon have died or gone mad. Five times had he been dragged before the judge, and submitted to the closest cross-examination. Yet, in spite of his fever, in spite of every effort to entrap him, no word had fallen from his lips which could in any way implicate either Wanda or Padlewsky.

Nothing but the powerful intervention of the Emperor himself could have availed to get him out of the prison into the hospital.

When Nadege first saw him she uttered a loud cry and fell weeping bitterly upon his bed. But amidst her sobs and her kisses she managed to whisper these words in his ear:

"Wanda is trying to manage your escape. Pretend to be very ill, so that you can remain here a few days."

Litzanoff's eyes glistened; his pale face colored. He pressed Nadege's hand.

"Tell Wanda that I thank her," he murmured.

Three days afterwards Litzanoff received through his surgeon a letter containing twenty thousand roubles. The letter, written in French, ran as follows:

"Tomorrow you must go down into the courtyard of the hospital to take the air. The doctor and the gatekeeper are already bribed. Corrupt the two sentinels who will be your escort. Outside the gate you will find a carriage, in which will be seated two men dressed as officers, with a black and yellow ribbon in their buttonholes. Get into the droschky and go with them."

A few moments after the receipt of this letter, the doctor went to the medical director of the hospital, to make his report. He said:

"Count Litzanoff cannot recover without air and exercise. It would be better for him to walk in the courtyard every morning about ten o'clock."

"But, doctor," answered the director, "if the prisoner escapes, I can get myself ready to go to that land whence no traveler returns."

"He is too weak to escape," said the doctor. "And how can he escape, with the two sentinels alongside of him and never leaving him for a moment?"

"That is true," said the director. "And besides, he is too weak to escape."

The next morning at ten o'clock, Litzanoff, who could hardly stand up, was dressed and taken down into the garden, supported by two sentinels.

As a precaution, the director had warned the gatekeeper and placed at the entrance of the hospital another sentinel.

The supplies for the day were being brought in. There were a number of wagons outside, and a great deal of coming and going peopled the courtyard.

Litzanoff was walking slowly up and down, leaning on a cane. His haggard face and wasted body imparted an air of great weakness to his appearance. Now and then he watched the gate with furtive eyes. Gradually he drew nearer and nearer to the vaulted gateway which separates the courtyard of the hospital from the outer street.

It seemed to him that it would be dangerous to try to bribe the sentinels. The gatekeeper was all right. He thought that with a little agility he might accomplish the rest.

A cart had just finished unloading some bags of flour; another one was coming up laden with wood. Everyone in the yard was busied in getting the flour out of the way to make room for the wood.

Litzanoff seized that moment to throw himself under the wheels of the first cart as it drove out of the gate. So suddenly did he transform himself from a sickly invalid to a brisk young man that his sentinels looked stupefied. Meanwhile he had caught sight of the promised droschky; with one leap he was inside. Raymond threw an officer's cloak over Litzanoff's shoulders; Korolef seized the reins.

They heard the cries of the soldiers; the sentinel placed to guard the gate rushed at them, but Koroletf gave the reins to his fiery black horse, and the droschky was soon lost in a labyrinth of streets.

They drove on for a quarter of an hour at this giddy pace. Neither Stepane nor Raymond nor Korolef said a word. At last they slackened their speed, and Korolef exclaimed:

"We are safe! They will never catch us now. But we must change our dress."

Under the seat of the droshky were three touloupe jackets. The three men put them on.

"Now," said Korolef, "we can breathe freely, as good mujiks who adore the Czar."

"To whom do I owe my deliverance?" inquired Litzanoff.

"To two nihilists," answered Korolef, "who are delighted to have it in their power to pay a good turn to the police."

"You owe it, above all, to Wanda Kryloff," said Raymond. "It is on her account that I am here."

These words were spoken in French. Litzanoff answered in the same tongue:

"I think I have had the pleasure of meeting you once before?"

"Yes, at Prince Kryloff's."

"Are you a Frenchman?"

"Yes."

"Do tell me your name, at least, so that I may know to whom I am indebted for the great service you have just now rendered me."

"My name is Raymond Chabert, but you are not in the least indebted to me. I am only an instrument of Princess Wanda."

Raymond had pronounced that name for the second time, in such a respectful, tender tone, that Stepane was jealous. He watched Raymond suspiciously.

"And what is your name?" he said to Korolef. "Is it by order of Princess

Wanda Kryloff that you are here too?"

"I am a revolutionist. I obey no one's orders. I have not exposed my life to please you. You owe me no gratitude whatever. You managed admirably. I saw them running after you, I heard them calling out. Well done! Well done! I say. Ah, my fine fellows, you are clever policemen, sharp and sly; but what do you say of this, eh? In open day, under the very nose of your three sentinels, we escaped with our prisoner, and you will not find us in a hurry." And as he spoke, he laughed and shook in his seat.

This man Korolef had a singular head and a very mobile face. His dark skin, his eyes, now grey, now black, his black curly hair, all betrayed his gypsy origin. His close-cropped head was almost always adorned with a red wig, and his small features made it easy for him to disguise himself as an old man. His slender and agile body had suppleness and vigor.

On his father's side, Korolef was a Russian. When he wished he had all the stolidity of the true Russian. He had been taken prisoner in a little uprising of the students, and had been sent to Siberia, but he had managed to escape. Venturing to return to Petersburg, he hourly ran the risk of being recognized. He was clever, quick, very powerful, very courageous, even rash. The nihilists entrusted him with their most difficult missions. He always had acquitted himself remarkably well.

"Ah," he said, "this is not the first time I have played off this trick upon the gentlemen of the Third Section." They stopped before a house. Korolef threw the reins to Raymond and opened the door.

"Come," he said to Litzanoff. But the latter, now that the excitement was over, was so weak that Korolef was almost obliged to carry him.

"Have you any message to send to Princess Wanda?" asked Raymond. "I am going at once to let her know that you are safe and sound."

"Tell her . . . oh, do not tell her anything, for I can find no words to express what I feel. Tell her that I long to see her, and that as soon as I am well I shall show her my gratitude by devoting myself entirely to the cause."

Raymond bowed, got into the droschky again, and in less than a quarter of an hour found himself before Prince Kryloff's door. Wanda was waiting for him in an inexpressible state of anxiety.

"Well?" said she.

"He is in safety," answered Raymond.

Wanda uttered no exclamation, but she strove to conceal the joy, the intense feeling, that she knew lurked in her eye.

"When are we to be married?" asked Raymond.

"Tomorrow evening," she said, smiling and giving him her hand.

CHAPTER XXXIII

A SECRET MARRIAGE

In Russia the priest's sanction alone rendered marriage valid. The Russians knew but two kinds of union: the church wedding and free love, which the common people called living in free grace.

The archimandrites perform those duties which in other countries of Europe devolve upon the notary public. The young lover is bound to make an offering to the monastery and also one to his parish church. His fair betrothed is held responsible for a canopy heavily enriched with precious stones, to be placed over an image of the Blessed Virgin.

The marriage is always preceded by a handsome entertainment where the two contracting parties exchange rings. The ceremony itself is celebrated in the church. Among the wealthier classes the young married couple receive a benediction at night by the light of consecrated tapers in their own drawing-room. The bride wears, as elsewhere, the time-honored white dress and wreath of orange flowers.

Gloom, dullness and sadness presided over Wanda's and Raymond's wedding in place of joy, festivity and delight. Instead of a pretty bridal dress, she wore a harsh brown frock. A hat trimmed with fur supplanted the white veil. It was a traveling-dress rather than a wedding dress. She had chosen this costume to make Raymond understand that theirs would not be a quiet life, full of domestic joy, but a long journey, a struggle, a life of work.

Raymond had come in full dress, as a bridegroom should.

"Alas, dear friend," said she, smiling, "we are not going to a ball! It is much more likely that we shall have to take a long journey across the Urals."

Raymond was pale and much agitated; Wanda, calm, but very sad.

In her youthful dreams, when her heart had first beat at the thoughts of love, surely this was not the union the thought of which had filled her soul with rapture. She by her beauty, her rank, her fortune, could hope for every happiness, every delight, every luxury. What faith, what self-sacrifice did it not require to induce her to contract such a union, without love, without enthusiasm, in a stranger's house, far from her kindred and her friends!

"You are very sad, Wanda," said Raymond. "Do you regret your decision?"

"No, I regret nothing. But have we the right to be happy, when so many millions of our fellow-beings are sunk in wretchedness?"

"That is carrying the idea of joint responsibility rather far."

"In this century of egotism, it cannot be pushed too far. We must give to the world startling and practical examples of our belief."

Narkileff performed the ceremony. Deprived of all religious rites, it was very short.

At the moment when Wanda pronounced the sacramental "yes," a terrible cry startled every one present.

Standing on the threshold of the door, trembling, pale as death, stood Count Litzanoff.

Padlewsky knew nothing of his relations with Wanda, and had asked him to be one of the witnesses. When he was told of Wanda's approaching marriage, he had bean seized with a violent attack of fever. Korolef warned Padlewsky that Litzanoff could not be present at the ceremony. But Litzanoff, finding out when it was to take place, mad with jealousy, raging with fever, had gotten out of bed, and in spite of Korolef, gone to Padlewsky's house.

At that cry Wanda turned, and Litzanoff fell senseless to the ground. They rushed towards him and unfastened his clothes. His breast was covered with blood; he had reopened his wound, clutching at his heart with his poor nervous fingers.

He was carried into an adjoining room and laid upon a sofa. As soon as he revived, he was conscious of two faces bending over him; they were Wanda and Raymond. He closed his eyes with a painful contraction of the lids.

"Leave me alone with him for a moment," said Wanda.

"Stepane," she murmured in a low voice, "do you think me capable of a lie?"

"No," answered Litzanoff.

"Then listen to me. I shall never be the wife of Raymond Chabert except in name."

"What, then, is the meaning of this farce?"

She explained to him, in a few words, her reasons for marrying.

"Perhaps," she added, "there may be still another reason. I may feel the need of something to separate me more completely from you."

Stepane opened his eyes and looked at her with a gaze in which his whole heart, his whole life, was concentrated.

She stooped over him and kissed him on the forehead. But he threw his arms around her and with all his remaining strength pressed her to his heart.

"Wanda! Wanda! Swear to me that you love me, and me only."

"Poor fool! I love you."

CHAPTER XXXIV

THE SEPARATION

Two days after her marriage, Wanda left Petersburg with her father for the Ukraine.

Before she went away she gave Padlewsky a letter for Litzanoff, with strict injunctions that he was not to receive it until he should be thoroughly recovered in health. She begged Padlewsky in the meanwhile to tell him that she would only be away for a few weeks.

The letter to Litzanoff ran as follows:

My dear friend,

I am going away, although my heart bleeds to have to leave you while you are still so ill. But my duty calls me, and you know what I have sacrificed to that.

We must not meet again. I felt last night that I cannot resist your love if I remain where you are. We cannot serve two masters; love is, of all masters, the most jealous, the most exacting.

I have a passionate nature; I can only love one thing at a time, and I have consecrated myself to the love of humanity; I must serve it alone.

I have told you once before, and I tell you again, we must not see each other, at least until the final triumph of the Cause, a triumph which I firmly believe is not far distant.

Besides, it is necessary for your safety that you quit Russia. Take Nadege with you and go to Italy or Switzerland. In either of those countries you will find refugees who will initiate you more thoroughly into our doctrines. The Cause is not essentially Russian; in every country the oppressed need a deliverer.

Farewell, my friend; we shall surely see one another some day, when, perhaps, time and distance may have moderated our unfortunate attachment.

Your devoted friend,
Wanda

When Padlewsky handed this letter to the convalescent, he was taken with a violent attack of fever and delirium which lasted for three days.

As soon as he came to himself, he wrote to Nadege:

My dear, sweet Nadege:

I am going to give you a great deal of pain, but it is necessary. You love me and I am unworthy of your love. Our characters are so unlike that we can never be happy together. You should have been married to a quiet, even-tempered, good man, resembling yourself in character.

The ties of marriage are more hateful to me than were the chains of my prison. I could obtain a divorce by paying for it; but that I will never do on your account.

I implore you silly dear child, do not trouble yourself any more about me. I am obliged to leave Russia. Where can I go? I do not know myself. At any rate, I do not wish you to sacrifice your youth and beauty to me. I have enough to reproach myself with; do not add your tears to the account.

What is to become of me? I cannot tell. Nadege, I am unhappy. Following the example of our sublime friend, I have determined to devote myself to the revolutionary cause. I wish to dedicate all my fortune to it. I have written to our steward to prepare our respective accounts, and he will hand over to you your own fortune. I shall leave Dimitri in charge of the revenue. He will forward it to the persons whose address I shall give him. A very little will suffice me; I intend to 'simplify' myself and give myself entirely to the cause.

If you will take my advice, you will sue for a divorce and marry some one else. You could not possibly find a worse match than myself.

Believe me, dear child, that I thoroughly and gratefully appreciate your love.

Most sincerely yours,
Stepane Litzanoff

He had a private interview with his steward and drew up a formal deed, bequeathing the larger portion of his fortune to *The Deliverance*. It was left to Woldeman Siline, in trust.

Then he cut off his hair and his moustache and dressed himself in the costume of a Lithuanian ballad-singer. Korolef had procured a hideous yellow garment for him to wear, but he threw it down with disgust.

"No," said he, "I would rather be sent to Siberia than put on that frightful thing."

"You are an aesthetic still," laughed Korolef.

"I acknowledge it; taste is innate; we do not need to make ourselves ugly, in order to feel kindly towards the common people. We need not lower ourselves to them; it would be much better to lift them up to us."

"Is it under this disguise that you expect to convert the peasants to socialism? Nobody will think you are in earnest."

"I propose," answered Litzanoff, "to change my costume every two or three days. This is only a traveling dress."

"Where are we going?" asked Korolef.

"Are you going with me ?"

"Yes, I have received orders not to leave you."

"Well, then, let us travel through Western Russia as far as Kiev. I expect to remain there some time."

"Here," said Korolef, "are two false passports, which will enable us to leave Petersburg."

That very night they set out for Moscow.

Doubtless, Stepane Litzanoff was an ardent lover of humanity, but above all was he a jealous lover of Wanda Kryloff.

CHAPTER XXXV

THE PROPAGANDA

It was towards the middle of May, 1878, when a troika drove rapidly along the road that leads from Alexandria to the summer residence of Prince Kryloff.

Three men were seated in the vehicle. In the driver, despite his Cossack disguise, one could easily recognize the curly head, mobile features, and gypsy skin of Korolef. Behind him sat a man prematurely grey, but still in the prime of life. He had a fine head and a calm and unmoved countenance, but a close observer could detect traces of suffering in that wrinkled brow, and a lurking bitterness about the corners of his mouth.

The third individual, dressed in a cloak of faded old velvet and wearing blue spectacles, was at the same time quiet and restless. It was Litzanoff. For three months he had been walking over Lithuania, Podolia and Wolhinia, scattering his tracts and preaching his doctrines in the country inns and in the factories. When about to leave Petersburg, he sent for one of his young friends, who was heavily in debt, and offered to pay off his liabilities if he would assume Litzanoff's name and pass himself off as the Count in some prominent capital of Europe. The proposition was greedily accepted, and the stratagem proved perfectly successful. Count Litzanoff was believed to be outside of Russia, and consequently all search for him had ceased. In fact, how could any one suppose for a moment that an escaped prisoner would remain within reach of the Czar's police?

Our three travelers were crossing the steppes washed by the waters of the Dnieper. The steppes are immense prairies, grassy oceans, with great green waves and limitless horizon. In winter, they resemble the Polar Sea: one wide waste of ice and snow. Now and then the green desert is broken by villages and cultivated fields. Narrow paths lead from hamlet to hamlet. An occasional stream glitters between verdant banks. Now a lordly castle breaks upon the eye; or a white church, with green and gilded cupola, stands out distinctly against the dark blue of the sky.

Our travelers, unconsciously affected by the dreamy loneliness of the steppe, were lost each in his own contemplation. The troika flew on and on, leaving behind it the track of its wheels.

For some time they had traveled in this manner, stopping at the post-houses to change horses. There they would take a cup of tea, always ready in the large samovar; then if there were any nihilists in the neighborhood they would stop over night and carefully disseminate their pamphlets, which were hidden away in a box under the seat of the troika. In this manner they had gone through nearly all of the provinces of Odessa, Kherson, and Ekaterinoslav.

Prince Kryloff's property was situated between Kiev, the Holy City, and Gitomir, the capital of Wolhinia. The travelers were approaching the village of Krylow, but a short distance from the Prince's residence. It was nearly dark as they entered the little town. They drove past the houses painted in stripes; the churches built with heavily gilded cupolas; the inns and numerous drinking houses, out of which the workmen, half drunk, tottered into the road; past the police station, past the Governor's house and the bazaar; until the troika, bounding over the rough stones of a Russian street, drove into the public square. Then the eldest of the three men said to Litzanoff, in a hollow voice:

"Here, twenty years ago, I received ninety-nine strokes of the knout."

Litzanoff shuddered. "You?" he said.

"Yes, by order of the Prince."

"Wanda's father?"

"By the order of that tyrannical savage."

"I understand why you are a nihilist."

"It is not humiliation that made me a nihilist; rather has it been the love of justice and of truth."

"Of course," replied Litzanoff, "but still your suffering caused you to think and to rebel; and rebellion and reflection brought about the discovery of the truth."

"That may be so," answered the person to whom Litzanoff was speaking.

This wise, grave man was the celebrated physician, Michael Federoff.

The troika at last drew up before the post house, at the extreme end of the village. Thanks to the provident care of Korolef, the three men were soon served with a frugal but excellent repast. As soon as they had appeased their hunger, they set out to find Zobolewsky, whose address Wanda had given them.

This Zobolewsky was formerly the foreman of the factory where Wanda and Katia had gone to begin their apprenticeship. Wanda had brought him to Krylow, where he superintended the Prince's factories, and was the leader of a band of anarchists.

There was a movement brewing at this time in the province of Kiev, but Wanda and Raymond did not care to join it, fearing the inexperience of the leaders. Zobolewsky was enthusiastic and excitable, and wished to hurry on the outbreak.

He gave all the details to the three travelers. Litzanoff and Korolef were for immediate action. The news that they brought with them from the South was favorable; it would be well to give the rest an example of courage and daring.

Michael listened to all that they had to say. When asked for his advice, he answered:

"I must see for myself. I am afraid that in your desire to hasten the movement, you mistake the disposition of the population, After I have gone through the country around Kiev, I can tell you my impressions."

"Padlewsky will be here tomorrow," said Litzanoff. "He has passed through Moscow, Rragair, Toula, Orel, Komsk, and Karkow; he has had an excellent opportunity to make observations, and he is very calm in his judgement. After his arrival we can have a meeting at Kiev. We must begin our movement in the Ukraine. The Southern Russian has a great deal of the Cossack in him: all his horror of the yoke, all his love of liberty; he is much less apathetic then the Russian peasant in general."

As they were talking, Raymond came in.

"Wanda could not get away," he said, "but she will try to be tomorrow night at the factory, where we are to have a meeting."

He joined in their discussion, and informed them that according to his observation not more than the tenth part of Russia was with them in their desire for the revolution.

"That may be," said Zobolewsky, "and yet we may lead on the other nine parts. This tenth part has all the intelligence and all the energy of the country. It is an incontrovertible fact that the peasants are greatly dissatisfied. They are dull, but once aroused, they surely will join with us. Their tithes and their taxes swallow up all they make. What is the good of their working when they can never lay anything up for a rainy day? That is the whole secret of their laziness. They must certainly, in the end, join a movement which will liberate them from fruitless toil and hopeless poverty."

"My friends," objected Michael, "you forget the clergy and the army, the two great supports of the Russian Empire. Remember, the Czar is the representative of God in Russia, and the army, although decimated in the late war, is still formidable."

"I assure you," said Litzanoff, "there is much discontent among the private soldiers, and even among the clergy."

"The recent trial of Vera Zassoulitch," added Zobolewsky, "has undoubtedly given a fresh impulse to the revolution. We must walk in the footsteps of that heroine, and endeavor to free our nation from bondage."

"We shall meet the envoy from Petersburg tomorrow," said Michael, "and we can then decide upon a plan of action. I have thought it well over, and I will then give you the result of my reflections."

They separated, to meet on the following day.

CHAPTER XXXVI

THE INQUIRY

Prince Kryloff's residence stood upon a hill a short distance from the Dnieper. It was built after the Italian manner, in the midst of a large park laid out in straight avenues and of formal shrubbery. This imposing structure was in harmony with the pompous and dictatorial character of the Prince.

Just behind this superb building, in a secluded, charming, fantastic part of the grounds, stood a little structure thoroughly Russian in its character, reminding one of a Swiss chalet. Along two sides of the house ran a wide piazza, supported on slender pillars, all enwrapped and entwined with English ivy, American trumpet-creeper, and strange climbing plants from China and Greece. At the four corners little projections, like large bay windows, stood out from the walls, adorned with numberless wood carvings. A double flight of steps led down from the front door into an English garden, which was full of fountains, waterfalls, flower beds, and rock work. At a short distance the Dnieper could be seen rolling its waters through the green sea of the illimitable steppe.

This was Wanda's summer home. She called it her cottage, and thither she would constantly retire, both for study and meditation, and also to escape from the numberless visitors who ceaselessly invaded Prince Kryloff's hospitable mansion. Every one knew that she was eccentric; on that account the frequent absence of the beautiful Princess was condoned.

Wanda had other reasons for preferring the cottage to the castle. From it she could easily, accompanied by Katia, take a little run into the factories.

She had established a school for the children of the workmen, quite near the cottage, and she superintended their instruction herself. This gave great scandal to the priest, for it was done entirely without his assistance or authority.

The Princess and Katia frequently passed the night away from home sometimes in one village, sometimes in another, sometimes with her mother, who was living for the time at Ekaterinoslav. In one of the factories she gave instruction in the doctrines of nihilism.

Once when the Prince was away, Princess Alexandra had ventured to visit Wanda in her cottage. Between these two women, knit together by the ties of both blood and friendship, there existed a perfect love, rendered only stronger by the mystery and danger that surrounded every interview.

It was early in May. Visitors were flocking to see the Prince. His castle was the center of attraction to all the nobility in the neighborhood. His receptions were splendid; nothing could exceed the hospitality and the splendor of the boyards. Among the guests visiting at Castle Kryloff were Stackelberg and Raymond Chabert.

Vassili Stackelberg had accepted the invitation so hospitably proffered him in Petersburg by Princess Wanda. He had made his headquarters at her father's house while he conducted his search and inquiry into the condition of the socialists throughout the neighboring provinces.

Thus far he had discovered nothing; for Wanda had secretly and adroitly frustrated all his plans and diverted all his suspicions. Moreover, he had fallen in love with the Princess, who alternately encouraged or discouraged him, according to circumstances. He loved her as well as his vile heart could love. His vanity and ambition were aroused and gave to his passion the semblance of a genuine feeling.

Raymond Chabert walked on air. There was a secret between him and Wanda. The bond between them touched him to the heart. He loved her so completely that no grosser thought could tarnish the purity of his affection. He worshiped rather than loved her. Besides, she loved Litzanoff, and Litzanoff loved her. He was jealous, and yet no self-love mingled with that jealousy. After all Litzanoff was not as happy as he was and could not be with her.

As for Prince Kryloff, his time was entirely taken up attending to his factories. He had sugar factories, paper factories and sawmills for working up the products of his forests. He employed a vast number of workmen. Raymond Chabert had been a great help to him. His knowledge of engineering had been most useful to the Prince, who was very grateful to the young Frenchman, not only for the past, but also for future services. This new railroad would double the Prince's income.

In spite of his royal generosity, his magnificence, and his exquisite manners, the Prince was very mean towards his workmen. Attached to every factory was a bazaar, fitted up with all the necessaries of life. Instead of money the men received checks for the several amounts due them. For these checks they could obtain anything contained in the bazaar. This sort of exchange was a considerable source of revenue to the Prince.

Throughout every factory and every village on her father's estate, Wanda scattered her tracts. Raymond busied himself in the neighboring provinces, wherever his work on the railroad led him, and Litzanoff was entrusted with the messages to be carried backwards and forwards between the different groups of nihilists, as nothing could be entrusted to the post.

So, without his knowledge, Prince Kryloff's country seat was the center of a formidable propaganda.

Vassili Stackelberg remained at the castle, daily watching and sighing for Wanda, ogling her as soon as he saw her, evidently seeking an opportunity to declare his love. This Wanda desired to prevent. However, one morning, coming through the park, she unexpectedly stumbled upon the German. It was a lovely morning; mother earth sent forth her sweet, fresh breath, the spring air breathed life into nature, the sun drew every heart up towards itself. The warblers were singing, the river rushed on with distant soothing murmur; the day was unspeakably brilliant, beautiful, magnificent. It told upon Vassili Stackelberg. He resolved to bare his love at once.

"Is this you, so early?" he exclaimed. "Where have you been, Wanda Petrowna?"

"I have been to see a poor sick woman."

"How good you are!" said Stackelberg.

"I am not good, but you know I am a nihilist," said she, laughing, "and I love the poor."

"You a nihilist! You, the personification of elegance and beauty and distinction! But enough of that. I want to see you, Wanda, to speak to you about something which is of the deepest importance to me."

"Do you! I should like so much to know what it is, but I have not time now; I am in a hurry to get some medicine to send to that poor woman."

"Let me go with you," persisted Vassili. "I shall be so glad to help you."

"No, you would make me waste my time, and I am in haste. I will take you with me another day."

"Will you promise to take me with you another day?"

"Yes, very soon."

She waved her hand to him and disappeared among the trees, thus for the twentieth time preventing Vassili from expressing his love. He walked up and down a long time, thinking, wondering what to make of Wanda. What did she mean? Did she love him, or did she not? Doubtless she acknowledged his superiority, his promising career. And yet why did she always avoid a declaration? Perhaps she did not feel sure of his affection for her. Perhaps . . .

Just then he found himself opposite the door of Wanda's cottage. He saw Raymond Chabert coming down the steps with a beaming countenance. This was a revelation! Wanda's conduct towards this young man had once or twice excited Vassili's suspicions, but she was so eccentric, so queer, that it was difficult to know what to think of her.

A terrible thought suddenly took possession of him. The blood rushed to his face. Was she pretending an interest in him to conceal her love for this Frenchman? Was she making a fool of him; of him, Prince Vassili

Stackelberg?

He went up to Raymond.

"Good morning, Monsieur Chabert," said he in French; "are you in the habit of paying such early visits to the Princess?"

"I have been to see her on business, my dear Prince," answered Raymond.

"Your business is an exceedingly convenient one, giving you, as it seems, the entry to a very pretty woman's boudoir! However, all Frenchmen love intrigue. You are born flirts and adventurers."

"Adventurers! What do you mean? There is nothing extraordinary in my visit to the Princess. In digging for my railroad, a few days ago, a bank of earth fell in and injured one of my workmen seriously. The Princess promised me some money for him, as he will not be able to work for some time, and has a wife, and five children. That explains the whole mystery of my early visit. I went to get the money."

"I thoroughly understand the Princess's benevolence, and I also understand that this poor devil's misfortune has been most fortunate for you. By the bye, Monsieur Chabert, I was informed yesterday by the Commissary of Police that there are a large number of nihilists among your laborers. Is that so?"

"I do not belong to the police, myself," answered Raymond. "The mujiks are reserved and suspicious, and they will not tell on one another. There is a tacit understanding between these oppressed creatures."

"Ah, Monsieur Chabert; you look upon our Russian peasants with pity, do you? Are your French peasantry so much better off than ours?"

"Not much, but whatever our faults may be, we are as a nation infinitely more civilized than you Russians."

"Do you look upon your heterogeneous republic as a proof of superior civilization? Was Napoleon III a more liberal ruler than Alexander? You Frenchmen consider yourselves the first nation in the world; whereas, we see only your inconstancy, your conceit, and your contemptible vanity, and look upon you generally as a race of jumping-jacks."

"Vassili Antonovitch, I allow no one to speak to me thus of the nation to which I belong!"

"Well, the expression 'jumping-jacks' is scarcely parliamentary, and I withdraw it," said Stackelberg, with a sneer upon his lips.

"I thoroughly appreciate the faults of our national character," answered Raymond, "but I also know that we have always taken the lead in every scientific, political, and social question. There is, inherent in the French character, a quick comprehension, an enthusiasm . . ."

"Your quickness and your enthusiasm combined go to make up your volatility."

"Your prudence and dishonesty combined go to make up the character of the German nation," answered Chabert, in a most insolent tone.

Stackelberg saw that he had gone too far, and having no desire to risk his precious life in a duel, he beat a retreat.

"That speech does not touch me, Monsieur Chabert, for I am a Russian. We all know that there is among Frenchmen a genuine chivalry."

"Which of course goes to make up the volatility of our character, eh?"

"I did not mean to say that you are volatile, in fact I do not understand French thoroughly; I speak it like a stupid German. Perhaps instead of volatility I should say instability."

"No, generosity is the proper word," cried Raymond, now very much excited.

"Just as you please, Monsieur Chabert; generosity let it be."

Raymond instantly bowed and walked away.

"This booby shall pay dear for his insolence," said Stackelberg to himself. "Besides, I am jealous of him. Wanda is entirely too polite to him. Who is he? Where does he come from? He is not even a gentleman, yet he dares to speak to me in this manner. He must be a nihilist. He must have somebody to back him, or he surely would not presume to take this attitude in Prince Kryloff's house. I will find it all out this very day."

CHAPTER XXXVII

THE DECLARATION OF LOVE

Wanda fully comprehended that the time had arrived for Stackelberg to propose. She saw it in his glowing eye, his trembling voice, his anxious eagerness to please. And she put off his avowal from day to day by every means in her power, knowing full well that the hour she refused him would be a dangerous one for the nihilists, and perhaps also for herself.

She kept out of his way all that morning, but in the evening after dinner, notwithstanding the number of guests that were present, he managed to find her alone.

"I have been waiting to speak to you all day long," he said.

"Yes! What can it be about?"

"I want to speak to you about something that concerns me very much."

"That sounds rather appalling. To be sure, I am of age, and eccentric in my habits and customs; still I do not usually grant private interviews to young men, especially when I suspect them of — what shall I say?"

"Have you guessed my secret?" asked the Prince. "That is not a very difficult thing to do."

"What is it?"

"That you want to make me a formal offer of your hand."

"Will you allow me to do so, Wanda?"

"First, tell me what you think of me."

"I am too much in love with you to form any critical analysis of your character. Very early this morning I met Monsieur Chabert coming out of your private cottage, and not withstanding that no suspicions of your conduct pressed my mind . . ."

"Thanks, Vassili Antonovitch, thanks."

"Will you not allow the same privileges that you allow to Monsieur Chabert?"

"But you do not want to see me about any money matters."

"No; but I have a great deal to say to you."

"Well, say it now."

"No, I must see you entirely alone."

"I do not like to appoint a time to meet you alone, now that I know your feelings towards me."

He looked at her fixedly; she cast down her eyes. He thought that she loved him, and was ashamed to let him detect that love in her face. He drew nearer and fastened upon her his greedy gaze. Wanda was trembling all over.

"Pity me!" he whispered.

"I cannot."

"Why?"

"I am so afraid of you."

"Afraid of me? You are not afraid of Raymond Chabert?"

"Oh, Monsieur Chabert — he is different."

"How different?"

"He lays no claim to my heart."

"How do you know that?"

"A woman can always tell."

"Can you see into every man's heart?"

"I think I can."

"What do you see in mine?"

"I would rather not tell you."

"Well, let me tell you what is in it."

"I do not want to hear that, either."

"Why not?"

"The idea of marriage terrifies me."

"Dear Wanda, love is the only thing that makes life worth living."

"That is because you do not love very deeply."

"What do you mean?"

"Why, I have always heard," explained the Princess, "that a strong love causes a man a great deal of suffering."

"Yes, but a man does not wish to be cured of that agony. Don't you think your indifference and your coldness cause me a great deal of pain?

Wanda, I love you passionately."

"Passionately?" said she, looking at him for the first time. "Would you lay down your life to please me?"

"Willingly! A hundred times!"

"That would he ninety-nine times too often. Would you, a sensible man, a future diplomat, would you throw away your life in that manner? I cannot believe it."

"Try me."

"I will think about it."

"Try me at once, I beg of you."

"Well, then, apologize to Monsieur Chabert for the manner in which you insulted him this morning."

"No, Wanda, he is a nihilist. All I can do for him is, for your sake, not to denounce him to the Third Section."

Wanda grew white as death, and Stackelberg noticed it; she was really frightened.

"He is no socialist," she said laughing. "If you can find any proof against him, I will deliver him up to you tied neck and heels. But if you cannot find anything against him, will you not apologize to him?"

"I will, upon one condition; that you will grant me a private interview."

"What for? You are very persistent."

"May I hope for it?"

"You can hope, that will not hurt anybody," answered Wanda with a bewitching smile.

"You are a flirt!" said Stackelberg. "Sometimes I feel as if I should like to kill you."

"Since when has it become the fashion to stab a woman for love?"

"I warn you, Princess, my passions are fierce."

"Yes, some of your passions."

"What do you mean?"

"Your ambition, for instance."

"Thank you."

"Are you not very ambitious?"

"I am ambitious to have you for my wife. I would make you the most distinguished woman in the whole Empire."

"That sounds much like an offer of marriage."

"Do you think for a moment, Wanda, that I would dare speak to you of love without also intending to ask your hand in marriage?"

"Indeed, I never think of marrying. So, naturally, it does not occur to me that others may be thinking of it."

"You never think of marrying, Wanda?"

"No, upon my word, I never do. I used to think about it, but I do not now."

"Well, that is a revelation. Is there any one upon whom you have fixed your affections?"

"It seems to me your questions are rather indiscreet."

"I am jealous, Wanda, jealous even of your past life."

Wanda stood still, apparently lost in thought, then she exclaimed abruptly: "You are too curious, Vassili Antonovitch," and turned away as though to leave him. But suddenly, as if repenting of her coldness, she looked back and sent one glance towards the Prince, who stood as though bewitched by it.

Stackelberg never closed his eyes that whole night through. He thought over every word that Wanda had spoken; he recalled her every look, her every gesture. "She is so strange," he said to himself, "so fearless, and still so reserved, so womanly! She is perfect! How she could love a man!" Then Raymond Chabert suddenly came into his mind. Vassili thought of Raymond's insolence and of his own pusillanimity. Perhaps Wanda despised him as much its she admired Chabert. How he hated that Frenchman!

CHAPTER XXXVIII

THE PROPOSAL

The enamored Vassili arose the next morning feverish and unrefreshed. He determined to go at once to Prince Kryloff and ask him for his daughter's hand in marriage. The Prince had been very polite to him, and would not, he thought, oppose the match. It would, in a pecuniary point of view, be very desirable, as both Vassili and Wanda were heirs to enormous wealth.

As he was dressing, he drew near the window, and carelessly looking out upon the beautiful view, he perceived Wanda and Chabert walking together down the broad avenue. Wanda was leaning on Raymond's arm.

Stackelberg was seized with a violent attack of jealousy. He had but one thought: to get down into the park and strive to overhear their conversation.

Meanwhile, Raymond was relating to Wanda the events of the previous evening; how Federoff, Litzanoff, and Korolef had arrived at Krylow, and the result of their discussion. He also told Wanda that her mother, not being very strong in health, had been left behind at Ekaterinoslav, there to wait until Federoff should send for her.

Wanda was naturally very anxious to see her mother. She told Raymond that she was seriously thinking of leaving her father's house altogether, so as to be free to go to her mother and do her own work for the cause.

"My situation is becoming more and more painful," she said. "Stackelberg is in love with me and will probably ask my father for my hand today. Then I shall have to undergo all sorts of terrible scenes, for my father desires the match. Stackelberg will be in a rage. He is jealous of you; he suspects you of being a nihilist; the next thing will be your arrest. If there is to be an outbreak in the neighborhood, I cannot help with the rebellion against my own father. I think I had better go away."

Just then Wanda noticed Stackelberg watching them.

"Here comes the inquisitor," she said. "We must take care what we say. Up to this time, I have managed to persuade him that there are no nihilists in this neighborhood, but since yesterday he suspects something. My father is going to have quite a party tomorrow, we can easily get off then without being noticed. Anyhow, I must see our friends and talk it over with them. Tell them that I wish to meet them tonight in the paper factory, at twelve o'clock. And I wish you would come for me this evening, in a droschky, at eleven o'clock."

Instead of giving Raymond her hand, she bowed to him quite distantly, as though dismissing him. Stackelberg noticed this, for he was now very near them. He also noticed that they had carefully kept away from the shrubbery, so as to allow no eavesdropping. All this meant, to his observant mind, a secret conversation.

As soon as he came near enough, Wanda addressed him in the most friendly manner.

"Good morning, Prince. What brings you out so soon? We very seldom have the pleasure of seeing you so early."

"I do not like early rising, but this morning I could not sleep."

"While you are lying in bed, my dear inquisitor, your favorite anarchists may be gamboling all over the country."

"In fact," he said, looking darkly after Raymond, who disappeared down the avenue, "I begin to believe in their existence."

Vassili walked slowly by Wanda's side. They were both agitated, both very much embarrassed. Suddenly, to her astonishment, without saying another word, he turned on his heel. He walked quickly in the direction of the house, mounted the steps, crossed the hall and knocked at the door of Prince Kryloff's private room.

The Prince admitted him, and Stackelberg, without any preface, asked him bluntly for his daughter's hand.

The Prince was delighted. "I am very anxious to marry off my daughter," he said to Stackelberg, "and you have my entire approval, but you must first gain her consent. I give you fair warning, she will not marry to please me, unless her future husband suits her own taste likewise. But she has always been very kind to you and invited you to stay with us here in the Ukraine."

"I have hesitated for some time before coming to you," answered Vassili, "for I cannot make up my mind what your daughter's feelings are towards me. Sometimes she encourages me, and then again she discourages me in the most pointed manner, without my being able to find out what is the reason of it."

"Women are all alike, Vassili Antonovitch, and Wanda is certainly a very singular girl. However, I will speak to her today, and if she gives her consent we can have the betrothal tomorrow. Then your marriage can be formally announced."

"The sooner the better," answered Vassili. "I am desperately in love, but I must tell you that I am uneasy about this great intimacy between the Princess and the Frenchman."

"Whom do you mean? Chabert?"

"I do indeed," answered Stackelberg.

"You surely are not in earnest, Prince Stackelberg. Princess Kryloff could never lower herself to fall in love with Chabert. Wanda is too proud, too dignified, to forget herself so far as that. Raymond Chabert has been of great use to me, and I have paid him well for his services. He is a very good engineer, but he is a mere nobody in society; he is not clever, and if a Frenchman is not clever, what is he?"

"I grant you all that," retorted Vassili, "but still, the Princess has undoubtedly a fancy for him."

"I think you are mistaken; however, as soon as this road through my property is finished, I shall politely ask him to take his departure. I agree with our late Emperor Nicholas concerning the French. To admit them into our country is to throw open the gates for the entrance of the Revolution."

"I depend upon you, then, dear Prince," answered Vassili, "to see the Princess and to obtain her consent?"

"I will go to her at once," answered her father, "and I hope to bring you a favorable answer."

Prince Kryloff found Wanda alone, sitting at her desk writing.

"My daughter," he exclaimed, in a glad tone, "I have good news for you. Prince Stackelberg has proposed for you."

"Well, what of that? He says I am a nihilist; what does he want with a nihilist for his wife?"

"You do not seem very well disposed towards him today?"

"All yesterday and all this morning he spent in watching me. I thought he came here look out for the rebels, but it seems he has come to look out for me."

"My child, he loves you."

"Well, that is no reason why he should be such a spy."

"He is jealous."

"Poor fellow."

"And he wants to marry you, and he has sent me to you to ask your consent."

"I am very sorry to hear it."

"Why? Why?"

"Because I positively refuse to marry him."

"What! You refuse him?"

"Certainly I do.

"The best match in the empire! Reflect for a moment: this is the best offer you have ever had. I beg of you do not throw away your prospects in a fit of bad humor."

"I do not refuse Prince Stackelberg because I am in a bad humor, but because I do not love him."

"You need not love him. There is nothing more stupid than a love-match. Look at me. I married for love, and I surely have paid dear for it."

"There is one other person who has paid still dearer," retorted Wanda.

"Whom do you mean?" said the Prince, frowning.

"I mean her."

He made no answer to this remark; he feared another outbreak.

"Wanda," he went on, "I very much desire your marriage, and this proposal suits me in every respect. Vassili has a large fortune, as do I. Your children will inherit it all, and . . ."

"I do not care for money," interrupted Wanda, "and I have other views for my marriage."

"What do you mean ? Whom do you desire to marry? Will you not tell me?"

"I know you will never give your consent. He is not a nobleman, and I do not even know whom his family are."

"What means has he?"

"He has no means."

"Then certainly you must be insane."

"I do not estimate people according to their rank. It is merely an accident of birth, and after all, what is birth? We nobles are all descended from some old robber or murderer, or . . ."

Upon hearing these words the anger of the Prince knew no bounds. The sweat stood in great beads on his forehead; his hands were clenched; his mouth was white with rage. His voice trembled so he could hardly speak.

"This is all sheer folly," he said at length. "Marriage is not a pastime, to last but for an hour; it is a serious thing to undertake, involving not only your own life, but the lives of your children. Do you wish to shame me before the eyes of the world?"

"I do not see what there is shameful in marrying an honorable, talented man."

"Is this person whom you fancy a Russian?"

"No, he is a Frenchman."

"Chabert! It is Chabert!" shrieked the Prince, utterly beside himself with rage. "Never, never! I would rather see you dead. I am afraid of myself! I am afraid of myself!"

He rushed toward the door, but Wanda stood in the way. "Father," she said, "do not mention our conversation to any one, above all, to Chabert, and do not send him away. He knows nothing of my feelings for him; he is perfectly respectful, and a pure-minded man. If you send him away, I know what I shall do."

"What?"

"I shall go with him."

"You would leave me to follow that fellow?"

"I certainly should."

"Wanda," said Prince Kryloff, "I give you two days for reflection, not about Chabert, but about your marriage with Vassili Stackelberg. If you wish to marry without my consent, and if you refer the question to the Assembly, you certainly will not obtain its sanction."

Wanda listened to her father with a smile upon her lips; she would have denied him openly had she not suddenly thought of the meeting that she was to attend that night.

"Very well," she said, "as you offer to give me two days to think over Prince Stackelberg's proposal, I will accept your terms. Day after tomorrow at this time, I will give you my answer."

"Is that a promise?"

"It is."

"And you will not do anything between now and then without letting me know?"

"I will not; I give you my word."

"That will do; now we must see about our party tomorrow. Have you asked Joseph if everything is attended to?"

"Not yet, but I am going to."

"My dear child," said the Prince, "do not forget that all the happiness and all the pride of my life depend wholly on you."

"If that is so," said Wanda, "do not forget that you promised me also to give a present of money to every one of your workmen tomorrow, if I would consent to take an interest in the party."

"Yes, I will do so, but I shall give the money in your name.

"Please do not. Please give it in your own name; I have a reason for asking you to do this."

"Well, I will think it over; but I do not care to be taxed with a liberalism which I do not feel. It would be undertaking to play a part for which I have no talent whatever."

CHAPTER XXXIX

THE SURPRISE

When Wanda found herself alone she hastened to write the following note:

My Dear Raymond,
    What I told you this morning has come to pass. My father wishes me to marry the German. I have not, as yet, told him of our marriage, but if he pushes me too far I shall tell him all. In that case I shall be obliged to quit his house; he will never accept you as a son-in-law. You must be very careful when you come for me tonight. Wait for me at the lower gate, and do not show yourself near the house today.

All that day Wanda appeared absorbed in the preparations for the entertainment that was to come off the next evening. She went from one room to the other giving orders, superintending the decorations, and always seeming very agreeable to Prince Stackelberg, who followed her about incessantly. He knew that she had requested two days in which to consider his proposal and never doubted that her decision would be favorable to him.

Night had fallen. Prince Kryloff was in bed, just going to sleep, when a terrible thought crossed his brain. What if Wanda's politeness to Stackelberg were but a ruse to throw them off the track? Where had Chabert been all day long? What if Wanda were to run off with him that very night?

It was eleven o'clock. He got up, dressed himself quickly, and hastened to the door of Wanda's cottage.

It was a lovely night, starlit and clear. There was no light in the windows. He listened; there was no sound. He looked around him for the night watchmen. At last he saw one stretched out on the ground, sound asleep. He pushed him with his foot. No answer. He shook him, but he could not arouse him; the man had evidently been drinking.

The Prince went around to the back of the house, and there he found another guard asleep upon a bench. He struck him violently. The watchman opened his great blue eyes for a moment and then closed them again. Evidently this man, too, was drunk.

He examined the shrubbery and tried to open the door, but it resisted all his efforts. Everything was perfectly silent. His suspicions began to fade away. He heard nothing but the nightingale trilling out her pearly notes on the silent night air. As he turned away, greatly relieved, to go to his own room, a slight noise, like the drawing of a bolt, made him pause and hide himself quickly behind a clump of trees. Then he saw a shadow on the gravel walk; a woman was coming out of the cottage.

It was Wanda.

The Prince stood terrified, dumbfounded, rooted to the earth. Wanda was walking very fast; somebody must be waiting for her; could it be Chabert?

He would follow her and find out what she was about. He suspected that she was going to the lower park gate, and crossing the park he made for that point.

He reached the gate and waited for her. In a few moments he heard a horse snorting on the other side of the wall. A man spoke to it: the voice was Chabert's!

The Prince saw Wanda coming towards the gate; as she put the key in the lock, her father sprang forward and seized her in his arms.

"You shall not go out!" he said, in a hollow voice.

Wanda gave a stifled cry. "I will go," she replied.

"Where?"

She made no answer.

"I know where you are going. You are going to run away with that Frenchman."

"I am engaged to be married to him," she said.

"Is that true? How long have you been engaged?"

"We have exchanged rings before witnesses, so you can no longer oppose our marriage."

"We shall see about that. Meanwhile, you shall not pass through this gate."

"I beg you, father, to let me go! I am not going to run away, I assure you. I shall be back in two hours, but I must go."

"Well, tell me where you are going."

"I am going to see a poor woman who is dangerously ill. I promised to send her something, and the preparations for tomorrow put it all out of my mind."

"Well, I will go with you."

"That is impossible."

"What a lie you are telling me! What is this woman's name?"

"Akoulina Federoff."

She was the doctor's sister; she was really very ill. Wanda had been intending to go to see her all day long to tell her about her brother Michael.

"Federoff!" cried the Prince. "How dare you pronounce that accursed name in my presence?"

His whole past life seemed to pass before him like a dream. "Wretched girl! Wretched girl! Tomorrow I shall take care that none of these Federoffs remain longer on my estate. Give me the key of the gate."

"I will not!" answered Wanda.

The Prince held a stick in his hand; Wanda knew this well. She was frightened — not about herself, but about Raymond.

"What are you going to do?" she asked, in a beseeching voice.

"Open the gate, I tell you!"

"No, I will not," repeated Wanda.

The moon was shining full upon the young girls face. Her resemblance to her mother was striking.

"Curses upon her!" cried the Prince, beside himself with rage; "it is Alexandra herself — her own devilish, infernal self!"

He raised his hand to strike, when he was seized from behind by a powerful arm. It was Raymond, who, hearing this violent altercation, had climbed the wall to find out what was the matter.

The Prince turned, and disengaging himself, brought down his stick upon Raymond's head with great force. The young Frenchman sprang lightly aside, and before the blow could be repeated, Wanda threw herself between them. Seizing her father's uplifted arm, she cried out:

"Do not strike him! Do not strike him! He is my husband!"

"Your husband!" shouted the Prince. "I do not believe a word of it! Get out of here, Sir! Get out of here, I tell you!"

Wanda quickly unlocked the gate, and pushed Raymond out.

"Go on," she said, "and tell the Federoffs that I cannot come to them tonight."

"The Federoffs! The Federoffs!" roared the Prince.

Wanda turned away to go back to the house, her father following her. They walked on without saying a word. Her father could hardly hold himself up. Wild with rage, he tottered from side to side like a drunken man.

Wanda began to regret the step she had taken. As she saw her father in such distress her heart softened towards him, but the thought of his violence, rage, and injustice, kept alive her rebellious feelings.

"Wanda," he said suddenly. "I have a right to insist upon an explanation. What Is the meaning of all this? You merely wished to frighten me, did you not? You are not engaged to Chabert? Still less is he your husband. Let us sit down here; I cannot stand."

He sank upon a seat, and Wanda took her place by his side.

"I have often," he continued, "been unjust and unkind and angry with you; but my whole nature is embittered by my past life. Look at your own eccentricities; your mysterious comings and goings, enough to exasperate the mildest father. Be loving to me, my child, and pity me. Tell me that you are not going to leave me. Above all, promise me that you will not think of marrying this Frenchman, this ambitious wretch, who covets your fortune much more than your heart. This low adventurer; this . . ."

"That is enough," said Wanda, rising; "I cannot allow you to speak in that manner of Raymond, whom I esteem deeply, and who is really my husband.

The Prince sprang to his feet.

"Your husband! Your husband!" he cried. "Oh, no! It cannot be. You must be joking with me. You are not married?"

"Yes, we are married."

"Since when?"

"For four months."

"Where were you married?"

"In Petersburg."

"In what parish ?"

"I shall not tell you."

"If I have to search through the whole forty-eight parishes of Petersburg, I shall find out. What priest has dared to perform this marriage without my consent? And if there is such a marriage, I shall have it broken, and the priest who has dared to break the canon law of the church shall be severely punished. I mean what I say, and you know I am not to be trifled with."

"I know it well."

"And still you do not fear me. Who has taught you to drive me to despair in this manner?"

"Do you really wish to know?"

"Yes; I do."

"Well, I will tell you," said Wanda. "For a long time I have been striving to awaken in you a sense of justice to make you understand that you are in no way superior to other men. I have wished by this marriage of mine to humiliate your pride, and thus to avenge those whom you harassed and oppressed. I wished to avenge my own noble mother whom you tortured. I wished to avenge Michael Federoff, whom you condemned to the most infamous punishment. These are not your only crimes. Daily you oppress the poor, strike the weak, outrage the defenseless. How often have I tried to check you in this criminal course."

"Criminal! I a criminal!" uttered the Prince. "Yes, Wanda, you are a nihilist like your mother!"

"I am exactly like her," replied Wanda, "and that is why I married Chabert. You dreamed of an alliance for me which would increase our wealth, and place me at the head of Russian society. You desired as my husband a Russian nobleman, powerful and haughty, imbued with all your ideas of authority. I on the contrary, desired a poor, honest man, kindly and generous, and I have found him in Raymond Chabert."

"Hush, Wanda, hush," repeated the Prince. "You will drive me crazy. You dare to pass judgement upon me and my actions? Come home at once.

Tomorrow I will talk this over with you. I cannot allow this marriage, nor do I entirely believe in it. Why have you kept it from me for four months? I suppose you have exchanged rings, but just now I can talk with you no more on this subject. I only ask one thing of you; give me two days' respite. Tomorrow two or three hundred persons will be here; after the fete is over, I will see you again about it. But no scandal, Wanda, I entreat you. If you knew how to treat me, you could do anything with me, but you shock me all the time."

"Father, you do not know how often you shock every one about you. Look at that stick in your hand, that was raised but a little while so to strike me and Raymond! Yesterday, when the work women in the paper mill sent to ask you to raise their wages, what was your answer? That instead of ten kopecks extra, you would give them ten blows of your stick extra."

"My child, you did not read their address; it was insolent beyond expression. They not only demanded more pay, but also shorter hours of work."

"Well, what if they did? It would not ruin you to grant their request."

"If I were to grant everything they ask, I should soon be ruined. I cannot increase their wages. You will — But I am taking cold; I am shaking all over. Kill me, Wanda! Ah, such ingratitude! There is no wish of yours that I have ever denied. And how many sacrifices I have made to ameliorate the condition of those workmen! But the more I grant them, the more do they strive to grasp. You can look through my books, and you will see that in some of the factories the outlay has far exceeded the income. Ah, these workmen! These vermin! These low wretches!"

Wanda sighed. "It will never be any better with him," she murmured.

They had reached Wanda's cottage. She bade her father good night and went into the house. As soon as she had shut the door behind her the Prince went up to one of the watchmen, who was still asleep, and kicked him. The man awoke and jumped up, looking at his master with a scared face.

"This is the way you do your duty, is it? Well, I will pay you what you have earned."

Raising his stick, the Prince beat him with all his might, and at last gave him such a violent blow that it knocked him out. He then went back where the other watchman of the house slept the drunkard's sleep and treated him in the same manner.

Wanda, hearing these cries and howls, threw open her window and looked out; she was witness to the whole scene.

"Ah, my dear Katia!" she said, turning to her friend, "surely the measure of his iniquity is full. He does not believe in my marriage as yet, but as soon as he finds the proof of it, he is fully capable of killing Raymond and me too."

"What are you going to do?" asked Katia.

"I don't know, but I feel that I must decide at once."

"You must indeed," said Katia. "It would be miserable weakness to sit still and look on at such scenes as the one we have just witnessed, without speaking."

"Listen to me, Katia; you know my whole heart; I have hid nothing from you. I know that my father is most culpable; no one knows it so well as me. But when I think of all the love he has bestowed on me, of all the hopes he has centered in me, I shrink from striking the blow which I feel will cut him to the heart. He is my father, Katia. I cannot help excusing his vices, which are but the result of the barbarous civilization of our land."

"But you owe it to the cause to withdraw your approval from his iniquitous actions. Besides, you are married. It is your duty to go with your husband."

"Tonight," answered Wanda, "our friends are to have a meeting in the paper mill. If I get up very early tomorrow morning, I shall be able to get there before they break up. I hope Padlewsky will be there, for I do not wish to determine upon any plan of action without consulting him."

"Have you not asked your mother for her advice?"

"Yes, but I want to speak to Michael and our Petersburg friends about it. As soon as it is daylight, go to Akoulina's house and tell her to say that she was expecting me there yesterday."

Meanwhile the Prince had sent two fresh watchmen to guard the cottage, with strict orders to allow no one to leave it.

CHAPTER XL

THE VILLAGE

Very early in the morning, Katia, who had not been able to sleep, opened her shutters to let in the light. The first thing that struck her eye was the two new guards. She instantly went to the Princess with the news.

Wanda dressed herself hastily, and leaning out of her window, called the men to her. All the servants adored her, for she treated them as her equals, and they would have gone through fire and water for her.

"My friends," she said, "Katia and I want to go out; we shall probably be away for three hours, and the Prince must know nothing about it. Do you understand?"

"Yes, your Excellency," they answered, "the Prince shall know nothing of it."

Wanda's coachman had also received a warning not to provide her with a carriage under any pretext, but he, like the watchmen, adored her. About five o'clock she and Katia stepped into a droschky, drawn by a spirited little horse, and drove rapidly away in the direction of Krylow.

Wanda stopped the carriage at a point where two roads crossed. Katia got out.

"It will take you about an hour," said Wanda, "to get to Akoulina's, and from there to the factory."

Katia walked away, while Wanda drove on to the paper mill, which was under the superintendence of Zobolewsky.

Before Katia had arrived at the Federoffs, she heard a sound of wheels behind her. Looking back, she saw a carriage rushing along at a tremendous pace. She hid behind a hedge, and the vehicle passed her. "It must be the Prince going to Federoff's cottage," she said. Not knowing exactly what to do, she walked slowly on.

In the meanwhile the Prince had driven into the little village, and had stopped his horses before the mayor's house. That functionary hastily coming out to give his respects to his lord, Prince Kryloff asked him to point out the Federoff's cottage, and instantly drove towards it.

It was a pretty little house, standing on the outskirts of a pine forest. The front door was adorned with some very good wood carvings. A little garden ran alongside, already glowing with early spring flowers.

The Prince got out of his carriage and knocked rudely at the door. As he entered, he was struck by the air of elegance which pervaded everything within. Numerous articles of fine porcelain and glass adorned the room; carved oaken chests and a large wardrobe, a fine samovar of brilliant copper: all indicated comparative comfort.

On a bed in the middle of the room, surrounded by her family, lay Akoulina, evidently very near death. A person who appeared to be a physician was sitting by her side holding her hand. The Prince took him for the village doctor.

"Has Princess Wanda been here?" he asked.

"We have not seen her, Your Excellency," answered one of the women, very timidly.

"Is your daughter Akoulina ill?" he inquired.

Old Federoff merely pointed to the bed, but spoke not a word.

"Did you expect the Princess here yesterday?"

No one answered.

"Answer me, I tell you! Did she promise you that she would be here?" asked the Prince again, impatiently.

"The Princess told us perhaps she might be here," answered the old man.

"Is the Princess here? Where is she?" cried Akoulina, struggling to arise.

"The Princess is not here," answered her sister-in-law. "It is the Prince."

The dying girl, hearing these words, by a terrible effort sat upright in her bed. Looking eagerly around, she hissed through her teeth: "Michael! Michael! Hide! Hide!" Then, speaking to the Prince, she continued with an obsequious, "Michael is not here, Your Excellency. He has not done anything wrong. Will you punish him with the knout again?"

"She is delirious," muttered old Federoff. "She takes the doctor for Michael."

But the Prince fixed his eyes on the stranger. Suddenly a strange look came upon his face. He rushed forward and, seizing the man by the arm, turned him round to the light.

"It is Michael, indeed," he said.

Michael looked him full in the face, as he spoke: "I came to be with my sister in her last moments; she is going to die."

The Prince did not hear him.

"Here?" he said. "Here? He dares to appear here, on my estate?"

"This is a free village," retorted Michael.

"But you are not free. You have been condemned to the mines, and there shall you go."

The whole family, weeping and gesticulating, surrounded the Prince, imploring him to pardon Michael.

"Pardon him!" he cried. "Surely there is a God in heaven, and he has brought him back to me, and there is such a thing as justice, and I will teach him to know it."

"There is neither God nor justice!" cried out old Federoff. "Or . . ."

"Or what?" said the Prince.

"Mercy! Mercy your Excellency!" said the younger sister.

"Hush!" said Michael. "What is the use of lowering yourself to this man?"

"This man!" screamed the Prince. "Of whom are you speaking? I will teach you how to behave yourself."

He lifted his stick to strike, but Michael avoided the blow by striking up the Prince's hand, and the cane flew across the room, shattering the crockery into myriad pieces.

"Stop!" cried the old man. "This shall not go on. Swear to me this moment that you will allow Michael to escape! Swear it before this shrine of the Virgin, or you shall not leave this house alive!"

"And who is to prevent me from leaving this house?" asked the Prince, with a sneer.

"We will!" said the old man.

Michael's brother, Michael himself, and their father stood before the door — three powerful enemies.

The Prince saw his danger, but with dignity he said, "I order you to let me pass."

The three men did not move.

He raised his hand to strike the old man, but the sons stopped him.

"What!" said he. "Dare you lift your hands against me?"

"You have not only raised your hand but your leathern thongs against us. In those days, the power was on your side; now, it is on ours. The law of force is the only law in which you believe. It is now your turn to submit. Down on your knees, and ask pardon of God, and also of your victims!"

"Ask pardon of you clowns?" roared the Prince, and he rushed upon Michael, but Ivan and his father pinioned his arms from behind.

They cried out, "Swear that you will not have Michael arrested."

Rage and indignation had rendered the Prince half blind. He was afraid that he would lose his conscious. He said, "I will not have him arrested," at last.

"Keep him here," cried Michael, "while I make my escape." He kissed Akoulina, and flew out of the door.

Korolef was waiting for him in a little thicket hard by, and they drove off hurriedly to the paper mill. The Prince was not allowed to quit the cottage until half an hour later. He was wild with fury. He had but one thought, and that was vengeance.

When he came to the public square, he found the priest, the mayor, and the two deputy mayors waiting for him. The season, they said, had been bad. They had also been obliged to buy expensive machinery, and they had met together to implore the Prince to grant them a twelvemonth longer in which to pay their land tax. But the Prince would not listen to them.

"I will not grant you a day!" he answered. "Not an hour! You are all rich! The Federoffs are rich! You are all nihilists!"

"Nihilists!" exclaimed the priest. "The Federoffs may be, Your Excellency, for they never set their foot inside of the church, but all of us are pious men, who love God and the Czar."

"Are you sure that the Federoffs are nihilists?"

"They are always talking against their betters," answered the priest. "They are in constant correspondence with the workmen in the mill, who are all revolutionists, and they even have been heard to say that the Princess is a nihilist herself."

Without hearing another word, the Prince got into his droschky.

"May we not hope, Your Excellency," said the mayor, very humbly, "that you will grant us a little delay?"

"Not one day!" answered the Prince. "You can borrow the money from the Jews."

"Drive to Krylow," he called out to the coachman.

CHAPTER XI

THE PAPER MILL

As Wanda drove up to the paper mill, Matcha ran down to receive her.

"Come in, come in, dear Wanda!" she said. "Padlewsky is here, and several others. Make haste, the workmen will be coming in before long, and we do not want them to see us."

They ran up a narrow, dirty little staircase to the superintendent's office. Several men were sitting around a table in the middle of the room, and lying on a sofa was a remarkably beautiful woman. She was not young, for her hair was white as snow, but her face and figure had preserved their youthful character.

As soon as Wanda entered the woman jumped up and threw her arms around the Princess, exclaiming, "My daughter! My child!"

Wanda could hardly speak. Presently she said: "How could you be so imprudent as to come here?"

"I could not stay away from you any longer," replied Princess Alexandra.

In a few moments Wanda looked around her and recognized Litzanoff and Padlewsky, although both of them were disguised.

"You are superb, Litzanoff!" she said, "and you too, Padlewsky. How much it must have cost you two to make yourselves so hideous. Where is Raymond?"

"He will be here soon," said Matcha. "He has gone to Krylow to get a carriage for use in case you make up your mind to run away tonight."

"I have come to ask your opinion about this matter," said Wanda, turning to Padlewsky.

"I have been opposed to it up to the present time, my dear Wanda, because it might damage the party seriously. Of course if you leave your father's house to join the nihilists, it will naturally make a great stir in the world, and we shall be watched much more closely than ever. Up to this time I had always hoped that you would be able to bring Prince Stackelberg over to us."

"Prince Stackelberg! "answered the Princess. "He would only betray us. He proposed to my father for me yesterday. When he hears that I have refused him, he will never forgive me. I cannot be in any more danger among the nihilists than I am now in my own father's house."

"My beloved child," cried Alexandra, much terrified, "do not stay another day under that tiger's roof! It is your mother who commands you. Remember what I endured."

She was interrupted by the entrance of Michael and Korolef. Michael, deathly pale, and still very much agitated, told his story.

"Oh, Michael! Michael!" exclaimed Alexandra. "If he gets you in his power again, you are lost!"

"Undoubtedly," said Korolef. "But just now we cannot leave this place. Nobody will ever suspect us of hiding here. While the soldiers are searching all over the country, we had better stay quietly in the paper mill."

But Alexandra did not seem satisfied, and was evidently very uneasy.

"At any rate," said Michael, "I can only make my escape in the night. It would be too dangerous to attempt it in the daytime. In the meanwhile, tell me, my dear Padlewsky, what news have you from Petersburg?"

Hardly were the words out of his lips when the sound of carriage wheels was heard.

Matcha ran to the window.

"It is the Prince!" she whispered, "and two soldiers with him."

"There may be no cause for alarm," said Wanda. "He has come to speak to Zobolewsky about the address that the female workers gave him. Go down at once, Zobolewsky, and keep him from coming up. Here are the workmen now, and I see the women on the road."

As Zobolewsky left the room, he said to Matcha, "You know you can get out through the storeroom."

For seventeen years, Princess Alexandra had not set eyes upon her husband. She cautiously drew near the window and looked out.

"Yes, that is he," she murmured. "That is he, the barbarian!"

The soldiers were stationed each side of the entrance to the paper mill. Between them, with a whip in his hand, stood the Prince. As each female worker passed by him, she received a blow from this whip, accompanied by these words: "That is for being a nihilist."

"We are not nihilists, Your Excellency," they said, one after another.

"You must be nihilists," he answered, "to dare send me such an address as I received from you yesterday."

All of them submitted uncomplainingly to this outrage, until the last woman came up. She was about thirty years old, muscular, and very thin.

"I have five children, Your Excellency," she said, "and I am a widow. I cannot feed them and clothe them with thirty-five kopecks a day."

"That is nothing to me," answered the Prince. "Here are some roubles for your children." He threw several roubles on the ground, contemptuously.

"Now, pick them up, but you shall be punished like the rest."

The woman did not pick them up.

She drew herself up, and looked straight into Prince Kryloff's eyes.

"I am not a beggar. I work for my living. I want my rights. I will not accept alms."

The Prince raised his whip; the woman snatched it from him and struck him smartly with it. Then, crossing her arms, with a fearless voice and gesture, she said:

"Now you can do what you choose; I am avenged!"

The Prince seized her, threw her down, and literally trampled her under his feet. She never uttered a cry nor a complaint, but all the time she uttered curses upon her master. The two soldiers looked on, unmoved.

"Arrest her, and lead her away to Krylow!" ordered the Prince.

Zobolewsky wished to interpose. "Are you one of them also?" inquired the Prince, looking at him angrily.

Prince Kryloff thought he heard a low murmur among the operatives. "Stop," said he. "Fasten her to the railing, and come with me; you must search the mill."

"I assure Your Excellency you will find nothing," said Zobolewsky. "I will answer for my men with my head." But as he spoke his voice trembled slightly, and the Prince detected it.

"Your head is very unsafe, I think," said he.

"Do you suspect me, Your Excellency?"

"Not more than any one else. I suspect everybody. Go ahead, I will follow you."

Just then four more soldiers arrived, under the charge of a captain, who went up to the Prince.

"Your Excellency, there are nihilists hidden here. We have received news that three of their leaders left Krylow in the night for your paper mill. I am obliged to institute a search."

The Prince turned to Zobolewsky. "What do you think of this?" he asked.

Zobolewsky answered with perfect coolness: "I merely wish to clear myself. If there are nihilists in the mill, I shall be the first to give them up. But how are they to get in here without my knowing it? I will go upstairs and get my keys, and open every place for you myself."

He turned to go up the steps, when the captain called him back, but Zobolewsky pretended not to hear, and ran on into his office. Litzanoff and Korolef had dragged away a heavy book-case which stood in front of a door leading to the storeroom, and Korolef was just going to open it, as Zobolewsky appeared.

"Not yet, not yet!" he whispered. "The door is hidden on the other side by the wallpaper. I am going to take them first through the storerooms. They have come to search the mill. Don't open the door until we have left the next room. Then, Matcha, put the bookcase back before the door, and go into the workroom. Don't make any noise."

He ran downstairs; in a few moments they heard the heavy tread of the soldiers.

In pausing in front of the superintendent's office, Prince Kryloff asked:

"What door is this?"

Michael, Wanda and Alexandra recognized that voice and they trembled.

"I will open it in one moment, Your Excellency, but we are going into the storerooms first."

He entered the room next to his office, the soldiers and the Prince following him. This room held the reams of paper, ready for use, piled up in some places as high as the ceiling.

"If the captain desires it, I will call the men to move this paper."

"Are there no closets?" questioned the captain, sounding the walls with the handle of his sword.

"No, no," said the Prince. "There are no closets."

"Then," said Zobolewsky, loud enough for Matcha to hear, "we can go into the next room, where the second quality paper is stored; then into the drying-room, then into the folding-room, and so we shall come back to our starting-point. Afterwards we can visit my room and my foreman's room."

As soon as they went out, Matcha pushed the door. The paper on the other side gave way, and they entered the store-room. Matcha then closed the door behind them, pushed the bookcase into its place, and went down stairs to the workroom.

Having gone through every place, the Prince found himself, for the second time, standing in front of the door that Zobolewsky had not allowed him to enter. It had been locked, and now it stood open. He said nothing, but he watched.

They walked into the room lately occupied by Matcha and the rest, and the captain began examining the books in the bookcase. Zobolewsky was very nervous, opening and shutting the drawers, and trying to hurry them away.

"Why was this door locked a few minutes ago?" said the Prince.

"I suppose my wife was dressing herself."

Suddenly the Prince cried out: "Move that bookcase aside! Don't you see those cobwebs on the floor? It has been pushed there for some purpose. Arrest this man — he is an accomplice!" The soldiers immediately seized him to carry him off.

"No," said the Prince; "tie his hands, but do not go away; there are but five of you, and there are probably ten of them."

Turning to Zobolewsky, he continued: "Now that all is discovered, speak: Who is here?"

"No one that I know of, unless they have been brought here in my absence."

"You lie! Look at yourself in that mirror! You are as white as a sheet!"

They drew the bookcase aside, and there stood the door wide open.

Zobolewsky, as quick as lightning, drew his keys from his pocket, and with all his might threw them through the opening into the storeroom.

"My friends!" he cried, "escape!"

Those words were his death sentence.

"Seize him, and fall upon them," ordered the Prince. "Two of you go round to the door of the storeroom and kill them there."

But in the meanwhile they had been busy at work in the storeroom and had built up two breast-works of paper.

Unfortunately the keys fell just between these two ramparts. Korolef, who was as nimble as a monkey, crept between the two piles, but just as he seized the keys, the first pile fell down on him. Litzanoff fired upon the soldiers. The captain fell; another man was wounded.

Korolef had crept out, and was struggling hand-to-hand with the third soldier.

Raymond, Padlewsky and Michael were protecting the women. Raymond was armed with a revolver.

"Come on to the door!" cried Korolef. "I have the keys."

"No, no! Do not go out!" screamed Zobolewsky. "The door is guarded!" But Korolef, with a mighty effort, freeing himself from his antagonist, drew a dagger from his belt and smote his enemy dead.

The Prince called for the two men who were guarding the entrance to the storeroom.

"You can go!" cried Zobolewsky. "The door is free."

The Prince raised his pistol and fired at Zobolewsky; the weapon was not loaded.

Korolef was wounded, but he still fought bravely. He managed to plunge his dagger into the body of the fourth soldier. But one remained.

The Prince called for the two others, whom he had left below; they did not hear him, and he rushed down after them.

"Quick! Quick!" cried Zobolewsky. "The Prince will soon return with reinforcements. Do not lose a minute! Go into the other storeroom. Raymond, Litzanoff and I can stop anybody that comes."

At this moment the Prince entered the workroom. The machines were all going; the air was filled with their noise, buzzing, humming, beating, whistling. No sound of the tumult above could be heard down there.

The workmen with their shirts tucked into their belts, the women in their faded cotton gowns, were hurrying past one another in the courtyard. The Prince put head out of a window and called aloud: "Murder! Murder!" But no one appeared to hear him. They all seemed deaf. Matcha had told them what to do. The Prince ran down and seized one of them by the arm. "Why don't you answer me when I call you."

"Were you calling me, Your Excellency?"

"They are murdering the soldiers up there."

"I have nothing to do with the soldiers. I am not paid to defend the soldiers."

At that moment, Matcha came flying into the yard. "Come upstairs! They are murdering Zobolewsky!"

Instantly, they all rushed to protect their superintendent, whom they adored.

Kryloff understood that his life was in danger. He went to look for his carriage.

"They are all nihilists, every one of them," he repeated. "Did not you hear me, Joseph, just now, when I was calling for help?"

"I heard nothing, Your Excellency. I was asleep," said the coachman. "You made me get up so early this morning."

"You lie!"

Joseph looked frightened.

So this servant whom Prince Kryloff trusted was deceiving him, too!

As he drove away he met Katia, who had walked all the way from the Federoffs. The Prince stopped the carriage.

"Where is Wanda?"

"I suppose she is at home!"

"You lie, you miserable creature. I saw you go out together. Where are you going now?"

"I am going to the mill."

"What for?"

"To see my friend Matcha."

"And your friend Zobolewsky?"

"Yes, Your Excellency."

"She is a nihilist, too. Listen to me, Katia; do you want to make two hundred roubles? If you do, tell me where Wanda is."

"I think, Your Excellency, that she must be at home, unless she has gone out to take a walk, as she very often does in the early morning."

"You impudent liar!" roared the Prince. Snatching the whip from Joseph's hand he struck Katia with it across the face.

"I will know the truth, and if I find out that you are deceiving me, too, I will have you whipped until I see the blood come." He drove off.

Katia walked on to the mill. She found her friends in a great state of excitement, all talking together. They wanted Wanda to take refuge in flight, but she would not.

"I must go home first," she said, "and look over my papers and letters; some of them must be destroyed. I will go away tonight. Katia, and I will be at the lower garden gate tonight, and Raymond and Korolef must be there to meet us."

"What am I to do?" implored Litzanoff.

"You must go with Padlewsky and Michael and my mother; they need you to protect them."

On the road back to the cottage, Katia told the Princess of the interview with her father.

"Oh, well," answered Wanda, "we shall get home before he does." She turned her light vehicle into a rough road which crossed the woods, and at the risk of breaking her carriage, arrived at the cottage some time before her father.

He came after awhile, and instantly attacked the two watchmen.

"Where Is the Princess?" he inquired.

"She is in the house, Your Excellency."

"Has she been out?"

"No, Your Excellency."

"Has Katia been out?"

"No, Your Excellency."

The Prince put his hands up to his head.

"I see," he cried, "I see they are all against me," and turning away, he walked rapidly towards Stackelberg's bedroom. Entering unceremoniously, the Prince related to him the events of the past four hours. It was yet only eight o'clock in the morning.

Stackelberg watched the Prince as he told his strange story, and wondered if he could be in his right mind.

"I see," said the Prince to Vassili, "that you think I am insane. I am not, I assure you. As you have discretionary powers, you must act at once. Telegraph to Heyking, the Chief of Police at Kiev."

"How many workers have you in the mill?"

"Three hundred men and two hundred women."

"Five hundred!" exclaimed Stackelberg. "I shall ask Heyking for a squadron of infantry to arrest them and take them to Kiev; there is no prison in this neighborhood large enough to hold them. I will go to Krylow at once and attend to it."

"Give special orders for the arrest of Michael Federoff and his entire family."

"Very well, I will," said Stackelberg.

"Be sure you don't fail me," added Kryloff; "without you my fete would not be a success."

"Are you still going to have it? What answer has the Princess given you about me? Has she said anything?"

"We will speak about it when you come back."

"Has the Princess refused me?"

"She has asked for two days in which to make up her mind."

On the road to Krylow, Stackelberg met several of the Prince's guests on their way to the house. Among them he recognized Alexis Verenine.

CHAPTER XII

THE ENGAGEMENT

When Wanda reached home, she felt perfectly exhausted. She threw herself down on her bed, all dressed as she was, and fell fast asleep.

It was high noon when she awoke. She heard the rolling of carriages and the sound of many voices and of merry laughter. She arose with a start, remembering that it was the morning of her father's fete.

Katia came to her bedside and handed her a letter that had arrived during her sleep. It was from Nadege, and ran as follows:

My Dear Wanda:

I am at Kiev. I have come here to be near you and to hear something about Stepane. I have been very ill; his desertion of me nearly killed me. I am stopping at Countess Kousmine's; you know she is a very dear friend of mine. To my astonishment, I have discovered that she is a nihilist. She tells me that all the young people in this town are of the same way of thinking. I hope to see you soon, when I shall be able to tell you more.

Your best friend,
Nadege

P. S. If Stepane is at your house, speak about me to him, but do not tell him where I am. I do not intend again to burden him with my presence, unless he desires it.

"Poor Nadege," sighed Wanda. "Why can I not give her back her husband's heart?"

"Is Countess Kousmine General Kousmine's wife?" asked Katia. "If she is, we can go to her house when we arrive at Kiev; no one will suspect the General of harboring socialists."

"That is a capital idea," answered Wanda; "I will write to Nadege at once, and . . ."

She was interrupted by the entrance of a footman, with a note. It was from Raymond.

"The inquisitor is at work. The paper mill has been evacuated. There has been a fight between the workers and the soldiery; several are killed and wounded. A company of soldiers is stationed at the village; they have placed sentinels around the mill. The Federoff's are arrested. Akoulina is entirely alone, dying. No one dares go near her. Michael begs you to send her assistance. Do you think it will be prudent for us to make our escape tonight?"

Wanda read this note, and then sat for several minutes lost in thought; her face glowed with indignation, her bosom heaved with rage. At last she took a pen, and wrote these words rapidly, in French: "Nothing is changed in my plans. Come for me at midnight."

"It took me some time to decide," she said to Katia, "but now my determination is fixed."

The servant had hardly left the room with the note before her father entered.

"What are you doing, Wanda?" he said. "Our guests have all arrived, and you are not even dressed yet."

"I have been thinking very hard, my father, and I have made up my mind."

"About what?"

"I have made up my mind that you can announce my engagement to Prince Vassili Stackelberg."

"Are you in earnest, my daughter?"

"You never believed that I was really married to Raymond Chabert, did you? I only wanted to frighten you, and to cure you of your horrid habit of spying on me. I hope you will forgive me now, in consideration of my present determination."

"You have given me a great deal of pain, Wanda, but I forgive you everything," and he pressed her to his heart. "My dear daughter, let us have no more quarrels! I give you my word of honor, I will not suspect you any more."

"Confess," said Wanda, laughing, "that you are glad to hand me over to someone else, who will spare you all trouble. I think Stackelberg is both jealous and suspicious."

The Prince left Wanda's room, beaming with delight. He was in such a good temper that he received his guests in that fine manner which gave him the reputation of being the most elegant gentleman of his day.

At four o'clock Stackelberg returned. "Now," he said, "we can enjoy ourselves in peace; the country is quiet."

"Well, Vassili Antonovitch," returned Prince Kryloff "You shall have your reward. My daughter consents to marry you, and I am the happiest man in Russia."

"Is that really so?" asked Vassili, violently agitated.

"Yes; I am going to announce your engagement today."

A few moments after this conversation, dinner was served. It was as magnificent as the Russian nobility's feasts proverbially are, but superb as it was, it was as nothing compared to the entertainment that the Prince had provided for the evening of that memorable day.

The night was warm; the air heavy with spring odors; the moon shone, but fitfully, one moment lighting up the scene with silvery splendor, then casting over all her dreamy shadows. A band of gypsy musicians, hidden among a clump of trees, gave to the air their weird and unfamiliar music. The brilliantly attired guests wandered through the park, which was lighted by colored lanterns. It was a dream of fairyland. The waters of the Dnieper caught the many-colored lights and reflected them back with shimmering brilliance.

Wanda was charming. She went from one group to the other, laughing, talking, bewitching them all by her beauty, her grace, and her wit. Her father was watching her anxiously; she seemed unnatural to him. Her laugh sounded forced; her eyes looked feverish.

It was eleven o'clock, and the Prince had ordered a beautiful display of fireworks to commence. Wanda was leaning on Stackelberg's arm.

"How can I thank you?" he whispered.

"I wished to reward you," she answered, with a coquettish smile, "for the zeal you have displayed against the nihilists."

"It is a perfect miracle that the Prince's life was spared," said Stackelberg.

"What a magnificent report you will have to send in, Vassili! You have a brilliant future before you."

"Say, rather, we have, dear Wanda; you will share all my labors and all my glory."

The servants were sending up some blue lights; at that moment the unearthly glare enveloped them as with a halo. Wanda wore a strange costume that night. It was made of steel-grey satin and red velvet. The front was of grey, laid in fine plaits; it looked like a coat of mail. In the midst of the light from the fireworks, the red of the dress resembled a lambent flame. Wanda herself, pale and dark, with a mocking smile upon her lips, might have been taken for a rebellious angel.

There was a murmur of admiration among the guests, breaking out at last into applause.

"How superb! How wonderful! Bravo! Hurrah for the fair Beelzebub!"

"You are beautiful," said Stackelberg, "but you are terrible. If I did not love you as I do, I should fear you."

"You ought to fear me. I think it will take a very brave man to marry me."

"I am a brave man, I hope. Don't you think so?"

"Yes . . . rather."

"What do you mean?" said Vassili.

"I remember a circumstance in which you did not show yourself particularly courageous."

"Please tell me what that was."

"Do you remember the time you challenged Litzanoff?"

"I do."

"The duel never came off, did it?"

"Litzanoff was arrested, and since that we have never met, but if you wish me to fight him, I will try and find out where he is."

"He has gone to Monte Carlo, I believe," said Wanda, carelessly.

"He was in love with you, and I was jealous of him; and . . ."

"You had him imprisoned!" exclaimed Wanda, excitedly.

"I — What makes you think that ? I swear to you . . ."

"There is no use of swearing, Prince Stackelberg. You only did your duty. The poor fool was a nihilist, or something very much like it . . . But I feel cold; let us go into the house."

They walked together as far as the entrance of the large drawing-room. Wanda drew her hand away from Vassili's arm, and leaned against the side of the door. Around her hung a portiere from Karamania's loom, a mingled weave of black and red.

Several gentlemen were in the room, discussing the political situation. They were interested and animated, representing the different shades of opinion among the higher classes of Russia. One of them, a small, elderly man, pleaded the cause of the people, although at the same time praising the Czar; another ardently desired reform, but dreaded a revolution; another maintained that religion alone, and its adoption by the masses, could set the country right.

"The common people," said Stackelberg, "must have religion. It is a necessity to them in the hard lives they lead."

"Do you acknowledge," broke in Wanda, "that the common people do lead a hard life?"

"Of course I do; it is very evident," he replied.

"But what does your Government do for them?" she continued. "Every man for himself and the devil take the hindmost — that is your motto. And then you are astonished at the existence of the nihilists. I am only astonished that the Government holds together as well as it does."

"Take care, Wanda Petrowna!" said Stackelberg, laughing, "people will say you are a nihilist yourself!"

Wanda walked forward until she had reached the middle of the room. Her long red train glided like a serpent behind her. The steely satin seemed molded to her breast; on her arms great rubies, set in steel, sent forth their darting light; upon her breast a ruby lizard held a spray of scarlet flowers.

She was dazzling; her costume fairly glittered; but, above all, shone her great dark eyes.

She stood before them all, and without a shade of fear, she spoke:

"Gentlemen, I am a nihilist. I can hide it no longer. I wish to overturn this Asiatic government. 'Zemlia y Volia' is my motto. Down with all governments, royal, imperial, autocratic, whatever you may call them! I am a revolutionist! Down with the nobles! Down with the infamous secret police, which arrests, tortures, and exiles every noble creature in Russia! Away with the hateful Third Section, of whom Mister Vassili Stackelberg is the fit representative!"

She waved her hand towards him with a gesture of the most superb disdain.

Stackelberg's eyes almost started from his head. Everyone thought himself dreaming.

"Yes," resumed Wanda, "I am for the free federation of all working corporations. I desire that the workman shall receive the proceeds of his work. I desire that capital shall not receive all the benefits of labor. I desire the complete renovation of society. Now, Mister Stackelberg, you, who understand the system of arrests, why do you not arrest me? Do you still desire to unite your fate with mine?"

The gentlemen in the room looked at one another. Vassili could neither speak nor move; he vaguely understood that something fearful was taking place.

Prince Kryloff, delighted with the success of his entertainment, just then wandered aimlessly into the drawing-room, and looking around, suddenly became aware that there was something wrong.

"What have you been saying, Wanda, to shock our guests?" he asked.

"I have been telling them that I am a nihilist, and that you, Prince Kryloff, have made me one. You, who grind the poor to the earth, who oppress the weak, who beat your servants as if they were dogs. And what difference is there between you and them? The lowest of them is better than you, for he has never committed the crimes you have. This very morning you have been beating the poor women who asked you for a few kopecks to buy bread for their children. You trampled one woman under your feet because she dared to reason with you. There are laws in Russia, but there are no judges brave enough to enforce them. So I will judge you! I will pronounce sentence upon you!"

She crossed the room with unfaltering step, and left it unhindered.

The Prince had already passed through too much for his strength that day. As he listened to his daughter, a mist passed before his eyes. He tried to speak; he tried to go to her and force her to be silent; but his knees bent beneath him and his tongue clove to the roof of his mouth.

Wanda's last words overpowered him. His face became purple; his eyelids twitched convulsively. His eyeballs rolled in their sockets like a maniac's and then glared before them with frightful fixedness. He tottered, and with a cry of "Stop her! Stop her!" he fell to the earth.

CHAPTER XLIII

FLIGHT

No one dared to stop Wanda. Calm, stately as a goddess, Princess Wanda walked through her father's halls. She was pale as death.

The night had grown dark. Rain was falling, and lightning darted through the heavens. The guests, with flying feet, were seeking shelter.

Verenine crossed Wanda's path. She held out her hand and took his, pressing it affectionately. "Farewell," she said.

"Where are you going, Wanda? What ails you? Are you ill? Are they forcing you to marry this German?"

"I shall not marry him," she replied. "I am going away."

"Where?"

"To Siberia, perhaps."

"I will go with you, Wanda, if you will let me."

"I will not let you. Goodbye."

They had reached the vestibule. She wrapped herself in a large waterproof cloak.

The storm was raging, the rain beating against the window panes. She had on a little pair of steel-gray satin slippers, fastened with bows of red velvet.

"Wait one moment, Wanda; you will get your feet wet."

"Oh, no matter," she answered.

But Verenine, to her astonishment, took her up in his arms, and bore her through the driving storm to her own cottage.

"I really did not think you were so strong," said Wanda, laughing. "You might be of some use to us."

"Shall I go with you?" he asked, anxiously.

"No, not now. But meet me at Kiev the day after tomorrow, at Countess Kousmine's. See that you tell no one where I shall be."

Everything was ready for her flight. She put on her dark traveling dress — her wedding dress. Then she unfastened her hair and let it fall in all its beauty upon her shoulders. It touched the ground.

"Cut it off, Katia," she said. Katia hesitated, and Wanda, impatiently taking up the scissors, began the work of destruction.

"It is no time now, Katia," she said, "for sentimental nonsense. Cut it off, and be done with it."

It was soon over. A red wig was placed upon her head and a pair of blue spectacles upon her nose. Then, clothing herself in her waterproof and a large bonnet, she went out into the storm.

It was midnight. They reached the park gate unmolested. A kibitka-style carriage was awaiting them, drawn by five spirited ponies. Two men were seated in the carriage; one held the horses. It was Korolef.

Wanda recognized Litzanoff seated by the side of Chabert.

"Here you are, all three," she said.

"Yes, Federoff has arranged it all," answered Stepane. "He thinks we had better come with you, as we may be attacked."

"Where are we all to meet again?"

"At Kiev, at Mentikoff, the printer's. Raymond has bought these horses so that we shall not have to stop at the post-houses."

They got into the carriage, Korolef mounted in front, and they drove off at a furious pace. They had no luggage. Katia held on her knees a little trunk containing Wanda's jewels and a large sum of money. Otherwise they were unencumbered. What good would trunks of fine clothes do them, entering now upon the apostle's life, a life without rest, without peace?

The rain was over. The wind had risen and was sweeping over the country furiously. It was still very dark, lighted only occasionally by fierce lightning flashes.

Our four travelers sat in perfect silence. They felt that this hour was the turning point of their existence.

Wanda was thinking. Did she hesitate? Did she fear? No; but she felt the deepest pity for her father, and her heart ached.

"What are you thinking about, Wanda?" asked Katia.

But she dared not speak to her inflexible friend the thoughts that troubled her.

"I am thinking of the past and of the future," she replied.

"Do you regret what you have done?"

"No."

Gradually the storm died away, and the two young girls, utterly worn out, fell asleep.

They were entering a dark wood when they heard a pistol-shot behind them, then the galloping of horses.

"What was that?" asked Wanda, waking up.

"There are probably soldiers hidden in the woods," answered Litzanoff, and he instantly loaded his revolver, as did also Raymond and Korolef.

A second shot was fired, and four mounted soldiers surrounded the kibitka.

"Stop!" they cried. But Korolef urged his horses on. The soldiers struck spurs into their beasts, rushed past the carriage, and fired all at once. One of the horses was shot through the head; the others galloped madly on for a few minutes, when a second horse fell. Then Korolef stopped. Litzanoff and Raymond fired.

Wanda and Katia held their pistols in their hands, loaded and ready for action.

"Do not fire." said Stepane. "When we have discharged our revolvers, you can hand us yours."

Litzanoff and Raymond fired again.

One of the soldiers fell to the ground, and his horse galloped away.

"That is all right, "said Litzanoff. "We are now even: three against three."

Day began to dawn in the east, and dimly lighted their struggle.

"Lie down in the carriage!" said Litzanoff to the two young women. "We have wounded the second man. We shall soon get the better of the other two."

"Are you hit?" asked Wanda.

"I am just touched on the shoulder."

"And you, Raymond?"

As she spoke, a ball struck him full in the breast; Wanda screamed aloud.

"That is a woman's voice," said one of the soldiers. "They are here!"

Raymond tore open his waistcoat to see where he was wounded.

"There is little harm done," he said. "The ball has flattened itself against my pocket book."

The cover of the kibitka was riddled with balls, but they had not touched the women, who were lying down in the bottom of the carriage.

The third soldier's horse fell, and the two others, believing the rebels to be more numerous than themselves, gave up the fight and galloped off in the direction of Bielaja, whose cupolas and towers could now be faintly seen in the distance.

There was, however, no time to lose, for they would certainly soon return with reinforcements.

The fugitives got out of the carriage. Korolef examined the beasts; two were badly wounded, but the other three could be driven.

While they were hitching up the horses again, Katia went to see if the two soldiers were really dead. One of them still breathed; she lifted his head and he opened his eyes.

"Whom are you looking for?" she asked.

"The nihilists from Krylow."

"What orders have you received?"

"To detain every carriage going from Krylow to Kiev."

"And to shoot the travelers?"

"Yes, if they resisted," he added, in a very feeble voice. "The nihilists! the nihilists! Djagguernot! The devils! Holy Virgin, have mercy upon me!"

He fell back insensible.

Katie took two pieces of paper from her pocket, and on them she wrote with a red pencil the words, "Killed for having fired upon the nihilists!" She pinned these two slips upon the coats of the two soldiers.

Now they had to change their route and avoid passing through Bielaja. So they plunged into the woods. At the end of half an hour, after having followed a road marked only by notches in the trunks of the trees, they reached a sort of clearing, where tall pine trees with gleaming trunks pointed their trembling spires heavenward. Here was a gypsy camp, and two jaded horses were browsing upon the scanty herbage.

"I have an idea," said Wanda. "Let us exchange our carriage for one of these carts, and we can dress as gypsies. The alarm has by this time been given all over the country, and before night we shall probably be arrested, if we do not take some prompt measures."

They all quickly accepted her proposal — as did likewise the poor nomads, when they saw the two hundred roubles that she offered them.

Katia took the fortune-teller's dress and Wanda the ballad-singer's. She wrapped her head up in a blue cotton handkerchief, put a gilt necklace round her neck, and carried a guitar in her hand. Raymond, Litzanoff, and Korolef exchanged their clothes for the gypsies' rags. This little incident amused them, and so they pursued their journey, avoiding the villages and hamlets. About eight o'clock in the evening they stopped at a little tavern where Litzanoff and Korolef had been before.

As they were getting out of the cart, two gray hooded soldiers poked their heads out of the inn door and examined them attentively.

The delicate skill and white hands of Wanda looked suspicious. She did not look like a gypsy. They accosted the little party, and asked them to give their names.

The fugitives hesitated. This hesitation was against them.

"Can't you see what I am?" said Korolef, as he took off his red wig and showed them his black curly hair.

"Where were you born?" asked one of the soldiers.

"Under a tree."

"Who were your parents?"

"My father was a crow, and my mother was a magpie."

The soldier reddened with anger. "Come in here, you vagabonds!" he cried and pushed them pell-mell into the tavern.

Litzanoff and Korolef knew this place: the inn-keeper was a socialist, and they had often stopped there before in their peregrinations. As they entered, Korolef exchanged glances with him. He recognized at once the danger of their situation.

"You think we are not gypsies," said Korolef to the soldiers. "Well, try us! Here is our fortune-teller who will tell you the past, present and future. And here is a singer who can beat all the artists in Petersburg. As for me, there is not a dancer on the steppes to compare with me."

As he spoke, he stretched upon the floor his old tattered cloak. "Sit down on this, Prima Donnas, and sing us the sword dance."

Wanda sat down in Turkish fashion and began chanting a strange wild melody that she had heard the peasants sing on her father's estate, playing an occasional chord upon the balalaika as accompaniment.

At first her voice sounded soft and low, but gradually the measure quickened, and the notes grew more intense, mingled occasionally with what seemed sighs of longing. Then the chant died away, leaving behind it a vibration of melodious language.

Korolef, in his dance, followed this disordered music. He began gently, scarcely raising his feet from the ground. Then he trampled and pawed; suddenly with one leap he cleared the room, bent over, crawled a few steps, and then lay flat down.

Wanda stopped; there was silence for a moment, until her voice, low, trembling, husky, began again. Suddenly she burst forth in a rapture of song.

Korolef had gone on with his dance, and he leaped up from the floor, then trampled and pawed the ground again, then turned round and round like a spindle, bounding, stamping, whirling, until it made one dizzy to look at him.

The soldiers, who, like all Russians, dearly love music and dancing, were fascinated. As they looked they emptied the glasses with which the innkeeper was plying them.

"Evidently there is nothing wrong about these people," they said.

The song, the dance, and the vodka all conspired to muddle their brains; they sat down on a bench, and their heads began to nod.

Wanda stopped playing for a moment. Instantly one of the men sat up. "Don't stop," he said, "go on, go on."

But gradually they ceased to speak or notice. They both slipped gently down upon the floor, fast asleep.

Then the fugitives crept out. The horses were hitched up, and they resumed their journey in the direction of Kiev. They went on all that day and the next, avoiding the high road as much as possible, until, as the sun was setting, they mounted a high hill, and a beautiful spectacle dazzled their eyes.

The holy city of Kiev lay at their feet, steeped in the golden vapors of the setting sun. The houses, built in little gardens; the many hills, crowned with lofty buildings; the fortress; the famous monastery of Kievo Pestchersk; the Tithe Church, one of the oldest in Russia; St. Andrew's spires and domes; farther on, the blue waters of the Dnieper flowing through the green valley — all this is as fair a sight as the sun looks down upon.

"We must enter the city through the faubourg Vasilcoff," said Korolef. "We can leave our cart at the first inn we come across, and then we can go on foot to Mentikoff's, where I hope we shall find our friends safe and sound."

But they had hardly entered the outskirts of the town before a squad of cavalry blocked their way. There was nothing to be done; for one moment Litzanoff and Korolef thought of resisting, but it was hopeless.

The soldiers surrounded their carriage, and under such an escort they drove through the town. The crowd gathered around them, growing larger and more dense every moment. Two carriages were coming up in the opposite direction; the street was narrow, and the wheels of one of them got entangled with the gypsy caravan. Seizing his opportunity, Korolef leaped lightly from the driver's seat, and plunged amongst the crowd. A soldier saw him, and jumped from his horse, running after him, and crying out, "Stop him! Stop him!"

It was of no use! The crowd looked on unmoved. They seemed a population very indifferent to their government and its police.

Raymond took the reins, which Korolef had dropped, and Litzanoff seated himself in Raymond's seat, by the side of Wanda.

These two days passed close to Wanda had increased Stepane's passion a thousand fold. Several times, in the woods, he had been tempted to kill Raymond and run off with Wanda. He was jealous of every word, of every look, that she addressed to that poor, fictitious husband.

Yet in these last two days he had been happy, To listen to her voice, to drink in her words, to be lost in the light of her eyes, to be intoxicated with her beauty, all this was great happiness.

But now, when he saw himself about to be separated from her, perhaps forever, his despair knew no bounds.

"Wanda," he said, "When I think that I am perhaps looking at you for the last time, I feel as if my heart were being torn out of my breast. Probably if they recognize me I shall be sent to Siberia, but the snows of Siberia cannot cool the fire that is consuming me. Before you leave me, give me one word that I can treasure forever in the depths of my heart."

Wanda gave him her hand. He held it a long time in his.

"I shall never forget you, Stepane," she said.

They drew up before Colonel Heyking's house.

Wanda threw her rain-cloak around her, and put on her blue spectacles.

CHAPTER XLIV

THE BLUE OFFICER

In any Russian city of any importance, the Third Section was represented by a colonel or a captain of dragoons, who wore the light blue uniform. His functions were not clearly defined, but he was recognized as the inspector of the governor, the inspector of the magistrates, the inspector of every one in the province.

This officer was generally an affable gentleman with distinguished manners. He was an honorary member of all the benevolent societies, but when the sun set, he was in the habit of receiving individuals whose conversation was not to be overheard by any ordinary subject of the Czar.

He was amiable as well as blue; he listened to every complaint; he was thoroughly incorruptible; he loathed a scandal; he was extremely polite; he tried to live on good terms with everybody, for he knew well that for the least cause he might be dismissed from the service. But he dismisses others to Siberia more frequently than he is dismissed himself. He was the most powerful man in the city, for he was accountable to no one except to his superior, the Chief of the Third Section.

Colonel Heyking was a fair type of this amiable but formidable individual. He was a young man, handsome, fair, with great auburn whiskers.

When the four fugitives were brought before him, he looked at them attentively, and bowing to Wanda, said, with much deference:

"Will you have the kindness to lay aside your cloak and spectacles?"

Wanda saw that she was recognized, and complied with his request.

"It is impossible, Princess," said Heyking, gallantly, "to forget your face, if a man has once seen it. Is this young girl your waiting maid? And is this Monsieur Chabert?"

He stood perplexed before Litzanoff. "I suppose this man is one of the operatives from the paper mill, is he not?"

"Colonel," said Wanda, "it is useless to try to hide anything from you. Monsieur Chabert is my husband; this young man is Monsieur Chabert's servant. He is in no way responsible for my flight, and I hope that you will set him at liberty."

"What is his name?"

"Ivan Zmuoff. And now, Colonel," added she, "will you please to tell me why we are obliged to give an account of everything that we do to the police?"

"And Princess Wanda Kryloff, will you please to tell me why you are dressed up in this manner?"

"Because my father would not acknowledge my husband as his son-in-law, and so I left his house."

"And is that the reason that these gentlemen killed two soldiers yesterday, on the road to Bielaja?"

"I do not know what you mean," answered Wanda.

"You will all four have the goodness to write your names upon this sheet of paper," said Heyking.

They did so. He examined carefully the four signatures, and laid the sheet upon which they were written side by side with two slips of paper that looked as if they had been torn from a notebook.

Turning towards Katia, he said: "Your notebook, if you please."

"I have none," she answered, turning deathly pale.

Heyking was watching her. "Give it up at once," he said, "or I shall have you searched."

Katia handed her notebook to the Colonel. Two pages had been torn out of it.

The two slips of paper, upon which was written with red crayon, "Killed for having fired upon the nihilists," exactly fit the place in the notebook where the two pages hall been torn out.

"You see," said Heyking, "you have denounced yourselves as nihilists. Your case is a very grave one."

"We only killed them in self-defense," answered Raymond. "In the dark night we could not tell who they were."

"You say," continued Heyking, "that you have been married to Monsieur Chabert without your father's consent?"

Wanda took from Katia's hands the box containing her papers and jewels. In it was the certificate of her marriage. She handed it to the Colonel, who read it attentively and curiously.

"It is a perfectly legal document," he said, restoring it to Wanda. With the most exquisite politeness, he added: "Indeed, Princess, I am exceedingly grieved to be obliged to put you under arrest. But you know that Prince Stackelberg has discretionary powers, and I must obey him. I shall telegraph to him immediately that you are here, for he is looking for you in the south. Day after tomorrow he will be here, and he will then decide himself what is to be your fate."

At these words, Wanda felt a cold sweat break out all over her. She had mortally offended this man, who could now take such terrible vengeance upon her, not only upon her, but upon Litzanoff and Raymond.

Litzanoff, too, trembled at the thought of meeting Stackelberg, but he trembled from hate and not from fear.

"I do not regard you as a prisoner, Princess," continued Heyking, with the same extreme politeness, "and I do not wish to treat you as such. If you and Monsieur Chabert will accept for tonight my hospitality, I shall be most happy to give you a room in my house."

Wanda noticed a strange light in Litzanoff's eyes. She understood him; she guessed his jealous thoughts.

"Can I not have my waiting-maid with me?" she inquired.

But the Colonel answered her in the most determined manner: "Until the arrival of Prince Stackelberg, Katia Lawinska and the person whom you call Ivan Zmuoff will be taken to the fortress."

He gave his orders to his soldiers, bowed coldly to the Princess, and left the room.

CHAPTER XLV

THE PRINTING OFFICE

Mentikoff's printing office stood in the most aristocratic part of Kiev, not far from the monastery of Kievo Pestchersk. Mentikoff was at the same time publisher and printer. He edited pious books, sold sacred images, and provided the monastery and its pilgrims with all manner of relics.

The Russians were very superstitious. Every cottage boasted of its picture of the Blessed Virgin, or of the patron-saint of its owner. Mentikoff's pictures were celebrated for their beauty. As he made a large number of them, he employed a great many workmen.

They were all anarchists, and they all pretended great devotion to conceal their real views. When the day's work was over, the operatives offered to work without remuneration in aid of the cause. The most incendiary revolutionary pamphlets came out of Mentikoff's holy printing press. Concealed within the pictures of saints or wrapped around some sacred relic, they found their way through the post into every corner of Holy Russia.

It was at Mentikoff's that Alexandra, Michael, Padlewsky, Matcha, and Zobolewsky, had taken refuge. Dressed as common workmen, they had entered the printer's shop unrecognized.

At eleven o'clock that night, Korolef appeared among them and told them the dreadful news. But he told them that he thought he had found a means to deliver the prisoners.

As he was talking, Countess Kousmine, Nadege, and Verenine entered. Verenine had sent word to Nadege that Wanda was coming to Kiev, and they were all three uneasy at her failure to appear. Countess Kousmine had constant intercourse with Mentikoff, and she hoped to hear from him something of the fugitives.

When Nadege was told that Stepane was again under arrest, she nearly fainted.

"He is lost! He is lost!" she cried. "Oh, Korolef! Save him this time, and I will give you my whole fortune; I will devote my whole life to the cause."

"Korolef," said Verenine, "I will do anything to deliver our friends; I am perfectly willing to lay down my life for them. I am a nihilist; I desire the revolution."

That very evening a number of students, the most active leaders of the revolutionary party, hearing that Padlewsky and Michael had arrived at Mentikoff's, came to get their instructions.

They asked this question: "Shall Heyking's death sentence be executed?"

For three months, despite of his warning, he had ceaselessly persecuted the nihilists. This evening's arrests filled the measure of his iniquity.

But in the interest of the prisoners, Michael and Padlewsky urged a little delay.

CHAPTER XLVI

A TERRIBLE POSITION

As Wanda and Chabert were ushered, by Colonel Heyking's order, into their bedroom, Chabert could not repress a violent emotion, but the Princess was perfectly calm and unmoved.

She was exhausted, and lay down upon a sofa. "Take that chair, Raymond," said she. "What is to become of us, dear friend? I am not uneasy about myself, on account of my high rank. But Russian justice is far from being just. My father and Stackelberg will pursue you relentlessly. You may be sent to Siberia. When you offered me your life, you did not think it would come to this, did you?"

"I foresaw everything, dear Wanda, and I never hesitated for a moment."

"But how will you be able to endure the dreadful Siberian climate? You are not accustomed to our cold."

"I have given you my life, Wanda; my greatest unhappiness would be to be separated from you."

"How good you are, Raymond," she said, holding out her hand to him.

But he, to conceal his agitation, arose and went to the window. "There is no means of escape," he said. "There is a sentinel right here, under our window."

Then he tried the door. "Not withstanding Heyking's politeness, we are held fast under lock and key."

"Yet I will trust Korolef's ingenuity to get us out," said Wanda. "If worst comes to worst and you are condemned, I shall ask permission to go with you, Raymond. I am your wife, and the Emperor has never refused to allow a wife to accompany her husband in exile."

"Would you follow me to Siberia, Wanda?" said Raymond, in a voice broken with emotion.

"Yes; it is my duty, and I will do it."

"But you are not my wife. Do you think that I seriously believe in this sham marriage?"

"This sham marriage, as you call it, is more binding in my eyes than if I were really your wife."

"No, no," exclaimed Chabert; "I shall never consent to your going with me. Besides, the cause needs you here in Russia."

"Raymond, you devoted yourself to me blindly. I owe you something in return. I know you have a noble heart, and that you would forgive me for deserting you, but I could never forgive myself. I could not accept my liberty when you had sacrificed yours for me."

"Who says that it is for you that I have sacrificed my liberty? Can you not see that I too am willing to die for my convictions? Did I not offer my life to the cause before I ever saw you? Grant me at least this merit, which is far above any mere personal feeling,"

"I know you well, Raymond, and I do not doubt the nobility of your sentiments. But would you have thrown yourself with the same ardor into the revolutionary movement, in this foreign land, had it not been for me?"

"My dear Wanda," said Raymond, "it is all one to me whether the revolution begins in Russia or Germany or England or America. It is bound to break out, and when it does, it will carry everything before it. To help on this great idea, is the object of my life. I am only too happy to have at my side a companion like you."

Wanda seized Raymond's hand and pressed it between her own.

"You are noble, Raymond! I am proud to bear your name. I knew that I understood you when I chose you for my husband."

"You were surrounded by men quite as generous and quite as noble as I am."

"Do you mean Stepane?"

"Do not think that I am jealous."

"I do not suspect you of anything so base. Stepane and my Cousin Verenine were only devoted to me personally. The cause was a secondary matter to them. That is why I have less confidence in them than I have in you."

At this moment the Colonel's footman entered with some refreshments.

"Can you eat anything?" asked Raymond.

"We must strengthen ourselves with food to keep up our spirits; so, my dear Raymond, let us make a good meal."

When their supper was over, Wanda lay down upon the bed, dressed as she was, and invited Raymond to repose upon the sofa.

"Grant me one favor, Wanda," he said. "For this one night, let me lie at your feet."

He wrapped himself in his fur cloak, and stretched himself on the carpet at the foot of her bed.

She was soon asleep, but Raymond could not close his eyes. The affection that Wanda had expressed for him had deeply touched him. He was thirty years old, and passionately loved this woman who lay there, trusting in his respect and in his love.

When Wanda awoke the next morning, Raymond was standing by her side. She noticed his altered countenance and his feverish eyes.

"Are you ill ?" she asked.

"Not at all," he answered, looking away from her.

"But what is the matter with you ?" she asked again. Raymond flushed crimson.

"Oh, my friend! My friend," she whispered, "forgive me."

At this moment the key turned in the lock, the door opened, and Vassili Stackelberg walked into the room.

CHAPTER XLVII

DEFIANCE

As he entered, he examined the prisoners' faces. Wanda's was calm and pure; Raymond's sad and full of passion.

Vassili felt a pain shoot through his heart, for he truly loved the Princess, although he was jealous, furious, and thirsting for vengeance. To make her suffer as he was suffering, to separate her forever from the man she loved, to torture, to annihilate the creature who had dared to be his rival, these were his frantic hopes.

Wanda rose as he entered and advanced to meet him. "Is it by your orders, Sir," she said, "that we are arrested?"

"It was indeed I who gave the order, upon the express desire of the Prince, your father."

"My father has no right to have me arrested, and less have you the right to arrest Monsieur Chabert, a foreigner accredited by his own government."

"I certainly had very serious reasons for giving that order," answered Stackelberg.

"Have the goodness to say what they are?"

"You forget that you have openly declared yourself, in the presence of twenty persons, to be a nihilist."

"I certainly did, but that is merely my own way of thinking. Does the Government, personified in you, intend to prevent me from thinking?"

"It does not intend to allow you to give utterance to revolutionary opinions."

"What! Not in my own drawing-room?"

"No, not in your own drawing-room."

"What is Monsieur Chabert accused of?"

"Of having mixed himself up in a rising of workmen."

"How will you prove that?"

"I shall not attempt to prove it. It is enough that I know it."

"I shall appeal to the French Embassy," said Raymond.

"Appeal, Sir, appeal as much as you please. I can show that you are an anarchist, a dangerous revolutionist, a plotter, not to say . . ."

"Sir," said Raymond, advancing upon him, "I am your prisoner, it is true, and if you are a gentleman, you will apologize for your insulting words."

Stackelberg laughed aloud. "This is some of your French boasting. You forget the distance between myself and an adventurer like you."

Without more ado, Raymond slapped him in the face. "Coward! You are coward!"

Wanda screamed aloud. "Oh, Raymond! what have you done!"

Stackelberg threw open the door and called to his soldiers, who stood without.

"Take this man and handcuff him! Let him be guarded with the greatest care."

Wanda understood that it was an eternal separation. Full of pity, remorse, and tenderness, she rushed towards Chabert and clasped him in her arms.

"Raymond," she sobbed, "my friend, my husband! Farewell, farewell!"

"Adieu, Wanda," said Raymond. "Regret nothing; I suffer gladly for you and for the cause."

He held her to his heart, while he pressed a lingering kiss upon her forehead.

The German, beside himself with rage, signed to his men to cut this scene short. They bore Raymond away.

Stackelberg was left alone with Wanda. For some minutes neither spoke. They watched each other like two men about to fight a duel.

At last Stackelberg broke the silence. "Pray be seated, Princess. We must speak together."

He took a seat also, and leaning his elbows upon the table, stooped over like a man bearing a heavy burden.

"And so you have been making game of me, Wanda Petrowna! Making game, too, of my love for you, a love so great, so all-absorbing, that I would have sacrificed everything to it!"

"What, for instance?" asked Wanda.

"My position in society, my convictions, even, if you had desired it."

"What do you mean by your convictions?"

"I mean my devotion to the Emperor."

"That is not a conviction, it is merely a sentiment, which translated into sensible language means personal interest or personal ambition."

"But I do believe in the principle of authority," said the Prince.

"What do you mean by that principle? Do you mean the right that certain men arrogate to themselves to rule over other men? Is that a part of the divine right?"

"In listening to you, in looking at you, Wanda Petrowna, I forget divine rights and all other rights. Your eyes convince me more than your words."

"Insipid compliments to a prisoner!" said Wanda, disdainfully.

"You look so beautiful! This gypsy costume is becoming to you. I am not paying you any compliments. You know what I have felt for you ever since my eyes first rested upon your face, at that ball at the Winter Palace."

"That was so long ago!"

"Five months ago! For five months your image has never once been out of my mind. You know it, don't you?"

"I have heard you say so."

"Do you believe me."

"Not altogether. The nihilists have occupied your attention also."

"You made me forget everything, even my duty. You said, 'There are no socialists,' and I believed you, and sought for them no longer. I could not tear myself from the place where you lived. A day passed away from you would have been a day of agony for me. Had you wished it, you could have brought me over to your views. Even now I feel my weakness. One look from you, one word of hope . . ."

"Well?"

"I would listen to you. I would obey your wishes. I would give up the search. I would set you and the other fugitives free."

"Would you liberate all the prisoners in Kiev?"

"I would do anything to be loved by you for one day, for one hour."

"Well, commence by opening the prison doors, and I will see what I can do for you. I will consent to remain in your hands as a hostage."

"You will consent?" said Vassili, rising from his seat. "Then pity me, and give me one kiss."

Wanda shrunk away from him with a look of disgust that he could not mistake.

"You hate me," he said, seating himself again. "Are you married?"

"I am, and I am not."

"What do you mean?"

"Legally, I bear Monsieur Chabert's name, but I am not his wife."

"You showed Heyking a marriage certificate. I should like to see it."

"What for?"

"If Monsieur Chabert is really your husband I will treat him with more consideration. "

Wanda hesitated, but at last she handed him the paper.

Stackelberg took it with trembling hand. At first, he could not understand it, but recovering himself, he looked at the date January 30th.

"So!" he hissed between his set teeth, "for four months you have been deceiving me I. For four months you have been playing the part of an infernal coquette!"

"I tried to make myself agreeable to you, as you were my guest, that was all."

"Did you not promise me your hand the very day that you ran away?

Did you not allow me to announce our engagement publicly?"

Wanda did not answer.

"You see yourself there is no excuse for such disloyal conduct."

"Disloyal?" retorted Wanda, raising her splendid eyes to his. "And were you very loyal, Vassili Antonovitch, when you had Count Litzanoff sent to prison?"

"I?"

"Yes, you, Sir. The judge who questioned him repeated word for word the conversation that you had with him, in my father's smoking room, the night of our ball."

"And so it was to avenge that man whom you loved, that you . . ."

"If I loved him, how could I have married Raymond Chabert?"

"I cannot explain your conduct, Wanda Petrowna."

"It is very simple. I married Raymond Chabert to get away from my father's rule. As I told you just now, he is only my husband in name."

"Then, if you have not given your heart to Raymond, it is because you love the other man."

"No."

"At the bottom of every female resolve, there is always a question of love. You are either in love with Litzanoff or with Chabert. Which is it?"

Wanda knew that if she gave him the least clue, it would be the destruction of one or the other of her friends. She therefore assured him that her whole desire was to devote herself to the nihilist cause.

"Well," said Stackelberg, "there is one more way to save you and your friends; that is to reveal to me all your nihilist secrets."

"Truly, Prince Stackelberg," replied Wanda, "you must have a strange opinion of me if you think me capable of betraying the cause to which I have devoted my life."

Stackelberg walked up and down the room, then suddenly stopped before his prisoner.

"Wanda," said he, "if you believe that I am thinking of the nihilists at this moment, you are mistaken. I hardly know what I am saying. I am only prolonging our interview because, strange, ridiculous as it is, I love you. Hell is in my heart. You have infamously deceived me. You are laughing at me now. I know that you hate me, and in spite of all, I love you. Tell me, what shall I do? I repeat it again, I will do anything if you will only smile upon me."

"And I repeat it again: open the prison doors to my friends."

"Will you remain with me as hostage? And you will grant me . . ."

"My friendship," and Wanda gave her hand to Stackelberg, who fell down upon his knees and kissed it over and over again.

"Wanda! Wanda!" he cried, "pity me! Give me one kiss, and I will be your slave forever!"

His face was so distorted that it frightened her.

"No," she said, stepping back.

But Stackelberg jumped up, took her in his arms, and strained her to his breast. "I will have one kiss," he said. Throwing his arm around her neck he pressed his trembling lips to hers.

Wanda, horrified, forgot to be prudent.

"I hate you! I loathe you!" she cried, breaking away from him and running to a little table on which lay her revolver, which she seized, and leveling it at the Prince, said, "Wretch! If you come near me, I will fire."

She accompanied these words with such a look that Vassili recoiled, terrified, for he was indeed a coward.

"Well," he said, "I will have nothing that I must obtain by force. But remember one thing, Madame Chabert, soon you will be on your knees to me, and then perhaps I may be inflexible."

He went out. Half an hour later two soldiers arrived to take Wanda to the fortress.

CHAPTER XLVIII

THE FALSE ARCHIMANDRITE

It was about eight o'clock on the evening of the following day when an archimandrite, dressed in his ecclesiastical robes, with his tall black hat upon his head and St. Andrew's cross upon his heart, walked briskly along the road to the fortress. His skin was very swarthy and his long beard snow-white.

It was none other than Korolef, for whom Mentikoff had procured this disguise, on the way to deliver Litzanoff from prison.

When he reached the fortress, he asked permission of the porter to see Ivan Zmuoff, producing a permit signed "Heyking." It was a false permit, but the Russians are so superstitious that the man never thought of critically examining a paper held out to him by a priest, and merely begging the archimandrite for his blessing, he hastened to open the gate, and conducted him to Litzanoff's cell.

"Leave me here, my friend," said Korolef to the jailor. "Come for me in half an hour."

The jailor went away, closing the door upon him whom he believed to be the head of the monastery.

Stepane gazed at his visitor with defiance in his face.

Then Korolef took off his hat, laid aside his beard, and said in his natural voice:

"Do you not know me? I have come to deliver you. There is not a moment to lose. We must change clothes; you will go out, and I will remain in your place."

"And you think I would accept such a sacrifice?"

"I am not sacrificing myself for you."

"Yes, I understand; it is for the cause. But yet I should have to leave you here in my place. No, my dear friend, I will not do it. After all, it is a perfect piece of selfishness; you take all the best parts in the play for yourself. I want an opportunity to show what I can do too."

"Listen to me, Stepane. My pockets are full of money. Your wife gave it to me for the purpose of getting you out of prison."

"Is my wife in Kiev?"

"Yes, and if I had not promised to get you out, she would certainly have gone to the Governor, and so made an end of everything."

"That is just like her,"said Stepane. "What are you going to do with the money?"

"Bribe the watchmen and the sentinels, and escape, all four of us."

"Are the Princess and Chabert both here?"

"Yes, they were brought in yesterday. One of our men, who is a servant at Heyking's, brought us word. But we have lost too much time already. Make haste: undress yourself."

Litzanoff still objected. "You can give me the money," he said. "I can bribe the men as well as you."

"No, no, it requires more care than you suppose; if you were to fail, they would take all your bank notes away from you, and you would be sent to the hole."

As he spoke, Korolef took off his robes, and impatiently held them out to Litzanoff. "If the jailor were to come in just now there would he a pretty mess," said he.

Litzanoff obeyed, and as he and Korolef were nearly of a size and as the shades of evening were falling fast, the change was hardly perceptible.

"Now," said Korolef, "Look down, lean your head forward, put on your hat, walk slowly and with dignity, raise your shoulders, draw your elbows into your side — that will do!"

The jailor opened the door. The passage outside was very dark; the man noticed nothing out of the way.

"My friend," said Stepane, "take me to the cell occupied by Princess Kryloff."

The jailor hastened to obey.

XLIX

THE FEMALE PRISONER

Four grey walls, a wooden stool, a tiny table, and an iron bedstead, composed the furniture of Wanda's cell.

She was sitting by the table leaning her head upon her hand.

She had been there for thirty-six hours, counting every hour as it was struck by the fortress clock, listening to the clank of chains, the click of the guns, and the noise of the locks, as the keys turned heavily in the doors.

Her appearance was already very much altered, but she never for one moment regretted her resolution. She was sad, but she was neither discouraged nor cast down. She was determined that she would follow out her convictions to the end, even to Siberia, even to death.

Yesterday she was one of the great ladies of Russia; today she was Madame Chabert, a nihilist, whose very name would send a shudder through Russia.

Behind her glittered all that she had lost; before her stood forth in grim reality all that she was called upon to endure.

She smiled bitterly at herself. In the palaces in which her youth had been passed, she had felt herself more of a prisoner than at this very moment, within these four bare walls, beneath these grated windows.

Korolef had said that he would deliver her, but how could he do it? Then Stackelberg would come again, most probably. She was at his mercy.

At this thought, she shuddered. He could do anything. He could with one word cause her to disappear forever, so that no one would ever know what had become of her.

So she sat, lost in thought, when the door grated on its hinges and then opened. To her great astonishment, she saw a priest enter. What did it mean? Were they going to try and convert her?

She stood up. "What do you want with me?" she said.

The jailor closed the door upon the archimandrite, who, falling on his knees, cried out, "Wanda! Wanda! It is I."

"You, Stepane! In this dress!"

After telling her how it had all happened, he added, "I could not resist the desire to see you, and declare to you once more my love and my devotion."

"Oh, how imprudent!" cried Wanda. "Go away! Go away, I suppose any one should come!"

"Let me stay here a few moments. I only accepted Korolef's suggestion so as to see you alone for one minute. You always manage to place some barrier between us, Wanda. Let me see you, let me tell you . . . I do not know what I am saying."

Wanda was leaning against the wall. Her breast was heaving, her eyes half-closed. She dared not speak, lest she should betray her emotion. Her nerves were unstrung by her imprisonment, and this unexpected visit found her very weak. She made no reply. He drew near, and took her hand; it was cold as ice.

"You are not angry with me, Wanda, are you?" he said.

She felt her knees tremble.

"Wanda, my idol, I have not displeased you, have I?"

"Stepane," she answered, struggling against the rising tenderness that threatened to overwhelm her, "I cannot be false to my promise."

"What promise? Your promise to this Raymond Chabert?"

"Remember, Stepane," she said, "he helped you to escape from prison."

Stepane dropped upon the stool, buried his face is his hands, and sobbed aloud.

"Stop, my dear friend," said Wanda. "Your presence here frightens me. We do not even know what is to become of us. Call the jailor; I am afraid of Stackelberg." Then she related to him the scene of the night before.

"The coward!" raged Litzanoff, "to insult a prisoner, a defenseless woman! The wretch! I will kill him!"

"I implore of you, Stepane, do not be rash; you may ruin us all."

"To please you, Wanda, I will try to control myself, but you must tell me that you love me."

Wanda gave him her hand, murmuring faintly, "I do love you."

But Stepane fell at her feet.

Wanda heard a footstep. "Get up, Stepane," she said. But he would not heed, he would not listen.

The door flew open. A man stood upon the threshold: Stackelberg.

At the sight of this priest on his knees at Wanda's feet, the terrible inquisitor stood for a moment stupefied.

"Who gave this man permission to enter?" he asked, turning to the jailor.

"The Governor."

"Where is the permit?"

"Will Your Excellency deign to show it?" faltered the trembling official.

Litzanoff hesitated for one instant, and then produced the false document.

This hesitation increased Stackelberg's suspicions.

"Go, bring a light, and summon the soldiers," he ordered.

The door had hardly closed, when Litzanoff, with one bound, seized Vassili, threw him down on the hard floor, pressed his knee against his breast, twined his fingers into his enemy's cravat, and twisted it round and round so as to choke him.

"We have an old account to settle, you coward!" he growled through his set teeth.

Wanda strove to free Stackelberg. "Oh Stepane!" she cried, "I implore you! I command you! Let this man alone!"

Litzanoff heeded her not. Stackelberg's face was black; his eyes seemed starting from their sockets; his tongue hung out of his mouth.

"Here are the soldiers!" exclaimed Wanda. Litzanoff arose. Stackelberg was unconscious, but not dead. He came to himself in a moment, and painfully raising himself upon his elbow said, "Handcuff that scoundrel! Put him in irons, and shut him up in the darkest of the casemates!"

But the soldiers would not lay their hands upon an archimandrite.

"He is an escaped prisoner who has profaned the religious habit," said Vassili.

"Ivan Zmuoff!" exclaimed the jailor, holding up his lantern to Litzanoff's face. "The real archimandrite has taken this man's place in the other cell."

"What does all this mean, Stepane Litzanoff?" inquired Stackelberg.

"You are a policeman, it is your place to find out," said Stepane, scornfully following the soldiers as he spoke.

"Will you, Madame, inform me how the Count Litzanoff came to be in your cell?"

Wanda would not speak. Stackelberg signed to the jailor to withdraw. They were left alone.

"So," he said, "Stepane is your lover? You love him, and he and you together have laughed at my love."

"No, we have never laughed at you."

"I seem to fill you with horror."

"Yes," said Wanda, "the secret police does fill me with horror. You are a disgrace to Russia. You stifle everything that is good and great in the country. Iniquity is so natural to you, that your very infamy seems to you all act of justice. Yes, your love does fill me with horror; for I despise you, and I hate you."

"Your lover shall pay for these insults, Madame Chabert."

"You would condemn him, whatever I might say."

"No, one word from you, and I will . . ."

"A man who is capable of proposing such terms to a woman in my situation is capable of anything. I do not trust your word, and I shall never lower myself before you."

"Is this your determination?"

"It is."

The soldiers, who had gone off with Litzanoff, returned.

"Take this woman to the casemates," ordered Stackelberg.

The men approached to seize her.

"It is unnecessary; I will follow you," she said, with an air so noble, so proud, that they dared not touch her.

Stackelberg followed her with his eyes, which literally glared with fury. He then proceeded to the cell in which Korolef was confined, and subjected him to a strict cross-questioning. He obtained nothing from him. Then he ordered him likewise to be shut up in a dungeon.

They forgot to search him, and Korolef bore away with him the bank notes hidden between the soles of his shoes, and his dagger carefully tucked away in his girdle.

CHAPTER L

THE RESCUE

In the meanwhile, as nothing was heard from Korolef, Alexandra and Nadege became terribly uneasy. Michael and Padlewsky had both gone to Moscow, and the women had no one to counsel or advise them.

The next day Mentikoff was informed, by the real archimandrite, of the remarkable trick that had been played upon the prison authorities, and Mentikoff reported it all to his friends. "We have still one resource left us," he said. "That is, to play upon the discontent of the garrison, and so effect the rescue of the prisoners by means of the soldiers of the guard."

News had arrived that morning of Prince Kryloff. He was still ill in bed, and so they had nothing to fear from him.

The colonel who commanded the regiment at the fort was a very young man and a very unpopular one. The soldiers hated him, and under his rule several of them had turned nihilists. Among these was a corporal, a great friend of Mentikoff's. He undertook to make the jailor drunk and to find out in which cell Korolef was confined. He managed to slip through the bars of the prisoner's window a little paper, on which was written:

"Try to get out, all five of you, this evening. The soldiers will let you pass."

Korolef lost no time. He had been arranging his plan for several days. He had concealed his bank-notes under his red wig, and he had stuck his dagger into his stool, on the under side, where no one thought of looking for it.

When the clock had struck seven, Korolef took out his banknotes and put them on the bench. Then he laid himself down on the floor, his head thrown hack, one arm stretched out and the other clutching at his heart. He closed his eyes; his mouth was drawn to one side, his limbs looked rigid.

It was time for the jailor to go his round. Soon his steps were heard, drawing nearer and nearer. He opened the door and came in. When he saw Korolef's body stretched out on the floor, he thought he was dead. He called him several times, but Korolef did not move. Then he came into the room, leaving the door open behind him, to see what was the matter. He leaned over the prisoner, who had a dagger in his hand.

Suicides are frequent in the Russian prisons, and this looked like one. As the jailor bent over him, the dead man leaped up, and placing himself in the doorway, exclaimed, "One cry, one movement, and you are a deadman!"

The jailor, seized with terror, stood motionless. Korolef continued, "On that bench are ten thousand roubles. That is a fortune to you. Choose between death and fortune. If you will help us to escape, me and my companions, those ten thousand roubles are yours, and besides, when we find ourselves outside of the prison walls, we will give you ten thousand roubles more. If you refuse, I will kill you."

The jailor was strongly tempted. "Wait a minute," said he. "I think I can arrange it. Follow me. I will point out to you the cells in which your friends are confined. Then I will come back, and lie down here in your place. You must wound me slightly, and I will say that I was wounded, and fainted from loss of blood. That while I was unconscious you went off with the keys."

"You can say whatever you please, but take care that no one finds out our escape for several hours, or you will never see that other ten thousand roubles. If you betray us, we will kill you; I give you my word of honor, and you can trust the word of a nihilist. Well, have you made up your mind? Will you take the money?"

"I will," answered the jailor, pocketing the bank notes.

Twenty minutes later, Wanda, Katia, Raymond, Litzanoff, and Korolef, came down into the prison yard, in which two sentinels were walking up and down. One of these was the corporal.

The prisoners had now to pass by the porter's lodge and open the grated door. The two sentinels rushed forward, entered the porter's room, tied his hands, seized his keys, and unlocked the gate.

Nothing remained but to get past the guard, which consisted of twenty men, but these men were all nihilists.

"My friends," said the corporal, "let us follow the prisoners! Let us fly with them; otherwise we shall all be shot tomorrow. Besides, Russia will soon be in a state of revolution, and you will be rewarded for having delivered the leading members of the revolutionary party from an unmerited punishment."

The soldiers went with them.

Once outside the fortress they separated and arrived at Mentikoff's by different roads.

It was now eight o'clock, and a great many persons were at the printer's. Their delight at seeing their friends once more was boundless. Alexandra pressed her daughter to her heart with rapture.

"Where is Nadege?" asked Wanda. No one knew; and they were so busy discussing the situation, and hearing Michael, who had just returned from Moscow, relate all he had seen and reflected upon during his absence, that the recollection of Nadege passed quite from their mind.

Michael and Padlewsky were reporting the views and opinions of some of the most prominent nihilists of Moscow, when the bell of the street door was rung violently.

"Who is that, coming here at this hour?" they asked anxiously of one another. They feared it might be the police. Had they already found out about the escape of the prisoners, and were they on their track?

The unexpected visitor was Nadege.

CHAPTER LI

THE ASSASSINATION

Nadege was pale. Her eyes looked wild. She recognized Stepane, in spite of his disguise; she rushed towards him and clasped him in her arms.

"You are here at last!" she said, looking around wildly.

She was panting. She hid her head in her hands, then she looked up, with eyes on fire: "I have just come from the Governor's. I have betrayed you all. Make haste! Go away! Do not lose a minute. Tomorrow, this very night perhaps, this house will be surrounded."

"Wretched woman! What have you done?" cried Litzanoff.

Nadege looked at him with terror. "Before you condemn me, listen to me," she said.

But in her agony she could not speak. Every one present, pale, silent, motionless, fixed angry and indignant eyes upon poor Nadege.

Wanda took pity on the feeble creature. "My friends," she said, "you see how unhappy she is. Before you pass sentence upon her, hear what she has to say."

"Death to all traitors!" said a voice from the end of the room.

"Speak!" said Litzanoff, no longer able to restrain his rage.

"My poor friend, tell us what it is that you have done," added Wanda, gently.

"Yes, yes," answered Nadege, "I must tell all. At five o'clock this evening I received an order to appear before Colonel Heyking. I thought that I had been accused of participating in the revolutionary movement. I was not afraid for myself; but it was not of myself and my opinions that the Chief of Police questioned me. It was about Countess Kousmine, her nihilist gatherings, and their results. I persisted in denying anything about it, when he suddenly said to me:

"Do you love your husband, Madame?"

"Certainly I do," said I, trembling.

"Well, he is at present in the casemates of the fortress."

"I know it," I answered.

"Who told you?" he asked.

I made no reply. He insisted upon my answering his question, but I would not.

"Speak, Madame, I beg you. If you do not, I must believe that you hold intercourse with the nihilists, and I shall be obliged to have you arrested."

I stood perfectly silent, expecting to be led away to the fortress, and happy in the hope of being near my husband, happy to prove my fidelity to the cause. But the Colonel did not give the order for my arrest, and after a moment of silence, continued:

"Do you know why Count Litzanoff has been imprisoned in the casemates?"

"No."

"Then I will tell you." He related to me the whole scene that was enacted in Wanda's cell.

"There has been, you see," he added, "an attempt to assassinate an eminent person, and you know what is the penalty of assassination."

"Is it work in the mines?" I asked.

"Worse than that. Prince Stackelberg has discretionary powers, and he can hang or shoot your husband, without any form of trial."

At these words, I felt all my strength leave me. I lost my head. I fell at his feet, at the feet of that man! Nadege shuddered as she spoke.

"There is but one way to save your husband," said the Colonel.

"What is it?" I cried.

"Tell me everything that you know about the nihilists in Kiev."

"Ah, I swear to you that if there had been a question of my life alone, I would never have betrayed you. But at the thought that they were going to hang or shoot Stepane, I lost my mind. He promised to set me at liberty, as well as Stepane, if I would tell him everything and I thought: I can tell him everything, and then I can run quickly and warn my friends, and so I can save them and my husband, too. I did not tell him everything, but I told him too much. You must fly; you must conceal yourselves. They may surround this house at any moment, for I told him that it is your meeting place. Heyking guessed that the secret printing press is in this house, the press that he has been hunting for the last six months.

"Now if I have deserved death," she added, "kill me, strike me, strike me. Stepane, I beg you to kill me with your own hand. I have been very unhappy, very unhappy for a long time. I would rather die than live despised by you."

"We have no time to lose in useless talk," said Mentikoff. "We must hide the printed matter and the nihilist pamphlets, and disperse as quickly as possible."

"I know a better way," said Litzanoff. "Give me some kind of arms; I don't care what."

Nadege thought that Stepane was going to kill her. "Yes," she said, "death at your hands will be sweet to me, but before I die, pardon me."

"Get up," said Litzanoff gently. "You are not to blame, but this scoundrel who has abused your weakness and your love to make you commit a cowardly action, this man who has dishonored you, he is the one to be blamed. It is for me, your husband, the guardian of your honor, to avenge you."

"What; are you going to do?" asked Nadege.

"I am going to kill him. The Revolutionary Committee passed sentence on him four months ago. He has forgotten the warning that he received. I will recall it to his mind."

"Stop! stop! I beg of you!" implored Nadege. "The soldiers are down stairs, I am sure!"

"No. I have time enough."

He tore himself from his wife's embrace and went towards the door. Wanda and Michael called him back.

"Wait," said they, "until we shall have deliberated upon Heyking's sentence."

"You mean wait till we all are in Siberia, don't you? He knows our secret; is he not now getting ready to surround this house and arrest us, every one? It is no crime that I am about to commit. I merely intend to put the man's sentence in execution. If I could challenge him and meet him in a duel, I would not assassinate him."

Once more Nadege renewed her entreaties, her embraces. It was in vain. He went out.

"Follow him!" said Wanda to Verenine. Verenine rushed after him.

As soon as Litzanoff went out into the street he saw a young man walking in his direction. He stopped him and asked him to show him the way to the police office.

"Do you want to see Colonel Heyking?" said the stranger. "He is not at home st this hour. He always dines at the Kriest-Catik restaurant."

"I wish you would show me where that is," answered Stepane.

The young man assented, merely stopping a few moments for Litzanoff, who turned into a shop and bought a dagger. Asking his companion to wait outside for him, they walked together to the door of the restaurant, where the young fellow left Litzanoff.

Stepane stood at the door for a long time; it seemed to him a year. At last, about ten o'clock, Heyking came out, arm-in-arm with one of his friends. Litzanoff followed them for some time. They did not notice him. He quickened his pace and passed them; then turned back and walked towards them, knocked against Heyking rudely, and as the latter turned quickly round with his arm raised, Litzanoff struck him suddenly, right under the arm. It was his death-blow.

"I am hit!" said Heyking, falling. His friend supported him, crying, "Murder! Murder! Stop the assassin!"

A passerby threw himself on Litzanoff, but he received a severe wound from the dagger in the fleshy part of his arm, and he let go his hold.

Still the cry rang out through the quiet street: "Murder! Murder! Stop the assassin!"

A watchman threw himself in the way. Litzanoff, seeing a policeman before him, struck him full in the heart. The man fell dead.

A crowd began to gather, but whether from fear of the assassin or from hatred to the police, Litzanoff was not arrested.

The police began flocking in. One man went forward to meet them, and told them what was the matter. This was Verenine, who had just caught up with Litzanoff.

In the mean while, Stepane had time to escape. Freed from the throng, he perceived a little alley, dark and deserted. He dashed down it, and made his way to Mentikoff's.

As he neared the house, he heard the sound of a fight, the report of firearms, and shrill cries. Then he saw a great light shoot up and redden the sky.

He asked the passers by what was going on; they could not tell him. He ran on. It was as he had expected. The soldiers were attacking Mentikoff's house.

CHAPTER LII

THE ATTACK

In the cellar under the printing office was a quantity of socialistic printed matter. There was time neither to take it away nor to destroy it. What was to be done? The nihilists, huddled together in Mentikoff's room, debated this question most anxiously.

Suddenly the sound of Heyking's cavalry was heard.

The house had two entrances.

"Let the bravest of us," said Michael, "defend the front door, so that we can get the women out the back."

They were fifty-three in all: the twenty soldiers who had composed the guard of the fortress, and eighteen men and fifteen women of the others.

The women all ran to the back door, but they found sentinels already stationed there, and the yard full of soldiers.

"There are only two squads of cavalry," said the corporal. "We can fight them."

"But they can send to the fortress for reinforcements," answered Michael.

"But their colonel is always gambling or drunk; he is not at the fortress now; he is in some low house or other. He will not trouble himself."

"Have we any arms?" asked Raymond. "If we have, I think we had better fight."

Wanda understood the danger. If they surrendered, the deserters would be shot, the escaped prisoners would be exiled to Siberia; her mother and Michael would be recognized, and would fall into the hands of her father. If they fought they would run the risk of being shot, every one of them.

"We must resist! We must fight!" said the valiant Katia. "The police have no right to control our meetings. We should not yield assent to this unjust and aggressive action. It is a principle that we should defend with our lives."

Mentikoff, although he saw that in any event he was ruined, showed a great deal of determination.

"We had better fight," he said. "There are papers in the house, that we have not time to destroy, which would ruin the whole party."

They had a few arms, which were distributed. Besides, among the nihilists present, several had daggers, and a few had revolvers.

Suddenly they saw a great light.

"They want to burn us alive! "cried Alexandra. "At whatever price, let us force our way out." She threw open a window to look out, and a ball struck her on the shoulder.

Wanda rushed towards her mother. "It has done no harm," said Alexandra. "My felted coat deadened the blow."

This decided Wanda; she took up a gun.

The balls now began to shower upon them, the window panes were shattered, and broken glass and bullets hailed in.

Raymond begged Wanda to come away from the window. "I am no weak woman," she said, "and I want to prove it to you, once for all."

Katia, perfectly cool, loaded the guns, while poor Nadege, seated in a corner, seemed sunk in a sort of stupor. She thought of no one but Stepane.

"What a pity Korolef is not here!" said Raymond.

"And Verenine too," added Wanda. She dared not trust herself even to think of Litzanoff.

Already several of the soldiers were killed, and some lay wounded on the ground, but still the printer's office held out.

The captain sent to inform Heyking of the state of affairs and to the fortress for reinforcements. The major came in a very little while with twenty men. He suspected that the house must be defended by the soldiers who had deserted.

The fight became more earnest; the major, seeing his men fall around him, tried to make terms.

"Yield!" he yelled to the nihilists. "Yield, and we will spare your lives." But at that moment a ball, which went right through his epaulet, put an end to his peaceful state of mind.

"Assassins! Robbers! Murderers!" he shouted. "You shall all be shot, every man of you!" He ordered his men to assault the house.

The dragoons and the soldiers rushed upon the building; it was built of bricks, but was entirely unprotected about the doors and windows. The front door fell in, but behind it they found a barricade of printing presses, furniture, and reams of paper. As they could not get through this, the soldiers planted ladders against the wall. In spite of every effort of the defenders to set these on fire, they reached the windows of the second story. As they did so, the news of Heyking's assassination was brought to the major. The two officers were now perfectly bloodthirsty.

The fight did not last much longer. At midnight everything was over.

Litzanoff, Korolef, and Verenine had watched it all from afar, burning to rush in, and not daring to.

The nihilists were all handcuffed. Wanda had been taken with a gun in her hand. When she was brought before the major he was struck by her beauty. "What is your name?" he asked.

"Vera Perowsky," she lied.

"And what is yours?" he said to Alexandra.

"Sophia Naznuff."

Katia and Nadege also gave assumed names.

Verenine and Litzanoff, mingling with the crowd, saw them pass in front of them. For one instant they were impelled to force their way through the soldiers and carry them off.

"It is madness!" said Korolef. "We could not save them. We should only be arrested, that is all. Believe me, we can be of more use to them outside the prison than inside."

The next morning upon hearing the events of the night before, the pious inhabitants of Kiev were struck with terror at the boldness of the nihilists. In one night five prisoners had escaped; a whole guard had deserted; the Chief of Police had been assassinated; the printing office of that good man Mentikoff transformed into a robber's cave; and a regular fight had taken place in one of the most fashionable parts of the city. Besides, they learned there had been a rising at Karkow and another at Pultowa. At Sartow whole villages had been set on fire. Later in the day a dispatch from the south brought the news that all the villages upon Prince Kryloff's estate were in open rebellion against the Government.

CHAPTER LIII

THE SENTENCE

Upon learning of the assassination of Heyking, Stackelberg had instantly telegraphed to Mezentzoff, the Chief of the Third Section. Mezentzoff had telegraphed back that until further orders Stackelberg should take the position left vacant by the death of Heyking. He also confirmed his discretionary powers, leaving him at liberty to take such measures as he thought necessary.

When they brought him the list of the names of the prisoners, he was astounded at not finding Wanda's among them. They reported to him, at the same time, that there were several women among the prisoners, among others, a remarkably beautiful girl, who had been taken with arms in her hand, and who had fought bravely, making a desperate resistance.

"What is her name?" he asked.

"Vera Perowsky."

"Bring her before me," he ordered, "but search her first, and see that she has no weapons concealed in her clothes."

An hour later, Wanda, dressed in a female worker's dress, with chains upon her feet and her arms tied behind her, was ushered into Stackelberg's office. Strange to say, this garb but enhanced her marvelous beauty, the pure white of her skin, and the strange luster of her dark eyes.

Stackelberg at first could not meet her gaze. "You have been arrested," he said, looking down on the ground, "with arms in your hands. What have you to say in your defense?"

"Nothing," she answered.

"Are you not, at least, sorry for what you have done?"

"No, I am not."

"Would you do it over again?"

"I would. In the stifling atmosphere in which we Russians live, there is but one means to diffuse our revolutionary doctrines, and that is daring and fearless bravery."

"You will be tried by a military commission, and martial law is inexorable."

"I know it."

"Do you know what penalty you have incurred?"

"Death," answered Wanda.

"Yes. But I can save you."

"I did not know that you are invested with absolute authority."

Stackelberg handed her Mezentzoff's dispatch.

"Do you see that? Heyking was assassinated yesterday evening by one of your men, and I have replaced him as master of police in Kiev."

"You are quite worthy of the position," answered Wanda, with an expression of the utmost contempt.

Stackelberg was silent for a moment, then he said, "Do you still despise me, Wanda Petrowna?"

Wanda made no answer.

"Has death no terror for you?"

"If it comes, I hope I shall bear it bravely and so prove my faith to the cause."

"But your death will not do any good to the cause. No one will see your execution. What glory will come to you from your unknown and unremembered loss of life?"

"We do not sacrifice ourselves for glory, Prince Stackelberg; we sacrifice ourselves for a great Idea."

"But what good will it do when no one knows anything about it? Wanda, I love you passionately; you know it. I want to save you. Only sign a retraction, only send in an appeal for pardon.

"I am not a coward, Monsieur de Stackelberg. I will not abjure my convictions for fear of death. "

Vassili rose from his seat, and walked up and down.

"She is mad, mad!" he repeated. "She will have it so."

Wanda watched him unmoved.

He came up to her suddenly. "Wanda, I ask only that you do not despise me, and I will save you in spite of everything."

"Indeed, Monsieur de Stackelberg, the fear of death has not turned my head so much that I forget in what country we are living. Certainly you are very powerful, and you can shoot as many poor girls as you choose, but you dare not shoot Prince Kryloff's daughter."

"But you forget," retorted Vassili, "that you have put down your name in the prison register as Vera."

"But I shall tell my real name to the military commission."

"And suppose I tell them that you lie?"

"You would be afraid to do that, for it would be known."

"Who will know it when you are no longer in the world to tell it?"

"My friends will."

"What friends?"

Wanda felt a cold chill run through her veins.

It was true! He could have her shot, without anyone knowing it. She was a brave woman, and yet the instinct of self-preservation within her rose in rebellion at the idea of this gloomy execution. But almost instantly her will conquered this instinct.

"In fact," she answered, "my life is no more precious than another's. I would rather die than lower myself before you."

Vassili looked at her almost stupefied.

"What pride! What obstinacy!" he exclaimed.

"Any lofty sentiment is so foreign to your nature," said Wanda, "that you cannot understand it."

"I will give you eight days," he said, "in which to think over this matter. Eight days of prison life may change your opinions and your views."

He threw open the door and summoned the soldiers.

"Conduct Vera Perowsky back to the fortress," he ordered.

Then he sat down, without even looking at Wanda. But as soon as she was gone, his rage broke out.

"I will tame her pride! I will bend her iron spirit or she shall die."

In the course of the day he went over to the fortress to inspect the prisoners. He hoped to find Litzanoff among them, and his disappointment was great at not finding him, but when he saw Raymond, a savage joy lighted up his blue eyes. "He at least shall not escape me!" he said to himself.

But Litzanoff could not he very far off, so Stackelberg ordered a search to be made through every suspected house in the town. Happily he never suspected the one in which Litzanoff had taken refuge.

The Prince then appointed a military commission for the trial of the rebels. As in all the nihilist trials of the last ten years, the prisoners showed themselves courageous and daring, to the astonishment of their judge.

The trial was short. It was enough that they had been taken in open rebellion against the agents of the government. Their sentence could be but one of three things: labor in the mines, exile to Siberia, or death.

The trial was held behind closed doors; notwithstanding, a report got abroad in the town that a great many of the prisoners had been sentenced to death. The rumor further ran that some ladies of very high rank were among those condemned.

These reports reached Litzanoff's ears. At the mere thought that Wanda might be among them, he was taken with a sort of delirium. "We must deliver her," he said, "at whatever price, if we have to burn down the city, to burn down the fortress. Korolef, can you think of no plan? We must get a message to her, must send her some word of encouragement."

"That is what I am thinking of all the time," answered Korolef. "How can we save them? Stackelberg is more careful than Heyking. The prisoners are closely guarded. Stackelberg goes through the prison himself every day. The major, since our escape, watches day and night."

"Then, you can think of nothing?"

"Yes; let Verenine go to Petersburg, and throw himself at the feet of Prince Alexander, the Czarowitch, and beg for the pardon of Wanda Kryloff. And you go at once to Moscow, where your man of business happens to be just now. Make him give you all the money he can lay his hands on: two hundred thousand roubles, if he call get them."

"You can have my whole fortune."

"Well, I will go to find Prince Kryloff, and tell him that his daughter is condemned to death. He can get her out of Stackelberg's clutches. For I have an idea that if Stackelberg is going to put her to death, he will do it quickly and privately. This we must try to hinder."

The three friends left Kiev that same night in different directions. Thanks to their excellent disguises they were not molested.

Prince Kryloff was still very feeble. He was out of bed, but the doctor had not allowed him, as yet, to leave the house. In order to gain admission to him, Korolef sent up his name as a messenger from Countess Kousmine, bringing news of Wanda.

The Prince knew nothing of what had taken place in the neighborhood. The very word "nihilist," mentioned in his presence, brought back his delirium. His mind was unsettled, and they feared for his reason.

When Korolef told him that his daughter was in prison, he was taken with a fit of raving which ended in unconsciousness. However, this passed off in a short while, and he determined to set out at once for Kiev. But suddenly he changed his mind, and thinking it was a trick, determined not to leave home. For two whole days, two precious days, Korolef pleaded with him, struggling with the irresolute fancies of an unsettled brain.

Verenine had obtained, through the Czarowitch, an interview with the Emperor. The Czar was stern at first, but, with his usual goodness, finally relented. He knew about the troubles at Kiev, and the assassination of Heyking. Upon Verenine's entreaty, he promised to order Princess Kryloff's sentence to be deferred until he himself could look into the affair.

Litzanoff, in spite of the lamentations of his faithful Dimitri, had mortgaged his entire property and obtained two hundred thousand roubles at an exorbitant rate. Korolef had said to him: "In Russia, you can do anything with money." He thought that with this amount he might be able to bribe the whole garrison of the fort.

Mezentzoff, under the directions of the Emperor, sent to Stackelberg the following despatch:

"By order of the Emperor, defer passing sentence upon Princess Kryloff. Tomorrow some one will be sent to supply your place as Chief of Police."

This telegram completely upset Stackelberg. Who had told the Emperor about this affair? He thought he had kept it perfectly secret. Was it true that the nihilists had their spies in the Emperor's palace, or even in the Third Section itself? He was frightened, but still he was determined not to give up his revenge.

Ever since Wanda had been in his power, he had been a prey to remorse and hesitation. One minute he wished to save her; another, to torture her, so as to avenge himself for all she had made him suffer.

When he received this telegram, and saw that Wanda might escape him, his rage know no bounds. He sat down and wrote:

"I have consulted the registers of all the prisons in Kiev. Princess Kryloff is not here."

He sent this telegram off, and went at once to the fortress.

The military commission had indeed sentenced Wanda to death, as also Raymond, Katia, Matcha, three other women and five men, and all the soldiers who had deserted. Although Wanda at her trial had declared her name to be Wanda Chabert, and her father's name Prince Kryloff, the court had sentenced her under the name of Vera Perowsky. The trial was a mockery. Stackelberg had ordered what sentences should be pronounced upon the different prisoners.

For three days she had known her sentence. For three days had she been in mortal agony. Already she had been in prison for ten days. Tell days of close confinement, of absolute solitude, within those four grey walls.

No one who has not tried it can imagine the terrible effect that this solitude has upon a person. Under it the nerves seem to relax, the fibers of the brain to disintegrate, often producing serious mental trouble, and even madness. The list of martyrs of the Russian socialists included a great number of prisoners who had gone mad, and many suicides.

Wanda was strong and brave, but she was a woman, and her whole being revolted at the idea of the terrible death in store for her. To die at twenty years of age, in all the strength of her life, the freshness of her youth, the perfection of her beauty! At this thought her whole being shuddered. And still she regretted neither happiness nor youth nor beauty; she regretted only having to die before she could see the triumph of the cause for which she was about to sacrifice her life. However, she had gradually grown resigned to the thought, except at night, when she would awake suddenly, and this idea of death stood out before her in the black darkness, like some hideous spirit of evil, and terror seized her soul.

As Stackelberg entered her cell, he remarked a great change in her appearance, and a nervous trembling, which shook her from head to foot, as soon as she saw him. From this physical weakness, he argued a corresponding moral weakness, which promised success to his designs.

For a few moments he did not speak. Wanda rose when he came in. Her proud disdainful look dismayed him.

"Well!" he asked at last, "have you thought over your determination?"

"Yes."

"Have you changed your mind?"

"Monsieur de Stackelberg, a conviction which it has taken three years to form cannot be uprooted in ten days. A conviction is not an opinion; it is a deep, perfect, unshaken belief."

"And yet, in the face of death one sometimes modifies one's way of looking at things. You know what your sentence is, do you not."

"By your orders, I suppose, they took good care to read it to me."

"I may as well tell you that tomorrow morning is fixed upon as the time of your execution."

Wanda grew white. Her teeth chattered, but she recovered herself almost instantly.

"I am quite prepared," she said.

"Are you prepared to die?" exclaimed Vassili, amazed at such courage. "No, you shall not die; I will not have it. Do you hear me, Wanda? I will not allow it. Your death would drive me mad. I have never loved any one but you. I can never love any one else. Listen to me."

"Monsieur de Stackelberg," she answered, haughtily, "my feelings have not changed any more than my convictions have."

"Do you mean that you still hate me?"

She made no reply.

"Wanda, is it not rather I who should hate you? Think of the manner in which you insulted me! Think of how you treated me in the presence of three hundred persons! There are some things that cannot easily be forgiven."

"And you have not forgiven me?"

"Not only have I forgiven you, but I love you still."

"And your love is perhaps the reason why I am now in this jail, under sentence of death."

"You were sentenced for resisting the officers of the law. But I could save you, and I would save you, in spite of all you have done to me."

"No, Monsieur de Stackelberg; I must show you what it is to know no fear."

"So, you refuse me?"

"I do."

He left the cell. As he stood in the doorway, he turned, made two steps forward, and stretched out his arms to Wanda with a gesture of impassioned longing. But Wanda stood unmoved, haughty and cold, gazing at him with such scorn that his hands fell to his side. With a hoarse groan, he went out.

What should he do? Set her at liberty? That meant to give her to Litzanoff, who had not been arrested, and who loved her, for she had told him so. She had only trifled with him to avenge Litzanoff. She had probably left her father's house to be with him, and share his life of peril and adventure.

In the presence of three hundred persons, Wanda had been openly declared to be betrothed to him. No, he would not be made ridiculous; to avoid that he would avenge himself in a terrible manner.

He went home, and sent for the Cossack colonel who had lately arrived at Kiev.

"I have received orders from Petersburg," he said. "The execution is fixed for tomorrow morning."

The colonel bowed.

"I myself shall leave Kiev today; another Chief of Police has been appointed."

The colonel withdrew.

The officer had hardly gone downstairs when Stackelberg rushed out and called for an orderly.

"Quick! Quick! Call the colonel back."

The orderly ran down into the street as fast as he could, but the colonel had galloped away, and could not be overtaken.

Then Stackelberg hesitated again. Should he countermand the order? What would she think of him if he did? He called for his valet, ordered him to pack up his clothes, then wrote several letters and gave several orders, without knowing what he was writing or what he was saying. At six o'clock dinner was served, but he could not eat. At seven o'clock he got into the train, with his head sunk upon his chest, like a guilty wretch flying from the specter of his guilt.

"If I stay here two hours longer, I shall go mad," he muttered to himself.

Prince Kryloff and Korolef arrived at Kiev that same night at eleven o'clock. While the Prince went to the police office, in hopes of finding Stackelberg, Korolef went to look for Litzanoff and Raymond.

Verenine had not come back, but he had sent a despatch to Litzanoff, who only awaited Korolef's return to see what money would do in the fortress. But Stepane was very restless and feverish; he seemed to foresee calamity.

"Korolef," he said, "do not let us lose a moment. Let us try this very night to get into the fort."

"It would be of no use," answered Korolef. "Prince Kryloff will do a great deal better than we can. If the Prince is unsuccessful, we will try tomorrow. But he will succeed, you may depend upon it, for he loves his daughter."

Litzanoff saw there was nothing he could do, but he could not sleep.

Kryloff, finding that Stackelberg had left the city, went to the Governor, who was a friend of his, but he assured the Prince that his fears were groundless.

"If the Princess had been among the prisoners," he said, "I certainly should have known of it." Yet, as the Prince insisted upon it, he gave him a permit to visit, the next morning, all the cells in the fortress occupied by the female prisoners.

The Governor, at the time, knew nothing of the orders that Stackelberg had given to the colonel of the Cossacks.

When Korolef came he found the Prince quite reassured, too much so; he had to disquiet him again. He told him that Wanda was certainly a prisoner, and was probably condemned to death.

The next morning at four o'clock the Prince arose, and accompanied by Korolef, went to the fortress where, thanks to his permit, he was allowed to enter.

They threw open the doors of all the cells in which the women were. Most of the prisoners were still asleep, and this early awakening gave them a great fright.

Alexandra was not asleep. She had been awakened about three o'clock by an unusual noise. All sorts of dreadful ideas had tormented her brain. A terrible anxiety oppressed her. She felt the same danger threatened Michael and Wanda. She knew that they had been sentenced to death.

She was sitting upon a bench listening, when she heard doors opening and shutting, and the sound of feet approaching. Suddenly the door of her cell flew open. She stood up; but in an instant she shrunk back.

Prince Kryloff stood upon the threshold. He did not recognize his wife; but he was struck by the resemblance.

"Who is this woman?" he said to the jailor.

"Sophia Lazareff."

"Is that your real name?" said the Prince to Alexandra.

She did not answer him.

"Where do you come from?"

Still no answer.

Then he entered the cell and went up close to her; he cried aloud, "Alexandra, is this you?"

"Yes, Alexandra, your victim," answered the Princess.

"It is she! It is she," repeated the Prince. "Yes, Wanda must be here. She has taken my child from me! Where is Wanda? Speak, where is she?" And then he turned to the jailor, saying, "Put this woman in chains. She is a devil. My daughter is here. Where is my child?"

"Yes, Wanda is here," said Alexandra. "And you alone can save her. Oh, save her! Save her!"

"I thought you told me, "said the Prince to the jailor, "that this was the last cell where the women are?"

"I did," said the jailor. "There were five others, but this morning . . ."

"This morning what!" exclaimed Alexandra.

"This morning they were removed."

"To where?"

The jailor made no reply.

"Speak I tell me!" said the Prince, shaking him by the arm.

"To be shot."

"Why did you not tell me this before?"

"Your Excellency did not ask me."

Alexandra, forgetting the past, half crazy, fell on her knees at her husband's feet, and with a choking voice said, "Pierre, run and save her,"

"There was no Princess Kryloff among the prisoners," said the jailor.

"She had taken the name of Vera Perowsky," said Alexandra.

"That is the name of one of the prisoners to be shot this morning," said the man.

"Too late! Too late!" cried the Princess; while something seemed to burst in Prince Kryloff's brain. He struggled against this terrible feeling, this terrible pain. All his paternal love aroused, he said to the jailor: "Lead me to the place of execution."

At that very instant they heard a discharge of musketry. The Prince, struggling against his weakness, ran out of the fortress. When he reached the gate, he found Korolef waiting for him. He, too, had heard the discharge.

CHAPTER LIV

THE EXECUTION

The distance of about half a verst was a flat of ground, gently sloping, which belonged to the fortress.

The day dawned grey and wan. There was a fine, chilly rain falling. It was just six o'clock. The platoon of soldiers, their arms in their hands, were drawn up on the flat of ground. The prisoners were led out. All walked with a firm step. What was the meaning of such fearlessness? These women and these men were upheld by the ardor of deep conviction. For a long time they had looked forward to this moment. Now that it had come, it could neither astonish nor frighten them.

The five women came first; Katia and Wanda walked side by side.

"My friend," said Katia, "they are going to shoot you under the name of Vera Perowsky. I think you had better give your real name. For the Russian people, who worship rank, your death will be a powerful example."

"No, Katia," answered Wanda, "I will have absolute equality. To recall my rank at the moment of death would be to recognize a difference between you and me. My death will be certainly known, and my contempt for birth and rank will be a sufficient lesson. Equality will be harder to establish in Russia than liberty, even."

Katia was the first one summoned. She walked forward, put aside the soldiers who wished to support her, advanced with unwavering step to the stake, to which they bound her. She would not let them bandage her eyes.

"My friends! My brothers!" she said, in a loud, ringing voice, "I die gladly for the cause of justice and liberty; the revolution is near at hand,

and we shall be avenged."

The adjutant gave the signal; fifteen balls struck her.

Wanda looked at this sight with heroic courage. They called out her name "Vera Perowsky." She walked calmly forward.

A terrible, heart-breaking cry burst from some one of the prisoners. It was Raymond, who up to that moment had not seen her, and who did not know that she was to die with him. He strove to break his bonds, and rush towards her, but the soldiers held him back.

They were tying Wanda to the stake. She cast one glance at Raymond.

"Do not shoot! Do not shoot!" he screamed in his agony. "That is not Vera Perowsky; it is Prince Kryloff's daughter, Princess Wanda!"

The adjutant hesitated a moment; then, obedient to his orders, he commanded the men to fire.

But not a gun was fired.

Raymond's cries, Wanda's beauty, the name of Prince Kryloff, intimidated and awed the men.

Raymond continued crying aloud: "Do not commit this murder!"

Then turning to the adjutant, he went on:

"Respect the life of this innocent girl!"

But the adjutant for the second time gave the order to fire. "Whoever will not obey me," he said, "shall be shot upon the spot!"

They raised their guns and fired; Wanda's head fell forward on her breast.

At that moment three men came upon the grounds. They were the Prince, Korolef, and the soldier who showed them the way.

The Prince ran forward, but the adjutant stood in his way. The Prince thrust him rudely aside.

"I am Prince Kryloff," he said. "Where is Vera Perowsky? where is she? She is my daughter, Princess Kryloff."

The officer turned ashy-pale, and pointed to the stake. The Prince ran to the place. The Prince recognized Katia, and shuddered. Then he went to the other body. He stood there perfectly motionless, looking down at his dead child with dilated eyes.

Suddenly his heart, contracted with agony, sent a rush of blood to his brain; it carried with it ruin to his already enfeebled mind. A horrible fit of laughter seized him. Burst after burst of this untimely merriment chilled the very blood in the veins of those who heard it. They tried to lead him away, so as to go on with the execution, but insane rage now had full possession of him. He rushed upon the men who tried to hold him, and with superhuman strength freed himself.

"The nihilists! The nihilists!" he howled. "I will exterminate them, every one." They succeeded at last in tying his hands, but still he roared, "The nihilists! The robbers! The assassins! They have murdered my child, my beautiful Wanda."

And then he was taken again with another irrepressible fit of laughter.

And now they saw an officer approach, in company with a tall, fair-haired young man. It was Verenine, bringing Wanda's pardon, signed by the Emperor with his own hand.

"Too late," said Korolef.

Verenine cast one look around, and understood all. He fell upon a mound of earth, and hiding his face in his hands, sobbed aloud.

Korolef went to find Litzanoff in his hiding place.

"Well?" said Stepane.

Korolef made a gesture of despair.

"Dead?" cried Litzanoff.

Korolef was silent. Litzanoff pressed his hands to his heart. He staggered back as if he had been shot. He could not speak. He panted, gasped for breath.

"Be calm," said Korolef.

"Oh, I am very calm," said Stepane, with a wan smile. "After all, what is life? Where is her body?"

"It has been taken to the fortress."

"Let us go there."

"What do you want to do?"

"Kill myself by her side," answered Stepane.

"What good would that do? "said Korolef. "If you really loved that noble woman, you should try to imbue yourself with her spirit, even after her death."

"I lived only through her and for her. She is dead; I have nothing to live for."

"But before you die, avenge her; kill her murderers."

At these words he arose. "You are right," he said, "let us avenge her. Who are her murderers?"

"First, Stackelberg," answered Korolef. "Then the principal Chief of Police, and all the oppressors of Russia."

CHAPTER LV

THE DEPARTURE FOR SIBERIA

At the moment of Wanda's execution, Raymond had fainted dead away. This saved his life. The new Chief of Police appointed to Kiev, brought with him orders emanating from the Emperor himself. Raymond's sentence was commuted to labor in the quicksilver mines. It was a slow instead of a violent death.

Alexandra, Michael, Matcha and Zobolewsky were condemned to hard labor.

At the beginning of July they all set out for Siberia, their destination being Irkutsk, five thousand versts from Petersburg.

As a usual thing, these sad processions start in the spring-time, but the prisons were full, and it was necessary to clear them.

The prisoners were on foot, about five hundred of them, guarded by Cossacks. These latter were armed with pistols, lances, and long whips.

The men walked first, each one clad in a gray cloak, with a number in copper fastened upon his breast, his feet shod with high boots, and his head covered with a sheep skin cap. Strapped upon his back was a warm woolen blanket, and stuck into each belt was a tin cup and a spoon.

The women, dressed in long black cloaks with hoods, came behind, at some distance from the men, surrounded, like them, by an escort of cavalry.

Behind them, a line of miserable carts picked up any who might fall down exhausted upon the road.

These noble women and glorious men walked side by side with the most infamous criminals. This was their sorest trial.

These melancholy processions were frequent in Russia. No one is permitted to speak to them. The condemned man was, as it were, excommunicated from the rest of the world.

The Cossacks cracked their whips to warn people away, and ran up and down the ranks with lanterns tied to the end of their lances, watching lest the prisoners should let fall any letters by the wayside.

Michael and Zobolewsky were strong enough to endure this three months' journey, but Raymond, weakened by his grief, arrived at Irkutsk in a state of complete exhaustion. Yet he was obliged at once to begin the fearful labor to which he was condemned.

Princess Alexandra, had she given her true name, could have been treated with the respect which is always paid to rank in Russia. Instead of being dragged in a miserable cart, she could have traveled to Siberia in a comfortable carriage with a private escort. But then she would have been separated from Michael and her other friends. She preferred to undergo the terrible journey with them.

The prisoners were allowed one hour every Sunday, after they had heard mass, when they might see and talk with one another.

Zobolewsky had tried to escape; he had been caught, and severely flogged as an example to the rest.

But they were still upheld by the hope that their friends would find out where they were, and perhaps deliver them.

General Kousmine obtained Nadege's pardon. Verenine, who had not been neglected, gave her news of her husband. Litzanoff refused to see her. He wrote her a letter, telling her that he had loved Wanda entirely, and that Wanda being dead, his heart was dead also, and that he could love no one else. He begged her to leave him alone, and never to seek to see him again. Besides, he told her he would soon make an end to an existence which had become unendurable.

She determined to return to Petersburg, and Verenine accompanied her.

CHAPTER LVI

VENGEANCE

As soon as Stackelberg got to Petersburg, he drew up a sensational account of the nihilist movement in Southern Russia, particularly in the Ukraine.

This report, which put the one published the year before by Count Pahlen to the blush, procured the author much praise, and gave him the reputation at the Third Section of being one of the bravest champions of the Czar's government.

He received the eight-pointed star of the order of St. Andrew. And yet in spite of all this, Stackelberg was terribly depressed. One recollection haunted him day and night. Wanda's image was constantly before him. He sought to divert his mind and to amuse himself. He had always been looked upon as the most sensible, proper, steady young man in Petersburg. Now there was nothing going on, no dissipation of any kind, in which he could not be found. He passed his evenings, and even his nights, in the fashionable club-houses of Petersburg, which the young men in society delight to keep up.

His coachman often would have to wait for him at the door of one or another of these clubs the whole night long. This man had frequently of late met two other coachmen, who always had an unlimited supply of vodka with them.

As might be foreseen, one night Prince Stackelberg's driver was dead drunk. One of the two strange coachmen carefully took off his coat, dressed himself in it, and mounted the box of the Prince's coupe. It was one o'clock in the morning before Vassili left the club, and he threw himself into his carriage without noticing anything out of the way. He was terribly depressed and gloomy, and never noticed that as soon as the carriage door was shut a second man mounted the box with the coachman.

The carriage rolled on. Within, tortured with remorse and gloomy despair, the Prince took no note of where it was going until his eye was attracted by an unwonted aspect of the street. He put his head out of the window and called to the driver, but the man made no reply, merely whipping up his horses to make them go faster.

"The fellow is drunk!" he said to himself. No other thought crossed his mind.

They had arrived at a lonely part of the city; it looked like a deserted stone quarry. The horses were suddenly stopped.

The door of the carriage was thrown open, and Stackelberg saw, instead of his own coachman, two strange faces.

"What is the meaning of this nonsense?" he asked, in a voice tremulous with rage.

"It means," answered one of the men, "that the Revolutionary Committee has determined to revenge upon your noble person the outrages that you have poured out upon us nihilists: the death of our friends, whom you sentenced at Kiev, and above all, the murder of Wanda Kryloff."

"An ambush! An ambush!" cried Stackelberg, straining his eyes to see where he was.

In the pale light he saw human figures like shadows rising out of the stone-quarry, and quickly advancing towards his coupe. At the same moment strong arms seized him, and in spite of his resistance, stripped him of every particle of clothing. Then the shadows spit in his face, slapped him, insulted him in and, last of all, they flogged him with whips.

Terrified, enraged, dreading death, he nevertheless spoke not one word, uttered no complaint, but he strove to see the faces of his enemies so that he might have his revenge.

At last they allowed him to put on his clothes, and to get into his carriage again. As he was about to step in, he saw two men already seated inside. He drew back, but a powerful hand pushed him in and a voice whispered in his ear, while he felt the cold touch of a pistol on his temple, "Speak one word, make one movement, and you are dead!"

So he sat down in his own coupe, between the two unknown men, and they drove off.

It was a beautiful night one of those exquisite northern nights when the light is so transparent, so luminous, that one cannot only distinguish faces, but every change of expression, and so at once Stackelberg recognized Litzanoff. The other man he did not know. It was Korolef.

"Do you recognize me, scoundrel?" asked Stepane.

Stackelberg trembled from head to foot.

"If I am not mistaken, this is Count Litzanoff, is it not ?" said he, bowing politely.

"You know that I loved Wanda Kryloff, did you not?" retorted Stepane.

"I did not, I assure you."

"Well, I did love her, wildly, passionately, and you ordered her death, you assassinated her."

"I swear to you that you are mistaken."

"Cowardly liar! Hold your tongue!"

"What proof have you?"

"I have every proof. In the first place, I see your guilt in your face. I have taken upon myself to avenge her death. So you must die."

Stackelberg tried to open the carriage door, but Korolef instantly pointed a revolver at his head.

"Mercy!" he cried; "before you condemn me; hear what I have to say."

"Did you listen to what she had to say?"

"She was tried by a judge."

"By what judge? By your accomplices, you mean. You richly deserve death, for you are a murderer. An eye for an eye, and a tooth for a tooth: that is our motto.

"I swear to you that I had orders which I could not disobey."

"You lie, coward!" said Litzanoff, striking him in the face. "You had express orders to delay the execution. Take back that statement."

"I take it back," said Stackelberg, humbly.

"Now ask pardon for your conduct to me."

"I give you my word . . ."

"No new falsehoods! Apologize, I tell you."

"I beg your pardon."

"Coward! Coward! You sicken me. Let us make an end of it."

And he plunged his dagger into Vassili Stackelberg's heart.

Stackelberg had time to give one terrible cry, "Help! They are murdering me!" But a second blow silenced him forever.

Then Korolef drew from his pocket a printed slip of paper; on it were these words: "Killed by order of the Revolutionary Committee."

They had reached the gates of the city. Korolef and Litzanoff jumped out of the carriage, leaving the horses to find their way to their stable alone.

This assassination made a great noise, and struck terror into the heart of all the officials in the Empire.

But this impression was soon effaced by a still more daring attempt upon the life of General Mezentzoff, Chief of the Third Section. The daily papers reported it as follows:

August, 1878. The General, who was in full uniform, was walking this morning at nine o'clock with Colonel Nakaroff, who was in civilian's dress. At the corner of Michael Square and Italian Street they met two young men, one of whom suddenly stabbed General Mezentzoff in the left breast, inflicting a dangerous wound.

Colonel Nakaroff threw himself upon the assassin, but his companion fired upon the Colonel with a revolver, happily without hitting him. The two young men got into a handsome droschky which was waiting for them, and drove off in the direction of Sadovaia very rapidly. At that moment there were no other hacks at the corner of Michael Square and Italian street. Was this an accident? It should be inquired into. It was hoped at first that the

General's wound would not prove fatal, but it is our painful duty to announce to our readers that General Mezentzoff expired nine hours after the attempt upon his life.

A few days after this event, large red placards, posted on the walls of every town in Russia, announced that Mezentzoff had been killed by order of the Revolutionary Committee.

CHAPTER LVII

CONCLUSION

It was the beginning of November. A post-carriage was driving rapidly upon the road to Irkutsk. The temperature was thirty degrees below zero. Two gentlemen, dressed as cavalry officers, wrapped in furs, were seated in the rozok. One of them was intensely sad. It was Litzanoff. The other, in spite of his huge mustache, could easily be recognized. It was Korolef.

"How cold it is," said the latter. "It is freezing enough to make one gnash one's teeth, as the Siberians say."

"Are we near Irkutsk?" asked Litzanoff.

"It is about five versts off. I assure you, I feel very uneasy about going to the Governor."

"What nonsense!" answered Litzanoff. "Haven't we the order for their liberation, even the signature of the Emperor, and the seal of the Third Section?"

"Yes, we have, but the signature is a forgery."

"Oh, it is very well imitated, and the seals are real."

"But what shall I tell him is the reason that they have not sent this order through the ordinary channels, instead of sending us with it?"

"Bah! Before the Emperor's signature the Governor will bow down as every body else has done on the road."

"The superior officers are more suspicious and watchful. They know what a terrible punishment awaits them if the prisoners escape."

"You are afraid," said Litzanoff, smiling sadly. "I don't care what becomes of me."

"I afraid?" answered Korolef. "I am afraid of not succeeding, that is all."

It was five o'clock in the morning. A gray fog wrapped the valley of Angora, the pine forests, and the surrounding mountains.

Korolef lowered the glass for a moment; it was so covered with the frost that they could not see out.

"What a beautiful sight!" he exclaimed. The fog was lifting; the heavens, scarlet towards the rising sun, glittered like silver at the zenith, where a million microscopic rubies seemed to shine. On one side could be seen the bell towers and the domes of the Monastery of Saint Irkout, surrounded with pines and larches draped in cloaks of snow, which made them look like gigantic white monks. Farther on, the city of Irkutsk stood boldly out, built upon many hills, surrounded by lofty walls, and adorned with innumerable domes and slender spires.

The postilion cracked his whip, and soon they drove under the massive gate of the city, and instantly bent their course to the Kousnetzoff, where the Governor lived.

Korolef and Litzanoff were announced as envoys extraordinary from the Third Section.

When Korolef presented his sealed orders, the Governor looked at him suspiciously.

"I see that you are surprised," said Korolef. "But this is not a matter of a private individual. Princess Kryloff has been condemned unjustly, under the name of Sophia Lazareff."

The Governor called for his secretary, and ordered him to consult the register.

He countersigned the order for the liberation of the prisoners, and returned it to Korolef, telling him at the same time where he could find them.

Michael and Zobolewsky were in the copper-mines, but Raymond had been sent to the quicksilver mines, not far from Lake Baikal.

Five years in these mines reduced the most robust man to a pale, fleshless, enfeebled skeleton. The poor wretches who work in them never see the light of the sun.

Matcha and the other women were employed in sifting ore. Alexandra, on account of her age, was allowed to board with a poor family, who, after serving out their term, had determined to remain in Siberia. She passed whole days perfectly motionless, stretched upon a bed of dried moss, with her eyes closed, feverish and wretched.

Litzanoff and Korolef delivered first Michael, Zobolewsky, and Matcha; then they went to find Alexandra. At the sight of Michael she fainted, and remained for a long time unconscious.

There was no time to lose; they took her up, wrapped her in furs, and laid her in the carriage.

Now they must free Raymond. They bent their way towards Lake Baikal.

When they saw him, they could hardly recognize him, so changed was he by his life, his grief at Wanda's death, and his utter hopelessness. At the sight of Litzanoff, he forgot his old jealousy. He saw only the man who had loved Wanda, like himself, and who, like himself, was wretched.

The two rushed together, and held each other in a long embrace; their hearts choking, their faces bathed in tears.

Korolef thought it would not be safe to return the same way they had come, so they crossed the lake, a vast expense of water, the largest lake in the world. Gaining the frontier of China, they embarked at Hong Kong in a vessel for Southampton, where they arrived safely in February.

As we write these lines, a letter has arrived from Petersburg, giving us some facts connected with the persons, who are all drawn from real life, mentioned in these papers.

Prince Kryloff is hopelessly insane.

It is said that Nadege is about to procure a divorce, to enable her to marry Alexis Verenine. Although they take no active part in the nihilist movement, in memory of Wanda they are still faithful to it.

Korolef and Litzanoff are in Petersburg. They are the implacable executors of the Revolutionary Committee. Vengeance is Stepane's one idea.

Every time the daily papers report some mysterious assassination, equally daring and fearless, we think that we know the authors.

Raymond has not returned to France. He has taken Wanda's mother for his own.

Michael remains the most intelligent member of the party. Unfortunately, his advice and Padlewsky's are not always heeded. But he remains unmoved and calm, seeing clearly that progress, to be lasting, must be slow.

But he sees the current that draws Russia along. He knows better than anyone the Russian character: the fierce power which leads it to extremes, and which shrinks from moderation. He would direct and control this power; he would stem this torrent which threatens to overwhelm his country. But he sees his impotence, and he awaits with unspeakable anxiety the denouement of that great social tragedy, of which Russia has as yet given us but the prologue.

THE END

Contemporary Nihilist Fiction from III Publishing

Deconstruction Acres by Tim W. Brown $10.00
When professor Race Fletcher, author of a best-selling book deconstructing *Green Acres,* shows up Ione dumps Underdog for him. The fight over Ione brings unexpected consequences in this satirical look at campus life.

The Last Days of Christ the Vampire by J.G. Eccarius $10.00
Jesus has set his sights on converting some teenagers in Providence, Rhode Island, but instead they resist and set out to hunt him down before he can release his Apocalypse. Arguably the best religious satire of the 20th century.

Virgintooth by Mark Ivanhoe $7.00
Elizabeth has not exactly died: she has been made into a vampire. Now she has not only all the problems she had when alive, but she must also get along with the other vampires.

Geminga, Sword of the Shining Path by Melvin Litton $9.95
Poised between a superstitious past and a surreal future of bioengineering and artificial consciousness, Geminga surfs the winds.

This'll Kill Ya by Harry Willson $6.00
The mystery that will have you laughing out loud and examining your own reactions to materials that surely should be censored.

A.D. by Saab Lofton $12.00
The future seen through African-American eyes: after decades of anti-utopian racist fascism in the 21st century, revolutionaries create a society based on Libertarian Socialist Democracy.

Down and Out in the Ivy League by J.G. Eccarius $10.00
George Orwell was *Down and Out in Paris and London*, and J.G. Eccarius was down and out in the Ivy League. A selection of great stories by this master story teller.

Pyrexia by Michel Méry $10.00
Abelard shares a tiny apartment on Mars with his anima, Kahani. For entertainment he hooks into the GUM (Global Un-Manifested) Station, which once took him to Pyrexia, the sex-goddess at the beginning of the universe.

Anarchist Farm by Jane Doe $10.00

An animal fable for adults and children. Pancho the pig is driven off a farm; raccoons lead him to the forest defenders, fighting to protect their forest from the Corporation's clear-cuts. The Corporation plans to grab the farm and slaughter the animals...

We Should Have Killed the King by J.G. Eccarius $5.00

The spirit of rebellion was reborn in America in the punk/anarchist movement during the 1980's and Jack Straw was there.

Resurrection 2027 by J.G. Eccarius $7.00

Ann Swanson remembers her life as a nurse before the Apocalypse. Resurrected years later by the grace of Mary the Mother of God, she is called to work at the Temple of the Resurrection. A brave new look at religious mind control.

My Journey With Aristotle to the Anarchist Utopia by Graham Purchase $7.00

No government? No taxes? No police? Wouldn't that be anarchy? Aristotle leads Tom down to Bear City where humans live happily without government or bosses of any kind.

Vampires or Gods? by William Meyers [non-fiction] $15.00

Vampires living thousands of years, commanding legions of human worshipers? Yes! Every major ancient civilization was associated with an immortal claiming to be a god. Egypt had Osiris, who rose from the dead after his body was hacked to pieces...

The Father, The Son, and The Walkperson by Michel Méry $10.00

A web of fractalled tales mixing science-fictionish absurdity with a quantum-improbability perspective of our information-oriented, reality-denying technoculture. By taking society spectacle to new heights, Méry prepares you to be dashed on the rocks of surreality below.

Individual orders: send cash, or check or money order for the listed price (postage & handling is free for orders of $10.00 or more in the US & Canada; otherwise add $2) made out to III Publishing, P.O. Box 1581 Gualala, CA 95445.

For an up to date list, information about authors, and samples of these books visit

www.iiipublishing.com